Praise for the Novels of
#1 *New York Times* Bestselling Author
Nicholas Sparks

The Best of Me

"A creative genius...This book is great for any love story enthusiast."　　　　　　　　　　　　　—HubPages.com

"Unforgettable...Makes you settle in for another romantic date with this well-respected and talented storyteller."
　　　　　　　　　　—*Fredericksburg Free Lance-Star* (VA)

"I could not put it down...a classic Nicholas Sparks tragedy but with a twist of hope...If I can pick my favorites from him, THE BEST OF ME will rank with *Message in a Bottle* and *The Notebook*—it was *that* good."　　　—BookReporter.com

"Sparks does it again! The author known for his tear-jerkers doesn't disappoint."　　　　　　　　—*RT Book Reviews*

"An emotional tale of passionate love, lost love, and reunited love."　　　　　　　　　　　　　—*Sacramento Bee*

"THE BEST OF ME is classic Nicholas Sparks....Sparks has a way with words. The writing is good."　　—WCFCourier.com

Safe Haven

"A compelling love story...a gripping tale of love and survival... a riveting 'read all night' page-turner."　　—BookReporter.com

The Lucky One

"A tale of redemption...holds readers in suspense until the final chapter...it will test readers' beliefs in the power of destiny and fate, and how they relate to choices one makes in life."

—*Chattanooga Times Free Press*

"An emotional roller coaster...The book is great...it will introduce you to a great storyteller."

—*Navajo Times* (AZ)

"In true Nicholas Sparks fashion, the reader is engaged from the first to last page. The characters are authentic and the plot is engrossing and emotionally charged."

—BookLoons.com

"Sparks gives his many fans another reason to adore him with this tale of a once-in-a-lifetime quest for true romance...a grand, destined love story...Romance fans will consider themselves more than fortunate to have discovered *The Lucky One*."

—TeenReads.com

The Choice

"A tender and moving love story."

—*Publishers Weekly*

"Provides subtle lessons in love and hope...reinforces the theory that all choices, no matter how seemingly unimportant...often have far-reaching, rippling effects. Sparks has become a favorite storyteller because of his ability to take ordinary people, put them in extraordinary situations, and create unexpected outcomes."

—BookReporter.com

"A heartrending love story...will have you entranced. And if *The Notebook* left you teary-eyed, his latest will have the same effect."

—*Myrtle Beach Sun News*

"Will unleash a torrent of tears...But the emotion will be emotionally cleansing for it involves a choice each of us is likely to face one day. This is the stuff of serious romance novels."

—ContemporaryLit.About.com

Dear John

"Beautifully moving...Has tremendous emotional depth, revealing the true meaning of unconditional love."

—*RT Book Reviews*

"Full of pathos."

—*Roanoke Times*

"For Sparks, weighty matters of the day remain set pieces, furniture upon which to hang timeless tales of chaste longing and harsh fate."

—*Washington Post Book World*

"Sparks lives up to his reputation...a tribute to courageous and self-sacrificing soldiers."

—*Booklist*

At First Sight

"An ending that surprises."

—*New York Times Book Review*

"Engrosses readers from the first page to the last."

—*RT Book Reviews*

"Nicholas Sparks is one of the best-known writers in America and overseas for good reason: He has written stories that reveal the yearning for our most prized possession: love."

—*Mobile Register* (AL)

"Highly recommended. Nicholas Sparks can take a simple plot and turn it into a masterwork of art...Be prepared for a surprise ending."

—BestsellersWorld.com

True Believer

"Time for a date with Sparks... The slow dance to the couple's first kiss is a two-chapter guilty pleasure." —*People*

"For romance fans, *True Believer* is a gem."

—EDGEBoston.com

"Another winner... a page-turner... has all the things we have come to expect from him: sweet romance and a strong sense of place." —*Charlotte Observer*

"Sparks does not disappoint his readers. He tells a fine story that entertains us." —*Oklahoman*

The Wedding

"Sweet but packs a punch... There is a twist that pulls everything together and makes you glad you read this."

—*Charlotte Observer*

"A slice of life readers will take to their hearts."

—*Tulsa World*

"Sparks tells his sweet story... [with] a gasp-inducing twist at the very end. Satisfied female readers will close the covers with a sigh." —*Publishers Weekly*

The Guardian

"An involving love story... an edge-of-your-seat, unpredictable thriller." —*Booklist*

"Nicholas Sparks is a top-notch writer. He has created a truly spine-tingling thriller exploring love and obsession with a kind of suspense never before experienced in his novels."

—RedBank.com

"Fans of Sparks won't be disappointed."

—*Southern Pines Pilot* (NC)

Nights in Rodanthe

"Bittersweet...romance blooms...You'll cry in spite of yourself."

—*People*

"Passionate and memorable...smooth, sensitive writing...This is a novel that can hold its own."   —Associated Press

"Extremely hard to put down...a love story, and a good love story at that."   —*Boston Herald*

A Bend in the Road

"Sweet, accessible, uplifting."   —*Publishers Weekly*

"A powerful tale of true love."

—*Booklist*

"Don't miss it; this is a book that's light on the surface but with subtle depths."

—BookLoons.com

The Rescue

"A romantic page-turner...Sparks's fans won't be disappointed."

—*Glamour*

"All of Sparks's trademark elements—love, loss, and small-town life—are present in this terrific read."   —*Booklist*

A Walk to Remember

"An extraordinary book...touching, at times riveting...a book you won't soon forget."   —*New York Post*

"Sparks knows how to tug at a reader's heartstrings."

—*Chicago Sun-Times*

"Bittersweet...a tragic yet spiritual love story."   —*Variety*

Message in a Bottle

"The novel's unabashed emotion—and an unexpected turn—will put tears in your eyes."   —People

"Glows with moments of tenderness...delve[s] deeply into the mysteries of eternal love."   —*Cleveland Plain Dealer*

"Deeply moving, beautifully written, and extremely romantic."

—*Booklist*

The Notebook

"Nicholas Sparks...will not let you go. His novel shines."

—*Dallas Morning News*

"Proves that good things come in small packages...a classic tale of love."   —*Christian Science Monitor*

"The lyrical beauty of this touching love story...will captivate the heart of every reader and establish Nicholas Sparks as a gifted novelist."   —*Denver Rocky Mountain News*

NICHOLAS SPARKS

The Best of Me

GRAND CENTRAL
PUBLISHING

NEW YORK   BOSTON

Copyright © 2011 by Willow Holdings, Inc.
Excerpt from *The Longest Ride* copyright © 2013 by Willow Holdings, Inc.
Reading Group Guide copyright © 2012 by Hachette Book Group, Inc.

Grand Central Publishing
Hachette Book Group
237 Park Avenue
New York, NY 10017

www.HachetteBookGroup.com

Printed in the United States of America

RRD-H

Originally published in hardcover by Hachette Book Group.

First media tie-in trade edition: August 2014

10 9 8 7 6 5 4 3 2 1

Grand Central Publishing is a division of Hachette Book Group, Inc.
The Grand Central Publishing name and logo are trademarks of Hachette Book Group, Inc.

The Hachette Speakers Bureau provides a wide range of authors for speaking events. To find out more, go to www.hachettespeakersbureau.com or call (866) 376-6591.

The publisher is not responsible for websites (or their content) that are not owned by the publisher.

Library of Congress Catalog Number: 2011933986

ISBN 978-1-4555-5655-7 (pbk.); 978-1-4555-3308-4 (Scholastic pbk.); 978-1-4555-6138-4 (Target pbk.)

For Scott Schwimer
A wonderful friend

Acknowledgments

Some novels are more challenging to write than others, and *The Best of Me* falls into that category. *The Best of Me* was difficult to write—I won't bore you with those reasons—and without the support of the following people, I'd probably still be working on it. So, without further ado, I want to offer my thanks.

For Cathy, my wife: When we first met, it was love *At First Sight*, and nothing has changed in all the years we've been together. You're the best, and I always consider myself lucky to call you my wife.

For Miles, Ryan, Landon, Lexie, and Savannah: You add joy to my life and I'm proud of all of you. As my children, you are, and always will be, *The Best of Me*.

For Theresa Park, my agent: After finishing the first draft of the novel, I came to *A Bend in the Road*, and you deserve my gratitude not only for your efforts to help me improve the novel, but for your patience as I tried to work through it. I'm fortunate to have you as an agent. Thank you.

For Jamie Raab, my editor: *The Rescue* you performed on this novel was, as always, amazing, and your suggestions "spot-on." You're not only a fabulous editor, but a wonderful person. Thank you.

For Howie Sanders and Keya Khayatian, my film agents: I'm a *True Believer* when it comes to the idea that honor, intelligence, and passion are the bedrock of any good working relationship. Both of you exemplify these attributes—always—and I'm thankful for everything you've done. I'm fortunate to work with you.

For Denise DiNovi: The producer of *Message in a Bottle*—and other film adaptations of mine, of course—you've become more than just someone with whom I work. You've become my friend, and my life is better for it. Thank you so much, for everything.

For Marty Bowen: You did a wonderful job as the producer of *Dear John*, and I appreciate not only your efforts on my behalf, but your friendship as well. Thank you for all you've done and I'm glad that we're working together again.

For David Young, CEO of Hachette Book Group: Without question, you've made me *The Lucky One*, and I appreciate all you do. Thank you.

For Abby Koons and Emily Sweet, at Park Literary Group: My sincerest thanks for all the work you do on my behalf. Both of you go above and beyond when it comes to helping me out, and I'm more appreciative than you know. Oh, and Emily? Congratulations on *The Wedding*...

For Jennifer Romanello, my publicist at GCP: *The Guardian* of my tour... *Grazie* for everything, as always. You're the best.

For Stephanie Yeager, my assistant: After working on the set of *Nights in Rodanthe*, you've been keeping my life running smoothly ever since. I appreciate it—and thank you—for all you do.

For Courtenay Valenti and Greg Silverman, at Warner Bros.: Thanks for taking a chance on me, and this novel, without reading it beforehand. It wasn't an easy decision, but I'm appreciative of *The Choice* you made. Above all, I'm thrilled to work with both of you again.

For Ryan Kavanaugh and Tucker Tooley, at Relativity Media, and Wyck Godfrey: I'm incredibly excited about the film adaptation of *Safe Haven*, and I'd like to thank all of you for giving me the opportunity to work with you again. It's an honor, and I won't forget it and I know you'll do a wonderful job.

For Adam Shankman and Jennifer Gibgot: Thank you for the great work you did on the film version of *The Last Song*. I trusted you, and you came through . . . something I'll never forget.

For Lynn Harris and Mark Johnson: Working with both of you, so long ago, was one of the best decisions of my career. I know you've both done many, many films since then, but just so you know, I will always, always be thankful for the film version of *The Notebook*.

For Lorenzo DiBonaventura: Thank you for the adaptation of *A Walk to Remember*. The passage of time does nothing to diminish my love for that movie.

For David Park, Sharon Krassney, Flag, and everyone else at Grand Central Publishing and United Talent Agency: While I once spent *Three Weeks with My Brother*, it's been fifteen years that I've been associated with all of you. Thanks for everything!

The Best of Me

1

——— 🌿 ———

For Dawson Cole, the hallucinations began after the explosion on the platform, on the day he should have died.

In the fourteen years he'd worked on oil rigs, he thought he'd seen it all. In 1997, he'd watched as a helicopter lost control as it was about to land. It crashed onto the deck, erupting in a blistering fireball, and he'd received second-degree burns on his back as he'd attempted a rescue. Thirteen people, most of them in the helicopter at the time, had died. Four years later, after a crane on the platform collapsed, a piece of flying metal debris the size of a basketball nearly took his head off. In 2004, he was one of the few workers remaining on the rig when Hurricane Ivan slammed into it, with winds gusting over a hundred miles an hour and waves large enough to make him wonder whether to grab a parachute in case the rig collapsed. But there were other dangers as well. People slipped, parts snapped, and cuts and bruises were a way of life among the crew. Dawson had seen more broken bones than he could count, two plagues of food poisoning that sickened the entire crew, and two years ago, in 2007, he'd watched a supply ship start to sink as it pulled away from the rig, only to be rescued at the last minute by a nearby coast guard cutter.

But the explosion was something different. Because there was no oil leak—in this instance, the safety mechanisms and their

backups prevented a major spill—the story barely made the
national news and was largely forgotten within a few days. But
for those who were there, including him, it was the stuff of nightmares. Up until that point, the morning had been routine. He'd
been monitoring the pumping stations when one of the oil storage tanks suddenly exploded. Before he could even process what
had happened, the impact from the explosion sent him crashing into a neighboring shed. After that, fire was everywhere. The
entire platform, crusted with grease and oil, quickly became an
inferno that engulfed the whole facility. Two more large explosions rocked the rig even more violently. Dawson remembered
dragging a few bodies farther from the fire, but a fourth explosion,
bigger than the others, launched him into the air a second time.
He had a vague memory of falling toward the water, a fall that for
all intents and purposes should have killed him. The next thing
he knew, he was floating in the Gulf of Mexico, roughly ninety
miles south of Vermilion Bay, Louisiana.

Like most of the others, he hadn't had time to don his survival suit or reach for a flotation device, but in between swells
he saw a dark-haired man waving in the distance, as if signaling
Dawson to swim toward him. Dawson struck out in that direction, fighting the ocean waves, exhausted and dizzy. His clothes
and boots dragged him down, and as his arms and legs began
to give out he knew he was going to die. He thought he'd been
getting close, though the swells made it impossible to know for
sure. At that moment, he spotted a lone life preserver floating among some nearby debris. Using the last of his remaining
strength, he latched on. Later, he learned that he was in the
water for almost four hours and had drifted nearly a mile from the
rig before being picked up by a supply ship that had rushed to the
scene. He was pulled on board, carried belowdecks, and reunited
with other survivors. Dawson was shivering from hypothermia,
and he was dazed. Though his vision was blurred—he was later
diagnosed with a moderate concussion—he recognized how

lucky he'd been. He saw men with vicious burns on their arms and shoulders, and others bleeding from their ears or nursing broken bones. He knew most of them by name. There were only so many places for people to go on the rig—it was essentially a small village in the middle of the ocean—and everyone made it to the cafeteria or the recreation room or gym sooner or later. One man, however, looked only vaguely familiar, a man who seemed to be staring at him from across the crowded room. Dark-haired and maybe forty years old, he was wearing a blue windbreaker that someone on the ship had probably lent him. Dawson thought he looked out of place, more like an office worker than a roughneck. The man waved, suddenly triggering memories of the figure he'd spotted earlier in the water—it *was* him—and all at once, Dawson felt the hairs on the back of his neck rise. Before he could identify the source of his unease, a blanket was thrown over his shoulders and he was ushered to a spot in the corner where a medical officer waited to examine him.

By the time he sat back down, the dark-haired man was gone.

Over the next hour, more survivors were brought aboard, but as his body began to warm, Dawson started to wonder about the rest of the crew. Men he'd worked with for years were nowhere to be seen. Later, he would learn that twenty-four people were killed. Most, but not all, of the bodies were eventually found. While he recovered in the hospital, Dawson couldn't stop thinking about the fact that some families had no real way to say good-bye.

He'd had trouble sleeping since the explosion, not because of any nightmares but because he couldn't shake the feeling of being watched. He felt . . . *haunted*, as ridiculous as that sounded. Day and night, he occasionally caught a glimpse of movement from the corner of his eye, but whenever he turned there was never anyone or anything there that could explain it. He wondered if he was losing his mind. The doctor suggested he was having a posttraumatic reaction to the stress of the accident and that his brain might still be healing from the concussion. It made sense and sounded logical, but it didn't feel right to Dawson. He nodded anyway. The doctor gave him a prescription for sleeping pills, but Dawson never bothered to fill it.

He was given a paid leave of absence for six months while the legal wheels began to grind. Three weeks later, the company offered him a settlement and he signed the papers. By then he'd already been contacted by a half-dozen attorneys, all of them racing to be the first to file a class action suit, but he didn't want the hassle. He took the settlement offer and deposited the check on the day it arrived. With enough money in his account to make some people think he was rich, he went to his bank and wired most of it to an account in the Cayman Islands. From there, it was forwarded to a corporate account in Panama that had been opened with minimal paperwork, before being wired to its final destination. The money, as always, was virtually impossible to trace.

He'd kept only enough for the rent and a few other expenses. He didn't need much. Nor did he want much. He lived in a single-wide trailer at the end of a dirt road on the outskirts of New Orleans, and people who saw it probably assumed that its primary redeeming feature was that it hadn't flooded during Hurricane Katrina in 2005. With plastic siding that was cracked and fading, the trailer squatted on stacked cinder blocks, a temporary foundation that had somehow become permanent over time. It had a single bedroom and bath, a cramped living area, and a kitchen with barely enough room to house a mini refrigerator. Insulation was almost nonexistent, and humidity had warped the floors over the years, making it seem as if he were always walking on a slant. The linoleum in the kitchen was cracking in the corners, the minimal carpet was threadbare, and he'd furnished the narrow space with items he'd picked up over the years at thrift stores. Not a single photograph adorned the walls. Though he'd lived there for almost fifteen years, it was less a home than a place where he happened to eat and sleep and take his showers.

Despite its age, it was almost always as pristine as the homes in the Garden District. Dawson was, and always had been, a bit of a neat freak. Twice a year, he repaired cracks and caulked seams to keep rodents and insects at bay, and whenever he prepared to return to the rig, he scrubbed the kitchen and bathroom floors with disinfectant and emptied the cupboards of anything that might spoil or mold. He generally worked thirty days on, followed by thirty days off, and anything that wasn't in a can would go bad in less than a week, especially during the summer. Upon his return, he scrubbed the place from top to bottom again while airing it out, doing his best to get rid of the musty smell.

It was quiet, though, and that was really all he needed. He was a quarter mile off the main road, and the nearest neighbor was even farther away than that. After a month on the rig, that was exactly what he wanted. One of the things he'd never gotten used to on the rig was the endless noise. Unnatural noise. From cranes continually repositioning supplies to helicopters to the pumps to the endless pounding of metal on metal, the cacophony never stopped. Rigs pumped oil around the clock, which meant that even when Dawson was trying to sleep, the clamor continued. He tried to tune it out while he was there, but whenever he returned to the trailer he was struck by the almost impenetrable silence when the sun was high in the sky. In the mornings he could hear birdsong drifting from the trees, and in the evenings he'd listen to the way the crickets and frogs sometimes synchronized their rhythm a few minutes after the sun went down. It was usually soothing, but every now and then the sound made him think of home, and when that happened he would retreat indoors, forcing the memories away. Instead, he tried to focus on the simple routines that dominated his life when he was back on solid ground.

He ate. He slept. He ran and lifted weights and tinkered on his car. He took long, wandering drives, going nowhere in particular. Now and then he went fishing. He read every night and wrote an occasional letter to Tuck Hostetler. That was it. He owned neither a television nor a radio, and though he had a cell phone, only work numbers were listed in the contact list. He picked up groceries and essentials and stopped at the bookstore once a month, but other than that he never ventured into New Orleans. In fourteen years, he'd never been to Bourbon Street or strolled through the French Quarter; he'd never sipped coffee at the Café Du Monde or had a hurricane at Lafitte's Blacksmith Shop Bar. Instead of visiting a gym, he worked out behind the trailer beneath a weathered tarp he'd strung between his home and nearby trees. He didn't go to the movies or kick back at a friend's place while the Saints played on Sunday afternoons. He was forty-two years old and hadn't been on a date since he was a teenager.

Most people wouldn't or couldn't have lived their lives that way, but they didn't know him. They didn't know who he had been or what he had done, and he wanted to keep it that way.

Then, out of the blue on a warm afternoon in mid-June, he received a phone call, and memories of the past rose anew. Dawson had been on leave for almost nine weeks. For the first time in nearly twenty years, he was finally going home. The thought made him uneasy, but he knew he had no choice. Tuck had been more than just a friend; he'd been like a father. And in the silence, as he reflected on the year that had been the turning point of his life, Dawson saw a flash of movement once more. When he turned, there was nothing there at all, and he wondered again whether he was going crazy.

*

The call had come from Morgan Tanner, an attorney in Oriental, North Carolina, who informed him that Tuck Hostetler had passed away. "There are arrangements best handled in person," Tanner explained. Dawson's first instinct after hanging up was to book his flight and a room at a local bed-and-breakfast, then call a florist and arrange for a delivery.

The following morning, after locking the front door to the trailer, Dawson walked around back, toward the tin shed where he kept his car. It was Thursday, June 18, 2009, and he carried with him the only suit he owned and a duffel bag he'd packed in the middle of the night when he hadn't been able to sleep. He unlocked the padlock and rolled up the door, watching sunlight stream onto the car he'd been restoring and repairing ever since high school. It was a 1969 fastback, the kind of car that turned heads when Nixon was president and still turned heads today. It looked as if it had just rolled off the assembly line, and over the years countless strangers had offered to buy it from him. Dawson had turned them down. "It's more than just a car," he told them, without further explanation. Tuck would have understood exactly what he meant.

Dawson tossed the duffel bag onto the passenger seat and laid the suit on top of it before sliding behind the wheel. When he turned the key, the engine came to life with a loud rumble, and he eased the car onto the gravel before hopping out to lock the shed. As he did, he ran through a mental checklist, making sure he had everything. Two minutes later, he was on the main road, and a half hour after that he was parking in the long-term lot at the New Orleans airport. He hated leaving the car but had no choice. He collected his things before starting toward the terminal, where a ticket was waiting for him at the airline counter.

The airport was crowded. Men and women walking arm in arm, families off to visit grandparents or Disney World, students shuttling between home and school. Business travelers rolled their carry-ons behind them, jabbering on cell phones. He stood in the slow-moving line and waited until a spot opened at the counter. He showed his identification and answered the basic security questions before being handed his boarding passes.

There was a single layover in Charlotte, a little more than an hour. Not bad. Once he landed in New Bern and picked up his rental car, he had another forty minutes on the road. Assuming there weren't any delays, he'd be in Oriental by late afternoon.

Until he took his seat on the plane, Dawson hadn't realized how tired he was. He wasn't sure what time he'd finally fallen asleep—the last time he'd checked, it had been almost four—but he figured he'd sleep on the plane. Besides, it wasn't as though he had much to do once he got to town. He was an only child, his mom had run off when he was three, and his dad had done the world a favor by drinking himself to death. Dawson hadn't talked to anyone in his family in years, nor did he intend to renew their acquaintance now.

Quick trip, in and out. He'd do what he had to do and didn't plan on hanging around any longer than he had to. He might have been raised in Oriental, but he'd never really belonged there. The Oriental he knew was nothing like the cheery image advertised by the area Visitors' Bureau. For most people who spent an afternoon there, Oriental came across as a quirky little town, popular with artists and poets and retirees who wanted nothing more than to spend their twilight years sailing on the Neuse River. It had the requisite quaint downtown, complete with antiques stores, art galleries, and coffee shops, and the place had more weekly festivals than seemed possible for a town of fewer than a thousand people. But the real Oriental, the one he'd known as a child and young man, was the one inhabited by families with ancestors who had resided in the area since colonial times. People like Judge McCall and Sheriff Harris, Eugenia Wilcox, and the Collier and Bennett families. They were the ones who'd always owned the land and farmed the crops and sold the timber and established the businesses; they were the powerful, invisible undercurrent in a town that had always been theirs. And they kept it the way they wanted.

Dawson found that out firsthand when he was eighteen, and

then again at twenty-three, when he finally left for good. It wasn't easy being a Cole anywhere in Pamlico County, Oriental in particular. As far as he knew, every Cole in the family tree going back as far as his great-grandfather had spent time in prison. Various members of the family had been convicted of everything from assault and battery to arson, attempted murder, and murder itself, and the rocky, wooded homestead that housed the extended family was like a country with its own rules. A handful of ramshackle cabins, single-wide trailers, and junk barns dotted the property that his family called home, and unless he had no choice, even the sheriff avoided the place. Hunters gave the land a wide berth, rightly assuming that the TRESPASSERS WILL BE SHOT ON SIGHT sign wasn't simply a warning but a promise. The Coles were moonshiners and drug dealers, alcoholics, wife beaters, abusive fathers and mothers, thieves and pimps, and above all, pathologically violent. According to an article that had been published in a now defunct magazine, they were at one point regarded as the most vicious, revenge-driven family east of Raleigh. Dawson's father was no exception. He'd spent most of his twenties and early thirties in prison for various offenses that included stabbing a man with an ice pick after the man had cut him off in traffic. He'd been tried and acquitted twice for murder after witnesses had vanished, and even the rest of the family knew enough not to rile him up. How or why his mom had ever married him was a question that Dawson couldn't begin to answer. He didn't blame his mom for running off. For most of his childhood, he'd wanted to run off, too. Nor did he blame her for not taking him. Men in the Cole family were strangely proprietary about their offspring, and he had no doubt his father would have hunted his mom down and taken him back anyway. He'd told Dawson as much more than once, and Dawson had known better than to ask his dad what he would have done had his mom refused to give him up. Dawson already knew the answer.

He wondered how many members of his family were still living on the land. When he'd finally left, in addition to his father,
there'd been a grandfather, four uncles, three aunts, and sixteen
cousins. By now, with the cousins grown up and having kids of
their own, there were probably more, but he had no desire to
find out. That might have been the world he'd grown up in, but
like Oriental, he'd never really belonged to them, either. Maybe
his mom, whoever she was, had something to do with it, but he
wasn't like them. Alone among his cousins, he never got in fights
at school and he pulled down decent grades. He stayed away from
the drugs and the booze, and as a teenager he avoided his cousins
when they cruised into town looking for trouble, usually telling
them that he had to check on the still or help disassemble a car
that someone in the family had stolen. He kept his head down
and did his best to maintain as low a profile as he could.

It was a balancing act. The Coles might have been a band of
criminals, but that didn't mean they were stupid, and Dawson
knew instinctively that he had to hide his differences as best he
could. He was probably the only kid in his school's history who
studied hard enough to fail a test on purpose, and he taught himself how to doctor his report cards so they appeared worse than
they really were. He learned how to secretly empty a can of beer
the moment someone had his back turned by poking it with a
knife, and when he used work as an excuse to avoid his cousins,
he often toiled until the middle of the night. That was successful for a while, but over time, cracks appeared in the facade. One
of his teachers mentioned to a drinking buddy of his dad's that
he was the best student in his class; aunts and uncles began to
notice that he alone among the cousins was staying within the
bounds of the law. In a family that prized loyalty and conformity
above all else, he was different, and there was no worse sin.

It infuriated his father. Though he'd been beaten regularly
since he was a toddler—his father favored belts and straps—by
the time he was twelve the beatings became personal. His father

would beat him until Dawson's back and chest were black and blue, then return an hour later, turning his attention to the boy's face and legs. Teachers knew what was happening, but, afraid for their own families, they ignored it. The sheriff pretended that he couldn't see the bruises and welts as Dawson walked home from school. The rest of the family had no problem with it. Abee and Crazy Ted, his older cousins, jumped him more than once, beating him as bad as his father—Abee because he thought Dawson had it coming, Crazy Ted just for the hell of it. Abee, tall and broad with fists the size of ham bones, was violent and short-tempered but smarter than he let on. Crazy Ted, on the other hand, was born mean. In kindergarten, he stabbed a classmate with a pencil in a fight over a Twinkie, and before he was finally expelled in the fifth grade he'd sent another classmate to the hospital. Rumor had it that he'd killed a junkie while still a teenager. Dawson figured out it was best not to fight back. Instead, he learned to cover up while absorbing the blows, until his cousins finally grew bored or tired or both.

He didn't, however, follow in the family business and grew more resolute that he never would. Over time, he learned that the more he screamed, the more his father beat him, so he kept his mouth shut. As violent as his father was, he was also a bully, and Dawson knew instinctively that bullies fought only the battles they knew they could win. He knew there would come a time when he'd be strong enough to fight back, when he would no longer be afraid of his father. As the blows rained down on him, he tried to imagine the courage his mom had shown by cutting all ties to the family.

He did his best to hasten the process. He tied a sack filled with rags to a tree and punched it for hours a day. He hefted rocks and engine parts as often as he could. He did pull-ups, push-ups, and sit-ups throughout the day. He put on ten pounds of muscle before turning thirteen, and another twenty by fourteen. He was growing taller as well. By fifteen, he was nearly as tall as his father.

One night, a month after he turned sixteen, his father came at him with a belt after a night of drinking, and Dawson reared up and ripped it from his father's grasp. He told his father that if he ever touched him again, he'd kill him.

That night, with nowhere else to go, he took refuge in Tuck's garage. When Tuck found him the following morning, Dawson asked him for a job. There was no reason for him to help Dawson, who was not only a stranger but a Cole as well. Tuck wiped his hands on the bandanna he kept in his back pocket, trying to read him before reaching for his cigarettes. At the time, he was sixty-one years old, a widower for two years. When he spoke, Dawson could smell the alcohol on his breath, and his voice was raspy with the residue of the unfiltered Camels he'd been smoking since he was a child. His accent, like Dawson's, was pure country.

"I figure you can strip 'em, but you know anythin' about puttin' 'em back again?"

"Yes, sir," Dawson had answered.

"You got schoolin' today?"

"Yes, sir."

"Then you be back here right afterwards and I'll see how you do."

Dawson showed up and did his best to prove his worth. After work, it rained most of the evening, and when Dawson sneaked back into the garage to take refuge from the storm, Tuck was waiting for him.

Tuck didn't say anything. Instead, he drew hard on his Camel, squinting at Dawson without speaking, and eventually went back into the house. Dawson never spent another night on the family land. Tuck didn't make him pay rent and Dawson bought his own food. As the months rolled on, he began to think about the future for the first time in his life. He saved as much as he could, splurging only to buy the fastback from a junkyard and gallon-size jugs of sweet tea from the diner. He repaired the car in the evenings after work while drinking the tea, and he fantasized about going to college, something no Cole had ever done. He considered joining the military or just renting his own place, but before he could make any decisions his father showed up unexpectedly at the garage. He'd brought Crazy Ted and Abee with him. Both of them carried baseball bats, and he could see the outline of a knife in Ted's pocket.

"Gimme the money you been earning," his father said without preamble.

"No," Dawson answered.

"I knew you'd say that, boy. That's why I got Ted and Abee here. They can beat it out of you and I'll take it anyway, or you can gimme what you owe for running off."

Dawson said nothing. His father picked at his gums with a toothpick.

"See, all it would take for me to end this little life of yours is a crime out there in town. Maybe a burglary, maybe a fire. Who knows? After that, we just plant some evidence, place an anonymous call to the sheriff, and let the law do the work. You're alone out here at night and you ain't gonna have no alibi, and for all I care, you can just rot away for the rest of your life surrounded by iron and concrete. Won't bother me none at all. So why don't you just hand it over?"

Dawson knew his father wasn't bluffing. Keeping his face expressionless, he took the money from his wallet. After his father counted the bills, he spat the toothpick onto the ground and grinned.

"I'll be back next week."

Dawson made do. He managed to squirrel away a little bit of the money he earned to continue his repairs on the Fastback and buy the sweet tea, but most of his money went to his father. Though he suspected that Tuck knew what was going on, Tuck never said anything directly to him. Not because he was afraid of the Coles, but because it wasn't his business. Instead, he began cooking dinners that were just a bit too large for him to eat on

his own. "Got some left, if you want it," he'd say after walking a
plate out to the garage. More often than not, he'd go back inside
without another word. That was the kind of relationship they
had, and Dawson respected it. Dawson respected Tuck. In his
own way, Tuck had become the most important person in his life,
and Dawson couldn't imagine anything that would change that.

Until the day Amanda Collier entered his world.

Though he'd known of Amanda for years—there was only
one high school in Pamlico County and he'd gone to school with
her most of his life—it wasn't until the spring of his junior year
that they exchanged more than a few words for the first time. He
always thought she was pretty, but he wasn't alone in that. She
was popular, the kind of girl who sat surrounded by friends at a
table in the cafeteria while boys vied for her attention, and she
was not only class president but a cheerleader as well. Throw in
the fact that she was rich, and she was as inaccessible to him as
an actress on television. He never said a word to her until they
were finally paired as lab partners in chemistry.

As they labored over test tubes and studied together for tests
that semester, he realized that she was nothing like he'd imagined
she would be. First, that she was a Collier and he a Cole seemed
to make no difference to her, which surprised him. She had a
quick, unbridled laugh, and when she smiled there was a mischievous hint about it, as though she knew something that no one
else did. Her hair was a rich honey blond, her eyes the color of
warm summer skies, and sometimes as they scribbled equations
into their notebooks, she would touch his arm to get his attention and the feeling would linger for hours. In the afternoons, as
he worked in the garage, he often found he couldn't stop thinking about her. It took him until spring before he finally worked up
the courage to ask if he could buy her an ice cream, and as the
end of the school year approached they began to spend more and
more time together.

That was 1984, and he was seventeen years old. By the time

summer ended, he knew he was in love, and when the air turned crisp and autumn leaves drifted to the ground in ribbons of red and yellow, he was certain that he wanted to spend the rest of his life with her, as crazy as that sounded. They stayed together the following year, growing even closer and spending every possible moment together. With Amanda, it was easy for him to be himself; with Amanda, he was content for the first time in his life. Even now, that final year together was sometimes all he could think about.

Or more accurately, Amanda was all he could think about.

On the airplane, Dawson settled into the flight. He had a window seat about halfway back, next to a young woman: red hair, midthirties, long-limbed, and tall. Not exactly his type, but pretty enough. She leaned into him as she searched for her seat belt and smiled in apology.

Dawson nodded, but sensing that she was about to strike up a conversation, he stared out the window. He watched the luggage cart pull away from the aircraft, drifting as he often did into distant memories of Amanda. He pictured the times they went swimming in the Neuse that first summer, their bodies slick as they brushed up against each other; or how she used to perch on the bench while he worked on his car in Tuck's garage, arms wrapped around her drawn-up knees, making him think that he wanted nothing more than to see her sitting just like that forever. In August, when he finally got his car to run for the first time, he took her to the beach. There they lay on their towels, fingers intertwined as they talked of their favorite books, the movies they enjoyed, their secrets and dreams for the future.

They argued as well, and then Dawson caught a glimpse of her fiery nature. Their disagreements weren't constant, but they weren't infrequent, either; remarkably, no matter how quickly things flared up, they almost always ended equally fast.

Sometimes it was about little things—Amanda was nothing if not opinionated—and they'd bicker furiously for a while, usually without any sort of resolution. Even in those instances where he became truly angry, he couldn't help admiring her honesty, an honesty rooted in the fact that she cared more about him than anyone else in his life.

Aside from Tuck, no one understood what she saw in him. Though they initially tried to conceal the relationship, Oriental was a small town, and people inevitably began to whisper. One by one, her friends withdrew, and it was only a matter of time before her parents found out. He was a Cole and she was a Collier, and that was more than enough cause for dismay. At first, they clung to the hope that Amanda was simply going through a rebellious phase, and they tried to ignore it. When that didn't work, things got harder for Amanda. They took away her driver's license and prohibited her from using the phone. In the fall, she was grounded for weeks at a time and forbidden to go out on weekends. Never once was Dawson allowed into their home, and the only time her father ever spoke to him he called Dawson "a worthless piece of white trash." Her mother begged Amanda to end it, and by December her father had stopped speaking to her altogether.

The hostility surrounding them only drew Amanda and Dawson closer together, and when Dawson began to take her hand in public, Amanda held tight, daring anyone to tell her to let go. But Dawson wasn't naive; as much as she meant to him, he always had the sense that they were on borrowed time. Everything and everyone seemed stacked against them. When his father found out about Amanda, he would ask about her when he came by to collect Dawson's wages. Though there was nothing overtly menacing in his tone, simply hearing him say her name left Dawson feeling sick to his stomach.

In January, she turned eighteen, but as furious as her parents were about the relationship, they stopped short of throwing her out of the house. By then Amanda didn't care what they thought—or at least that was what she always told Dawson. Sometimes, after yet another bitter argument with her parents, she would sneak out her bedroom window in the middle of the night and strike out for the garage. Often he would be waiting for her, but sometimes he'd awaken to her nudging him as she joined him on the mat he'd unrolled on the floor of the garage office. They'd wander down to the creek and Dawson would slip his arm around her while they sat on one of the low-slung branches of an ancient live oak. In the moonlight, as the mullets were jumping, Amanda would rehash her arguments with her parents, sometimes with a quaking voice and always careful to protect his feelings. He loved her for that, but he knew exactly how her parents felt about him. One evening, while tears spilled from beneath her lids after yet another argument, he gently suggested that it might be better for her if they stopped seeing each other.

"Is that what you want?" she whispered, her voice ragged.

He pulled her closer, slipping his arms around her. "I just want you to be happy," he whispered.

She'd leaned into him then, resting her head on his shoulder. As he held her, he'd never hated himself more for being born a Cole.

"I'm happiest when I'm with you," she finally murmured.

Later that night they made love for the first time. And for the next two decades and beyond, he carried those words and the memories of that night inside him, knowing that she had been speaking for them both.

❦

After landing in Charlotte, Dawson flung his duffel bag and suit over his shoulder and walked through the terminal, barely registering the activity around him as he sifted through memories of his final summer with Amanda. That spring, she'd received notice of her acceptance to Duke, a dream of hers since she'd been a little girl. The specter of her departure, coupled with the isolation from her family and friends, only intensified their desire to pass as much time together as possible. They spent hours at the beach and took long drives while the radio blasted, or they simply hung around Tuck's garage. They swore little would change after she left; either he'd drive to Durham or she'd come back to visit. Amanda had no doubt that they'd find a way to somehow make it work.

Her parents, however, had other plans. On a Saturday morning in August, a little more than a week before she was supposed to leave for Durham, they cornered her before she was able to escape the house. Her mom did all the talking, though she knew her father stood firmly in agreement.

"This has gone on long enough," her mother began, and in a voice that was surprisingly calm, she told Amanda that if she continued to see Dawson, she would have to move out of the house in September and start paying her own bills, and they wouldn't pay for her to attend college, either. "Why should we waste money on college when you're throwing your life away?"

When Amanda started to protest, her mother talked right over her.

"He'll drag you down, Amanda, but right now you're too young to understand that. So if you want the freedom of being an adult, you'll also have to assume the responsibilities. Ruin your life by staying with Dawson—we're not going to stop you. But we're not going to help you, either."

Amanda ran straight out of the house, her only thought to find Dawson. By the time she reached the garage, she was crying so hard she couldn't speak. Dawson held her close, letting bits and pieces of the story trickle out as her sobs finally subsided.

"We'll move in together," she said, her cheeks still damp.

"Where?" he asked her. "Here? In the garage?"

"I don't know. We'll figure it out."

Dawson remained silent, studying the floor. "You need to go to college," he finally told her.

"I don't care about college," Amanda protested. "I care about you."

He let his arms fall to his sides. "I care about you, too. And that's why I can't take this from you," he said.

She shook her head, bewildered. "You're not taking anything from me. It's my parents. They're treating me like I'm still a little girl."

"It's because of me, and we both know that." He kicked at the dirt. "If you love someone, you're supposed to let them go, right?"

For the first time, her eyes flashed. "And if they come back, it's meant to be? Is that what you think this is? Some sort of cliché?" She grabbed his arm, her fingers digging into him. "We're not a cliché," she said. "We'll find a way to make it work. I can get a job as a waitress or whatever, and we can rent a place."

He kept his voice calm, willing it not to break. "How? You think my dad is going to stop what he's doing?"

"We can move somewhere else."

"Where? With what? I have nothing. Don't you understand that?" He let the words hang, and when she didn't answer, he finally went on. "I'm just trying to be realistic. This is your life we're talking about. And...I can't be part of it anymore."

"What are you saying?"

"I'm saying your parents are right."

"You don't mean that."

In her voice, he heard something almost like fear. Though he yearned to hold her, he took a deliberate step backward. "Go home," he said.

She moved toward him. "Dawson—"

"No!" he snapped, taking a quick step away. "You're not listening. It's over, okay? We tried, it didn't work. Life moves on."

Her expression turned waxy, almost lifeless. "So that's it?"

Instead of answering, he forced himself to turn away and walk toward the garage. He knew that if he so much as glanced at her he'd change his mind, and he couldn't do that to her. He wouldn't do that to her. He ducked under the open hood of the fastback, refusing to let her see his tears.

When she finally left, Dawson slid to the dusty concrete floor next to his car, remaining there for hours, until Tuck finally came out and took a seat beside him. For a long time, he was silent.

"You ended it," Tuck finally said.

"I had to." Dawson could barely speak.

"Yep." He nodded. "Heard that, too."

The sun was climbing high overhead, blanketing everything outside the garage with a stillness that felt almost like death.

"Did I do the right thing?"

Tuck reached into his pocket and pulled out his cigarettes, buying time before he answered. He tapped out a Camel.

"Don't know. There's a lot of magic between you, ain't no denying that. And magic makes forgettin' hard." Tuck patted him on the back and got up to leave. It was more than he'd ever said to Dawson about Amanda. As he walked away, Dawson squinted into the sunlight and the tears started again. He knew that Amanda would always be the very best part of him, the self he would always long to know.

What he didn't know was that he would not see or speak to her again. The following week Amanda moved into the dorms at Duke University, and a month after that Dawson was arrested.

He spent the next four years behind bars.

2

Amanda stepped out of her car and surveyed the shack on the outskirts of Oriental that Tuck called home. She'd been driving for three hours and it felt good to stretch her legs. The tension in her neck and shoulders remained, a reminder of the argument she'd had with Frank that morning. He hadn't understood her insistence on attending the funeral, and looking back, she supposed he had a point. In the nearly twenty years that they'd been married, she'd never mentioned Tuck Hostetler; had their roles been reversed, she probably would have been upset, too.

But the argument hadn't really been about Tuck or her secrets, or even the fact that she would be spending another long weekend away from her family. Deep down, both of them knew it was simply a continuation of the same argument they'd been having for most of the past ten years, and it had proceeded in the typical fashion. It hadn't been loud or violent—Frank wasn't that type, thank God—and in the end Frank had muttered a curt apology before leaving for work. As usual, she'd spent the rest of the morning and afternoon doing her best to forget the whole thing. After all, there was nothing she could do about it, and over time she'd learned to numb herself to the anger and anxiety that had come to define their relationship.

During the drive to Oriental, both Jared and Lynn, her two

older children, had called, and she'd been thankful for the distraction. They were on summer break, and for the past few weeks the house had been filled with the endless noise typical of teenagers. Tuck's funeral couldn't have been better timed. Jared and Lynn already had plans to spend the weekend with friends, Jared with a girl named Melody and Lynn with a friend from high school, boating at Lake Norman, where her friend's family owned a house. Annette—their "wonderful accident," as Frank called her—was at camp for two weeks. She probably would have called as well were cell phones not prohibited. Which was a good thing, otherwise her little chatterbox would no doubt have been calling morning, noon, and night.

Thinking about the kids brought a smile to her face. Despite her volunteer work at the Pediatric Cancer Center at Duke University Hospital, her life largely revolved around the kids. Since Jared was born, she'd been a stay-at-home mom, and while she'd embraced and mostly relished that role, there'd always been a part of her that chafed at its limitations. She liked to think she was more than just a wife and mother. She'd gone to college to become a teacher and had even considered pursuing a PhD, with thoughts of teaching at one of the local universities. She'd taken a job teaching third grade after graduation... and then life had somehow intervened. Now, at forty-two, she sometimes found herself joking to people that she couldn't wait to grow up so she could figure out what she wanted to do for a living.

Some might call it a midlife crisis, but she wasn't sure that was exactly it. It wasn't as though she felt the need to buy a sports car or visit a plastic surgeon or run off to some island in the Caribbean. Nor was it about being bored; Lord knows, the kids and the hospital kept her busy enough. Instead, it had more to do with the sense that somehow she'd lost sight of the person she'd once meant to be, and she wasn't sure she'd ever have the opportunity to find that person again.

For a long time, she'd considered herself lucky, and Frank had been a big part of that. They'd met at a fraternity party during her sophomore year at Duke. Despite the chaos of the party, they'd somehow managed to find a quiet corner where they'd talked until the early hours of the morning. Two years older than her, he was serious and intelligent, and even on that first night she knew he'd end up being successful at whatever he chose to do. It was enough to get things started. He went off to dental school at Chapel Hill the following August, but they continued to date for the next two years. An engagement was a foregone conclusion, and in July 1989, only a few weeks after she'd finished her degree, they were married.

After a honeymoon in the Bahamas, she started her teaching job at a local elementary school, but when Jared came along the following summer, she took a leave of absence. Lynn followed eighteen months later, and the leave of absence became permanent. By then, Frank had managed to borrow enough money to open his own practice and buy a small starter house in Durham. Those were lean years; Frank wanted to succeed on his own and refused to accept offers of help from either family. After paying the bills, they were lucky if they had enough money left over to rent a movie on the weekend. Dinners out were rare, and when their car died, Amanda found herself stranded in the house for a month, until they could afford to get it fixed. They slept with extra blankets on the bed in order to keep the heating bills down. As stressful and exhausting as those years had sometimes been, when she thought back on her life, she also knew they'd been some of the happiest years of their marriage.

Frank's practice grew steadily, and in many respects their lives settled into a predictable pattern. Frank worked while she took care of the house and kids, and a third child, Bea, followed just as they sold their starter house and moved into the larger one they had built in a more established area of town. After that, things got even busier. Frank's practice began to flourish while she shuttled Jared to and from school and brought Lynn to parks and playdates, with Bea strapped in a car seat between them. It was during those years that Amanda began to revisit her plans to attend graduate school; she even took the time to look into a couple of master's programs, thinking she might enroll when Bea started kindergarten. But when Bea died, her ambitions faltered. Quietly, she set aside her GRE exam books and stowed her application forms in a desk drawer.

Her surprise pregnancy with Annette cemented her decision not to go back to school. Instead, if anything, it awakened a renewed commitment in her to focus on rebuilding their family life, and she threw herself into the kids' activities and routines with a single-minded passion, if only to keep the grief at bay. As the years passed and memories of their baby sister began to fade, Jared and Lynn slowly regained a sense of normalcy, and Amanda was grateful for that. Bright-spirited Annette brought a new kind of joy into their home, and every now and then Amanda could almost pretend that they were a complete and loving family, untouched by tragedy.

She had a hard time pretending the same about her marriage.

She wasn't, nor ever had been, under the illusion that marriage was a relationship characterized by endless bliss and romance. Throw any two people together, add the inevitable ups and downs, give the mixture a vigorous stir, and a few stormy arguments were inevitable, no matter how much the couple loved each other. Time, too, brought with it other challenges. Comfort and familiarity were wonderful, but they also dulled passion and excitement. Predictability and habit made surprises almost impossible. There were no new stories left to tell, they could often finish each other's sentences, and both she and Frank had reached the point where a single glance was filled with enough meaning to make words largely superfluous. But losing Bea had changed them. For Amanda, it spurred a passionate commitment to her volunteer work at the hospital; Frank, on the other hand, changed from someone who drank occasionally into a full-blown alcoholic.

She knew the distinction, and she'd never been a prude about drinking. There'd been several occasions in college when she'd had one too many at a party, and she still enjoyed a glass of wine with dinner. Sometimes she might even follow that with a second glass, and that almost always sufficed. But for Frank, what started as a way to numb the pain had morphed into something he could no longer control.

Looking back, she sometimes thought she should have seen it coming. In college, he'd liked to watch basketball games while drinking with his friends; in dental school, he'd often wanted to unwind with two or three beers after his classes had finished for the day. But in those dark months when Bea was sick, two or three beers a night gradually became a six-pack; after she died, it became a twelve-pack. By the time they reached the second anniversary of Bea's death, with Annette on the way, he was drinking to excess even when he had to work the following morning. Lately, it was four or five nights a week, and last night had been no different. He'd staggered into the bedroom after midnight, as drunk as she'd ever seen him, and had begun to snore so loudly that she'd had to sleep in the guest room. His drinking, not Tuck, had been the real reason for their argument this morning.

Over the years, she'd witnessed it all, from a simple slurring of his words at dinnertime or at a barbecue to drunk and passed out on the floor of their bedroom. Yet because he was widely regarded as an excellent dentist, rarely missed work, and always paid the bills, he didn't think he had a problem. Because he didn't become mean or violent, he thought he didn't have a problem. Because it was usually only beer, it couldn't possibly be a problem.

But it was a problem, because he'd gradually become the kind of man she couldn't have imagined marrying. She couldn't count the number of times that she'd cried about it. And talked to him about it, exhorting him to think of the kids. Begged him to attend couples counseling to find a solution, or raged about his selfishness. She'd given him the cold shoulder for days, forced him to sleep in the guest room for weeks, and had prayed fervently to God. Once a year or so, Frank would take her pleas to heart and stop for a while. Then, after a few weeks, he'd have a beer with dinner. Just one. And it wouldn't be a problem that night. Or maybe even the next time he had one. But he'd opened the door and the demon would enter and the drinking would spiral out of control again. And then she'd find herself asking the same questions she'd asked in the past. Why, when the urge struck, couldn't he simply walk away? And why did he refuse to accept that it was destroying their marriage?

She didn't know. What she did know was that it was exhausting. Most of the time, she felt she was the only parent who could be trusted to take care of the kids. Jared and Lynn might be old enough to drive, but what would happen if one of them got into some kind of accident while Frank was drinking? Would he hop in the car, strap Annette into the backseat, and race to the hospital? Or what if someone got sick? It had happened before. Not to the kids, but to her. A few years ago, after eating some spoiled seafood, Amanda had spent hours throwing up in the bathroom. At the time, Jared had his learner's permit and wasn't allowed to drive at night, and Frank had been on one of his binges. When she was nearing dehydration, Jared ended up taking her to the hospital around midnight while Frank lolled in the backseat and pretended to be more sober than he really was. Despite her near delirium, she noticed Jared's eyes flicking constantly to the rearview mirror, disappointment and anger warring in his expression. She sometimes thought that he shed a large part of his innocence that night, a child confronting his parent's awful shortcomings.

It was a constant, exhausting source of anxiety, and she was tired of worrying what the kids were thinking or feeling when they saw their dad stumbling through the house. Or worrying because Jared and Lynn no longer seemed to respect their father. Or worrying that, in the future, Jared or Lynn or Annette might begin to emulate their father, escaping regularly into booze or pills or God knows what else, until they ruined their own lives.

Nor had she found much in the way of help. Even without Al-Anon, she understood that there was nothing she could do to make Frank change, that until he admitted he had a problem and focused on getting better, he would remain an alcoholic. And yet what did that mean for her? That she had to make a *choice*. That she had to *decide* whether or not she would continue to put up with it. That she had to form a list of *consequences* and stick to them. In theory, that was easy. In practice, though, all it did was make her angry. If he was the one with the problem, why was she the one who had to take responsibility? And if alcoholism was a disease, didn't that mean he needed her help, or at least her loyalty? How, then, was she—his wife, who'd taken a vow to remain with him in sickness and in health—supposed to justify ending the marriage and breaking up their family, after everything they had been through? She'd either be a heartless mother and wife or a spineless enabler, when all she really wanted was the man she'd once believed him to be.

That's what made every day so hard. She didn't want to divorce him and break up the family. As compromised as their marriage might be, part of her still believed in her vows. She loved the man he'd been, and she loved the man she knew he could be, but here and now, as she stood outside Tuck Hostetler's home, she felt sad and alone, and she couldn't help wondering how her life had come to this.

§

She knew that her mother was expecting her, but Amanda wasn't ready to face her just yet. She needed a few more minutes, and as dusk began to settle in she picked her way across the overgrown yard to the cluttered garage where Tuck had spent his days restoring classic cars. Parked inside was a Corvette Stingray, a model from the 1960s, she guessed. As she ran her hand over the hood, it was easy to imagine that Tuck would return to the garage any minute, his bent figure outlined against the setting sun. He would be dressed in stained overalls, his thinning gray hair would barely cover his scalp, and the creases of his face would be so deep they'd almost resemble scars.

Despite Frank's probing questions about Tuck this morning, Amanda had said little, other than to describe him as an old family friend. It wasn't the whole story, but what else was she supposed to say? Even she admitted that her friendship with Tuck was a strange one. She'd known him in high school but hadn't seen Tuck again until six years ago, when she was thirty-six. At the time, she'd been back in Oriental visiting her mother, and while lingering over a cup of coffee at Irvin's Diner she'd overheard a group of elderly men at a nearby table gossiping about him.

"That Tuck Hostetler's still a wizard with cars, but he's sure gone crazy as a loon," one of them said, and laughed, shaking his head. "Talking to his dead wife is one thing, but swearing that he can hear her answer is another."

The old man's friend snorted. "He was always an odd one, that's for sure."

It sounded nothing like the Tuck she'd known, and after paying for her coffee, she got into her car and retraced the almost forgotten dirt drive that led to his house. They ended up spending the afternoon sitting in rockers on his collapsing front porch, and since then she'd made a habit of dropping by whenever she was in town. At first it was once or twice a year—she couldn't handle visiting her mother any more than that—but lately she'd visited Oriental and Tuck even when her mother was out of town. More often than not, she cooked dinner for him as well. Tuck was getting on in years, and though she liked to tell herself that she was simply checking in on an old man, both of them knew the real reason she kept coming back.

The men in the diner had been right, in a way. Tuck had changed. He wasn't the mostly silent and mysterious, sometimes gruff figure she remembered, but he wasn't crazy, either. He knew the difference between fantasy and reality, and he knew his wife had died long ago. But Tuck, she eventually decided, had the ability to make something real simply by wishing it into existence. At least it was real for him. When she'd finally asked him about his "conversations" with his dead wife, he'd told her matter-of-factly that Clara was still around and always would be. Not only did they talk, he confessed, but he saw her as well.

"Are you're saying she's a ghost?" she asked.

"No," he answered. "I'm just sayin' she don't want me to be alone."

"Is she here now?"

Tuck peered over his shoulder. "Don't see her, but I can hear her puttering around inside the house."

Amanda listened but heard nothing other than the squeak of the rockers on the floorboards. "Was she around...back then? When I knew you before?"

He drew a long breath, and when he spoke, his voice sounded weary. "No. But I wasn't trying to see her then."

There was something undeniably touching, almost romantic, about his conviction that they loved each other enough to have found a way to stay together, even after she was gone. Who wouldn't have found that romantic? Everyone wanted to believe that endless love was possible. She'd believed in it once, too, back when she was eighteen. But she knew that love was messy, just like life. It took turns that people couldn't foresee or even understand, leaving a long trail of regret in its wake. And almost always, those regrets led to the kinds of *what if* questions that could never be answered. *What if* Bea hadn't died? *What if*

Frank hadn't become an alcoholic? *What if* she'd married her one true love? Would she even recognize the woman who now looked back at her in the mirror?

Leaning against the car, she wondered what Tuck would have made of her musings. Tuck, who ate eggs and grits at Irvin's every morning and dropped dry-roasted peanuts into the glasses of Pepsi that he drank; Tuck, who'd lived in the same house for almost seventy years and had left the state only once, when he'd been called to serve the country in World War II. Tuck, who listened to the radio or phonograph instead of watching television, because that's what he'd always done. Unlike her, Tuck seemed to embrace the role that the world had laid out for him. She recognized that there was probably wisdom in that kind of unflinching acceptance, even if she'd never be able to achieve it.

Of course, Tuck had Clara, and maybe that had something to do with it. They'd married at seventeen and had spent forty-two years together, and as Tuck talked to Amanda, she'd gradually learned the story of their lives. In a quiet voice, he'd told her about Clara's three miscarriages, the last of which came with serious complications. According to Tuck, when the doctor informed her that she'd never be able to have children, Clara had cried herself to sleep for almost a year. Amanda learned that Clara kept a vegetable garden and had once won a statewide competition for growing the largest pumpkin, and she saw the faded blue ribbon that was still tucked behind the mirror in the bedroom. Tuck told her that after he'd established his business, they built a small cottage on a small plot of land on the Bay River near Vandemere, a town that made Oriental seem like a city, and they spent weeks there every year, because Clara thought it was the most beautiful spot in the world. He described the way Clara used to hum to the radio when she was cleaning the house, and he revealed that every now and then he used to take her dancing at Red Lee's Grill, a place that Amanda frequented during her own teenage years.

It was a life, she eventually concluded, that had been lived in the middle ground, where contentment and love were found in the smallest details of people's lives. It was a life of dignity and honor, not without sorrows yet fulfilling in a way that few experiences ever were. She knew Tuck understood that more than anyone.

"With Clara, it was always good," was how he'd once summed it up.

Maybe it was the intimate nature of his stories, or maybe her growing loneliness, but over time, Tuck became a sort of confidant to her as well, something Amanda could never have predicted. It was with Tuck that she shared her pain and sadness about Bea's death, and it was on his porch that she was able to unleash her rage at Frank; it was to him that she confessed her worries about the kids, and even her growing conviction that she'd somehow made a wrong turn in her life somewhere along the line. She shared with him stories about the countless anguished parents and impossibly optimistic children she met at the Pediatric Cancer Center, and he seemed to understand that she found a kind of salvation in her work there, even if he never said as much. Mostly, he just held her hand in his gnarled, grease-stained fingers, soothing her with his silence. By the end, he'd become her closest friend, and she'd come to feel that Tuck Hostetler knew her, the real her, better than anyone in her current life.

Now, though, her friend and confidant was gone. Missing him already, she ran her gaze over the Stingray, wondering if he'd known it was the last car he'd ever work on. He'd said nothing to her directly, but thinking back, she realized that he'd probably had his suspicions. On her last visit, he'd given her an extra key to his house, telling her with a wink "not to lose it, or you might have to break a window." She'd tucked it in her pocket, not thinking much of it, because he'd said other curious things that night. She could remember rummaging through his cupboards, looking for something to make for dinner while he sat at the table, smoking a cigarette.

"You like red wine or white wine?" he suddenly asked, apropos of nothing.

"It depends," she answered, sorting through cans. "Sometimes I have a glass of red wine with dinner."

"I got me some red wine," he announced. "Over yonder, in that cabinet over there."

She turned. "Do you want me to open a bottle?"

"Never did much care for it. I'll stick with my Pepsi and peanuts." He tapped ashes into a chipped coffee cup. "I always got fresh steaks, too. Have 'em delivered from the butcher every Monday. Bottom shelf of the icebox. Grill's out back."

She took a step toward the refrigerator. "Do you want me to make you a steak?"

"No. Usually save those for later in the week."

She hesitated, unsure where this was leading. "So . . . you're just telling me?"

When he nodded and said nothing more, Amanda chalked it up to age and fatigue. She ended up making him eggs and bacon and tidied up the house afterward while Tuck sat in the easy chair near the fireplace with a blanket over his shoulders, listening to the radio. She couldn't help noticing how shriveled he looked, immeasurably smaller than the man she'd known as a girl. As she prepared to leave, she adjusted the blanket, thinking that he'd fallen asleep. His breaths were heavy and labored-sounding. She bent down and kissed him on the cheek.

"I love you, Tuck," she whispered.

He shifted slightly, probably dreaming, but when she turned to leave she heard him exhale. "I miss you, Clara," he mumbled.

Those were the last words she would ever hear him say. There was an ache of loneliness in those words, and all at once she understood why Tuck had taken Dawson in so long ago. Tuck, she figured, had been lonely, too.

After calling Frank to let him know that she'd arrived—his voice already sounded slurry—Amanda hung up with a curt few words and thanked God that the kids were otherwise engaged this weekend.

On the workbench she found the garage clipboard and wondered what to do about the car. A quick perusal showed the Stingray was owned by a defenseman for the Carolina Hurricanes, and she made a mental note to discuss the matter with Tuck's estate lawyer. Setting the clipboard aside, she found her thoughts drifting to Dawson. He, too, had been part of her secret. Telling Frank about Tuck would have entailed telling him about Dawson, and she hadn't wanted to do that. Tuck had always understood that Dawson was the real reason she'd come to visit, especially in the beginning. He didn't mind, for Tuck more than anyone understood the power of memory. Sometimes, when the sunlight slanted through the canopy, bathing Tuck's yard in a liquid, late summer haze, she could almost sense Dawson's presence beside her and she was reminded again that Tuck had been anything but crazy. Like Clara's, Dawson's ghost was everywhere.

Although she knew it was pointless to wonder how different her life might have been if she and Dawson had stayed together, lately she'd felt the need to return to this place with increasing regularity. And the more she'd visited, the more intense the memories had become, long-forgotten events and sensations resurfacing from the depths of her past. Here it was easy to remember how strong she'd felt when she was with Dawson, and how unique and beautiful he'd always made her feel. She could recall with utter clarity her certainty that Dawson was the only person in the world who really understood her. But most of all, she could remember how completely she'd loved him and the single-minded passion with which he'd loved her back.

In his own quiet way, Dawson had made her believe that anything was possible. As she drifted through the cluttered garage, with the smell of gasoline and oil still lingering in the air, she

felt the weight of the hundreds of evenings she'd spent here. She
trailed her fingers along the bench where she used to sit for hours,
watching as Dawson leaned over the open hood of the fastback,
occasionally cranking the wrench, his fingernails black with
grease. Even then, his face had held none of the soft, youthful
naïveté she saw in others their age, and when the ropy muscles
of his forearm flexed as he reached for another tool, she saw the
limbs and form of the man he was already becoming. Like everyone else in Oriental, she knew that his father had beaten him
regularly, and when he worked without his shirt, she could see
the scars on his back, no doubt inflicted by the buckle end of a
belt. She wasn't sure whether Dawson was even aware of them
anymore, which somehow made the sight of them even worse.

He was tall and lean, with dark hair that fell over darker eyes,
and she'd known even then that he would become only more
handsome as he grew older. He looked nothing like the rest of
the Coles, and she'd asked him once whether he resembled his
mother. At the time, they were sitting in his car while raindrops
splashed over the windshield. Like Tuck's, his voice was almost
always soft, his demeanor calm. "I don't know," he said, rubbing
the fog from the glass. "My dad burned all her pictures."

Toward the end of their first summer together, they'd gone
down to the small dock on the creek, long after the sun went
down. He'd heard there was going to be a meteor shower, and
after spreading out a blanket on the planks of the dock, they
watched in silence as the lights streaked across the sky. She knew
her parents would be furious if they knew where she was, but at
the time nothing mattered but shooting stars and the warmth of
his body and the gentle way he held her close, as if he couldn't
imagine a future without her.

Were all first loves like that? Somehow she doubted it; even
now it struck her as being more real than anything she'd ever
known. Sometimes it saddened her to think that she'd never
experience that kind of feeling again, but then life had a way of

stamping out that intensity of passion; she'd learned all too well
that love wasn't always enough.

Still, as she looked out into the yard beyond the garage, she
couldn't help wondering whether Dawson had ever felt such passion again, and whether he was happy. She wanted to believe he
was, but life for an ex-con was never easy. For all she knew, he
was back in jail or hooked on drugs or even dead, but she couldn't
reconcile those images with the person she'd known. That was
part of the reason she'd never asked Tuck about him; she'd been
afraid of what he might have told her, and his silence only reinforced her suspicions. She'd preferred the uncertainty, if only
because it allowed her to remember him the way he used to be.
Sometimes, though, she wondered what he felt when he thought
of that year they spent together, or if he ever marveled at what
they'd shared, or even whether he thought of her at all.

3

Dawson's flight landed in New Bern hours after the sun had begun its steady descent toward the western horizon. In his rental car, he crossed the Neuse River into Bridgeton and turned onto Highway 55. On either side of the highway, farmhouses were set back from the road and interspersed with the occasional tobacco barn that had fallen into ruin. The flat landscape shimmered in the afternoon sunlight, and it seemed to him that nothing had changed since he'd left so many years ago, maybe not even in a hundred years. He passed through Grantsboro and Alliance, Bayboro and Stonewall, towns even smaller than Oriental, and it struck him that Pamlico County was like a place lost in time, nothing but a forgotten page in an abandoned book.

It was also home, and though many of the memories were painful, it was here where Tuck had befriended him and it was here where he'd met Amanda. One by one, he began to recognize landmarks from his childhood, and in the silence of the car he wondered who he might have become had Tuck and Amanda never entered his life. But more than that, he wondered how differently his life might have turned out had Dr. David Bonner not stepped out for a jog on the night of September 18, 1985.

Dr. Bonner had moved to Oriental in December of the previous year with his wife and two young children. For years, the town had been without a physician of any kind. The previous physician had retired to Florida in 1980, and Oriental's Board of Commissioners had been trying to replace him ever since. There was a desperate need, but despite the numerous incentives that the town offered, few decent candidates were interested in moving to what was essentially a backwater. As luck would have it, Dr. Bonner's wife, Marilyn, had grown up in the area and, like Amanda, was considered to be almost royalty. Marilyn's parents, the Bennetts, grew apples, peaches, grapes, and blueberries in a massive orchard on the outskirts of town, and after he finished his residency, David Bonner moved to his wife's hometown and opened his own practice.

He was busy from the beginning. Tired of traveling the forty minutes to New Bern, patients flocked to his office, but the doctor was under no illusion that he'd ever become rich. It simply wasn't possible in a small town in a poor county, no matter how busy the practice was and despite the family connections. Though no one else in town knew it, the orchard had been heavily mortgaged, and on the day David had moved to town, his father-in-law had hit him up for a loan. But even after he'd helped his in-laws with money, the cost of living was low enough to allow him to buy a four-bedroom colonial overlooking Smith Creek, and his wife was thrilled to be back home. In her mind, Oriental was an ideal place to raise children, and for the most part she was right.

Dr. Bonner loved the outdoors. He surfed and swam; he bicycled and ran. It was common for people to see him jogging briskly up Broad Street after work, eventually heading past the curve on the outskirts of town. People would honk or wave, and Dr. Bonner would nod without breaking stride. Sometimes, after a particularly long day, he wouldn't start until just before dark, and on September 18, 1985, that was exactly what happened. He left the house just as dusk was settling over the town. Though

Dr. Bonner didn't know it, the roads were slick. It had rained earlier that afternoon, steadily enough to raise the oil from the macadam but not hard enough to wash it away.

He started out on his usual route, which took about thirty minutes, but that night he never made it home. By the time the moon had risen, Marilyn started to get anxious, and after asking a neighbor to watch the kids, she hopped in the car to search for him. Just beyond the curve at the edge of town, near a copse of trees, she found an ambulance, along with the sheriff and a slowly growing crowd of people. It was there, she learned, that her husband had been killed when the driver of a truck lost control and skidded into him.

The truck, Marilyn was told, was owned by Tuck Hostetler. The driver, who would soon be charged with felony death by motor vehicle and involuntary manslaughter, was eighteen years old and already in handcuffs.

His name was Dawson Cole.

Two miles from the outskirts of Oriental—and the curve he'd never forget—Dawson spotted the old gravel turnoff that led to the family land and automatically found himself thinking about his father. When Dawson was in the county jail awaiting trial, a guard had appeared suddenly and informed him that he had a visitor. A minute later, his father was standing before him, chewing on a toothpick.

"Runnin' off, seeing that rich girl, making plans. And where do you end up? In jail." He saw the malicious glee in his father's expression. "You thought you was better than me, but you ain't. You're just like me."

Dawson said nothing, feeling something close to hatred as he glared at his father from the corner of his cell. He vowed then and there that whatever happened, he would never speak to his father again.

There was no trial. Against the advice of the public defender, Dawson pleaded guilty, and against the advice of the prosecutor, he was given the maximum sentence. At Caledonia Correctional in Halifax, North Carolina, he worked on the prison farm, helping to grow corn, wheat, cotton, and soybeans, sweating beneath a blistering dog-day sun as he harvested or freezing in icy northern winds as he tilled. Though he corresponded with Tuck through the mail, in four years he never had a single visitor.

After his release, Dawson was placed on parole and returned to Oriental. He worked for Tuck and heard the townsfolk's whispers on his occasional supply runs to the automotive store. He knew he was a pariah, a no-good Cole who'd killed not only the Bennetts' son-in-law but the town's only doctor, and the guilt he felt was overwhelming. In those moments, he would pay a visit to a florist in New Bern, then later to the cemetery in Oriental where Dr. Bonner had been buried. He would place the flowers on the grave, either early in the morning or late at night, when few people were around. Sometimes he stayed for an hour or more, thinking about the wife and children Dr. Bonner had left behind. Other than that, he spent that year largely in the shadows, trying his best to stay out of sight.

His family wasn't through with him, though. When his father came to the garage to start collecting Dawson's money again, he brought Ted with him. His father had a shotgun, Ted had a baseball bat, but it was a mistake to have come without Abee. When Dawson told them to get off the property, Ted moved quickly but not quick enough: Four years of working in the sun-packed fields had hardened Dawson, and he was ready for them. He broke Ted's nose and jaw with a crowbar and disarmed his father before cracking the old man's ribs. While they were lying on the ground, Dawson aimed the shotgun at them, warning them not to come back. Ted wailed that he was going to kill him; Dawson's father simply scowled. After that, Dawson slept with the shotgun by his side and seldom left the property. He knew they could have come for him at any time, but fate is unpredictable. Crazy Ted ended up stabbing a man in a bar less than a week later and was hauled off to prison. And for whatever reason, his daddy never came back. Dawson didn't question it. Instead, he counted the days until he would finally be able to leave Oriental, and when his parole ended he wrapped the shotgun in an oilcloth, boxed it up, and buried it at the foot of an oak tree near the corner of Tuck's house. Afterward he packed his car, said good-bye to Tuck, and hit the highway, finally ending up in Charlotte. He found a job as a mechanic, and in the evenings he took classes in welding at the community college. From there, he made his way to Louisiana and took a job at a refinery. That eventually led to the job on the rigs.

Since his release he'd kept a low profile, and for the most part he was alone. He never visited friends because he didn't have any. He hadn't dated anyone since Amanda because, even now, she was all he could think about. To get close to someone, anyone, meant allowing that person to learn about his past, and the thought made him recoil. He was an ex-con from a family of criminals, and he'd killed a good man. Though he'd served his sentence and had tried to make amends ever since, he knew he'd never forgive himself for what he'd done.

🍃

Getting close now. Dawson was approaching the spot where Dr. Bonner had been killed. Vaguely, he noticed that the trees near the curve had been replaced by a low, squat building fronted by a gravel parking lot. He kept his eyes on the road, refusing to look.

Less than a minute later, he was in Oriental. He passed through downtown and crossed the bridge that spanned the confluence of Greens Creek and Smith Creek. As a boy, when trying to avoid his family, he'd often sit near the bridge, watching the sailboats and imagining the faraway harbors they might have visited and the places he one day wanted to go.

He slowed the car, as captivated by the view as he'd once been. The marina was crowded, and people were moving about on their boats, carrying coolers or untying the ropes that held their boats in place. Peering up at the trees, he could tell by the swaying branches that there was enough wind to keep the sails full, even if they intended to sail all the way to the coast.

In the rearview mirror, he glimpsed the bed-and-breakfast where he'd be staying, but he wasn't ready to check in just yet. Instead, on the near side of the bridge, he pulled the car over and climbed out, relieved to stretch his legs. He vaguely wondered whether the delivery from the florist had arrived, but he supposed he'd find out soon enough. Turning toward the Neuse, he recalled that it was the widest river in the United States by the time it reached Pamlico Sound, a fact that few people knew. He'd won more than a few bets on that piece of trivia, especially on the rigs, where practically everyone guessed the Mississippi. Even in North Carolina it wasn't common knowledge; it was Amanda who had first told him.

As always, he wondered about her: what she was doing, where she lived, what her daily life was like. That she was married, he had no doubt, and over the years he'd tried to imagine the kind of man she would have picked. Despite how well he'd known her, he couldn't picture her laughing with or sleeping next to another man. He supposed it didn't matter. The past can be escaped only by embracing something better, and he figured that was what she'd done. It seemed as though everyone else was able to, after all. Everyone had regrets and everyone had made mistakes, but Dawson's mistake was different. It was strapped to his back forever, and he thought again of Dr. Bonner and the family he'd destroyed.

Staring out at the water, he suddenly regretted his decision to return. He knew that Marilyn Bonner still lived in town, but he didn't want to see her, even inadvertently. And though his family would no doubt learn that he'd come back, he didn't want to see them, either.

There was nothing here for him. Though he could understand why Tuck had made arrangements for the attorney to call him after he'd died, he couldn't figure out why Tuck's express wish had been for Dawson to return home. Since receiving the message, he'd turned the question over and over in his mind, but it didn't make sense. Never once had Tuck asked him to come and visit; more than anyone, he knew what Dawson had left behind. Nor had Tuck ever traveled to Louisiana, and though Dawson wrote regularly to Tuck, he infrequently received a response. He had to think that Tuck had his reasons, whatever they might be, but right now he couldn't figure them out.

He was about to return to the car when he noticed the now familiar flash of movement just beyond his periphery. He turned, trying without success to locate the source, but for the first time since he was rescued, the hairs on his neck started to prickle. There was something there, he suddenly knew, even if his mind couldn't identify it. The setting sun glittered sharply off the water, making him squint. He shaded his eyes as he scanned the marina, taking in the scene. He spotted an elderly man and his wife pulling their sailboat into a slip; halfway down the dock, a shirtless man was peering into an engine compartment. He observed a few others as well: a middle-aged couple puttering around on a boat deck and a group of teenagers unloading a cooler after a day spent on the water. At the far end of the marina, another sailboat was pulling out, intent on capturing the late afternoon breeze—nothing unusual. He was about to turn away again when he spotted a dark-haired man wearing a blue windbreaker and staring in his direction. The man was standing at the foot of the dock and, like Dawson, was shading his eyes. As Dawson slowly lowered his hand, the dark-haired man's movements mirrored his own. Dawson took a quick step backward; the stranger did the same. Dawson felt his breath catch as his heart hammered in his chest.

This isn't real. It can't be happening.

The sun was low behind him, making the stranger's features difficult to discern, but despite the waning light Dawson was suddenly certain it was the man he'd seen first in the ocean and then again on the supply ship. He blinked rapidly, trying to bring the man into better focus. When his vision finally cleared, though, he saw only the outline of a post on the dock, fraying ropes tied at the top.

*

The sighting left Dawson rattled, and he suddenly felt the urge to go directly to Tuck's place. It had been his refuge years before, and all at once he recalled the sense of peace he'd found there. Somehow he didn't relish the thought of making small talk at the bed-and-breakfast as he checked in; he wanted to be alone to ponder the sighting of the dark-haired man. Either the concussion had been worse than the doctors had suspected or the doctors were right about the stress. As he edged back onto the road, he resolved to check with the doctors in Louisiana again, although he suspected they'd tell him the same thing they had before.

He pushed away the troubling thoughts and rolled down the window, breathing in the earthy scent of pine and brackish water as the road wound among the trees. A few minutes later, Dawson made the turn onto Tuck's property. The car bounced along the rutted dirt drive, and as he rounded the corner the house came into view. To his surprise, a BMW was parked out front. He knew it wasn't Tuck's. It was too clean, for one thing, but more than that, Tuck would never have driven a foreign car, not because he didn't trust the quality, but because he wouldn't have had the metric tools he'd need to repair it. Besides, Tuck had always favored trucks, especially those built in the early 1960s. Over the years, he'd probably bought and restored half a dozen of them, driving them for a while before selling them to whoever happened to make an offer. For Tuck, it was less about the money than the restoration itself.

Dawson parked beside the BMW and stepped out of the car, surprised at how little the house had changed. The place had never been much more than a shack even when Dawson had been around, and there had always been a half-finished-and-in-need-of-repair appearance to the exterior. Amanda had once bought Tuck a flowering planter to spruce up the place, and it still stood in the corner of the porch, though the flowers had long since withered away. He could recall how excited she'd been when they'd presented Tuck with it, even if he hadn't known quite what to make of it.

Dawson surveyed the area, watching a squirrel as it skittered along the branch of a dogwood tree. A cardinal called a warning from the trees, but other than that, the place seemed deserted. He started around the side of the house, walking toward the garage. It was cooler there, shaded by the pines. As he rounded the corner and stepped into the sun, he caught sight of a woman standing just inside the garage, examining what was probably the last classic car that Tuck had ever restored. His first thought was that she was probably from the attorney's office, and he was about to call out a greeting when she suddenly turned around. His voice died in his throat.

Even from a distance, she was more beautiful than he remembered, and for what seemed an endless span of time, he couldn't say anything. It occurred to him that he might be hallucinating again, but he slowly blinked and realized that he was wrong. She was real, and she was here, in the refuge that had once been theirs.

It was then, while Amanda was staring back at him from across the years, that he suddenly knew why Tuck Hostetler had insisted he come back home.

4

Neither one of them was able to move or speak as surprise gradually turned to recognition. Dawson's first thought was how much more vivid she was in person than in his memories of her. Her blond hair caught the late afternoon light like burnished gold, and her blue eyes were electric even at a distance. But as he continued to stare, subtle differences slowly came into focus. Her face, he noticed, had lost the softness of youth. The angles of her cheekbones were more visible now and her eyes seemed deeper, framed by a faint tracing of lines at the corners. The years, he realized, had been more than kind: Since he'd seen her last, she'd grown into a mature and remarkable beauty.

Amanda was also trying to absorb what she was seeing. His sand-colored shirt was tucked casually into faded jeans, outlining his still-angular hips and wide shoulders. His smile was the same, but he wore his dark hair longer than he had as a teenager, and she noticed a wash of gray at his temples. His dark eyes were as striking as she remembered, but she thought she detected a new wariness in them, the sign of someone who'd lived a life that had been harder than expected. Perhaps it was the result of seeing him here, in this place where they'd shared so much, but in the sudden rush of emotion she could think of nothing to say.

"Amanda?" he finally asked, beginning to walk toward her.

She heard the wonder in his voice as he said her name, and it was that, more than anything, that let her know he was real. *He's here*, she thought, *it's really him*, and as he closed the distance between them, she felt the years slowly falling away, as impossible as that seemed. When he finally reached her, he opened his arms and she went into them naturally, as she'd done so long ago. He pulled her close, holding her like the lovers they once had been, and she leaned into him, suddenly feeling eighteen again.

"Hello, Dawson," she whispered.

They embraced for a long time, holding each other close in the waning sunlight, and for an instant he thought he felt her tremble. When they finally pulled apart, she could sense his unspoken emotion.

She studied him up close, noting the changes the years had wrought. He was a man now. His face was weathered and tanned, like someone who spent long hours in the sun, and his hair had thinned only slightly.

"What are you doing here?" he asked, touching her arm as if to reassure himself that she was real.

The question helped her regain her bearings, reminding her of who she'd become, and she took a tiny step backward. "I'm here probably for the same reason that you are. When did you get in?"

"Just now," he said, wondering at the impulse that had driven him to make this unplanned visit to Tuck's. "I can't believe you're here. You look...amazing."

"Thank you." Despite herself, she could feel the blood in her cheeks. "How did you know I'd be here?"

"I didn't," he said. "I had the urge to swing by and I saw the car out front. I came around back and..."

When he trailed off, Amanda finished for him. "And here I was."

"Yeah." He nodded, meeting her eyes for the first time. "And there you were."

The intensity of his gaze hadn't changed, and she took another step backward, hoping the space would make things easier. Hoping he wouldn't get the wrong impression. She motioned toward the house. "Were you planning to stay here?"

He squinted at the house before turning back to her. "No, I have a room at the bed-and-breakfast downtown. You?"

"I'm staying with my mom." When she noticed his quizzical expression, she explained, "My dad passed away eleven years ago."

"I'm sorry," he said.

She nodded, saying nothing further, and he remembered that, in the past, it was how she'd usually closed a subject. When she glanced toward the garage, Dawson took a step toward it. "Do you mind?" he asked. "I haven't seen the place in years."

"No, of course not," she said. "Go ahead."

She watched him move past her and felt her shoulders relax, unaware that she'd been tensing them. He peeked into the small cluttered office before trailing his hand along the workbench and over a rusting tire iron. Wandering slowly, he took in the plank walls, the open beamed ceiling, the steel barrel in the corner where Tuck disposed of excess oil. A hydraulic jack and snap-on tool chest stood along the back wall, fronted by a pile of tires. An electronic sander and welding equipment occupied the side opposite the workbench. A dusty fan was propped in the corner near the paint sprayer, electric lights dangled from wires, and parts lay strewn on every available surface.

"It looks exactly the same," he commented.

She followed him deeper into the garage, still feeling a little shaky, trying to keep a comfortable distance between them.

"It probably is the same. He was meticulous about where he put his tools, especially in the last few years. I think he knew he was beginning to forget things."

"Considering his age, I can't believe he was still working on cars at all."

"He'd slowed way down. One or two a year, and then only when he knew he could do the work. No major restorations or anything like that. This is the first car I've seen here in a while."

"You sound like you spent a lot of time with him."

"Not really. I saw him every few months or so. But we were out of touch for a long time."

"He never mentioned you in his letters," Dawson mused.

She shrugged. "He didn't mention you, either."

He nodded before turning his attention back to the work-bench again. Folded neatly on the end was one of Tuck's bandan-nas, and lifting it up, he tapped his finger on the bench. "The initials I carved are still here. Yours, too."

"I know," she said. Below them, she also knew, was the word *forever*. She crossed her arms, trying not to stare at his hands. They were weathered and strong, a workingman's hands, yet tapered and graceful at the same time.

"I can't believe he's gone," he said.

"I know."

"You said he was forgetting things?"

"Just little things. Considering his age and how much he smoked, he was in pretty good health the last time I saw him."

"When was that?"

"Late February, maybe?"

He motioned toward the Stingray. "Do you know anything about this?"

She shook her head. "Just that Tuck was working on it. There's a work order on the clipboard with Tuck's notes about the car, but other than the owner, I can't make heads or tails of it. It's right over there."

Dawson found the order and scanned the list before inspect-ing the car. She watched as he opened the hood and leaned in to look, his shirt stretching tight around his shoulders, and Amanda turned away, not wanting him to realize that she'd noticed. After a minute, he turned his attention to the small boxes on the workbench. He pried back the lids, nodding as he sorted through the parts, his brow furrowing.

"That's strange," Dawson said.

"What?"

"It wasn't a restoration at all. It's mainly engine work, and minor stuff at that. Carburetor, the clutch, a few other things. My guess is he was just waiting for these parts to arrive. Sometimes, with these old cars, it can take a while."

"What does that mean?"

"Among other things, it means there's not a chance the owner can drive it out of here."

"I'll have the attorney contact the owner." She brushed a strand of hair from her eyes. "I'm supposed to meet with him anyway."

"The attorney?"

"Yeah." She nodded. "He's the one who called about Tuck. He said it was important that I come."

Dawson closed the hood. "His name wouldn't happen to be Morgan Tanner, would it?"

"Do you know him?" she asked, startled.

"Just that I'm supposed to meet with him tomorrow, too."

"What time?"

"Eleven. Which I'm guessing is the same time as your appointment, right?"

It took a few seconds before she grasped what Dawson had already figured out—that Tuck had obviously planned this little reunion all along. Had they not met here at Tuck's, they would have done so tomorrow no matter what. As the implication became clear, she suddenly didn't know whether she wanted to punch Tuck in the arm or kiss him for it.

Her face must have telegraphed her feelings, because Dawson said, "I take it that you had no idea what Tuck was up to."

"No."

A flock of starlings broke from the trees, and Amanda watched as they veered overhead, changing direction, tracing abstract patterns in the sky. By the time she faced him again, Dawson was leaning against the workbench, his face half in shadow. In this place, with so much history surrounding them, she swore she could see the young man Dawson used to be, but she tried to remind herself that they were different people now. Strangers, really.

"It's been a long time," he said, breaking the silence.

"Yes, it has."

"I have about a thousand questions."

She raised an eyebrow. "Only a thousand?"

He laughed, but she thought she heard an undercurrent of sadness in it. "I have questions, too," she went on, "but before that . . . you should know that I'm married."

"I know," he said. "I saw your wedding band." He tucked a thumb in his pocket before leaning against the workbench and crossing one leg over the other. "How long have you been married?"

"Twenty years next month."

"Kids?"

She paused, thinking of Bea, never sure how to answer the question. "Three," she finally said.

He noticed her hesitation, unsure what to make of it. "And your husband? Would I like him?"

"Frank?" She flashed on the anguished conversations she'd had with Tuck about Frank and wondered how much Dawson already knew. Not because she didn't trust Tuck with her confidences, but because she had the sudden sense that Dawson would know immediately whether she was lying. "We've been together a long time."

Dawson seemed to evaluate her choice of words before finally pushing off the workbench. He walked past her, heading toward the house, moving with the liquid grace of an athlete. "I suppose Tuck gave you a key, right? I need something to drink."

She blinked in surprise.

"Wait! Did Tuck tell you that?"

Dawson turned around, continuing to walk backward. "No."

"Then how did you know?"

"Because he didn't send one to me, and one of us has to have it."

She stood in place, debating, still trying to figure out how he knew, before finally following him up the path.

He climbed the porch steps in a single fluid motion, stopping at the door. Amanda fished a key from her purse, brushing against him as she slipped it into the lock. The door swung open with a squeak.

It was mercifully cool inside, and Dawson's first thought was that the interior was an extension of the forest itself: all wood and earth and natural stains. The plank walls and pine flooring had dulled and cracked over the years, and the brown curtains did little to hide the leaks beneath the windows. The armrests and cushions on the plaid sofa were almost completely worn through. The mortar on the fireplace had begun to crack, and the bricks around the opening were black, charcoaled remnants of a thousand roaring fires. Near the door was a small table bearing a stack of photo albums, a record player that was probably older than Dawson, and a rickety steel fan. The air smelled of stale cigarettes, and after opening one of the windows, Dawson switched on the fan, listening as it began to rattle. The base wobbled slightly.

By then, Amanda was standing near the fireplace, staring at the photograph sitting on the mantel. Tuck and Clara, taken on their twenty-fifth anniversary.

He walked toward Amanda, stopping when he was beside her. "I remember the first time I saw that picture," he offered. "I'd been here for about a month before Tuck let me inside the house, and I remember asking who she was. I didn't even know he'd been married."

She could feel the heat radiating from him and tried to ignore it. "How could you not know that?"

"Because I didn't know him. Until I showed up at his place that night, I'd never talked to Tuck before."

"Why did you come here, then?"

"I don't know," he said with a shake of his head. "And I don't know why he let me stay."

"Because he wanted you here."

"Did he tell you that?"

"Not in so many words. But Clara hadn't been gone that long when you came along, and I think you were just what he needed."

"And here I used to think it was just because he was drinking that night. Most nights, for that matter."

She searched her memory. "Tuck wasn't a drinker, was he?"

He touched the photo in its plain wooden frame, as if still trying to comprehend a world without Tuck in it. "It was before you knew him. He had a liking for Jim Beam back then, and sometimes he'd stagger out to the garage still holding the half-empty bottle. He'd wipe his face with his bandanna and tell me that it would be better if I found someplace else to stay. He must have said that every night for the first six months I was sleeping out there. And I'd lie there all night, hoping that by the next morning he would have forgotten what he'd told me. And then, one day, he just stopped drinking, and he never said it again." He turned toward her, his face only inches from hers. "He was a good man," he said.

"I know," she said. He was close enough that she could smell him; soap and musk, mingling together. Too close. "I miss him, too."

She stepped away, reaching over to fiddle with one of the threadbare pillows on the sofa, creating distance again. Outside, the sun was dropping behind the trees, making the small room even darker. She heard Dawson clear his throat.

"Let's get that drink. I'm sure that Tuck has some sweet tea in the refrigerator."

"Tuck doesn't drink sweet tea. He's probably got some Pepsi, though."

"Let's check," he said, making for the kitchen.

He moved with the grace of an athlete, and she shook her head slightly, trying to force away the thought. "Are you sure we should be doing this?"

"I'm pretty sure it's exactly what Tuck wanted."

Like the living room, the kitchen might have been stored in a time capsule, with appliances straight from a 1940s Sears, Roebuck catalog, a toaster the size of a microwave oven and a boxy refrigerator with a latch handle. The wooden countertop was black with water stains near the sink, and the white paint on the cabinets was chipping near the knobs. The flower-patterned curtains—obviously something Clara had hung—had turned a dingy grayish yellow, stained by the smoke from Tuck's cigarettes. There was a small, barrel-top table with room for two, and a clump of paper napkins had been stuffed beneath it to keep it from wobbling. Dawson swung the latch on the refrigerator door, reached in, and pulled out a jug of tea. Amanda entered as he set the tea on the counter.

"How did you know that Tuck had sweet tea?" she asked.

"The same way I knew you had the keys," he answered as he reached into the cupboard and pulled out a pair of jelly jars.

"What are you talking about?"

Dawson filled the jars. "Tuck knew we'd both end up here eventually, and he remembered that I like sweet tea. So he made sure he had some waiting in the refrigerator."

Of course he did. Just as he'd done with the attorney. But before she could dwell on it, Dawson offered her the tea, bringing her back to the present. Their fingers brushed as she took it.

Dawson held up his tea. "To Tuck," he said.

Amanda clinked her glass with his, and all of it—standing close to Dawson, the tug of the past, the way she'd felt when he'd held her, the two of them alone in the house—was almost more than she could handle. A little voice inside her whispered that she needed to be careful, that nothing good could come of this, and reminded her that she had a husband and children. But that only made things more confusing.

"So, twenty years, huh?" Dawson finally asked.

He was asking about her marriage, but in her distracted state it took her a moment to grasp. "Almost. How about you? Were you ever married?"

"I don't think it was in the cards."

She eyed him over the rim of her glass. "Still playing the field, huh?"

"I keep pretty much to myself these days."

She leaned against the counter, unsure what to read into his response. "Where do you live now?"

"Louisiana. In a parish just outside New Orleans."

"Do you like it?"

"It's okay. I'd forgotten until I came back here how much it looks like home. There are more pines here and more Spanish moss there, but other than that I'm not real sure I could tell the difference."

"Except for the alligators."

"Yeah. Except for that." He offered a faint smile. "Your turn. Where's home these days?"

"Durham. I stayed there after I got married."

"And you come back a few times a year to see your mom?"

She nodded. "When my dad was alive, they used to visit us because of the kids. But after my dad died, it got harder. My mom never liked to drive, so now I have to come here." She took a sip before nodding toward the table. "Do you mind if I sit? My feet are killing me."

"Feel free. I'll stand for a bit, though. I've been stuck on an airplane all day."

She picked up her glass and started toward the table, feeling his eyes on her.

"What do you do in Louisiana?" she asked, sliding into her seat.

"I'm a derrick hand on an oil rig, which basically means that I assist the driller. I help guide the drill pipe in and out of the elevator, I make sure all the connections are proper, I keep on the pumps to make sure they're running right. I know that probably doesn't make much sense since you've probably never been on a rig, but it's kind of hard to explain without actually showing you."

"That's a long way from fixing cars."

"It's less different than you think. Essentially, I work with engines and machines. And I still work with cars, too, in my spare time anyway. The fastback runs like new."

"You still have it?"

He grinned. "I like that car."

"No," she challenged, "you *love* that car. I used to have to drag you away from it whenever I came by. And half the time, I didn't succeed. I'm surprised you don't carry a picture of it in your wallet."

"I do."

"Really?"

"I was kidding."

She laughed, the same free-spirited laugh from long ago. "How long have you been working on rigs?"

"Fourteen years. I started as a roustabout, worked up to rough-neck, and here I am, a derrick hand."

"Roustabout to roughneck to derrick hand?"

"What can I say? We speak our own language out there on the ocean." He absently picked at one of the grooves etched into the ancient countertop. "And what about you? Do you work? You used to talk about becoming a teacher."

She took a sip, nodding. "I taught for a year, but then I had Jared, my oldest son, and I wanted to stay at home with him. After that Lynn was born and then...we had a few years when a lot happened, including my dad passing away, a really tough time." She paused, conscious of how much she was leaving out, knowing it wasn't the time or place to talk about Bea. She straightened up, keeping her voice steady. "A couple of years after that, Annette came along, and by then there was no reason for me to go back to work. But I've spent a lot of time over the past ten years volunteering at Duke University Hospital. I also do some fund-raising luncheons for them. It's hard sometimes, but it makes me feel like I'm making a little bit of difference."

"How old are your kids?"

She ticked them off on her fingers. "Jared turns nineteen in August and just finished his first year of college, Lynn is seventeen and starting her senior year. Annette, my nine-year-old, just finished third grade. She's a sweet and happy-go-lucky little girl. Jared and Lynn, on the other hand, are at the age when they think they know everything and I, of course, know absolutely nothing."

"In other words, you're saying they're kind of like we were?"

She thought about it, her expression almost wistful. "Maybe."

Dawson fell silent, staring out the window, and she followed his gaze. The creek had turned the color of iron and the slow-moving water reflected the darkening skies. The old oak tree near the bank hadn't changed much since the last time he'd been here, but the dock had rotted away, leaving only the pilings.

"A lot of memories there, Amanda," he observed, his voice soft.

Maybe it was the way he sounded when he said it, but she felt something click inside at his words, like a key turning in a distant lock.

"I know," she said at last. She paused, wrapping her arms around herself, and for a while the hum of the refrigerator was the only sound in the kitchen. The overhead light cast a yellowish glow on the walls, projecting their profiles in abstract shadows. "How long are you planning on staying?" she finally asked.

"I have a flight out early Monday morning. You?"

"Not long. I told Frank I'd be back on Sunday. If my mom had her way, though, she would rather I had stayed in Durham all weekend. She told me it wasn't a good idea to come to the funeral."

"Why?"

"Because she didn't like Tuck."

"You mean she didn't like me."

"She never knew you," Amanda said. "She never gave you a chance. She always had ideas about the way I was supposed to live my life. What I might want never seemed to matter. Even though I'm an adult, she still tries to tell me what to do. She hasn't changed a bit." She rubbed at the moisture on the jelly jar. "A few years ago, I made the mistake of telling her that I'd dropped in on Tuck, and you would have thought that I'd just committed a crime. She kept haranguing me, asking why I visited him, wanting to know what we talked about, all the while scolding me like I was still a child. So after that, I just stopped telling her about it. Instead, I'd tell her I was going shopping, or that I wanted to have lunch with my friend Martha at the beach. Martha and I were roommates in college and she lives in Salter Path, but even though we talk, I haven't actually seen her in years. I don't want to deal with my mother's prying questions, so I just lie to her."

Dawson swirled his tea, thinking about what she'd said, watching as the drink finally went still again. "As I was driving here, I couldn't help thinking about my father, and how for him it was always about control. I'm not saying your mom is anything like him, but maybe it's just her way of trying to keep you from making a mistake."

"Are you saying it was a mistake to visit Tuck?"

"Not for Tuck," he said. "But for you? It depends on what you hoped to find here, and only you can answer that."

She felt a flash of defensiveness, but before she could respond the feeling gave way as she recognized the pattern they'd shared so long ago. One would say something that challenged the other, often leading to an argument, and she realized how much she'd missed that. Not because they fought, but because of the trust it implied and the forgiveness that inevitably followed. Because, in the end, they'd always forgiven each other.

Part of her suspected that he'd been testing her, but she let the comment pass. Instead, surprising herself, she leaned forward over the table, the next words coming almost automatically.

"What are you doing for dinner tonight?"

"I don't have any plans. Why?"

"There are some steaks in the fridge if you want to eat here."

"What about your mom?"

"I'll call and tell her that I got a late start."

"Are you sure that's a good idea?"

"No," she said. "I'm not sure about anything right now."

He scratched a thumb against the glass, saying nothing as he studied her. "Okay." He nodded. "Steaks it is. Assuming they're not spoiled."

"They were delivered Monday," she said, remembering what Tuck had told her. "The grill's out back if you want to get it started."

A moment later he was out the door; his presence, however, continued to linger, even as she fished her cell phone from her purse.

5

―――― ❧ ――――

When the coals were ready, Dawson went back inside to retrieve the steaks from Amanda, who'd already buttered and seasoned them. Pushing open the door, he saw her staring into the cupboard while absently holding a can of pork and beans.

"What's going on?"

"I was trying to find some things to go with the steak, but other than this," she said, holding up the can, "there's not much."

"What are our choices?" he asked as he washed his hands at the kitchen sink.

"Aside from the beans, he has grits, a bottle of spaghetti sauce, pancake flour, a half-empty box of penne pasta, and Cheerios. In the fridge, he has butter and condiments. Oh, and the sweet tea, of course."

He shook off the excess water. "Cheerios is a possibility."

"I think I'll go with the pasta," she said, rolling her eyes. "And shouldn't you be outside grilling the steaks?"

"I suppose," he answered, and she had to suppress a smile. From the corner of her eye, she watched him pick up the platter and leave, the door behind him closing with a gentle click.

The sky was a deep, velvety purple and the stars were already ablaze. Beyond Dawson's figure, the creek was a black ribbon and the treetops were beginning to glow silver with the slowly rising moon.

She filled a pan with water, tossed in a little salt, and turned on the burner; from the fridge she retrieved the butter. When the water boiled, she added the pasta and spent the next few minutes searching for the strainer before finally locating it in the back of the cabinet near the stove.

When the pasta was ready, she drained it and put it back into the pan, along with butter, garlic powder, and a dash of salt and pepper. Quickly, she heated up the can of beans, finishing just as Dawson came back in carrying the platter.

"It smells great," he said, not bothering to hide his surprise.

"Butter and garlic," she nodded. "Works every time. How are the steaks?"

"One's medium rare, the other's medium. I'm good with either, but I wasn't sure how you wanted yours. I can always put one back on the grill for a few more minutes."

"Medium is fine," she agreed.

Dawson set the platter on the table and riffled through the cabinets and drawers, pulling out plates, glasses, and utensils. She caught sight of two wine glasses in the open cupboard and was reminded of what Tuck had said on her last visit.

"Would you like a glass of wine?" she asked.

"Only if you join me."

She nodded, then opened the cabinet that Tuck had pointed out, revealing two bottles. She picked out the cabernet and opened it while Dawson finished setting the table. After pouring them each a glass, she handed one to him.

"There's a bottle of steak sauce in the fridge, if you want some," she said.

Dawson found the sauce while Amanda poured the pasta into one bowl and the beans into another. They arrived at the table at the same time, and as they surveyed the intimate dinner setting, she noticed the gentle rise and fall of his chest as he stood beside her. Breaking the moment, Dawson reached for the bottle of wine on the counter, and she shook her head before sliding into her seat.

Amanda took a sip of wine, the flavor lingering at the back of her throat. After they served themselves, Dawson hesitated, staring at his plate.

"Is it okay?" She frowned.

The sound of her voice brought him back to her. "I was just trying to remember the last time I had a meal like this."

"Steak?" she asked, slicing into the meat and spearing a first bite.

"Everything." He shrugged. "On the rig, I eat in the cafeteria with a bunch of guys, and at home it's just me, and I usually end up doing something simple."

"What about when you go out? There are lots of great places to eat in New Orleans."

"I hardly ever get to the city."

"Even on a date?" she quizzed between bites.

"I don't really date," he said.

"Ever?"

He began to cut his steak. "No."

"Why not?"

He could feel her studying him as she took a sip, waiting. Dawson shifted in his seat.

"It's better that way," he answered.

Her fork paused in midair. "It's not because of me, is it?"

He kept his voice steady. "I'm not sure what you want me to say," he said.

"Surely you're not suggesting . . . ," she began.

When Dawson said nothing, she tried again. "Are you seriously trying to tell me that you—that you haven't dated anyone since we broke up?"

Again Dawson remained silent, and she put her fork down. She could hear a trace of belligerence creeping into her tone.

"You're saying that I'm the cause of this . . . this life you've chosen to lead?"

"Again, I'm not sure what you want me to say."

Her eyes narrowed. "Then I'm not sure what I'm supposed to say, either."

"What do you mean?"

"I mean that you're making it sound like I'm the reason you're alone. That it's . . . that it's somehow *my fault*. Do you know how that makes me feel?"

"I didn't say it to hurt you. I just meant—"

"I know exactly what you meant," Amanda snapped. "And you know what? I loved you back then as much as you loved me, but for whatever reason, it wasn't meant to be and it ended. But I didn't end. And you didn't end, either." She put her palms on the table. "Do you really think I want to leave here thinking that you're going to spend the rest of your life alone? Because of *me*?"

He stared at her. "I never asked for your pity."

"Then why would you say something like that?"

"I didn't say much of anything," he said. "I didn't even answer the question. You read into it what you wanted to."

"So I was wrong?"

Instead of answering, he reached for his knife. "Didn't anyone ever tell you that if you don't want to know the answer to a question, don't ask?"

Despite the fact that he'd deflected her question back at her— he'd always been able to do that—she couldn't help herself. "Well, even so, it's not my fault. If you want to ruin your life, go ahead. Who am I to stop you?"

Surprising her, Dawson laughed. "It's good to know you haven't changed a bit."

"Trust me. I've changed."

"Not much. You're still willing to tell me exactly how you think, no matter what it is. Even if you're of the opinion that I'm ruining my life."

"You obviously need someone to tell you."

"Then how about I try to ease your mind, okay? I haven't changed, either. I'm alone now because I've always been alone. Before you knew me, I did everything I could to keep my crazy family at a distance. When I came here, Tuck sometimes went days without talking to me, and after you left, I went up to Caledonia Correctional. When I got out, no one in the town wanted me around, so I left. I eventually ended up working for months of the year on a rig out in the ocean, not exactly a place conducive to relationships—I see that firsthand. Yes, there are some couples who can survive that kind of regular separation, but there's a fair share of broken hearts, too. It just seems easier this way, and besides, I'm used to it."

She evaluated his answer. "Do you want to know whether I think you're telling the entire truth?"

"Not really."

Despite herself, she laughed. "Can I ask you another question, then? You don't have to answer if you'd rather not talk about it."

"You can ask whatever you'd like," he said, taking a bite of steak.

"What happened on the night of the accident? I heard bits and pieces from my mom, but I never got the whole story and I didn't know what to believe."

Dawson chewed in silence before answering. "There's not much to tell," he finally said. "Tuck had ordered a set of tires for an Impala he was restoring, but for whatever reason, they ended up being delivered to a shop over in New Bern. He asked if I'd go pick them up, and I did. It had rained a little, and by the time I was getting back to town it was already dark."

He paused, trying yet again to make sense of the impossible. "There was an oncoming car and the guy was speeding. Or woman. I never did find out. Anyway, whoever it was crossed over the centerline just as I was closing in, and I jerked the wheel to make room. Next thing I knew, he was flying past me and the truck was halfway off the road. I saw Dr. Bonner, but..." The images were still clear, the images were *always* clear, an unchanging nightmare. "It was like the whole thing was happening in slow motion. I slammed on the brakes and kept turning the wheel, but the roads and grass were slick, and then..."

He trailed off. In the silence, Amanda touched his arm. "It was an accident," she whispered.

Dawson said nothing, but when he shuffled his feet, Amanda asked the obvious. "Why did you go to jail? If you weren't drinking or speeding?"

When he shrugged, she realized she already knew the answer. It was as clear as the spelling of his last name.

"I'm sorry," she said, the words sounding inadequate.

"I know. But don't feel sorry for me," he said. "Feel sorry for Dr. Bonner's family. Because of me, he never came home. Because of me, his kids grew up without a father. Because of me, his wife still lives alone."

"You don't know that," she countered. "Maybe she remarried."

"She didn't," he said. Before she could ask how he knew this, he started in on his plate again. "But what about you?" Dawson asked abruptly, as if stowing their previous conversation away and slamming the lid shut, making her regret she'd brought it up. "Catch me up on what you've been doing since we last saw each other."

"I wouldn't even know where to start."

He reached for the bottle of wine and poured more for both of them. "How about you start with college?"

Amanda capitulated, filling him in on her life, initially in broad strokes. Dawson listened intently, asking questions as she talked, probing for more detail. The words began to come easily. She told him about her roommates, about her classes and the professors who had most inspired her. She admitted that the year she spent teaching was nothing like she expected, if only because she could barely grasp the idea that she was no longer a student. She talked about meeting Frank, though saying his name made her feel strangely guilty, and she didn't mention him again. She told Dawson a little about her friends and some of the places she'd traveled over the years, but mainly she talked about her kids, describing their personalities and challenges and trying not to boast too much about their accomplishments.

Occasionally, when she'd finished a thought, she'd ask Dawson about his life on the rig, or what his days at home were like, but usually he'd steer the conversation back to her. He seemed genuinely interested in her life, and she found that it felt oddly natural to ramble on, almost like they were picking up the thread of a long-interrupted conversation.

Afterward, she tried to recall the last time she and Frank had talked like this, even when they were out alone. These days, Frank would drink and do most of the talking; when they discussed the kids, it was always about how they were doing in school or any problems they might be having and how best to solve them. Their conversations were efficient and purpose-driven, and he seldom asked about her day or her interests. Part of that, she knew, was endemic to any long marriage; there was little new to talk about. But somehow she felt that her connection with Dawson had always been different, and it made her wonder whether life would have taken its toll eventually on their relationship, too. She didn't want to think so, but how was she to know for sure?

They talked on into the night, the stars blurring through the kitchen window. The breeze picked up, moving through the leaves on the trees like rolling ocean waves. The wine bottle was empty and Amanda was feeling warm and relaxed. Dawson brought the dishes to the sink and they stood next to each other as Dawson washed while she dried. Every now and then, she'd catch him studying her as he passed her one of the dishes, and though in many ways a lifetime had elapsed in the years they had been apart, she had the uncanny feeling that they'd never lost contact at all.

When they finished in the kitchen, Dawson motioned toward the back door. "Do you still have a few minutes?"

Amanda glanced at her watch, and though she knew she probably should go, she found herself saying, "Okay. Just a few."

Dawson held the door open and she slipped past him, descending the creaking wooden steps. The moon had finally crested, lending the landscape a strange and exotic beauty. Silvery dew blanketed the ground cover, dampening the open toes of her shoes, and the smell of pine was heavy in the air. They walked side by side, the sound of their footfalls lost among the song of crickets and the whispering of the leaves.

Near the bank, an ancient oak spread its low-hanging limbs, the image reflecting on the water. The river had washed away part of the bank, making the limbs almost impossible to reach without getting wet, and they stopped. "That's where we used to sit," he said.

"It was our spot," she said. "Especially after I had an argument with my parents."

"Wait. You argued with your parents back then?" Dawson feigned amazement. "It wasn't about me, was it?"

She nudged him with her shoulder. "Funny guy. But anyway, we used to climb up and you'd put your arm around me and I'd cry and yell and you'd just let me rant about how unfair it all was until I finally calmed down. I was pretty dramatic back then, wasn't I?"

"Not that I noticed."

She stifled a laugh. "Do you remember how the mullets used to jump? At times, there were so many it was like they were putting on a show."

"I'm sure they'll be jumping tonight."

"I know, but it won't be the same. When we came out here, I

needed to see them. It was like they always knew that I needed
something special to make me feel better."

"I thought I was the one who made you feel better."

"It was definitely the mullets," she teased.

He smiled. "Did you and Tuck ever come down here?"

She shook her head. "The slope was a little too steep for him.
But I did. Or I tried, anyway."

"What does that mean?"

"I guess I wanted to know if this place would still feel the same
to me, but I didn't even get this far. It's not like I saw or heard
anything on the way down here, but I got to thinking that anyone could be out in the woods, and my imagination just . . . ran
away with me. I realized I was all alone, and if something happened there wouldn't be anything I could do. So I turned around
and went back inside and I never came down here again."

"Until now."

"I'm not alone." She studied the eddies in the water, hoping a
mullet would jump, but there was nothing. "It's hard to believe it's
been as long as it has," she murmured. "We were so young."

"Not too young." His voice was quiet, yet strangely certain.

"We were kids, Dawson. It didn't seem that way at the time,
but when you become a parent, your perspective changes. I mean,
Lynn is seventeen, and I can't imagine her feeling the way I did
back then. She doesn't even have a boyfriend. And if she was
sneaking out her bedroom window in the middle of the night, I'd
probably act the same way my parents did."

"If you didn't like the boyfriend, you mean?"

"Even if I thought he was perfect for her." She turned to face
him. "What were we thinking?"

"We weren't," he said. "We were in love."

She stared at him, her eyes capturing bits and pieces of the
moonlight. "I'm sorry I didn't visit or even write. After you were
sent up to Caledonia, I mean."

"It's okay."

"No, it's not. But I thought about it...about us. All the time." She reached out to touch the oak tree, trying to draw strength from it before continuing. "It's just that every time I sat down to write, I felt paralyzed. Where should I begin? Should I tell you about my classes or what my roommates were like? Or ask what your days were like? Every time I started to write something, I'd read over it and it didn't seem right. So I'd tear it up and promise that I'd start over again the next day. But one day just kept turning into the next. And then, too much time had passed and—"

"I'm not angry," he said. "And I wasn't angry then, either."

"Because you'd already forgotten me?"

"No," he answered. "Because back then I could barely face myself. And knowing that you'd moved on meant everything to me. I wanted you to have the kind of life that I'd never have been able to give you."

"You don't mean that."

"I do," he said.

"Then that's where you're wrong. Everyone has things in their past they wish they could change, Dawson. Even me. It's not as though my life has been perfect, either."

"Want to talk about it?"

Years ago, she'd been able to tell Dawson everything, and though she wasn't ready yet, she sensed that it was only a matter of time before it happened again. The recognition scared her, even as she admitted that Dawson had awakened something inside her that she hadn't felt in a long, long time.

"Would you be angry if I told you I'm not ready to talk about it yet?"

"Not at all."

She offered the ghost of a smile. "Then let's just enjoy this for a few more minutes, okay? Like we used to? It's so peaceful out here."

The moon had continued its slow ascent, lending an ethereal

cast to the surroundings; farther from its glow, stars flickered faintly, like tiny prisms. As they stood beside each other, Dawson wondered how often she'd thought of him over the years. Less often than he'd thought of her, he was certain of that, but he had the sense that they were both lonely, albeit in different ways. He was a solitary figure in a vast landscape while she was a face in a nameless crowd. But hadn't it always been so, even when they were teenagers? It had been what brought them together, and they had somehow found happiness with each other.

In the darkness, he heard Amanda sigh. "I should probably go," she said.

"I know."

She was relieved by his response, but also a bit disappointed. Turning from the creek, they made their way back toward the house in silence, both of them wrapped in their own thoughts. Inside, Dawson turned out the lights while she locked up, before they slowly strolled toward their cars. Dawson reached over, opening her door.

"I'll see you tomorrow at the attorney's office," he said.

"Eleven o'clock."

In the moonlight, her hair was a silver cascade, and he resisted the impulse to run his fingers through it. "I had a great time tonight. Thanks for dinner."

As she stood in front of him, she had the sudden, wild thought that he might try to kiss her, and for the first time since college she felt almost breathless under someone's gaze. But she turned away before he could even attempt it.

"It was good to see you, Dawson."

She slid behind the wheel, breathing a sigh of relief as Dawson closed the door for her. She started the engine and put the car in reverse.

Dawson waved while she backed up and turned around, and he watched as she headed down the gravel drive. The red taillights of her car bounced slightly until the car rounded a curve and vanished from sight.

Slowly, he walked back to the garage. He flipped the switch, and as the single overhead bulb came on, he took a seat on a pile of tires. It was quiet now, nothing moving except for a single moth that fluttered toward the light. As it batted against the bulb, Dawson reflected on the fact that Amanda had moved on. Whatever sorrows or troubles she was hiding—and he knew that they were there—she'd still managed to construct the kind of life that she'd always wanted. She had a husband and children and a house in the city, and her memories now were about all those things, which was exactly the way it should be.

As he sat alone in Tuck's garage, he knew he'd been lying to himself in thinking that he'd moved on as well. He hadn't. He always assumed she'd left him behind, but it was confirmed now. Somewhere deep inside, he felt something shift and break loose. He'd said good-bye a long time ago, and since then he'd wanted to believe that he had done the right thing. Here and now, though, in the quiet yellow light of an abandoned garage, he wasn't so sure. He'd loved Amanda once and he'd never stopped loving her, and spending time with her tonight hadn't changed that simple truth. But as he reached for his keys, he was conscious of something else as well, something he hadn't quite expected.

He rose and turned out the light, then headed for his car, feeling strangely depleted. It was one thing, after all, to know his feelings for Amanda hadn't changed; it was another thing entirely to face the future with the certainty that they never would.

6

———— ❧ ————

The curtains in the bed-and-breakfast were thin, and sunlight woke Dawson only a few minutes after dawn. He rolled over, hoping to go back to sleep, but he found it impossible. Instead, he stood and spent the next few minutes stretching. In the mornings, everything ached, especially his back and shoulders. He wondered how many more years he could continue working on the rig; there was a lot of accumulated wear and tear in his body, and every passing year seemed to compound his injuries.

Reaching into his duffel bag, he grabbed his running gear, dressed, and quietly descended the stairs. The bed-and-breakfast was about what he'd expected: four bedrooms upstairs, with a kitchen, dining room, and seating area downstairs. The owners, unsurprisingly, favored a sailing theme; miniature wooden sailboats adorned the end tables, and paintings of schooners hung on the walls. Above the fireplace was an ancient boat wheel, and tacked to the door was a map of the river, marking the channels.

The owners weren't yet awake. When he'd checked in the night before, they'd informed him that they'd left the delivery of flowers in his room, and that breakfast was at eight. That gave him plenty of time before his meeting to do what he needed to do.

Outside, the morning was already bright. A thin layer of haze on the river hovered like a low-level cloud, but the sky above was a brilliant blue and clear in every direction. The air was already warm, foretelling hotter weather to come. He rolled his shoulders a few times and was jogging before he hit the road. It took a few minutes before his body began to feel limber and he settled into an easy pace.

The road was quiet as he entered Oriental's small downtown. He passed two antiques stores, a hardware store, and a few real estate offices; on the opposite side of the street, Irvin's Diner was already open for business, with a handful of cars parked out front. Over his shoulder, the fog on the river had begun to lift, and breathing deeply, he caught the living scent of salt and pine. Near the marina, he passed a bustling coffee shop, and a few minutes later, with the stiffness almost completely gone, he was able to pick up his pace. At the marina, gulls circled and sounded their calls as people carried coolers to their sailboats, and he jogged past a rustic bait shop.

He passed the First Baptist Church, marveling at the stained-glass windows and trying to recall whether he'd even noticed them as a child, before searching for Morgan Tanner's office. He knew the address and finally spotted the placard on a small brick building wedged between a drugstore and a coin dealer. Another attorney was listed as well, though they didn't seem to share the same practice. He wondered how Tuck had chosen Tanner. Until the call, he'd never heard of the man.

As downtown Oriental came to an end, Dawson turned off the main road, branching out onto neighborhood streets, running without any particular destination in mind.

He hadn't slept well. Instead, his mind had cycled endlessly between Amanda and the Bonners. In prison, aside from Amanda, Marilyn Bonner was all he could think about. She had testified at the sentencing hearing, and her testimony underscored the fact that he'd not only robbed her of the man she loved and the father of her children, but also destroyed her entire way of life. In a breaking voice, she'd admitted that she had no idea how she was going to provide for her family, or what would become of them. Dr. Bonner, it turned out, had neglected to buy life insurance.

Eventually, Marilyn Bonner lost the house. She moved back in with her parents at the orchard, but her life continued to be a struggle. Her father had already retired and had early-stage emphysema. Her mom suffered from diabetes, and the loan payments on the property ate up almost every dollar the orchard brought in. Because her parents needed almost full-time care between them, Marilyn was able to work only part-time. Even when she combined her small salary with her parents' social security, there was barely enough to cover the basics, and sometimes not even that. The old farmhouse they lived in was beginning to fall apart, and the loan payments on the orchard eventually fell into arrears.

By the time Dawson got out of prison, things had become desperate for the Bonner family. Dawson didn't learn of that until he went to the farmhouse to apologize almost six months later. When Marilyn answered the door, Dawson barely recognized her; her hair had turned gray and her skin looked sallow. She, on the other hand, knew exactly who he was, and before he could say a word, she began screaming at him to leave, shrieking that he'd ruined her life, that he'd killed her husband, that she didn't even have enough money to fix the leaking roof or hire the workers she needed. She screamed that the bankers were threatening to foreclose on the orchard, and then that she was going to call the police. She warned him never to come back. Dawson left, but later that night he returned to the farmhouse and studied the decaying structure; he walked the rows of peach and apple trees. The following week, after receiving his paycheck from Tuck, he went to the bank and had a cashier's check sent to Marilyn Bonner for almost the entire amount, along with everything he'd saved since he'd gotten out of prison, with no note attached.

In the years since then, Marilyn's life had gotten better. Her parents eventually died and the farmhouse and orchard passed to her; though it had been a struggle at times, she'd slowly been able to make up the outstanding loan payments and carry out the necessary repairs. She now owned the land free and clear. She'd started a mail-order business a few years after he'd left town, selling homemade canned preserves. With the help of the Internet, her business had grown to the point where she no longer worried about paying the bills. Though she'd never remarried, she'd been dating an accountant named Leo for almost sixteen years.

As for the kids, Emily graduated from East Carolina University and eventually moved to Raleigh, where she worked as a manager in a department store, preparing most likely to take over her mom's business one day. Alan lived in the orchard in a double-wide that his mom had purchased for him and hadn't gone to college, but he had a steady job and in the photographs that were sent to Dawson, he always seemed happy.

Once a year, the photographs arrived in Louisiana along with a brief update on Marilyn, Emily, and Alan; the private detectives he'd hired had always been thorough but had never pried too deeply.

He sometimes felt guilty about having the Bonners followed, but he had to know whether he'd been able to make even the smallest positive difference in their lives. That's all he'd wanted since the night of the accident, and it was the reason he'd been sending checks monthly for the past two decades, almost always through anonymous offshore bank accounts. He was, after all, responsible for the greatest loss their family had experienced, and as he ran the quiet streets he knew he was willing to do whatever he could to make amends.

❦

Abee Cole could feel the fever inside him making him sick, and he shivered despite the heat. Two days ago, he'd taken his baseball bat to a guy who had provoked him, and the guy had surprised him with a box cutter. A dirty one that left an evil-looking slash yawning across his gut. Earlier this morning, he noticed green pus oozing out, smelling like a sewer despite the drugs that were supposed to help. If the fever didn't break soon, he had half a mind to take the bat to his cousin Calvin, since he'd sworn the antibiotics he'd stolen from the veterinary office would work.

Right now, though, he was distracted by the sight of Dawson running on the opposite side of the street, and he considered what to do about him.

Ted was in the convenience store behind him, and he wondered whether he'd spotted Dawson. Probably not; otherwise he'd be rushing out of the store like a wild boar. Ever since he'd heard that Tuck went toes up, Ted had been waiting for Dawson to show up. Probably while sharpening his knives and loading his guns and checking his grenades or bazookas or whatever the hell other weapons he kept at that rat hole he shared with Ella, that little tramp whore of his.

Ted wasn't quite right in the head. Never had been right. Just a bundle of rage, that one. Nine years in prison hadn't taught him how to keep it in check, either. In the past few years, it had gotten to the point where it was almost impossible to keep Ted in line, but as Abee often reflected, that wasn't always such a bad thing. It made him an effective enforcer, ensuring that everyone involved in producing crank on their property followed his rules. Ted scared the crap out of everybody these days, family included, and that suited Abee just fine. They kept their noses out of Abee's business and did what they were told. While he didn't particularly care for his younger brother, Abee did find him useful.

But now Dawson was back in town, and who the hell knew what Ted was going to do. Abee had figured that Dawson would show up on account of Tuck dying, but he hoped that Dawson would have had the sense to stay just long enough to pay his respects and leave before anyone knew he'd even come home. That's what anyone with a lick of sense would have done, and he was sure that Dawson was smart enough to know that Ted wanted to kill him every time he looked in the mirror and saw that crooked nose staring back at him.

Abee didn't give two licks what happened to Dawson, one way or the other. But he didn't want Ted creating unnecessary trouble. It was hard enough to keep things going already, what with the Feds and the staties and the sheriff poking their noses into the family business. It wasn't like the old days, when the law was afraid of them. These days, the cops had helicopters and dogs and infrared and snitches everywhere. Abee had to think about such things; Abee alone had to plan for such things.

Thing was, Dawson was a lot smarter than the meth-head tweakers Ted usually dealt with. Say what you want about Dawson, but he'd beaten the crap out of both Ted and his daddy when both of them were armed, and that meant something. Dawson wasn't afraid of Ted or Abee, and he'd be prepared. He could be ruthless when necessary, and that should have been enough to give Ted pause. But it wouldn't, because Ted wasn't going to be thinking straight.

The last thing he needed was for Ted to be sent away again. He needed him, what with half the family tweaking and prone to doing stupid things. But if Abee couldn't prevent Ted from going off the rails when he saw Dawson, Ted just might find himself standing before the judge again. The thought made his stomach burn, compounding his nausea.

Abee leaned over, vomiting onto the asphalt. He wiped his mouth with the back of his hand as Dawson finally disappeared around the corner. Ted still hadn't come out. Abee gave a mental sigh of relief and decided not to tell him about the sighting. He shivered again, his gut on fire. Jesus, he felt like crap. Who would have thought the guy was carrying a box cutter?

It wasn't like Abee was trying to kill the guy—he just wanted to send a message to him and anyone else who might be getting ideas about Candy. Next time, though, Abee wasn't going to take a chance. Once he started swinging, he wasn't going to stop. He'd be careful—he was always careful when the law might get involved—but everyone needed to understand that his girl-friend was off-limits. Guys better not look at her or talk to her, let alone get any ideas about getting into her pants. She'd probably get huffy, but Candy needed to understand that she was his now. He really didn't want to mess up that pretty face of hers to make a point.

≰

Candy wasn't sure what to do about Abee Cole. Sure, they'd gone out a few times, and she knew he probably thought he could boss her around now. But he was a guy, and she'd figured out guys a long time ago, even bull-headed types like Abee. She might be only twenty-four years old, but she'd been on her own since seventeen, and she'd learned that as long as she wore her blond hair long and loose and stared up at guys with *that look*, she could pretty much make them do whatever she wanted. She knew how to make a man feel fascinating, no matter how dull he might really be. And for the past seven years, it had served her well. She owned a Mustang convertible, courtesy of some old guy in Wilmington, and a small Buddha statue that she displayed on her windowsill, which was supposedly made of gold and was from a sweet Chinese man in Charleston. She knew that if she were to tell Abee that she was running low on cash, he'd probably give some to her and feel like a king.

Then again, maybe that wasn't such a good idea. She wasn't from around here and hadn't known who the Coles were when she'd arrived in Oriental a few months ago. The more she'd learned about them, the more uncertain she felt about letting Abee get too close to her. Not because Abee was a criminal. She'd taken a coke dealer in Atlanta for almost twenty thousand dollars over a few months, and he'd been as delighted with their overall arrangement as she'd been. No, it partly had to do with her discomfort around Ted.

They were often together when Abee came in, and frankly, Ted scared her. It wasn't just the pockmarked skin or brown teeth that freaked her out; it was more his overall...*vibe*. When he grinned at her, there was a gleeful malevolence about it, like he couldn't decide whether to strangle her or kiss her, but thought that both would be equally fun.

Ted had given her the serious creeps from the get-go, but she had to admit that the more she'd gotten to know Abee, the more she worried that the two were cut from the same cloth. Abee was getting a little...*possessive* lately, and that was beginning to scare her. In all honesty, it was probably time to move on. Drive north to Virginia or south to Florida, it didn't really matter. She'd leave tomorrow, except that she didn't have the cash to make the trip yet. She'd never been good at holding on to money, but she figured that if she really worked the customers at the bar this weekend and played her cards just right, she could earn enough by Sunday to get the hell out of here, before Abee Cole even realized she was gone.

❧

The delivery truck lurched from the centerline to the shoulder and back again, the result of Alan Bonner trying to free a cigarette by bouncing the pack against his thigh while simultaneously trying not to spill the cup of coffee he had wedged between his legs. On the radio, a country song was blaring, something about a man who'd lost his dog or wanted a dog or liked eating dogs or whatever, but lyrics had never been as important as rhythm, and this tune had *serious* rhythm. Add in the fact that it was Friday, which meant he had only seven more hours of work time left before the long, glorious weekend ahead, and he was already in a good mood.

"Shouldn't you turn that down?" Buster asked.

Buster Tibson was a new trainee with the company, which was

the only reason he was even in the truck, and all week long he'd been complaining about this or asking questions about that. It was enough to drive anyone crazy.

"What? You don't like this song?"

"It says in the manual that playing the radio loud causes distractions. Ron mentioned that specifically when he hired me."

That was another annoying thing about Buster. He was a stickler for the rules. It was probably why Ron had hired him.

Alan finished tapping out the cigarette and stuck it between his teeth while he searched for his lighter. Thing was wedged deep into his pocket and it took a bit of concentration to keep the coffee from spilling as he began to dig it out.

"Don't worry about it. It's Friday, remember?"

Buster seemed dissatisfied with his answer, and when Alan glanced over he noticed that Buster had ironed his shirt this morning. No doubt he'd made sure that Ron had noticed. Probably went into the office with a notepad and pen, too, so that he could write down everything Ron said while simultaneously complimenting Ron on his wisdom.

And what about the guy's name? That was another thing. What kind of a parent named their kid Buster?

The delivery van lurched onto the shoulder again as Alan finally freed his lighter.

"Hey, where the hell did you get the name Buster, anyway?" he asked.

"It's a family name. On my mom's side." Buster frowned. "How many deliveries today?"

All week long, Buster had been asking that question, and Alan had yet to figure out why the specific number was so important. They delivered nabs and nuts and chips and trail mix and beef jerky to gas stations and convenience stores, but the key was not to speed through the route, or Ron would just add more stops. Alan learned that last year and he wasn't about to make that mistake again. His territory already covered all of Pamlico County, which meant driving endlessly along the most boring roads in the history of mankind. Even so, this was far and away the best job he'd ever had. Way better than construction or landscaping or washing cars or anything else he'd done since he graduated from high school. Here, there was fresh air blowing through the window, music as loud as he wanted, and no boss constantly breathing down his neck. The pay wasn't half bad, either.

Alan cupped his hands, steering with his elbows while he lit his cigarette. He blew the smoke through the open window. "Enough. We'll be lucky if we finish."

Buster turned toward the passenger window, speaking under his breath. "Then maybe we shouldn't take such long lunches."

The kid was seriously irritating. And that's what he was—a kid, even if, technically, Buster was older than him. Still, the last thing he wanted was for Buster to report back to Ron that he was slacking off.

"It not about the lunches," Alan said, trying to sound serious. "It's about customer service. You can't just run in and run out. You have to talk to people. Our job is about making sure our customers are happy. That's why I always make sure that I do things by the book."

"Like smoking? You know you're not supposed to smoke in the van."

"Every man's got a vice."

"And blasting the radio?"

Uh-oh. The kid had obviously been compiling a list, and Alan had to think fast.

"I just did that for you. Kind of a celebration, you know? It's the end of your first week and you've done a great job. And when we finish up today, I'll make sure Ron knows that."

Mentioning Ron like that was enough to make Buster quiet down for a few minutes, which didn't seem like much, but after a week in the car with the guy, any silence was a good thing. The day couldn't end soon enough, and next week he'd have the van to himself again. Thank God.

And tonight? That was all about getting the weekend started right, which meant doing his best to forget all about Buster. Tonight he'd end up at the Tidewater, a hole-in-the-wall just outside town that was almost the only place nearby that offered any kind of nightlife. He'd drink some beer, play some pool, and if he was lucky, that cute bartender might even be there. She wore tight jeans that hugged her in all the right places, and she leaned forward in her skimpy top whenever she handed him a beer, which made it taste that much better. Same thing Saturday night and Sunday night, too, for that matter, assuming his mom had plans with her longtime boyfriend, Leo, and didn't drop by his double-wide like she had last night.

Why she didn't just marry Leo was beyond him; maybe then she'd have better things to do than check on her grown son. What he didn't want this weekend was for his mom to expect him to keep her company, because that just wasn't going to happen. Who cared if he was a little worse for the wear on Monday? By then, Buster would be in his own delivery truck, and if that didn't call for a little celebrating, nothing did.

Marilyn Bonner worried about Alan.

Not all the time, of course, and she did her best to keep her worries in check. He was an adult, after all, and she knew he was old enough to make his own decisions. But she was his mother, and Alan's primary problem as she saw it was that he always opted for the easy path, which led to nowhere, instead of the more challenging path that had a chance of turning out better. It bothered her that he lived his life more like a teenager than someone who was twenty-seven years old. Last night, when she'd dropped by his double-wide, he'd been playing a video game, and his first reaction had been to ask whether she wanted to give it a try. As she stood there in the doorway, she'd found herself wondering how she could have raised a son who didn't seem to know her in the slightest.

Still, she knew it could be worse. A lot worse. The bottom line was that Alan had turned out okay. He was kind and had a job and never got into trouble, and that was pretty good, in this day and age. Say what you want, but she read the papers and heard the scuttlebutt around town. She knew that a lot of his friends, young men she'd known since they were boys, even some from the *better* families, had descended into drug use or drank too much or even ended up in prison. It made sense, considering where they lived. Too many people glorified small-town America, making it seem like a Norman Rockwell painting, but the reality was something else entirely. With the exception of doctors and lawyers or people who owned their own businesses, there were no high-paying jobs in Oriental, or in any other small town for that matter. And while it was in many ways an ideal place to raise young children, there was little for young adults to aspire to. There weren't, nor would there ever be, middle management positions in small towns, nor was there much to do on the weekends, or even new people to meet. Why Alan still wanted to live here was beyond her, but as long as he was happy and paid his own way in the world, she was willing to make things a bit easier for him, even if that meant she'd had to buy a double-wide a stone's throw from the farmhouse to get him started off in life.

No, she didn't have any illusions about the kind of town Oriental was. In that way, she wasn't like the other blue bloods in town, but then losing a husband as a young mother of two tended to adjust your perspective. Being a Bennett and having attended UNC didn't stop the bankers from trying to foreclose on the orchard. Nor did her family name or connections help her support her struggling family. Even her fancy economics degree from UNC didn't buy her a pass.

In the end, everything came down to money. It came down to

what a person actually *did*, as opposed to who they thought they *were*, which was why she couldn't stomach the Oriental status quo anymore. These days, she'd hire a hardworking immigrant over a UNC or Duke society belle who believed that the world owed her a good living. The very notion probably struck people like Evelyn Collier or Eugenia Wilcox as blasphemous, but she'd long since come to view Evelyn and Eugenia and their ilk as dinosaurs, clinging to a world that no longer existed. At a recent town meeting, she'd even said as much. In the past it would have caused a commotion, but Marilyn's was one of the few businesses in town that was actually expanding, and there was nothing much anyone could say—including Evelyn Collier and Eugenia Wilcox.

In the years since David had died, she'd come to treasure her hard-won independence. She'd learned to trust her instincts, and she had to admit that she liked being in control of her own life, without anyone's expectations getting in the way. She supposed that was why she'd rejected Leo's repeated marriage proposals. An accountant in Morehead City, he was smart, well-to-do, and she enjoyed spending time with him. Most important, he respected her, and the kids had always adored him. Emily and Alan couldn't understand why she kept saying no.

But Leo knew she'd always say no, and that was okay with him, because the truth was they were both comfortable with the way things were. They'd probably see a movie tomorrow night, and on Sunday she'd attend church and then visit the cemetery to pay her respects to David, as she'd done every weekend for nearly a quarter century. She'd meet Leo later for dinner. In her own way, she loved him. It might not be the kind of love that others understood, but that didn't matter. What she and Leo had was good enough for both of them.

🍂

Halfway across town, Amanda was drinking coffee at the kitchen table and doing her best to ignore her mother's pointed silence.

The night before, after Amanda had come in, her mom had been waiting in the parlor, and even before Amanda had the chance to sit down, the questions had begun.

Where have you been? Why are you so late? Why didn't you call?

I did call, Amanda reminded her, but instead of being drawn into the incriminating conversation her mom obviously wanted, Amanda mumbled that she had a headache and that what she really needed to do was lie down in her room. If her mother's demeanor this morning was any indication, she was obviously displeased by that. Aside from a quick good morning as she'd entered the kitchen, her mom had said nothing. Instead, she went straight to the toaster, and after punctuating her silence with a sigh, she popped some bread in. As it was browning, her mom sighed again, a little louder this time.

I get it, Amanda wanted to say. *You're upset. Are you done now?* Instead, she sipped her coffee, resolving that no matter how many buttons her mom pressed, she wouldn't be drawn into an argument.

Amanda heard the toast pop up. Her mother opened the drawer and pulled out a knife before closing it with a rattle. She began to butter her toast.

"Are you feeling any better?" her mom finally asked without turning around.

"Yes, thank you."

"Are you ready to tell me what's going on? Or where you were?"

"I told you, I had a late start." Amanda tried her best to keep her voice even.

"I tried to call you, but I kept getting your voice mail."

"My battery died." That lie had come to her last night, on her way over. Her mom was nothing if not predictable.

Her mother picked up her plate. "Is that why you never called Frank?"

"I talked to him yesterday, about an hour after he got home

from work." She picked up the morning paper, scanning the headlines with studied nonchalance.

"Well, he also called here."

"And?"

"He was surprised you hadn't arrived yet," Amanda's mother sniffed. "He said that as far as he knew, you left around two."

"I had to run some errands before I left," she said. The lies came way too easily, she thought, but then she'd had a lot of practice.

"He sounded upset."

No, he sounded like he was drinking, Amanda thought, and I doubt if he'll even remember. She got up from the table and refilled her cup of coffee. "I'll call him later."

Her mother took a seat. "I was invited to play bridge last night."

So that's what this was about, Amanda thought. Or at least part of it, anyway. Her mom was addicted to the game and had been playing with the same group of women for almost thirty years. "You should have gone."

"I couldn't, because I knew you were coming and I thought we'd have dinner together." Her mother sat down stiffly. "Eugenia Wilcox had to fill in for me."

Eugenia Wilcox lived just down the street, in another historic mansion that was as gorgeous as Evelyn's. Though they supposedly were friends—her mom and Eugenia had known each other all their lives—there'd always been an unspoken rivalry between the two of them, encompassing who had the better house and the better garden and everything in between, including which of them made the better red velvet cake.

"I'm sorry, Mom," Amanda said, sitting back down again. "I should have called you earlier."

"Eugenia doesn't know the first thing about bidding and it ruined the entire game. Martha Ann already called and complained to me about it. But anyway, I told her that you were in town and one thing led to another and she invited us over for dinner tonight."

Amanda frowned and put down her coffee cup. "You didn't say yes, did you?"

"Of course I did."

An image of Dawson flashed in her mind. "I don't know if I'm going to have time," she improvised. "There might be a wake tonight."

"There might be a wake? What does that mean? Either there's a wake or there isn't one."

"I mean that I'm not sure if there is one. When the lawyer called, he didn't give me any specifics about the funeral."

"That's kind of strange, isn't it? That he wouldn't tell you anything?"

Maybe, Amanda thought. *But no stranger than Tuck arranging for Dawson and me to have dinner at his house last night.* "I'm sure he's just doing what Tuck wanted."

At the mention of Tuck's name, her mom fingered the pearl necklace she was wearing. Amanda had never known her to leave the bedroom without makeup and jewelry, and this morning was no exception. Evelyn Collier had always embodied the spirit of the Old South and would no doubt continue to until the day she died.

"I still don't understand why you had to come back for this. It's not as if you really knew the man."

"I knew him, Mom."

"Years ago. I mean, it's one thing if you were still living here in town. Maybe then I could understand it. But there was no reason to make a special trip down here for it."

"I came to pay my respects."

"He didn't have the best reputation, you know. A lot of people thought he was crazy. And what am I supposed to say to my friends about why you're here?"

"I don't know why you have to say anything."

"Because they're going to ask why you're here," she said.

"Why would they ask?"

"Because they find you *interesting*."

Amanda heard something in her mother's tone she didn't quite understand. As she tried to figure it out, she added some cream to her coffee. "I didn't realize I was such a hot topic of conversation," she remarked.

"It's really not that surprising if you think about it. You hardly ever bring Frank or the kids with you anymore. I can't help it if they find it strange."

"We've gone over this before," Amanda said, unable to hide her exasperation. "Frank works and the kids are in school, but that doesn't mean that I can't come. Sometimes, daughters do that. They go visit their mother."

"And sometimes, they don't see their mother at all. That's what they really find interesting, if you want to know the truth."

"What are you talking about?" Amanda narrowed her eyes.

"I'm talking about the fact that you come to Oriental when you know I won't be around. And that you stay in my house, without so much as even letting me know about it." She didn't bother to disguise her hostility before going on. "You didn't realize that I knew about it, did you? Like when I went on the cruise last year? Or when I went to visit my sister in Charleston the year before that? It's a small town, Amanda. People saw you. My friends saw you. What I don't understand is why you believed I wouldn't find out."

"Mom—"

"Don't," she said, raising a perfectly manicured hand. "I know exactly why you came. I might be older, but that doesn't mean I'm senile. Why else would you be here for the funeral? It's obvious you came here to see him. And that's where you went all those times you told me that you were going shopping, am I correct? Or when you said you were visiting your friend at the beach? You've been lying to me all along."

Amanda dropped her gaze and said nothing. There was really nothing she could say. In the silence, she heard a sigh. When her mom finally went on, her voice had lost its edge.

"You know what? I've been lying for you, too, Amanda, and I'm tired of it. But I'm still your mother and you can talk to me."

"Yes, Mom." In her voice she heard the petulant echo of her teenage self and hated herself for it.

"Is something going on with the kids that I should know about?"

"No. The kids are great."

"Is it Frank?"

Amanda rotated the handle on her coffee cup to the opposite side.

"Do you want to talk about it?" she asked.

"No." Amanda's voice was flat.

"Is there anything I can do?"

"No," she said again.

"What's going on with you, Amanda?"

For some reason, the question made her think about Dawson, and for an instant she was back in Tuck's kitchen, basking in Dawson's attention. And she knew then that she wanted nothing more than to see him again, no matter what the consequences.

"I don't know," she finally murmured. "I wish I did, but I don't."

❧

After Amanda went up to shower, Evelyn Collier stood on the back porch, staring at the fine layer of mist that hovered over the river. Normally, it was one of her favorite times of the day and had been, ever since she was a girl. Back then, she hadn't lived on the river; she'd lived near the mill her father owned, but on weekends she used to wander out to the bridge, where she sometimes sat for hours, watching the sun gradually dissipate the mist. Harvey had known she'd always wanted to live on the river, and it was the reason he'd bought the house only a few months after they'd been married. Of course, he'd bought it from his father for a song—the Colliers owned a lot of property back then—so it hadn't been a terrible stretch for him, but that wasn't important. What was important was that he'd cared, and she wished he were still around, if only to talk to him about Amanda. Who on earth knew what was going on with her these days? But then Amanda had always been a mystery, even as a girl. She had her own ideas about things, and from the time she could walk she'd always been as stubborn as a warped door on a humid summer day. If her mom told her to stay close, Amanda would wander off the first chance she got; if she told Amanda to wear something pretty, Amanda would skip down the steps wearing something from the back of the closet. When she was very young it had been somewhat possible to keep Amanda under control and on the right track. She was a Collier, after all, and people had expectations. But once Amanda became a teenager? Lord knows, it was like the devil had gotten into her. First Dawson Cole—a *Cole!*—and then the lies and sneaking out and the endless moodiness and fresh responses whenever she tried to talk some sense into her daughter. Evelyn's hair actually began to turn gray from the stress, and though Amanda didn't know it, if it wasn't for a steady supply of bourbon, she wasn't sure how she would have made it through those awful years.

Once they'd managed to separate her from the Cole boy and Amanda went off to college, things started to improve. There were some good, solid years, and the grandchildren were a delight, of course. Sad about the baby girl, just a toddler and a beautiful creature, but the Lord never promised anyone a life without tribulation. Why, she'd had a miscarriage herself a year before Amanda was born. Still, she was pleased that Amanda had been able to get back up on her horse after a respectable period of time—Lord knows the family needed her—and even take up some noteworthy charity work. Evelyn would have preferred something a little less *taxing*, like the Junior League, perhaps, but Duke University Hospital was still a fine institution, and she didn't mind telling her friends about the fund-raising luncheons Amanda hosted, or even her volunteer work there.

Recently, Amanda seemed to be slipping back into her old ways—lying like a teenager, of all things! Oh, they'd never been all that close, and she'd long resigned herself to the fact that they probably never would be. It was a myth that every mother and daughter were best friends, but friendship was far less important than family. Friends came and went; family was always there. No, they didn't really confide in each other, but confiding was often just another word for complaining, which was usually a waste of time. Life was messy. Always had been and always would be and that was just the way it was, so why bother complaining? You either did something about it or you didn't, and then you lived with the choice you made.

It didn't take a rocket scientist to figure out that Amanda and Frank were having problems. She hadn't seen much of Frank in recent years, since Amanda usually came alone, and she did recall that he liked his beer a little too much. Then again, Amanda's own father had been awfully fond of his bourbon, and no marriage was entirely blissful. There'd been years when she could barely stand the sight of Harvey, let alone want to stay married to him. If Amanda had asked, Evelyn would have admitted that, and she also would have reminded her daughter in the same breath that the grass isn't always greener on the other side. What the younger generation didn't understand was that the grass was greenest where it's watered, which meant that both Frank and Amanda had to get out their hoses if they wanted to make things better. But Amanda hadn't asked.

Which was a shame, because Evelyn could tell that Amanda was only adding more problems to an already troubled marriage— the lying was part of that. Because Amanda had been lying to her mom, it wasn't hard to surmise that she'd been lying to Frank as well. And once the lies started, where did they end? Evelyn wasn't sure, but Amanda was obviously confused, and people made mistakes when they were confused. Which meant, of course, that she'd have to be extra vigilant this weekend, whether Amanda liked it or not.

Dawson was back in town.

Ted Cole was standing on the front steps of the shack, smoking a cigarette and idly staring at the meat trees, which is what he always called them when the boys came back from hunting. A pair of deer carcasses, gutted and skinned, was strung up on sagging branches, and flies were buzzing and crawling over the flesh while the innards pooled in the dirt below.

The morning breeze made the rotting torsos rotate slightly, and Ted took another long drag on his cigarette. He'd seen Dawson, and he knew that Abee had seen him, too. But Abee had lied about it, which pissed him off almost as much as Dawson's bold-as-you-please appearance did.

He was getting a little tired of his brother, Abee. Tired of being ordered around, of wondering where all the family money was going. The time was coming when old Abee just might find himself staring down the wrong end of the Glock. His dear brother had been slipping lately. The guy with the box cutter had nearly killed him, something that never would have happened even a few years ago. It wouldn't have happened had Ted been there, but Abee hadn't told him what he'd been planning, and that was just another sign that Abee was getting careless. That new girl of his had him all twisted up—Candy, or Cammie, or whatever the hell she called herself. Yeah, she had a pretty face and a body that Ted wouldn't mind taking some time to explore, but she was a woman and the rules were simple: You wanted something from them, you got it, and if they got angry or gave you lip, you showed them the error of their ways. Might take a few lessons, but in the end all women came around. Abee seemed to have forgotten all that.

And he'd lied to him, right to his face. Ted flicked his cigarette butt off the porch, thinking that he and Abee were going to have a little come-to-Jesus soon enough, no doubt about it. But first things first: Dawson had to go. He'd been waiting a long time for this. Because of Dawson, his nose was crooked and his jaw had been wired shut; because of Dawson, that dude had made a crack about Ted's condition that Ted couldn't ignore, and nine years of his life had gone up in smoke. No one screwed with him and got away with it. No one. Not Dawson, not Abee. No one. Besides, he'd been looking forward to this for a long, long time.

Ted turned and went back inside. The shack had been built around the turn of the century, and the single overhead light that dangled from a string barely broke the shadows. Tina, his three-year-old, was perched on the ratty couch in front of the television, watching something from Disney. Ella walked past her without saying anything. In the kitchen, the skillet was coated with a thick layer of bacon grease, and Ella went back to feeding the baby, who sat there squealing in his high chair, his face covered in something yellow and goopy. Ella was twenty, with narrow hips, thin brown hair, and a fan of freckles on her cheeks. The dress she wore did little to hide the bump in her belly. Seven months along and feeling tired. She was always tired.

He grabbed his keys from the counter and she turned.

"You goin' out?"

"Don't be buttin' into my business," he said. When she turned around, he patted the baby's head before making for the bedroom. He removed the Glock he kept beneath the pillow and tucked it into his waistband, feeling excited, feeling like all was right in the world.

It was time to take care of things once and for all.

7

When Dawson returned from his run, several other guests were sipping coffee in the parlor, reading free copies of *USA Today*. He could smell the aroma of bacon and eggs wafting from the kitchen as he climbed the stairs to his room. After showering, he threw on a pair of jeans and a short-sleeved shirt before going down to breakfast.

By the time he got to the table, most of the others had already eaten, so Dawson ate alone. Despite the run, he wasn't very hungry, but the owner—a woman in her sixties named Alice Russell, who'd moved to Oriental to retire eight years ago—filled his plate, and he had the sense she'd be disappointed if he didn't eat everything. She had a grandmotherly look about her, right down to the apron and plaid housedress.

While he ate, Alice explained that, like so many others, she and her husband had retired to Oriental for the sailing. Her husband had grown bored, though, and they'd ended up buying the business a few years back. Surprisingly, she addressed him as "Mr. Cole" without any sign of recognition, even after he'd mentioned that he'd grown up in town. She was clearly still an outsider here.

His family was around, though. He'd seen Abee at the

convenience store, and as soon as he'd rounded the corner he'd ducked between some houses and made his way back to the bed-and-breakfast, avoiding the main road whenever possible. The last thing he wanted was any trouble with his family, especially Ted and Abee, but he had the disquieting feeling that things weren't quite settled.

Still, there was something he needed to do. After he finished eating, he picked up the flower bouquet he'd ordered while still in Louisiana and had sent to the bed-and-breakfast, then got in his rental car. As he drove, he kept his eyes on the rearview mirror, making sure that no one was watching him. At the cemetery, he wound his way through the familiar headstones to Dr. David Bonner's grave.

As he'd hoped, the cemetery was deserted. He laid the flowers at the base of the headstone and said a short prayer for the family. He stayed for only a few minutes before driving back to the bed-and-breakfast. Getting out of the car, he looked up. Blue skies stretched to the horizon, and it was already growing warm. Thinking the morning was too beautiful to waste, he decided to walk.

The sun glared off the waters of the Neuse and he slipped on a pair of sunglasses. Crossing the street, he surveyed the neighborhood. Even though the shops were open, the sidewalks were largely empty, and he found himself wondering how they were able to stay in business.

Eyeing his watch, he saw he still had half an hour until his appointment. Up ahead, he spied the coffee shop he'd passed earlier on his run, and though he didn't want more coffee, he decided he could use a bottle of water. Feeling a breeze pick up as he set his sights on the coffee shop, he saw the door swing open. He watched as someone stepped out, and almost immediately he began to smile.

Amanda stood at the counter of the Bean, adding cream and sugar to a cup of Ethiopian coffee. The Bean, once a small home that overlooked the harbor, offered about twenty different kinds of coffee along with delicious pastries, and Amanda always enjoyed coming here when she visited Oriental. Along with Irvin's, it was a place where locals congregated to catch up on whatever was happening in town. Behind her, she could hear the murmurs of conversation. Although the morning rush had long since passed, the café was more crowded than she'd expected. The twenty-something-year-old behind the counter hadn't stopped moving since Amanda had walked in.

She desperately needed coffee. The exchange with her mom this morning had left her feeling listless. Earlier, while she'd been in the shower, she'd briefly considered returning to the kitchen to attempt a real conversation. By the time she'd toweled off, though, she'd changed her mind. While she had always hoped that her mother would evolve into the sympathetic, supportive mother she had often longed for, it was easier to imagine the shocked, disappointed expression her mom would flash when she heard Dawson's name. After that, the tirade would commence, no doubt a repeat of the outraged, condescending lectures she had delivered when Amanda was a teenager. Her mother, after all, was a woman of old-fashioned values. Decisions were good or bad, choices were right or wrong, and certain lines were not to be crossed. There were nonnegotiable codes of conduct, especially regarding family. Amanda had always known the rules; she'd always known what her mom believed. Her mother stressed responsibility, she believed in consequences, and she had little tolerance for whining. Amanda knew that wasn't always a bad thing; she'd adopted a bit of the same philosophy with her own kids, and she knew they were better for it.

The difference was that her mother had always seemed so sure about everything. She had always been confident about who she was and the choices she'd made, as though life were a song and all she had to do was march in rhythm to it, knowing that every-thing would work out as planned. Her mother, Amanda often thought, had no regrets at all.

But Amanda wasn't like that. Nor could she ever forget how brutal her mother's reaction to Bea's illness and eventual death had been. She'd expressed her sympathy, of course, and stayed to take care of Jared and Lynn during many of their frequent vis-its to the Pediatric Cancer Center at Duke; she'd even cooked a meal or two for them in the weeks after the funeral. But Amanda could never quite grasp her mother's stoic acceptance of the situ-ation, nor could she stomach the lecture she'd delivered three months after Bea died, about how Amanda needed to "get back on her horse" and "stop feeling sorry" for herself. As if losing Bea were nothing more than a bad breakup with a boyfriend. She still felt a surge of anger every time she thought about it, and she sometimes wondered whether her mom was capable of any sort of compassion.

She exhaled, trying to remind herself that her mother's world was different from hers. Her mom had never gone to college, her mom had never lived anywhere but Oriental, and maybe that had something to do with it. She accepted things because there was nothing else to compare them to. And her own family had been anything but loving, from what little her mother had shared about her own upbringing. But who knew? All she knew for sure was that confiding in her mom would lead to more trouble than it was worth, and right now, she wasn't ready for that.

As she was putting the lid on her coffee, Amanda's cell phone rang. Seeing that it was Lynn, she stepped out onto the small porch as she answered, and they spent the next few minutes chatting. Afterward, Amanda called Jared on his cell phone, waking him and listening to his drowsy mumbles. Before hang-ing up, he said he was looking forward to seeing her on Sunday. She wished she could call Annette as well but consoled herself with the knowledge that she was almost certainly having a great time at camp.

After some hesitation, she also called Frank at the office. She hadn't had a chance earlier that morning, despite what she'd told her mom. As usual, she had to wait until he had a free minute between patients.

"Hey, there," he greeted her when he came on the line. As they talked, she deduced that he didn't remember calling the house last night. Nonetheless, he sounded glad to hear her voice. He asked about her mom, and Amanda told him that they were going to have dinner later; he told her that he had plans to go golfing on Sunday morning with his friend Roger and that they might watch the Braves game afterward at the country club. Experience told her that those activities would inevitably involve heavy drinking, but she tried to suppress her surge of anger, knowing that challenging him wouldn't do any good. Frank asked about the funeral and what else she planned to do in town. Though Amanda answered the questions honestly—she didn't know much yet—she could feel herself avoiding Dawson's name. Frank didn't seem to notice anything amiss, but by the time they finished their conversation, Amanda felt a distinct and uncomfortable frisson of guilt. Alongside her anger, it was enough to leave her feeling unusually unsettled.

Dawson waited in the shade of a magnolia tree until Amanda slipped the phone back into her purse. He thought he saw something troubled in her expression, but as she straightened the strap on her shoulder she became unreadable again.

Like him, she was wearing jeans, and as he started toward her he noticed the way her turquoise blouse deepened the color of her eyes. Lost in thought, she started when she recognized him.

"Hey," she said, breaking into a smile. "I didn't expect to see you here."

Dawson stepped onto the porch, watching as she ran a hand over her neat ponytail. "I wanted to grab some water before our meeting."

"No coffee?" Amanda gestured behind her. "It's the best in town."

"I had some at breakfast."

"Did you go to Irvin's? Tuck used to swear by the place."

"No. I just ate at the place where I'm staying. Breakfast comes with the room and all, and Alice had everything ready."

"Alice?"

"Just some swimsuit supermodel who happens to own the place. No reason for you to be jealous."

She laughed. "Yeah, I'm sure. How was your morning?"

"Good. Went for a nice run and had a chance to take in the changes around here."

"And?"

"It's like stepping into a time warp. I feel like Michael J. Fox in *Back to the Future*."

"It's one of Oriental's charms. When you're here, it's easy to pretend the rest of the world doesn't exist and that all your problems will simply float away."

"You sound like a commercial for the Chamber of Commerce."

"That's one of *my* charms."

"Among many others, I'm sure."

As he said it, she was struck again by the intensity of his gaze. She wasn't used to being scrutinized this way—on the contrary, she often felt virtually invisible as she went through the well-worn circuit of her daily routines. Before she could dwell on her self-consciousness, he nodded at the door. "I'm going to get that bottle of water, if that's okay."

He went inside, and from her vantage point Amanda noted the way the pretty twenty-something cashier tried not to stare at him as he walked toward the refrigerator case. When Dawson neared the back of the store, the clerk checked her appearance in the mirror behind the counter, then greeted him with a friendly smile at the register. Amanda turned away quickly, before he caught her watching.

A minute later, Dawson emerged, still trying to end his exchange with the clerk. Amanda forced herself to keep a straight face, and by unspoken agreement they moved off the porch, eventually wandering toward a spot with a better view of the marina.

"The girl at the counter was flirting with you," she observed.

"She's just friendly."

"She made it pretty obvious."

He shrugged as he unscrewed the cap of his bottle. "I didn't really notice."

"How could you not notice?"

"I was thinking about something else."

By the way he said it, she knew there was more, and she waited. He squinted out at the line of boats bobbing in the marina.

"I saw Abee this morning," he finally said. "When I was out for my run."

Amanda stiffened at the sound of his name. "Are you sure it was him?"

"He's my cousin, remember?"

"What happened?"

"Nothing."

"That's good, right?"

"I'm not sure yet."

Amanda tensed. "What does that mean?"

He didn't answer right away. Instead, he took a sip of water, and she could almost hear the wheels turning in his mind. "I guess it means I stay out of sight as much as possible. Other than that, I guess I'll play things as they come."

"Maybe they won't do anything."

"Maybe," he agreed. "So far, so good, right?" He screwed the cap back on the bottle, changing the subject. "What do you think Mr. Tanner's going to tell us? He was pretty mysterious when we talked on the phone. He wouldn't tell me anything about the funeral."

"He didn't say much to me, either. My mom and I were talking about the very same thing this morning."

"Yeah? How's your mom doing?"

"She was a bit upset that she missed her bridge game last night. But to make up for it, she was nice enough to coerce me into having dinner at a friend's house tonight."

He smiled. "So . . . that means you're free until dinner?"

"Why? What did you have in mind?"

"I don't know. Let's find out what Mr. Tanner has to say first. Which reminds me that we should probably get going. His office is just down the block."

After Amanda secured the lid on her coffee, they started down the sidewalk, moving from one patch of shade to the next.

"Do you remember when you asked if you could buy me an ice cream?" she asked. "That first time?"

"I remember wondering why you said yes."

She ignored his comment. "You took me to the drugstore, the one with the old-fashioned fountain and the long counter, and we both had hot fudge sundaes. They made the ice cream there, and it's still the best I've ever had. I can't believe they ended up tearing the place down."

"When was that, by the way?"

"I don't know. Maybe six or seven years ago? One day, on one of my visits, I noticed it was just gone. Kind of made me sad. I used to take my kids there when they were little, and they always had a good time."

He tried to picture her children sitting next to her at the old drugstore but couldn't quite conjure up their faces. Did they resemble her, he wondered, or take after their father? Did they have her fire, her generous heart?

"Do you think your kids would have liked growing up here?" he asked.

"When they were little, they would have. It's a beautiful town, with a lot of places to play and explore. But once they got older, they probably would have found it confining."

"Like you?"

"Yeah," she said. "Like me. I couldn't wait to leave. I don't know if you recall, but I applied to NYU and Boston College, just so I could experience a real city."

"How could I forget? They all sounded so far away," Dawson said.

"Yes, well...my dad went to Duke, I grew up hearing about Duke, I watched Duke basketball on television. I guess it was pretty much etched in stone that if I got in, that's where I'd go. And it ended up being the right choice, because the school was great and I made a lot of friends and I grew up while I was there. Besides, I don't know that I would have liked living in New York or Boston. I'm still a small-town girl at heart. I like to hear the crickets when I go to sleep."

"You'd enjoy Louisiana then. It's the bug capital of the world."

She smiled before taking a sip of her coffee. "Do you remember when we drove down to the coast when Hurricane Diana was coming? How I kept begging you to take me, and how you kept trying to talk me out of it?"

"I thought you were crazy."

"But you took me anyway. Because I wanted you to. We could barely get out of your car, the winds were so strong, and the ocean was just...wild. It was whitecaps all the way to the horizon, and you just stood there holding me, trying to convince me to get back in the car."

"I didn't want you to get hurt."

"Are there storms like that when you're on the oil rig?"

"Less often than you'd think. If we're in the projected path, we usually get evacuated."

"Usually?"

He shrugged. "Meteorologists get it wrong sometimes. I've been on the fringe of some hurricanes and it's unnerving. You're really at the mercy of the weather, and you just have to hunker down while the rig sways, knowing that no one's coming to the rescue if it goes over. I've seen some guys completely lose it."

"I think I'd be like one of those guys who lost it."

"You were fine when Hurricane Diana was coming in," he pointed out.

"That's because you were there." Amanda slowed her pace. Her voice was earnest. "I knew you wouldn't let anything happen to me. I always felt safe when you were around."

"Even when my dad and my cousins came by Tuck's? To get their money?"

"Yeah," she said. "Even then. Your family never bothered me."

"You were lucky."

"I don't know," she said. "When we were together, I'd see Ted or Abee in town sometimes, and every now and then I'd see your father. Oh, they'd have those little smirks on their faces if our paths happened to cross, but they never made me nervous. And then later, when I'd come back here in the summers, after Ted had been sent away, Abee and your dad kept their distance. I think they knew what you'd do if anything ever happened to me." She came to a full stop under the shade of a tree and faced him. "So no, I've never been afraid of them. Not once. Because I had you."

"You're giving me too much credit."

"Really? You mean you would have let them hurt me?"

He didn't have to answer. She could tell by his expression that she was right.

"They were always afraid of you, you know. Even Ted. Because they knew you as well as I did."

"You were afraid of me?"

"That's not what I meant," she said. "I knew you loved me and that you'd do anything for me. And that was one of the reasons it hurt so much when you ended it, Dawson. Because I knew even then how rare that kind of love is. Only the luckiest people get to experience it at all."

For a moment Dawson seemed unable to speak. "I'm sorry," he finally said.

"So am I," she said, not bothering to hide the old sadness. "I was one of the lucky ones, remember?"

After reaching Morgan Tanner's office, Dawson and Amanda sat in the small reception area replete with scuffed pine floors, end tables stacked with outdated magazines, and fraying upholstered chairs. The receptionist, who looked old enough to have been drawing social security for years, was reading a paperback novel. Then again, there wasn't much else for her to do. In the ten minutes they waited, the phone never rang.

Finally, the door swung open, revealing an elderly man with a shock of white hair, gray caterpillars for eyebrows, and a rumpled suit. He waved them into his office. "Amanda Ridley and Dawson Cole, I presume?" He shook their hands. "I'm Morgan Tanner, and I'd like to express my sympathies to both of you. I know this must be hard."

"Thank you," Amanda said. Dawson simply nodded.

Tanner ushered them to a pair high-backed leather chairs. "Please sit down. This shouldn't take long."

Tanner's office was nothing like the reception area, with mahogany shelving neatly stacked with hundreds of law books and a window that overlooked the street. The desk, an ornate antique with detailed molding on the corners, was topped with what appeared to be a Tiffany lamp. A walnut box sat in the center of the desk, which faced the leather armchairs.

"I want to apologize for being late. I was tied up on the phone, taking care of some last-minute details." He kept talking as he shuffled around the desk. "I suppose you're wondering why all the secrecy about the arrangements, but that was the way Tuck wanted it. He was rather insistent and had his own ideas about things." He inspected them from beneath his bushy eyebrows. "But I suppose you two already know that."

Amanda stole a look at Dawson as Tanner took his seat and reached for the file in front of him. "I also appreciate that both of you were able to make it. After listening to him talk about you, I know that Tuck would have appreciated it as well. I'm sure you both have questions, so let me go ahead and get started." He shot them a quick smile, revealing surprisingly even and white teeth. "As you know, Tuck's body was discovered on Tuesday morning by Rex Yarborough."

"Who?" Amanda asked.

"The mailman. It turns out that he'd made it a point to check in on Tuck fairly regularly. When he knocked at the door, no one answered. The door was unlocked, though, and when he went in, he found Tuck in his bed. He called the sheriff, and the determination was made that no foul play was involved. That was when the sheriff called me."

"Why did he call you?" Dawson asked.

"Because Tuck had asked him to. He'd made it known to the sheriff's department that I was his executor and should be contacted as soon as possible after he passed."

"You make it sound like he knew he was dying."

"I think he had a sense that it was coming," Tanner said. "Tuck Hostetler was an old man, and he wasn't afraid to confront the realities of his advancing age." He shook his head. "I just hope I can be as organized and resolute when my time approaches."

Amanda and Dawson exchanged glances but said nothing.

"I urged him to let you both know about his final wishes and plans, but he wanted to keep them secret for some reason. I still can't explain it." Tanner sounded almost paternal. "He also made it obvious that he cared deeply about you two."

Dawson sat forward. "I know it isn't important, but how did you two know each other?"

Tanner nodded, as if he'd expected the question. "I met Tuck eighteen years ago, when I brought in a classic Mustang for him to restore. At the time, I was a partner at a large firm in Raleigh. I was a lobbyist, if you want to know the truth. Did a lot of work with agriculture. But to make a long story short, I stayed down here for a few days to monitor the progress. I only knew of Tuck by reputation and I didn't quite trust him with my car. Anyway, we kind of got to know each other, and I realized I liked the pace of life around here. A few weeks later, when I finally came back to pick up my car, he didn't charge me near what I thought he would, and I was amazed at his work. Fast-forward fifteen years. I was feeling burned out and I decided on a whim to move down here and retire. Only it didn't quite take. After a year or so, I opened a small practice. Not much, just wills mainly and a real estate closing now and then. I don't need to work, but it gives me something to do. And my wife couldn't be happier that I'm out of the house for a few hours a week. Anyway, I happened to see Tuck at Irvin's one morning and told him that if he ever needed anything, I'd be around. And then, last February, surprising no one more than me, he took me up on the offer."

"Why you and not—"

"Another attorney in town?" Tanner asked, finishing for him. "I got the impression that he wanted an attorney who didn't have deep roots in this town. He didn't put much faith in attorney-client privilege, even when I assured him it was absolute. Is there anything more I can add that I didn't cover?"

When Amanda shook her head, he pulled the file closer to him and slipped on a pair of reading glasses. "Then let's get started. Tuck left instructions on how he wanted me to handle things as his executor. You should know those wishes included the fact that he didn't want a traditional funeral. Instead, he asked that, after his death, I arrange for cremation, and per his wishes as to the timing,

Tuck Hostetler was cremated yesterday." He motioned toward the box on his desk, leaving no doubt that it held Tuck's ashes.

Amanda paled. "But we arrived yesterday."

"I know. He'd asked that I try to take care of it before you arrived."

"He didn't want us there?"

"He didn't want anyone there."

"Why not?"

"All I can say is that he was specific in his instructions. But if I were to guess, I think he was under the impression that having to make any of the arrangements might have been upsetting to you." He lifted a page from the file and held it up. "He said— and I'm quoting him here—'ain't no reason my death should be a burden to 'em.'" Tanner removed his reading glasses and leaned back in his chair, trying to gauge their reactions.

"In other words, there's no funeral?" Amanda asked.

"Not in the traditional sense, no."

Amanda turned toward Dawson and back to Tanner again. "Then why did he want us to come?"

"He asked that I contact you in the hope that you would do something else for him, something more important than the cremation. Essentially, he wanted the two of you to scatter his ashes at a place he said was very special to him, a place apparently neither of you has ever visited."

It took Amanda only a moment to figure it out. "His cottage at Vandemere?"

Tanner nodded. "That's it. Tomorrow would be ideal, at whatever time you choose. Of course, if you're uncomfortable with the idea, I'll have it taken care of. I have to go up there anyway."

"No, tomorrow's fine," Amanda said.

Tanner lifted a slip of paper. "Here's the address, and I took the liberty of printing directions as well. It's a bit off the beaten path, as you might suspect. And there's one other thing: He asked that I give you these," he said, removing three sealed envelopes from the file. "You'll notice that two have your names on them. He asked that you read the unmarked one aloud first, sometime prior to the ceremony."

"Ceremony?" Amanda repeated.

"The scattering of the ashes, I meant," he said, handing over the directions and the envelopes. "And of course, feel free to add anything either of you might want to say."

"Thank you," she said, taking them. The envelopes felt oddly heavy, weighted with mystery. "But what about the other two?"

"I assume you're to read those afterward."

"You assume?"

"Tuck wasn't specific about that, other than to say that after you've read the first letter, you'll know when to open the other two."

Amanda took the envelopes and slipped them in her purse, trying to digest everything Tanner had told them. Dawson seemed equally perplexed.

Tanner perused the file again. "Any questions?"

"Did he give specifics on where at Vandemere he wanted the ashes scattered?"

"No," Tanner answered.

"How will we know, since we've never been there?"

"That's the same question I asked him, but he seemed sure that you would understand what to do."

"Did he have a particular hour of day in mind?"

"Again, he left that up to you. However, he was adamant in his desire that it remain a private ceremony. He asked me to make sure, for instance, that no information be given to the newspaper regarding his death, not even an obituary. I got the sense that he didn't want anyone, aside from the three of us, to know that he'd even died. And I followed his wishes, to the greatest extent possible. Of course, word inevitably leaked out despite my best attempts, but I want you to know that I've done all that I could."

"Did he say why?"

"No," Tanner answered. "Nor did I ask. By that time, I'd figured out that unless he volunteered it, he probably wasn't going to tell me." He looked at Amanda and Dawson, waiting to see if they had further questions. When they stayed quiet, he flipped the top page in the folder. "Moving on to the subject of his estate, you both know that Tuck had no surviving family. While I understand that your grief may make this feel like an inopportune time to discuss his will, he did ask that I let you know what he intended to do while you were both here. Would that be all right?" When they nodded, he went on. "Tuck's assets weren't insubstantial. He owned quite a bit of land, in addition to having funds in several accounts. I'm still working through the numbers, but what you should know is this: He asked that you help yourselves to any of his personal property that you may desire, even if it's only a single item. He simply asked that if there was disagreement about anything, the two of you work it out while you're here. I'll be handling the probate over the next few months, but essentially, the remainder of his estate will be sold, with the proceeds to benefit the Pediatric Cancer Center at Duke University Hospital." Tanner smiled at Amanda. "He thought you'd want to know that."

"I don't know what to say." She could feel Dawson's quiet alertness beside her. "It's so generous of him." She hesitated, more affected than she wanted to admit. "He—I guess he knew what it would mean to me."

Tanner nodded before sorting through the pages and finally set them aside. "I think that's it, unless you can think of anything."

There was nothing else, and after their good-byes Amanda rose while Dawson lifted the walnut box from the desk. Tanner stood but made no motion to follow them out. Amanda accompanied Dawson to the door, noticing the frown forming on his face. Before they reached the door, he paused and turned around.

"Mr. Tanner?"

"Yes?"

"You said something I'm curious about."

"Oh?"

"You said that tomorrow would be ideal. I assume you meant tomorrow as opposed to today."

"Yes."

"Can you tell me why?"

Tanner moved the file to the corner of his desk. "I'm sorry," he said. "But I can't."

※

"What was that about?" Amanda asked.

They were walking toward her car, which was still parked outside the coffee shop. Instead of answering, Dawson put his hand in his pocket.

"What are you doing for lunch?" he asked.

"You're not going to answer my question?"

"I'm not sure what to say. Tanner didn't give me an answer."

"But why did you ask the question in the first place?"

"Because I'm a curious person," he said. "I've always been curious about everything."

She crossed the street. "No," she finally said, "I don't agree. If anything, you lived your life with an almost stoic acceptance of the way things are. But I know exactly what you're doing."

"What am I doing?"

"You're trying to change the subject."

He didn't bother to deny it. Instead, he shifted the box beneath his arm. "You didn't answer my question, either."

"What question?"

"I asked what you were doing for lunch. Because if you're free, I know a great place."

She hesitated, thinking about small-town gossip, but as usual Dawson was able to read her.

"Trust me," he said. "I know just where to go."

※

Half an hour later, they were back at Tuck's, sitting near the creek on a blanket that Amanda had retrieved from Tuck's closet. On the way over, Dawson had picked up sandwiches from Brantlee's Village Restaurant, along with some bottles of water.

"How did you know?" she asked, reverting to their old short-hand. With Dawson, she was reminded of what it was like to have her thoughts divined before she uttered them. When they were young, a momentary glimpse or the subtlest of gestures had often been enough to signal a world of thought and emotion.

"Your mom and everyone she knows still live in town. You're married, and I'm someone from your past. It wasn't too hard to figure out that it might not be a good idea for us to be seen spend-ing the afternoon together."

She was glad he understood, but as he pulled two sandwiches from the bag, she nonetheless felt a quiver of guilt. She told herself that they were simply having lunch, but that wasn't the full truth, and she knew it.

Dawson didn't seem to notice. "Turkey or chicken salad?" he asked, holding both of them out to her.

"Either," she said. Then changing her mind, she said, "Chicken salad."

He passed the sandwich to her, along with a bottle of water. She surveyed her surroundings, relishing the quiet. Thin, hazy clouds drifted overhead, and near the house she saw a pair of squirrels chase each other up the trunk of an oak tree shrouded in Spanish moss. A turtle sunned itself on a log on the far side of the creek. It was the environment she had grown up in, and yet it had come to feel strangely foreign, a radically different world from the one she lived in now.

"What did you think about the meeting?" he asked.

"Tanner seems like a decent man."

"What about the letters Tuck wrote? Any ideas?"

"After what I heard this morning? Not a clue."

Dawson nodded as he unwrapped his sandwich and she did the same. "The Pediatric Cancer Center, huh?"

She nodded, thinking automatically of Bea. "I told you I volunteered at Duke University Hospital. I also do some fund-raising for them."

"Yes, but you didn't mention where at the hospital you worked," Dawson replied, his sandwich unwrapped but still untouched. She heard the question in his voice and knew that he was waiting. Amanda absently twisted the cap on her bottle of water.

"Frank and I had another child, a baby girl, three years after Lynn was born." She paused, gathering her strength, but knowing that, somehow, saying the words to Dawson wouldn't feel awkward or painful the way it so often did with others.

"She was diagnosed with a brain tumor when she was eighteen months old. It was inoperable, and despite the efforts of an incredible team of doctors and staff at the Pediatric Cancer Center, she died six months later." She looked out over the ancient creek, feeling the familiar, deep-seated ache, a sadness she knew would never go away.

Dawson reached over and squeezed her hand. "What was her name?" he asked, his voice soft.

"Bea," she said.

For a long time, neither said anything, the only sounds the burbling of the creek and the leaves rustling overhead. Amanda didn't feel that she needed to say more, nor did Dawson expect her to. She knew he understood exactly how she was feeling, and she had the sense that he felt an ache as well, if only because he couldn't help her.

❧

After lunch, they gathered the remains of their picnic along with the blanket and started back toward the house. Dawson followed Amanda inside, watching as she vanished around the corner to put the blanket away. There was something guarded about her, as if she were afraid of having crossed an unspoken line. After retrieving glasses from a cupboard in the kitchen, he poured some sweet tea. When she came back to the kitchen, he offered her one.

"You okay?" he asked.

"Yeah," she said, taking the glass. "I'm fine."

"I'm sorry if I upset you."

"You didn't," she said. "It's just that talking about Bea is still hard for me sometimes. And it's been an...unexpected weekend so far."

"For me, too," he agreed. He leaned back against the counter. "How do you want to do this?"

"Do what?"

"Go through the house. To see if there's anything you want."

Amanda exhaled, hoping her jumpiness wasn't obvious. "I don't know. It feels wrong to me somehow."

"It shouldn't. He wanted us to remember him."

"I'll remember him no matter what."

"Then how about this? He wants to be more than just a memory. He wants us to have a piece of him and this place, too."

She took a sip, knowing he was probably right. But the idea of rooting through his things to find a keepsake right now just felt like too much. "Let's hold off for a bit. Would that be all right?"

"It's fine. Whenever you're ready. You want to sit outside for a while?"

She nodded and followed him out to the back porch, where they seated themselves in Tuck's old rockers. Dawson rested his glass on his thigh. "I imagine that Tuck and Clara used to do this quite a bit," he commented. "Just sit outside and watch the world go by," he said.

"Probably."

He turned toward her. "I'm glad you came to visit him. I hated the thought that he was always all alone out here."

She could feel the moisture from the sweating glass as she held it. "You know he used to see Clara, right? After she was gone."

Dawson frowned. "What are you talking about?"

"He swore she was still around."

For an instant, his mind flashed on the images and movement that he'd been experiencing. "What do you mean, he saw her?"

"Just what I said. He saw her and talked to her," she said.

He blinked. "Are you saying that Tuck believed he was seeing a ghost?"

"What? He never told you?"

"He never talked to me about Clara, period."

Her eyes widened. "Ever?"

"The only thing he ever told me was her name."

So Amanda set her glass aside and began to tell him some of the stories that Tuck had shared with her over the years. About how he'd dropped out of school when he was twelve and found a job in his uncle's garage; how he'd first met Clara at church when he was fourteen years old and knew in that instant that he was going to marry her; how Tuck's entire family, including his uncle, had moved north in search of work a few years into the Great Depression and never came back. She told Dawson about his early years with Clara, including the first miscarriage, and his backbreaking work for Clara's father on the family farm while he worked on building this house at night. She said that Clara had two more miscarriages after the war and talked about Tuck building the garage before gradually beginning to restore cars in the early 1950s, including a Cadillac owned by an up-and-coming singer named Elvis Presley. By the time she finished telling him about Clara's death and how Tuck talked to Clara's ghost, Dawson had emptied his tea and was staring into the glass, no doubt trying to reconcile her stories with the man he'd known.

"I can't believe he didn't tell you any of that," Amanda marveled.

"He had his reasons, I guess. Maybe he liked you better."

"I doubt that," she said. "It's just that I knew him later in life. You knew him when he was still hurting."

"Maybe," he said, sounding unconvinced.

Amanda went on. "You were important to him. He let you live here, after all. Not once, but twice." When Dawson finally nodded, she set her glass aside. "Can I ask a question, though?"

"Anything."

"What *did* the two of you talk about?"

"Cars. Engines. Transmissions. Sometimes we talked about the weather."

"Must have been scintillating," she cracked.

"You can't imagine. But back then, I wasn't much of a talker, either."

She leaned toward him, suddenly purposeful. "All right. So now we both know about Tuck and you know about me. But I still don't know about you."

"Sure you do. I told you about me yesterday. I work on an oil rig? Live in a trailer out in the country? Still drive the same car? No dates?"

In a languid motion, Amanda draped her ponytail over one shoulder, the movement almost sensual. "Tell me something I don't know," she coaxed. "Something about you that no one knows. Something that would surprise me."

"There's not much to tell," he said.

She scrutinized him. "Why don't I believe you?"

Because, he thought, *I could never hide anything from you.* "I'm not sure," he said instead.

She grew quiet at his answer, working through something else in her mind. "You said something yesterday that I'm curious about." When he fixed her with a quizzical expression, she went on. "How did you know that Marilyn Bonner never remarried?"

"I just do."

"Did Tuck tell you?"

"No."

"Then how do you know?"

He laced his fingers together and leaned back in his rocker, knowing that if he didn't answer, she'd simply ask again. In that, she hadn't changed, either. "It's probably better if I start from the beginning," he said, sighing. He told her then about the Bonners—about his visit to Marilyn's crumbling farmhouse so long ago, about the family's years of struggle, that he'd begun sending them money anonymously when he got out of prison. And finally, that over the years he'd had private detectives report on the family's welfare. When he finished, Amanda was quiet, visibly struggling with a response.

"I don't know what to say," she finally burst out.

"I knew you were going to say that."

"I'm serious, Dawson," she said, her anger evident. "I mean, I know that there's something noble about what you're doing, and I'm sure it made a difference in their lives. But...there's something sad about it, too, because you can't forgive yourself for what so clearly was an accident. Everyone makes mistakes, even if some are worse than others. Accidents happen. But having someone follow them? To know exactly what's happening in their lives? That's just wrong."

"You don't understand—," he started.

"No, *you* don't understand," she interrupted. "Don't you think they deserve their privacy? Taking photos, digging through their personal lives—"

"It's not like that," he protested.

"But it is!" Amanda slapped the armrest of her rocker. "What if they ever found out? Can you imagine how terrible that would be? How betrayed and invaded they'd feel?" Surprising him, she placed a hand on his arm, her grasp firm and yet urgent to make sure he heard her. "I'm not saying I agree with what you're doing; what you do with your money is your business. But the rest? With the detectives? You've got to stop. You've got to promise me you'll do that, okay?"

He could feel the heat radiating from her touch. "All right," he said finally. "I promise I won't do it again."

She studied him, making sure he was telling the truth. For the first time since they'd met, Dawson looked almost tired. There was something defeated in his posture, and as they sat together she found herself wondering what would have happened to him had she never left that summer. Or even if she'd gone to visit him while he'd been in prison. She wanted to believe that it might have made a difference, that Dawson would have been able to live a life less haunted by the past. That Dawson, if not happy, would have at the very least been able to find a sense of peace. For him, peace had always been elusive.

But then he wasn't alone in that, was he? Wasn't that what everyone wanted?

"I have another confession," he said. "About the Bonners."

She felt her breath as it left her lungs. "More?"

He scratched the side of his nose with his free hand, as if to buy time. "I brought flowers to Dr. Bonner's grave earlier this morning. It was something I used to do when I got out of prison. When it got to be too much, you know?"

She stared at him, wondering if he was about to tack on another surprise, but he didn't. "That's not quite on the level of the other things you've been doing."

"I know. I just thought I should mention it."

"Why? Because now you want my opinion?"

He shrugged. "Maybe."

She didn't answer for a moment. "I think flowers are fine," she finally said, "as long as you don't overdo it. That's actually . . . appropriate."

He turned toward her. "Yeah?"

"Yes," she said. "Placing flowers at his grave is meaningful, but not invasive."

He nodded but said nothing. In the silence, Amanda leaned even closer. "Do you know what I'm thinking?" she asked.

"After everything I've said, I'm almost afraid to guess."

"I think you and Tuck are more alike than you realize."

He turned toward her. "Is that good or bad?"

"I'm still here with you, aren't I?"

🌿

When the heat became stifling even in the shade, Amanda led them back inside. The screen door banged shut gently behind them.

"You ready?" he asked, surveying the kitchen.

"No," she said. "But I suppose we have to do this. For the record, it still seems wrong to me. I don't even know how to start."

Dawson paced the length of the kitchen before turning to face her. "Okay, let's do this: When you think about your last visit with Tuck, what comes to mind?"

"It was the same as always. He talked about Clara, I made him dinner." She gave a small shrug. "I put a blanket over his shoulders when he fell asleep in the chair."

Dawson drew her into the living room and nodded toward the fireplace. "Then maybe you should take the picture."

She shook her head. "I couldn't do that."

"You'd rather it be thrown away?"

"No, of course not. But you should take it. You knew him better than I did."

"Not really," he said. "He never talked to me about Clara. And when you see it, you'll think about both of them, not just him, and that's why he told you about her."

When she hesitated, he stepped toward the fireplace and gently removed it from the mantel. "He wanted this to be important to you. He wanted the two of them to be important to you."

She reached for the photo, staring at it. "But if I take this, what's left for you? I mean, there's not much here."

"Don't worry. There's something I saw earlier that I'd like to keep." He moved toward the door. "Come on."

Amanda followed him down the steps. As they approached the garage it dawned on her: If the house was where she and Tuck had forged their bond, the garage had been that place for Dawson and Tuck. And even before he found it, she already knew what he wanted.

Dawson reached for the faded bandanna folded neatly on the workbench. "This is what he wanted me to have," he said.

"You sure?" Amanda squinted at the square of red cloth. "It's not much."

"It's the first time I've ever noticed a clean one around here, so it has to be for me." He grinned. "But yeah, I'm sure. To me, this is Tuck. I don't think I ever saw him without one. Always the same color, of course."

"Of course," she agreed. "We're talking about Tuck, right? Mr. Constant-in-All-Things?"

Dawson tucked the bandanna into his back pocket. "It's not such a bad thing. Change isn't always for the best."

The words seemed to hang in the air, and Amanda didn't reply. Instead, when he leaned against the Stingray, it triggered something in her memory, and Amanda took a step toward him. "I forgot to ask Tanner what to do with the car."

"I was thinking that I might as well finish it. Then Tanner can just call the owner to pick it up."

"Really?"

"As far as I can tell, all the parts are here," he said, "and I'm pretty sure Tuck would have wanted me to finish it. Besides, you're going to dinner with your mom, so it's not like I have anything else to do tonight."

"How long will it take?" Amanda scanned the boxes of spare parts.

"I don't know. A few hours, maybe?"

She turned her attention to the car, walking its length before facing him again. "Okay," she said. "Do you need help?"

Dawson gave a wry smile. "Did you learn how to fix engines since I saw you last?"

"No."

"I can take care of it after you leave," he said. "No big deal." Turning around, he gestured toward the house. "We can go back inside if you'd rather. It's pretty hot out here."

"I don't want you to have to work late," she said, and like an old habit rediscovered, she moved to the spot that had once been hers. She pushed a rusty tire iron out of the way and lifted herself onto the workbench before making herself comfortable. "We've got a big day tomorrow. And besides, I always liked watching you work."

He thought he heard something akin to a promise in that, and it struck him that the years seemed to be looping back on themselves, allowing him to revisit the time and place where he'd been happiest. Turning away, he reminded himself that Amanda was married. The last thing she needed was the kind of complication that comes from trying to rewrite the past. He drew a slow, deliberate breath and reached for a box on the other end of the workbench.

"You're going to get bored. This will take a while," he said, trying to mask his thoughts.

"Don't worry about me. I'm used to it."

"Being bored?"

She tucked her legs up. "I used to sit here for hours waiting for you to finish so we could finally go and do something fun."

"You should have said something."

"When I couldn't take it anymore, I would. But I knew that if I pulled you away too often, Tuck wouldn't have let me come around anymore. That's also why I didn't keep you talking the whole time."

Her face was partly in shadow, her voice a seductive call. Too many memories, with her sitting there the way she used to, talking like this. He lifted the carburetor from the box, inspecting it. It was refurbished but obviously done well, and he set it aside before skimming the work order.

He moved to the front of the car, popped the hood, and peered in. When he heard her clear her throat, he peeked at her.

"Well, considering Tuck's not around," she said, "I suppose we can talk all we want now, even if you are working."

"Okay." He stood straighter and stepped toward the work-bench. "What do you want to talk about?"

She thought about it. "Okay, how about this? What do you remember most about the first summer we were together?"

He reached for a set of wrenches, considering the question. "I remember wondering why on earth you wanted to spend time with me."

"I'm serious."

"So am I. I had nothing and you had everything. You could have dated anyone. And though we tried to lie low, I knew even then that it would only cause you problems. It didn't make sense to me."

She rested her chin on her knees, hugging them tightly to her body. "You know what I remember? I remember the time you and I drove to Atlantic Beach. When we saw all the starfish? It was like they'd all washed up at once, and we walked the entire length of the beach, tossing them back into the water. And later, we split a burger and fries and watched the sun go down. We must have talked for twelve straight hours."

She smiled before going on, knowing that he was remember-ing as well. "That's why I loved being with you. We could do the simplest things, like toss starfish into the ocean and share a burger and talk and even then I knew that I was fortunate. Because you were the first guy who wasn't constantly trying to impress me. You accepted who you were, but more than that, you accepted me for me. And nothing else mattered—not my family or your family or anyone else in the world. It was just us." She paused. "I don't know that I've ever felt as happy as I did that day, but then again, it was always like that when we were together. I never wanted it to end."

He met her eyes. "Maybe it hasn't."

She understood then, with the distance that age and maturity brings, how much he'd loved her back then. *And still did*, something whispered inside her, and all at once she had the strange impression that everything they'd shared in the past had been the opening chapters in a book with a conclusion that had yet to be written.

The idea should have scared her, but it didn't, and she ran her palm over the outline of their worn initials, carved into the workbench so many years ago. "I came here when my father died, you know."

"Where? Here?" When she nodded, Dawson reached again for the carburetor. "I thought you said you started visiting Tuck only a few years ago."

"He didn't know. I never told him I came."

"Why not?"

"I couldn't. It was all I could do to keep myself together, and I wanted to be alone." She paused. "It was about a year after Bea died, and I was still struggling when my mom called to tell me that my dad had had a heart attack. It didn't make any sense. He and my mom had visited us in Durham the week before, but the next thing I knew, we were loading up the kids to go to his funeral. We drove all morning to get here, and when I walked in the door, my mom was dressed to the nines and almost immediately began to brief me on our appointment at the funeral home. I mean, she showed hardly any emotion at all. She seemed to be more worried about getting the right kind of flowers for the service and making sure that I called all the relatives. It was like this bad dream, and by the end of the day, I just felt so...alone. So I left the house in the middle of the night and drove around, and for some reason I ended up parking down by the road and walking up here. I can't explain it. But I sat here and cried for what must have been hours." She exhaled, the tide of memories surging back. "I know my dad never gave you a chance, but he wasn't really a bad person. I always got along better with him than I did with my mom, and the older I got, the closer we became. He loved the kids—especially Bea." She was quiet before finally offering a sad smile. "Do you think that's strange? That I came here after he died, I mean?"

Dawson considered it. "No," he said. "I don't think it's strange at all. After I served my time, I came back here, too."

"You didn't have anywhere else to go."

His raised an eyebrow. "Did you?"

He was right, of course: While Tuck's had been a place of idyllic memories, it had also been the place she'd always come to cry.

She clasped her fingers tighter, forcing the memory away, and settled in, watching Dawson as he began to piece the engine back together. As the afternoon wound down, they talked easily of everyday things, past and present, filling in pieces of their lives and exchanging opinions on everything from books to places they had always dreamed of visiting. She was struck by a sense of déjà vu as she listened to the familiar clicks of the socket wrench when he adjusted it into place. She saw him struggle to loosen a bolt, his jaw clenching until it finally came free, before carefully setting it aside. Just as he had when they were young, he would stop what he was doing every now and then, reminding her that he was listening intently to everything she said. That he wanted to let her know, in his own understated way, that she had been and always would be important to him, struck her with almost painful intensity. Later, when he took a break from his labors and went to the house before returning with two glasses of sweet tea, there was a moment, just a moment, when she was able to imagine a different life that might have been hers, the kind of life she knew that she'd always really wanted.

When the late afternoon sun hung low over the pines, Dawson and Amanda finally left the garage, walking slowly back toward her car. Something had changed between them in the last few hours—a fragile rebirth of the past, perhaps—that both thrilled and terrified her. Dawson, for his part, ached to slip his arm around her as they walked side by side, but sensing her confusion he stopped himself.

Amanda's smile was tentative when they finally reached her door. She looked up at him, noticing his thick, full eyelashes, the kind that any woman would envy.

"I wish I didn't have to go," she admitted.

He shifted from one foot to the other. "I'm sure you and your mom will have a good time."

Maybe, she thought, *but probably not.* "Will you lock up when you go?"

"Of course," he said, noticing the way the sunlight skimmed over her glowing skin, the stray wisps of hair that lifted in the gentle breeze. "How do you want to do this tomorrow? Should I meet you up there or do you want me to follow you?"

She weighed the options, feeling conflicted. "There's no reason to bring two cars, is there?" she finally asked. "Why don't we just meet here around eleven and drive up together?"

He nodded and looked at her, neither of them moving. Finally, he took a slight step backward, breaking the spell, and Amanda felt herself exhale. She hadn't realized she'd been holding her breath.

After she slid onto the front seat of her car, Dawson closed the door behind her. His body was outlined against the setting sun, almost giving her the impression that he was a stranger. Feeling suddenly awkward, she pawed through her purse to find her keys, noting that her hands were trembling.

"Thanks for lunch," she said.

"Anytime," he answered.

Peeking in the rearview mirror as she pulled away, she saw that Dawson was still standing where she'd left him, as if hoping she'd change her mind and turn the car around. She felt the stirrings of something dangerous, something she'd been trying to deny.

He still loved her, she was certain of that now, and the realization was intoxicating. She knew it was wrong, and she tried to force the feeling away, but Dawson and their past had taken root once more, and she could no longer deny the simple truth that for the first time in years, she'd felt like she'd finally come home.

8

Ted watched little miss cheerleader pull out onto the road in front of Tuck's and decided that she looked pretty damn good for her age. But then she'd always been a looker, and back in the day, there'd been many times when he'd thought about having his way with her. Just throw her into the car and use her up and bury her where no one could find her. But Dawson's daddy had intervened, saying the girl was off-limits, and back then Ted used to think that Tommy Cole knew what he was doing.

But Tommy Cole didn't know anything. Took Ted until prison to figure that out, and by the time he was free he hated Tommy Cole almost as much as he hated Dawson. Tommy hadn't done anything after his son had humiliated them both. He had turned them into laughingstocks, which was why Tommy ended up being first on Ted's list once he got out. Wasn't hard to make it seem like Tommy had drunk himself to death that night. All he'd had to do was shoot him up with grain alcohol once he'd passed out, and the next thing you know, Tommy had choked on his own vomit.

And now Dawson was finally going to get crossed off Ted's list, too. As he waited for Amanda to clear out, he wondered what the two of them had been doing up there. Probably making up for all those years apart, all twisted up in the sheets and screaming each other's names. If he had to guess, he'd say she was married, and he wondered if her husband suspected what was going on. Probably not. It wasn't the kind of thing a woman liked to advertise, especially a woman who drove a car like that. She probably married some rich peckerhead and spent her afternoons at the salon getting her nails done, just like her mama did. Her husband was probably some doctor or lawyer, too vain to even consider that his wife might be fooling around behind his back.

She was probably good at keeping secrets, though. Most women were. Hell, he should know. Married or not, made no difference to him; if they offered, he took. Didn't matter if it was kin, either. He'd been with half the women out on the property, even the ones married to his cousins. Their daughters, too. He and Claire, Calvin's wife, had been going at it a couple of times a week for the past six years, and Claire hadn't said a thing to anyone. Ella probably knew what was going on, since she was the one who washed his drawers, but she kept her mouth shut, too, and she'd keep it shut if she knew what was good for her. A man's business was his own.

The taillights of the car flashed red as Amanda finally rounded the curve, vanishing from sight. She hadn't spotted his truck— no surprise, since he'd pulled off the road, hiding it as best he could in a thicket. He figured he'd wait a few minutes, just to make sure she wasn't coming back. Last thing he wanted was witnesses, but he was still wondering how best to handle this. If Abee had seen Dawson this morning, it was sure as hell certain that Dawson had seen Abee, which would have gotten him thinking, so maybe Dawson was just sitting up there waiting, too, shotgun in his lap. Maybe he had plans of his own, just in case his kin did indeed show up.

Like the last time.

Ted tapped the Glock against his thigh, thinking that the key was to surprise Dawson. Get close enough to take the shot, then pitch the body in the trunk and ditch the rental car somewhere out on the property. File off the VIN and set the whole thing on fire, until it was nothing but a husk. Getting rid of the body wouldn't be hard, either. Just weight it down, toss it in the river, and let water and time do the rest. Or maybe bury it somewhere in the forest, where no one was likely to find it. It was hard to prove murder without a body. Little miss cheerleader or even the sheriff could suspect all they wanted, but suspicion was a long way from proof. Things would get riled up, of course, but they'd eventually pass. After that, he and Abee were going to sort things out. And let's just say that if Abee wasn't careful, he might find himself at the bottom of the river, too.

Finally ready, Ted exited the car and began his advance into the woods.

Dawson set the wrench aside and closed the hood, finished with the engine. Ever since Amanda left, he'd been unable to shake the sensation of being watched. The first time it had happened, he'd gripped the wrench hard as he'd peeked out around the hood, but there was no one there.

Now, walking to the entrance of the garage, he scanned the area, taking in the scene. He saw the oaks and pines with kudzu climbing their trunks and noticed that the shadows had begun to lengthen. A hawk passed overhead, its outline flickering across the drive, and starlings called from the branches above. All else was quiet in the early summer heat.

But someone was watching him. Someone was out there, he was sure of it, and he flashed on an image of the shotgun he had buried beneath the oak tree near the corner of the house all those years ago—not deep, maybe a foot down, wrapped in oil-cloth and sealed from the elements. Tuck had guns in the house, too, probably under his bed, but Dawson wasn't sure they were warranted. There was nothing out here as far as he could tell, but in that instant a blur of movement flashed near a clump of trees on the far side of the drive.

When he tried to zero in on it, though, he saw nothing. He

blinked, waiting for more and trying to decide whether it had been his imagination, when the hairs on the back of his neck slowly began to rise.

✿

Ted moved cautiously, knowing that rushing in would be foolish. He suddenly wished he'd brought Abee along. Would have been good to have Abee close in from another direction. But at least Dawson was still up there, unless he'd decided to walk out of the place. Ted would have heard the car start up.

He wondered where Dawson was exactly. House or garage, or somewhere outside? He hoped he wasn't inside; hard to get up to the house without being noticed. Tuck's place was set in a small clearing, with the creek out back, but there were windows on all sides and Dawson might see him approach. In that case, it might be better if he hung back and waited until Dawson finally came out. Problem with that was Dawson could go out the front or the back, and Ted couldn't be in two places at once.

What he really needed to do was cause a distraction. That way, when Dawson came out to investigate, he could wait until Dawson was close enough before pulling the trigger. He felt confident with the Glock up to about thirty feet.

What kind of distraction, though? That was the question.

He crept forward, avoiding the loose piles of rocks spreading out in front of him; this whole area of the county had marlstone everywhere. Simple but effective. Toss a few, maybe even clank one off the car or break a window. Dawson would come outside to check it out and Ted would be waiting.

He grabbed a handful of marlstone and shoved it in his pocket.

✿

Dawson quietly made his way to the spot where he'd seen the movement, replaying the hallucinations he'd experienced since the explosion on the platform, thinking it all felt too familiar. He reached the edge of the clearing and peered into the woods, try-ing to calm the racing of his heart.

He stopped, hearing the starlings chirp, a hundred of them calling from the trees. Thousands, maybe. As a kid, he'd always been fascinated by the swarmlike way they would break from the trees when he clapped, as though they were tethered together. They were calling now, calling for something.

A warning?

He didn't know. Beyond him, the forest was a living thing; the air was briny and thick with the scent of rotting wood. Branches of low-slung oaks crawled along the ground before reaching to the sky. Kudzu and Spanish moss obscured the world less than a few feet away.

From the corner of his eye, he saw movement again and turned quickly, his breath catching in his chest as a dark-haired man in a blue windbreaker stepped behind a tree. Dawson could hear the sound of his own thudding heartbeat in his ears. No, he thought, it wasn't possible. It wasn't real, it couldn't be real, and he knew he was seeing things.

But pushing aside the branches, he followed the man deeper into the woods.

Getting close now, Ted thought. Through the foliage, he spot-ted the top of the chimney and he bent over, stepping carefully. No noise, no sounds. That was the key to hunting, and Ted had always been good at it.

Man or animal, it was all the same if the hunter was skilled enough.

Dawson pushed through the undergrowth, veering around trees. He was breathing hard as he tried to close the distance. Afraid to stop but growing more frightened with every passing step.

He reached the spot where he'd seen the dark-haired man and kept going, searching for any sign of him. Sweat poured off him, slicking his shirt to his back. He resisted the sudden urge to call out, wondering whether he could if he tried. His throat was like sandpaper.

The ground was dry, pine straw crackling underfoot. As he hopped over a fallen tree, he spotted the dark-haired man pushing through the branches, ducking behind a tree, his windbreaker flapping behind him.

Dawson broke into a flat-out run.

🌿

Ted had finally inched his way forward to the woodpile, which sat at the edge of the clearing. The house loomed directly behind it. From his vantage point, he could peer into the garage. The light was still on and Ted watched for almost a minute, looking for signs of movement. Dawson had been in there working on the car, he was almost sure of it. But he wasn't there now, or anywhere out front.

He was either in the house or in the back. Ted ducked down, moving into the cover of the forest before circling around to the rear of the house. Not there, either. Retracing his steps, he made his way back to the woodpile. Still no sign of Dawson in the garage. Which meant he had to be in the house. Probably to get a drink, or maybe take a leak. Either way, he'd be out soon enough.

He settled in to wait.

🌿

Dawson saw the man a third time, this time closer to the road. He sprinted after him, the branches and bushes slapping at him, but couldn't seem to close the distance. Panting, he gradually began to slow before coming to a stop at the edge of the road.

The man was gone. If, of course, he'd ever been in the woods at all, and Dawson suddenly wasn't so sure about that. The prickling sensation of being watched had dissipated, as had the icy fear; all he was left with was a feeling of being hot and tired, with a sense of frustration and foolishness mixed in.

Tuck used to see Clara, and now Dawson was seeing a dark-haired man wearing a windbreaker in the early summer heat. Had Tuck been as crazy as he was? He stood still, waiting for his breathing to return to normal. He was sure the man was following him, but if so, who was he? And what did the man want with him?

He didn't know, but the more he tried to focus on what he'd actually seen, the more it began to slip away. Like dreams only minutes after waking, it faded, until he was no longer sure of anything.

He shook his head, glad he was nearly finished with the Stingray. He wanted to return to the bed-and-breakfast to take a shower and lie down and think about things. The dark-haired man, Amanda...ever since the accident on the rig, his life had been in upheaval. He looked in the direction he'd come, deciding there was no point in traipsing back through the woods. It would be easier to follow the road and just hike up the drive. Stepping onto the macadam, he started walking, only to notice an old truck parked off the road behind a clump of bushes.

He wondered what it was doing out here; there was nothing to be found in this part of the woods except for Tuck's place. The tires weren't flat, and though he supposed the truck could have broken down, whoever it was probably would have come up the drive in search of help. Stepping into the underbrush, Dawson noticed that the truck was locked; he reached over and placed his hand on its hood. Warm, but not hot. Probably been there for an hour or two.

Nor did it make sense that it was tucked away, parked behind the bushes. If it needed a tow, it would have been better to keep it near the side of the road. It almost seemed that the driver didn't want anyone to notice the truck at all.

Like someone meant to keep it hidden?

With that, everything began to fall into place, beginning with the sighting of Abee that morning. This wasn't Abee's truck—the one he'd run past that morning—but that didn't mean anything. Carefully, Dawson traced a path around the far side of the truck, stopping when he noticed some branches twisted to the side.

The entry point.

Someone had come this way, heading toward the house.

Tired of waiting, Ted pulled out a chunk of marlstone, thinking that if he broke a window while Dawson was inside, Dawson might just decide to stay holed up. But a noise was different. When something loud cracked against the side of the house, you went outside to check what happened. He'd probably walk right past the woodpile, just a few feet away. Impossible to miss.

Satisfied, he reached into his pocket and pulled out the first chunks of marlstone. Cautiously, he peeked over the woodpile, seeing no one in the windows. Then, rising quickly, he threw the piece as hard as he could and was already ducking back down as it shattered against the house, the sound loud and sharp.

Behind him, the flock of starlings broke noisily from the trees.

Dawson heard a muted pop, and a cloud of starlings swarmed above him before quickly settling again. The noise hadn't been gunfire; it was something else. He slowed his approach, moving silently toward Tuck's house.

Someone was there. He was sure of it. His kin, no doubt.

Ted was on pins and needles, wondering where the hell Dawson was. There was no way he couldn't have heard the noise, but where was he? Why didn't he come out?

He pulled another stone from his pocket, this time throwing it as hard as he could.

🌿

Dawson froze at the sound of a second, louder report. Gradually, he relaxed and crept closer, pinpointing the source of the noise.

Ted, hiding behind the woodpile. Armed.

His back was to Dawson, and he was peering over the top of the woodpile at the house. Was he waiting for Dawson to emerge from the house? Making noise, hoping to lure him out to investigate?

Dawson suddenly wished he had dug up the shotgun. Or brought a weapon of any sort, for that matter. There were items in the garage, but there was no way he could get to them without Ted spotting him. He debated retreating to the road, but Ted wasn't likely to go away, unless he had a reason. All the same, he could tell from Ted's twitchy posture that he was getting antsy, and that was good. Impatience was the hunter's enemy.

Dawson ducked behind a tree, thinking, hoping for an opportunity to take care of this without getting shot in the process.

🌿

Five minutes passed, then ten, while Ted continued to seethe. Nothing, absolutely nothing. No movement out front, or even in the damn windows. But a rental car was parked in the drive—he could see the bumper sticker—and someone had been working in the garage. It sure as hell wasn't Tuck or Amanda. So if Dawson wasn't out front and he wasn't out back, he had to be in the house.

But why hadn't he come out?

Maybe he was watching television or listening to music...or sleeping or showering or God knows what else. For whatever reason, he must not have heard anything.

Ted crouched there another few minutes, growing even angrier, before finally deciding he wasn't going to just wait around. Ducking out from behind the woodpile, he scurried to the side of the house and peeked around to the front. Seeing nothing, he moved again, tiptoeing up to the porch. He pressed himself flat against the wall between the door and window.

He strained to hear the sounds of movement inside without success. No creaking floorboards, no blaring television or thumping music. Once he was certain he hadn't been spotted, he peered around the frame of the window. He took hold of the doorknob and turned it slowly.

Unlocked. Perfect.

Ted readied the gun.

※

Dawson watched Ted slowly push the door open. As soon as it closed behind him, Dawson raced for the garage, figuring he had maybe a minute, probably less. He seized the rusted tire iron from the workbench and sprinted silently for the front of the house, figuring that Ted was most likely in the kitchen or the bedroom by now. He prayed that he was right.

He jumped up onto the porch before flattening himself in the same spot where Ted had stood, gripping the tire iron and readying himself. It didn't take long; inside, he heard Ted cussing as he stomped toward the front door. When it swung open, Dawson flashed on Ted's panicked expression as he caught sight of Dawson an instant too late.

Dawson swung the tire iron, feeling the vibration in his arm as it crushed Ted's nose. Even as Ted staggered backward, blood spurting in a hot red gush, Dawson was already in pursuit. Ted hit the floor and Dawson brought the tire iron down hard on Ted's outstretched arm, sending the gun skittering away. At the sound of his bones breaking, Ted finally began to scream.

As Ted writhed on the floor, Dawson reached for the gun, leveling it at Ted.

"I told you not to come back."

Those were the last words Ted heard before his eyes rolled up, the blinding pain causing him to pass out.

✦

As much as he hated his family, he couldn't bring himself to kill Ted. At the same time, he wasn't sure what to do with him. He supposed he could call the sheriff, but once he left town he knew that, trial or not, he wasn't coming back, so nothing would happen to Ted anyway. Dawson would still be tied up for hours, giving his account of events, which would no doubt be met with suspicion. After all, he was still a Cole and he had a record. No, he decided, he didn't want the hassle.

But he couldn't just leave Ted out here, either. He needed medical attention, and dropping him off at the medical clinic would no doubt involve the sheriff again. Same thing with calling an ambulance.

Reaching down, he rummaged through Ted's pockets, finding a cell phone. After flipping it open, he punched some buttons and pulled up the contact list. A few names in there, most of which he recognized. Good enough. He fished around again for the keys to Ted's truck, then jogged out to the garage and gathered some bungee cords and wire, which he used to truss Ted up. Then, after the sun went down, he slung his cousin over his shoulder.

He carried Ted down the drive and tossed him into the bed of the truck. Then he climbed into the driver's seat, started the truck, and pointed it in the direction of the parcel of land where he'd been raised. Not wanting to draw attention, he shut off the headlights as he made his way to the edge of the Coles' property before stopping at the NO TRESPASSING sign. There he dragged Ted from the bed of the truck and propped his cousin against the post.

He opened the phone and hit the entry labeled "Abee." The phone rang four times before Abee answered. Dawson could hear loud music in the background.

"Ted?" he shouted over the noise. "Where the hell are you?"

"It's not Ted. But you need to come get him. He's hurt bad," Dawson answered. Before Abee could respond, Dawson told him where to find Ted. Hanging up, he tossed the phone to the ground between Ted's legs.

Back in the truck, he accelerated off the property. After disposing of Ted's gun in the river, he figured he'd swing by the bed-and-breakfast right away and grab his things. Then he'd trade out cars, leaving Ted's truck where he'd originally parked it, and find a hotel outside Oriental, where he could finally shower and eat before turning in for the night.

He was tired. After all, it had been a long day. He was glad it was over.

9

Abee Cole's stomach felt like someone was branding it, and the fever had yet to break, making him think that he should probably ask the doctor about his wound the next time he came into the room to check on Ted. Course, they'd probably want to admit him, too, and that wasn't gonna happen. Might bring up questions that Abee didn't feel like answering.

It was late, coming up on midnight, and the hospital had finally begun to quiet down. In the dim light, he looked over at his brother, thinking that Dawson had done a real number on him. Just like last time. Abee thought he was dead when he'd found him. Face covered in blood, arm bent sideways, and all he could think was that Ted had gotten careless. Either that, or Dawson had been waiting for him—which got him to thinking that maybe Dawson had plans of his own.

Abee felt the pain flare in his gut, triggering waves of nausea. The hospital wasn't helping. It was like a damn furnace here. The only reason Abee was still in the room was because he wanted to be around if Ted woke up, so he could find out if Dawson was up to something. He felt a shiver of paranoia but assumed that maybe he wasn't thinking straight. The antibiotics had better kick in, and soon.

The night had gone to hell, and not just because of Ted. He'd decided to swing by and see Candy earlier, but by the time he got to the Tidewater, half the guys in the bar were crowding around her. One look was enough for him to know that she was up to something. She was wearing a halter top that showed off everything she owned and a pair of shorty shorts that barely covered her rear. When she saw him walk in, she instantly got all nervous, like she'd been caught doing something wrong, and she sure as hell didn't seem happy to see him. He'd wanted to drag her out of the bar right there, but with so many people around he decided that might not be such a good idea. Later, he knew, they'd *talk* and she'd see the light of day. No question about that, but for the time being, it was better to figure out exactly why she'd been acting so guilty when he'd walked in. Or rather, who she was feeling guilty about.

Because that's what was going on, clear as day. Some guy at the bar, no doubt, and even though he was still light-headed with fever and his stomach was on fire, he was going to find out exactly which one of them it was.

So he'd settled in to wait, and after a little while he'd identified someone who just might be the one. Young guy, dark hair, flirting just a little too much with Candy for it to be a casual thing. He watched her touch his arm and give him an eyeful of her cleavage when she brought him his beer, and he'd just gotten up to take care of it when his phone started ringing, with Dawson on the other end. The next thing he knew, he was pounding on the steering wheel as he made his way to the hospital, Ted sprawled in the seat behind him. Even as he raced to New Bern, he pictured Candy with that cocky loser, taking off her halter top and moaning in his arms.

Right now, she was getting off work, and the thought filled him with rage. Because he knew exactly who was walking her to her car, and he couldn't do anything about it. Right now, he had to find out what Dawson was up to.

Ted drifted in and out of consciousness throughout the night, drugs and the concussion keeping him hazy, even when he was awake, but by midmorning the following day, all he could feel was rage. At Abee, because he kept asking whether Dawson was going to come after him; at Ella, because she kept whining and worrying and sniffling; and for the whispering he could hear from his kinfolk in the hallway, like they were wondering whether they should still be afraid of him. Mainly, though, the rage was focused on Dawson, and Ted lay in the bed, still trying to figure out exactly what had happened. The last thing he remembered before waking up in the hospital was Dawson standing over him, and it took a long time for him to make any sense of what Abee and Ella were telling him. By the end, the doctors had to put him in restraints and were threatening to call the police.

He'd been acting calmer since then because it was the only way he was going to get out of here. Abee was in the chair and Ella was on the bed beside him. She kept fussing over him, and he stifled the urge to backhand her, even though he was strapped to the bed and couldn't do it even if he tried. Instead, he tested the straps again, thinking about Dawson. He was going to die, no doubt about it, and Ted didn't give a rat's ass about the doctor's recommendation that he stay another night for observation, or his warning that moving around might be dangerous. Dawson might be leaving town at any minute. And when he heard Ella start to hiccup through her sobs, he spoke through gritted teeth.

"Go away," he said. "I gotta talk to Abee."

Ella wiped her face and exited the room without a sound. When she was gone, Ted turned toward Abee, thinking his brother looked like crap. Red in the face, sweating. The infection. Abee was the one who needed to be in the hospital, not him.

"Get me out of here."

Abee winced as he leaned forward. "You going back to get him?"

"It ain't over."

He pointed to the cast. "And just how you gonna get him with your arm all broken up like that? If you couldn't get him yesterday with two good arms?"

"'Cause you're going out with me. First you're going to bring me home so I can get another Glock. Then you and me are going to end this."

Abee leaned back in his chair. "And why would I want to do that?"

Ted held his gaze, thinking about Abee's earlier stream of anxious questions.

"'Cause last thing I remember before I blacked out, he told me that you were next."

10

---- ❧ ----

Dawson ran on the packed sand near the water's edge, half-heartedly chasing the terns as they darted in and out of the waves. Despite the early hour, the beach was crowded with other joggers and people walking their dogs, kids already building sandcastles. Beyond the dune, people were on their decks drinking coffee, feet propped on the railings as they enjoyed the morning.

He'd been lucky to get a room. At this time of year, hotels at the beach were usually booked solid, and it had taken a few calls to find a place that had a cancellation. His choices were to find a room around here or at a hotel in New Bern. And since the hospital was located in New Bern, he decided it was better to remain farther away. He would have to lie low. Ted, he suspected, wasn't about to let this go.

Despite his best efforts, he couldn't stop thinking about the dark-haired man. If he hadn't gone after him, he would never have known that Ted was lying in wait. The image—the ghost—had beckoned to him and he'd followed, just as he had in the ocean after the platform had exploded.

The two incidents chased each other around in his brain, an endless loop. Saving his life once might have been an illusion, but twice? For the first time, he began to wonder if the visits by the dark-haired man might have some greater purpose, as though he were being saved for a reason, even if he wasn't sure what that might be.

Trying to escape his thoughts, Dawson increased his pace, his breaths coming harder. He removed his shirt without slowing down and used it as a towel to wipe the sweat from his face. He zeroed in on the pier in the distance, resolving to run even faster until he reached it. Within minutes, the muscles in his legs were burning. He pushed on, trying to focus narrowly on driving his body to the limit, but his eyes kept flicking from side to side, unconsciously scanning the beachgoers for a sight of the dark-haired man.

After reaching the pier, instead of slowing down he maintained his pace until he got back to the hotel. For the first time in years, he finished his run feeling worse than when he'd started. He bent over, trying to catch his breath, no closer to any concrete answers. He couldn't help feeling a sea change in his internal world since he'd arrived in town. Everything around him felt indefinably different. Not because of the dark-haired man or Ted or because Tuck had passed away. Everything felt different because of Amanda. She wasn't simply a memory anymore; she'd suddenly become undeniably real—a vibrant, living version of the past that had never really left him. More than once, a young version of Amanda had visited him in his dreams, and he wondered whether his dreams of her would change in the future. Who would she be? He wasn't sure. All he knew for certain was that being with Amanda made him feel complete in a way few others would ever know.

The beach had reached its quiet hour, early morning visitors heading back to their cars and vacationers yet to spread out their towels. The waves rolled in a steady rhythm, the sound hypnotic. Dawson squinted toward the water, thoughts of the future filling him with despair. No matter how much he cared for her, he had to accept that she had a husband and children. It had been hard enough to end it once; the thought of ending things again seemed suddenly unbearable. The breeze picked up, whispering to him that his time with her was running out, and he started toward the lobby, drained by the knowledge and wishing with all his heart that things could somehow be different.

🌿

The more coffee Amanda drank, the more fortified she felt to deal with her mother. They were on the back veranda, overlooking the garden. Her mom was sitting posture-perfect in a white wicker chair, dressed as though she were expecting the governor to drop by for a visit, and dissecting the events of the previous night. She seemed to delight in finding endless conspiracies and hidden judgments in the tones and words her friends had used during dinner and bridge.

Thanks to the extended bridge game, an evening that Amanda had expected to last an hour, maybe two, lasted until half past ten. Even then, Amanda sensed that none of the others really wanted to go home. Amanda had begun to yawn by that point, and she really couldn't recollect what her mom was talking about. As far as she could tell, the conversations were no different than they'd been in the past, or than those in any other small town for that matter. Talk ran from neighbors to grandchildren, to who was teaching the latest Bible study or how to properly hang a set of curtains or the escalating price of rib roast, all seasoned with a bit of harmless gossip. The mundane, in other words, but leave it to her mother to raise the conversation to the level of national importance, no matter how misguided. Her mother could find fault or drama in her closet, and Amanda was just happy that her mom hadn't commenced her litany of complaints until after Amanda had finished her first cup of coffee.

What made focusing even more difficult was that she couldn't stop thinking about Dawson. She'd tried to convince herself she had everything under control, but then why did she keep visualizing the fall of his thick hair over his collar, or the way he looked in his jeans, or how natural it felt as they'd held each other in those first few moments after he'd arrived? She'd been married long enough to know that those things were less important than simple friendship and trust, forged by common interests; a few days together after more than twenty years wasn't long enough to even begin to form those bonds. It takes a long time to grow an old friend, and trust is built a single moment at a time. Women, she sometimes thought, had a tendency to see what they wanted to see in men, at least in the beginning, and she wondered whether she was making the same mistake. Meanwhile, as she pondered these unanswerable questions, her mom was incapable of silence. She kept droning on and on—

"Are you listening to me?" her mother asked, interrupting her thoughts.

Amanda lowered her cup. "Of course I'm listening."

"I was saying that you need to work on your bids."

"It's been a while since I've played."

"That's why I said you should join a club, or start one," she prompted. "Or didn't you hear that part?"

"I'm sorry. I've got a lot on my mind today."

"Yes. The little ceremony, right?"

Amanda ignored the dig because she wasn't in the mood to argue. Which was exactly what her mom wanted, she knew. Her mom had been working herself up all morning, using the imaginary skirmishes of the night before as justification for the inevitable invasion.

"I told you that Tuck wanted his ashes scattered," she explained, keeping her voice steady. "His wife, Clara, was cremated as well. Maybe he saw it as a way for them to be together again."

Her mother didn't seem to hear her. "What would one wear to something like that? It sounds so...dirty."

Amanda turned toward the river. "I don't know, Mom. I haven't thought about it."

Her mom's expression was as still and artificial as a manne-quin's. "And the kids? How are they?"

"I haven't talked to Jared or Lynn this morning. But as far as I know, they're fine."

"And Frank?"

She took a sip of her coffee, stalling. She didn't want to talk about him. Not after the argument they'd had last night, the same one that had become almost routine for them, the same one he would have already forgotten. Marriages, both good and bad, were defined by repetition.

"He's okay."

Her mom nodded, waiting for more. Amanda said nothing.

In the silence, her mom straightened the napkin in her lap before going on. "So how does this work today? You just dump the ashes where he wanted you to?"

"Something like that."

"Do you need a permit to do something like that? I'd hate to think that people were just allowed to do it anywhere they wanted."

"The lawyer didn't say anything, so I'm sure it's all worked out. I'm just honored that Tuck wanted me to be part of whatever he'd planned."

Her mom leaned forward slightly and smirked. "Oh, that's right," she said. "Because you were friends."

Amanda turned, suddenly tired of all this—her mother, Frank, all the deceptions that had come to characterize her life. "Yes, Mom, because we were friends. I enjoyed his company. He was one of the kindest people I've ever known."

For the first time, her mother seemed discomfited. "Where is this ceremony supposed to take place?"

"Why do you care? It's obvious you don't approve."

"I was just making conversation." She sniffed. "There's no rea-son to be rude."

"Maybe I sound rude because I'm hurting inside. Or maybe it's because you've yet to say anything supportive about any of this.

Not even an, 'I'm sorry for your loss. I know he meant a lot to you.' It's what people generally say when someone close passes away."

"Perhaps I would have if I'd known about this *relationship* in the first place. But you've been lying about it all along."

"Did you ever stop to consider that you're the reason I had to lie in the first place?"

Her mom rolled her eyes. "Don't be ridiculous. I didn't put the words in your mouth. I wasn't the one sneaking back here. You made the decision, not I, and every decision has consequences. You need to learn to take responsibility for the choices you make."

"You don't think I know that?" Amanda felt herself flush.

"I think," her mom said, drawing the words out, "you can be a little too self-centered at times."

"Me?" Amanda blinked. "You think *I'm* self-centered?"

"Of course," her mother said. "Everyone is, to a degree. I'm just saying that you take it a bit too far sometimes."

Amanda stared across the table, too stunned to speak. That her mother, of all people—*her mother!*—was suggesting this only fueled her outrage. In her mother's world, other people had never been anything but mirrors. She chose her next words carefully. "I don't think it's a good idea to talk about this."

"I think it is," her mother responded.

"Because I didn't tell you about Tuck?"

"No," she answered. "Because I think it has something to do with the problems you're having with Frank."

Amanda felt herself flinch inside at the comment, and it took everything she had to keep her tone and expression steady. "What makes you think I'm having problems with Frank?"

Her mom kept her tone neutral, but there was little warmth in it. "I know you better than you think, and the fact that you didn't deny it just proves my point. I'm not upset by the fact that you'd rather not talk about what's going on between the two of you. That concerns you and Frank, and there's nothing I could ever say or do to help. We both know that. Marriage is a partnership, not a democracy. Which begs the question, of course, of what you've been sharing with Tuck all these years. If I had to guess, it wasn't just that you wanted to visit him. It was that you also felt the need to *share* with him."

Her mom let the comment hang, her eyebrow a questioning arch, and in the silence Amanda tried to swallow her shock. Her mother adjusted her napkin. "Now, I assume you'll be here for dinner. Would you prefer to go out or stay in?"

"So that's it?" Amanda blurted out. "You throw out your assumptions and accusations, then close the subject?"

Her mom folded her hands in her lap. "I didn't close the subject. You're the one who refuses to talk about it. But if I were you, I'd think about what you really want, because when you get back home, you're going to have to make some decisions about your marriage. In the end, it's either going to work or it isn't. And a big part of that is up to you."

There was a brutal truth to her words. It wasn't just about her and Frank, after all; it was about the children they were raising. Amanda suddenly felt drained. Setting her cup on the saucer, she felt the anger leach out of her, leaving only a sense of defeat.

"Do you remember the family of otters that used to play out near our dock?" she finally asked, not waiting for an answer. "When I was a little girl? Dad would scoop me up whenever they appeared and bring me out back. We'd sit on the grass watching them splash and chase each other around. I used to think they were the happiest animals in the world."

"I fail to understand what this has to do with anything—"

"I saw the otters again," Amanda continued, talking over her mother. "Last year, when we took our vacation at the beach, we visited the aquarium at Pine Knoll Shores. I was excited to see the new otter exhibit. I must have told Annette about the otters behind our house a dozen times, and she couldn't wait to see them, but when we finally got there it wasn't the same as when I was a girl. The otters were there, of course, but they were sleeping up on a ledge. Even though we stayed at the aquarium for hours, they never moved at all. On our way out, Annette asked me why they weren't playing and I didn't really have an answer. But after we left, I felt…sad. Because I knew exactly why those otters didn't play."

She stopped to run her finger around the rim of her coffee cup before meeting her mother's gaze.

"They weren't happy. The otters knew they weren't living in a real river. They probably didn't understand how it happened, but they seemed to understand that they were in a cage and couldn't get out. It wasn't the life that they were meant to live, or even wanted to live, but there was nothing they could do to change it."

For the first time since she'd been at the table, her mom looked unsure about what to say. Amanda pushed her cup away before rising from the table. As she walked away, she heard her mom clear her throat. She turned.

"I assume you had some point with that story?" her mother asked.

Amanda gave a weary smile. "Yes," she said, her voice soft. "I did."

11

⚜

Dawson lowered the top of the Stingray and leaned against the trunk, waiting for Amanda. There was a sultry, heavy feel to the air, portending a storm later that afternoon, and he wondered idly whether Tuck had an umbrella stashed in the house somewhere. He doubted it. He could no more imagine Tuck using an umbrella than he could imagine him in a dress, but who knew? Tuck, he'd learned, was a man of surprises.

A shadow moved across the ground and Dawson watched an osprey make slow, lazy circles overhead until Amanda's car finally rolled up the drive. He could hear the sound of gravel crunching beneath the tires as she pulled into the shady spot next to his.

Amanda stepped out of the car, surprised by the black pants and crisp white shirt Dawson was wearing, but the combo definitely worked. With the jacket casually slung over his shoulder, he was almost too handsome for his own good, which only made what her mother had said even more prescient. She drew a deep breath, wondering what she was going to do.

"Am I late?" she asked, starting toward him.

Dawson watched her approach. Even from a few feet away, the morning rays illuminated the clear blue depths of her eyes, like the sunlit waters of a pristine lake. She was wearing a black pantsuit, with a sleeveless silk blouse and a silver locket around her neck.

"Not at all," he said. "I got here early because I wanted to make sure the car was ready."

"And?"

"Whoever fixed it knew exactly what he was doing."

She smiled as she reached him and then, acting on impulse, kissed him on the cheek. Dawson seemed unsure what to make of it, his confusion mirroring her own as she heard again the echo of her mother's words. She motioned to the car, trying to escape them. "You took the top down?" she asked.

Her question brought him back to her. "I thought we might take it up to Vandemere."

"It's not our car."

"I know," he said. "But it needs to be driven so I can make sure everything is working right. Believe me, the owner will want to know it's in perfect working order before he decides to take it out for a night on the town."

"What if it breaks down?"

"It won't."

"You're sure?"

"Positive."

A smile played on her lips. "Then why would we need to test-drive it?"

He opened his hands, caught. "Okay, maybe I just want to drive it. It's practically a sin to let a car like this sit in the garage, especially considering the owner won't know and the keys are right here."

"And let me guess—when we're done, we'll put it on blocks and run it in reverse, so the odometer goes backward, right? So the owner won't know?"

"That doesn't work."

"I know. I learned that when I watched *Ferris Bueller's Day Off*." She smirked.

He leaned back slightly, taking in the sight of her. "You look stunning, by the way."

She felt the heat travel up her neck at his words and wondered if she would ever stop blushing in his presence. "Thank you," she said, tucking a strand of hair behind her ear as she studied him in return, keeping a bit of distance between them. "I don't think I've ever seen you in a suit before. Is it new?"

"No, but I don't wear it much. Just special occasions."

"I think Tuck would have approved," she said. "What did you end up doing last night?"

He thought about Ted and all that had happened, including his subsequent move to the beach. "Not much. How was dinner with your mom?"

"Not worth talking about," she said. She reached into the car, running her hand over the wheel before looking up at him. "We had an interesting conversation this morning, though."

"Yeah?"

She nodded. "It got me to thinking about these last couple of days. About me, you...life. Everything. And on the drive over, I realized that I was glad that Tuck never told you about me."

"Why would you say that?"

"Because yesterday, when we were in the garage..." She hesitated, trying to find the right words. "I think I was out of line. The way I was acting, I mean. And I want to apologize."

"Why would you apologize?"

"It's hard to explain. I mean..."

When she trailed off, Dawson watched her before finally taking a step closer. "Are you all right, Amanda?"

"I don't know," she said. "I don't know anything anymore. When we were young, things were so much simpler."

He hesitated. "What are you trying to say?"

She looked up at him. "You have to understand that I'm not the girl I used to be," she said. "I'm a wife and a mother now, and like everyone else I'm not perfect. I struggle with the choices I've made and I make mistakes, and half the time I wonder who I really am or what I'm doing or whether my life means anything at all. I'm not special at all, Dawson, and you need to know that. You have to understand that I'm just...ordinary."

"You're not ordinary."

Her look was pained but unflinching. "I know you believe that. But I am. And the problem is that there's nothing ordinary about any of this. I'm completely out of my element. I wish that Tuck had mentioned you, though, so that I could have been more prepared for this weekend." Without even being aware of it, she reached up to touch the silver locket. "I don't want to make a mistake."

Dawson shifted from one foot to the other, understanding exactly why she'd said what she had. It was one of the reasons he'd always loved her, even if he knew he shouldn't say those words out loud. It wasn't what she wanted to hear. Instead, he kept his voice as gentle as he could. "We talked, we ate, we reminisced," he pointed out. "That's all. You haven't done anything wrong."

"Yes, I have." She smiled but couldn't hide the sadness in it. "I haven't told my mother that you're here. Nor have I told my husband."

"Do you want to?" he asked.

That was the question, wasn't it? Without even being aware of it, her mother had asked her the same thing. She knew what she should say, but here and now the words simply wouldn't come. Instead, she found herself slowly beginning to shake her head. "No," she whispered finally.

Dawson seemed to sense the fear that seized her at her own admission, because he reached for Amanda's hand. "Let's go to Vandemere," he said. "Let's honor Tuck, okay?"

She nodded, letting herself succumb to the gentle urgency of his touch, feeling yet another part of herself slip away, beginning to accept the fact that she was no longer fully in control of whatever might happen next.

Dawson led her around to the other side of the car and opened her door. Amanda took a seat, feeling light-headed as Dawson retrieved the box holding Tuck's ashes from his rental car. He wedged it into the space behind the driver's seat, along with his jacket, before getting in. After taking out the directions, Amanda stowed her purse behind the seat as well.

Dawson pumped the pedal before turning the key, and the engine came to life with a roar. He revved the engine a few times, the car shimmying slightly. When the idle finally held, Dawson backed it out of the garage and drove slowly down to the main road, avoiding the potholes. The sound of the engine quieted only slightly as they made their way back through Oriental and onto the quiet highway.

As Amanda began to settle in, she discovered that she could see all she really needed from the corner of her eye. Dawson had one hand on the wheel, a posture achingly familiar to her from the meandering drives they used to take. That was when he'd always been most relaxed, and she sensed that feeling in him again as he shifted from one gear to the next, the muscles of his forearm bunching and relaxing.

Amanda's hair lashed around her as the car picked up speed, and she twisted it into a ponytail. It was too loud for either of them to speak, but that was fine with her. She was content to be alone with her thoughts, alone with Dawson, and as the miles began to pass she felt her earlier anxiety begin to dissipate, as if blown away by the wind itself.

Dawson kept the speed steady, despite the empty expanse of the road. He wasn't in a rush, and she wasn't, either. Amanda was in a car with a man she'd once loved, journeying to a place unknown to either of them, and she reflected that the idea would have struck her as preposterous even a few days ago. It was crazy and unimaginable, but there was something thrilling about it as well. For a little while, at least, she wasn't a wife or mother or a daughter, and for the first time in years she felt almost free.

But Dawson had always made her feel that way, and when he propped an elbow out the window, she glanced at him, trying to think of anyone who even remotely resembled him. There was pain and sadness etched in the lines around the corners of his eyes and intelligence as well, and she found herself wondering what he would have been like as a father. A good one, she suspected. It was easy to imagine him as the kind of dad who'd gamely toss a baseball back and forth for hours, or try to braid his daughter's hair, even if he had no clue how to do it. There was something strangely tantalizing and forbidden about the idea.

When Dawson looked over at her then, she knew he was thinking about her, and she wondered how many nights on the oil rig he'd done the same thing. Dawson, like Tuck, was one of those rare people who could love only once, and if anything, separation had only made his feelings grow stronger. Two days ago, that realization had been disconcerting, but she now understood that, for Dawson, there had been no other choice. Love, after all, always said more about those who felt it than it did about the ones they loved.

A southerly breeze settled in, bringing with it the scent of open water, and Amanda closed her eyes, giving herself over to the moment. When they finally reached the outskirts of Vandemere, Dawson unfolded the directions Amanda had given him and scanned them quickly before nodding to himself.

Vandemere was less a town than a hamlet, home to only a few hundred people. She saw a scattering of houses set back from the road and a small country store with a single gas pump out front. A minute later, Dawson made a turn onto a rutted dirt drive just off the highway. She had no idea how he'd even seen it—the overgrowth made it nearly invisible from the highway—and they began to roll forward, cautiously rounding one curve and then another, skirting the decaying trunks of storm-toppled trees and following the gently rising contours of the landscape. The engine, so loud on the highway, seemed almost muted now, absorbed by a lush landscape that pressed in on them from all sides. The drive narrowed even more as they went on, and low-hanging branches draped with Spanish moss grazed the car as they passed. Azaleas, their withering blossoms lush and untamed, competed with the kudzu for sunlight, obscuring the view on either side.

Dawson leaned closer to the wheel, making slight adjustments as he inched forward, careful not to scratch the car's paint. Above them, the sun dipped behind another cloud, deepening the verdant world around them.

The drive widened slightly once they rounded one curve and then another. "This is crazy," she said. "Are you sure we're going the right way?"

"According to the map, this is the place."

"Why so far off the main road?"

Dawson shrugged, as puzzled as she was, but after edging around the last curve, he instinctively braked the car to a stop, both of them suddenly knowing the answer.

12

The final stretch of the drive ended at a small cottage nestled in a grove of ancient live oaks. The weathered structure, with chipping paint and shutters that had begun to blacken at the edges, was fronted by a small stone porch framed by white columns. Over the years, one of the columns had become enshrouded in vines, which climbed toward the roof. A metal chair sat near the edge, and at one corner of the porch, adding color to the world of green, was a small pot of blooming geraniums.

But their eyes were drawn inevitably to the wildflowers. Thousands of them, a meadow of fireworks stretching nearly to the steps of the cottage, a sea of red and orange and purple and blue and yellow nearly waist deep, rippling in the gentle breeze. Hundreds of butterflies flitted above the meadow, tides of moving color undulating in the sun. Bounding the field was a small, slatted wooden fence, barely visible through the lilies and gladiolas.

Amanda stared at Dawson in wonder, then at the field of flowers again. It seemed like a fantasy, one person's imagined vision of heaven. She wondered how and when Tuck had first planted it, but even then, in that moment, she'd known that Tuck had planted the wildflowers for Clara. He'd planted them to express what she meant to him.

"It's incredible," she breathed.

"Did you know about this?" His voice mirrored her own sense of wonder.

"No," she answered. "This was something that was meant for just the two of them."

As she said it, she had a clear picture of Clara sitting on the porch while Tuck leaned against a column, reveling in the heady beauty of the wildflower garden. Dawson finally removed his foot from the brake and the car rolled forward toward the house, the colors blurring like droplets of living paint stretching for the sun.

After parking near the house, they climbed out and continued to take in the scene. A small, winding pathway was visible through the flowers. Mesmerized, they waded into the sea of color beneath a patchy sky. The sun reemerged from behind a cloud, and Amanda could feel its warmth dispersing the perfumed scent that surrounded her. All her senses felt amplified, like the day had been created specifically for her.

Walking beside her, she felt Dawson reach for her hand. She let him take it, thinking how natural it felt, and she imagined she could trace the years of labor etched into his calluses. Tiny wounds had scarred his palms but his touch was improbably gentle, and she knew then, with sudden certainty, that Dawson would have created a garden like this for her as well if he'd known she wanted it.

Forever. He'd carved the word into Tuck's workbench. A teenage promise, nothing more, yet somehow he'd been able to keep it alive. She could feel the strength of that promise now, filling the distance between them as they drifted through the flowers. From somewhere far away, she heard the distant rumble of thunder and she had the strange sense that it was calling to her, urging her to listen.

Her shoulder brushed against his, making her pulse quicken. "I wonder if these flowers grow back, or if he had to sow seed every year," he mused.

The sound of his voice brought her out of her reverie. "Both," she answered, her voice sounding strange to her own ears. "I recognize some of them."

"So he came up earlier this year? To plant more seeds?"

"He must have. I see some Queen Anne's lace. My mom has it at the house and it dies out when winter settles in."

They spent the next few minutes wandering along the path while she pointed out the annuals she knew: black-eyed Susans, blazing stars, morning glories, and prairie asters, intermingled with perennials like forget-me-nots, Mexican hats, and Oriental poppies. There seemed to be no formal organization to the garden; it was as if God and nature intended to have their way, no matter what Tuck's plans might have been. Somehow, though, the wildness only enhanced the beauty of the garden, and as they walked through the chaotic display of color, all she could think was that she was glad Dawson was with her so they could share this together.

The breeze picked up, cooling the air and ushering in more clouds. She watched as he raised his eyes to the sky. "It's going to storm," he observed. "I should probably put the top up on the car."

Amanda nodded but didn't let go of his hand. Part of her feared that he might not take it again, that the opportunity might not arise. But he was right; the clouds were getting darker.

"I'll meet you inside," he said, sounding equally reluctant, and only slowly did he untwine his fingers from hers.

"Do you think the door's unlocked?"

"I'd be willing to bet on it." He smiled. "I'll be there in a minute."

"Could you grab my bag while you're out there?"

He nodded, and as she watched him walk away, she recalled that before she'd loved him, she'd been infatuated with him. It had started out as a girlhood crush, the kind that made her doodle his name on her notebooks while she was supposed to be doing her homework. No one, not even Dawson, knew that it hadn't been an accident that they'd ended up as chemistry partners. When the teacher asked the students to pair up, she'd excused herself to go to the bathroom, and by the time she got back Dawson was, as usual, the only one left. Her friends had sent her pitying glances, but she was secretly thrilled to be spending time with the quiet, enigmatic boy who somehow seemed wise beyond his years.

Now, as he closed up the car, history seemed to be repeating itself, and she felt that same excitement. There was something about him that spoke only to her, a connection she'd missed in the years they'd been apart. And she knew on some level that she had been waiting for him, just as he'd been waiting for her.

She couldn't imagine never seeing him again; she couldn't release Dawson to become nothing but a memory. Fate—in the form of Tuck—had intervened, and as she started walking toward the cottage she knew there'd been a reason for it. All of this had to mean something. The past was gone, after all, and the future was the only thing they had left.

As Dawson had predicted, the front door was unlocked. Entering the small house, Amanda's first thought was that this had been Clara's refuge.

Though it had the same scuffed pine flooring, cedar walls, and general layout as the house in Oriental, here there were brightly colored pillows on the couch and black-and-white photographs artfully arranged on the walls. The cedar planking had been sanded smooth and painted light blue, and the large windows flooded the room with natural light. There were two white built-in bookshelves, filled with books and interspersed with porcelain figurines, something Clara had obviously collected over the years. An intricate handmade quilt lay over the back of an easy chair, and there wasn't a trace of dust on the country-style end tables. Floor lamps stood on either side of the room, and a smaller version of the anniversary photograph perched near the radio in the corner.

Behind her, she heard Dawson step into the cottage. He stood silently in the doorway, holding his jacket and her bag, seemingly at a loss for words.

She couldn't hide her own amazement. "It's something, isn't it?"

Dawson slowly took in the room. "I'm wondering if I brought us to the wrong house."

"Don't worry," she said, pointing to the picture. "It's the right place. But it's pretty obvious that this place was Clara's, not his. And that he never changed it."

Dawson folded his jacket over the back of a chair, setting Amanda's bag alongside it. "I don't remember Tuck's house ever being this clean. I figure that Tanner must have hired someone to get the place ready for us."

Of course he did, Amanda thought. She recalled Tanner mentioning his plans to come here, and his instructions that they wait until the day after their meeting to make the trip. The unlocked door only confirmed her suspicions.

"Have you already seen the rest of the place?" he asked.

"Not yet. I was too busy trying to figure out where Clara let Tuck sit down. It's pretty obvious she never let him smoke in here."

He thumbed over his shoulder, in the direction of the open door. "Which explains the chair on the porch. That's probably where she made him sit."

"Even after she was gone?"

"He was probably afraid that her ghost would show up and scold him if he lit up inside."

She smiled, and they set off to tour the cottage, brushing up against each other as they navigated through the living room. Just as in the house in Oriental, the kitchen was at the rear, overlooking the river, but here the kitchen was all about Clara, too, from the white cabinets and intricate scrollwork in the moldings to the blue-and-white tile backsplash above the counters. There was a teapot on the stove and a vase of wildflowers on the counter, obviously plucked from the garden out front. A table nestled beneath the window; on it stood two bottles of wine, red and white, along with two sparkling glasses.

"He's getting predictable now," Dawson commented, taking in the bottles.

She shrugged. "There are worse things."

They admired the view of the Bay River through the window, neither of them saying anything more. As they stood together, Amanda basked in the silence, comforting in its familiarity. She could sense the slight rise and fall of Dawson's chest as he breathed, and she had to suppress the urge to reach for his hand again. In unspoken agreement they turned from the window and continued their tour.

Across from the kitchen was a bedroom centered by a cozy four-poster bed. The curtains were white and the bureau had none of the dings and scratches of Tuck's furniture back in Oriental. There were two matching crystal lamps, one on each of the nightstands, and an Impressionist landscape painting hung on the wall opposite the closet.

Connected to the bedroom was a bathroom with a claw-foot tub, the kind that Amanda had always wanted. An antique mirror hung above the sink, and she caught sight of her reflection next to Dawson's, the first time she'd seen an image of them together since they'd returned to Oriental. It occurred to her that in all the time they'd been teenagers, they'd never once been photographed as a couple. It had been something they'd talked of doing but had never gotten around to.

She regretted it now, but what if she'd had a photo to keep? Would she have tucked it away in a drawer and forgotten it, only to rediscover it every few years? Or would she have stored it somewhere special, a place known only to her? She didn't know, but seeing Dawson's face next to hers in the bathroom mirror felt distinctly intimate. It had been a long time since anyone had made her feel attractive, but she felt that way now. She knew that she was drawn to Dawson. She reveled in the way his gaze traveled over her, and the graceful ease of his body; she was acutely aware of their almost primal understanding of each other. Though it had been only a matter of days, she trusted him instinctively and knew she could tell him anything. Yes, they'd argued on that first night over dinner and again about the Bonners, but there'd also been an unvarnished honesty in what they'd said. There were no hidden meanings, no secret attempts to pass judgment; as quickly as their disagreements had flared up, they'd passed.

Amanda continued to study Dawson in the mirror. He turned and caught her gaze in the reflection. Without looking away, he gently reached out to smooth back a stray lock of hair that had fallen across her eyes. And then he was gone, leaving her with the certainty that whatever the consequences, her life had already been irrevocably altered in ways she'd never imagined possible.

After she retrieved her bag from the living room, Amanda found Dawson in the kitchen. He'd opened a bottle of wine and poured two glasses. He handed one of them to her, and they made their way wordlessly to the porch. Dark clouds at the horizon had rolled in, bringing with them a light mist. On the sloping, wooded bank that led to the river, the foliage took on a deep green vibrancy.

Amanda set her wine aside and rummaged through her bag. She pulled out two of the envelopes, handing the one with Dawson's name to him and holding the other, the one they were meant to read before the service, in her lap. She watched as Dawson folded his envelope and slipped it into his back pocket.

Amanda offered him the blank envelope. "Are you ready for this yet?"

"As I'll ever be."

"Do you want to open it? We're supposed to read it prior to the ceremony."

"No, you go ahead," he said, moving his chair closer. "I'll read it from here."

Amanda lifted the corner of the seal, then gently pried it open. Unfolding the letter, Amanda was struck by the scrawl on the pages. Here and there, words were crossed out, and the uneven lines exhibited a general shakiness, reflecting Tuck's age. It was long, three pages front and back, making her wonder how long it had taken him to write it. It was dated February 14 of this year. Valentine's Day. Somehow that seemed appropriate.

"You ready?" she asked.

When Dawson nodded, Amanda leaned in and both of them began to read.

Amanda and Dawson,

Thank you for coming. And thank you for doing this for me. I didn't know who else to ask.

I'm not much of a writer, so I guess that the best way to start is to tell you that this is a love story. Mine and Clara's, I mean, and while I suppose I could bore you with all the details of our courtship or the early years of our marriage, our real story—the part that you'll want to hear—began in 1942. By then, we'd been married three years, and she'd already had her first miscarriage. I knew how much that hurt her, and I hurt, too, because there was nothing I could do. Hardships drive some people apart. Others, like us, grow even closer.

But I'm drifting. Happens a lot when you get older, by the way. Just wait and see.

It was 1942, like I said, and for our anniversary that year, we went to see For Me and My Gal, *with Gene Kelly and Judy Garland. It was the first time either of us had ever seen a flicker* show, and we had to drive clear to Raleigh to do it. When it was over, we just sat there in the seats after the lights came up, thinking about it. I doubt you've ever seen it, and I won't trouble you with the details, but it's about a man who maims himself to avoid going off to the Great War, and then has to woo back the woman he loves, a woman who now believes him to be a coward. By then, I'd received my draft notice from the Army, so there were parts of it that hit home a little bit since I didn't want to leave my girl to go to war, either, but neither of us wanted to think about that. Instead, we talked about the title song, which had the same name as the flicker show. It was the catchiest, prettiest thing either of us had ever heard. On the drive home, we sang it over and over. And a week after that, I enlisted in the Navy.

It's kind of strange, since, as I said, I was about to be drafted into the Army, and knowing what I do now, the Army probably would have been a better fit, considering what I do with engines and the fact that I didn't know how to swim. I might have ended up in the motor pool making sure the trucks and jeeps could roll through Europe. Armies can't do much if vehicles ain't running, right? But even though I was nothing but a country boy, I did know that the Army puts you where it wants, not where you want to go, and by then folks knew it was only a matter of time before we hit Europe for good. Ike had just gone into North Africa. They needed infantry, men on the ground, and as excited as I was about the thought of taking on Hitler, the thought of joining the infantry just didn't sit with me.

At the enlistment office, they had this recruiting poster on the wall. For the Navy. Man the Guns, it said. It showed a shirtless seaman loading a shell, and something about it just spoke to me. I can do that, I thought to myself, so I walked over to the Navy desk, not the Army's, and signed up right there. When I got home, Clara cried for hours. Then she made me promise to come back to her. And I promised her I would.

I went through basic training and ordinance school. Then, in November 1943, I got posted to the USS Johnston, a destroyer out in the Pacific. Don't ever let anyone tell you that being in the Navy was less dangerous than being in the Army or the marines. Or less terrifying. You're at the mercy of the ship, not your own wits, because if the ship went down, you died. If you went overboard, you died, because none of the convoys would risk stopping to rescue you. You can't run, you can't hide, and the idea that you have no control at all just gets into your head and it sticks there. In my time in the Navy, I was never so scared in my life. Bombs and smoke everywhere, fires on the deck. Meanwhile, the guns are booming and the noise is like nothing you've ever heard. Thunder times ten, maybe, but that doesn't describe it. In the big battles, Japanese Zeros strafed the deck continually, the shots ricocheting all over the place. While this is going on, you're supposed to keep doing your job, like nothing unusual is happening.

In October 1944, we were cruising near Samar, getting ready to help lead the invasion of the Philippines. We had thirteen ships in our group, which sounds like a lot, but aside from the carrier, it was mainly destroyers and escorts, so we didn't have much firepower. And then, on the horizon, we saw what seemed like the entire Japanese fleet coming toward us. Four battleships, eight cruisers, eleven destroyers, hell-bent on sending us to the bottom of the sea. I heard later that someone said we were like David against Goliath, except we didn't even have a slingshot. And that's about right. Our guns couldn't even reach them when they opened fire. So what do we do? Knowing we didn't stand a chance? We engaged. The Battle of Leyte Gulf, they call it now. Went straight for them. We were the first ship to start firing, the first to launch smoke and torpedoes, and we took on both a cruiser and a battleship. Did a lot of damage, too. But because we were out front, we were the first to go dead in the water. A pair of enemy cruisers closed in and began firing, and then we went down. There were 327 men on board, and 186 men, some of them close friends, died that day. I was one of the 141 that made it out alive.

I'll bet you're wondering why I'm telling you this—you're probably thinking I'm drifting again—so I might as well get to it. On the raft, with this big battle raging all around us, I realized that I wasn't afraid anymore. All of a sudden, I knew I'd be okay because I knew that Clara and I weren't done yet, and this feeling of peace just came over me. You can call it shell shock if you want, but I know what I know, and right there, under an exploding sky filled with gun smoke, I remembered our anniversary from a couple of years ago and I started singing "For Me and My Gal," just like Clara and I did on the car ride home from Raleigh. Just boomed it out at the top of my lungs, like I didn't have a care in the world, because I knew that somehow Clara could hear me, and she'd understand that there was no reason to worry. I'd made her a promise, you see. And nothing, not even going down in the Pacific, was enough to stop me from keeping it.

Crazy, I know. But like I said, I got rescued. I got reassigned to a crew ship and hauled marines to Iwo Jima the next spring. Next thing I knew, the war was over and I was home. I didn't talk about the war when I got back. I couldn't. Not a single word. It was just too painful and Clara understood that, so little by little, we settled back into our lives. In 1955, we started building the cottage here. I did most of the work myself. One afternoon, just after I'd finished up for the day, I walked toward Clara, who was knitting in the shade. And I heard her singing "For Me and My Gal."

I froze, and the memories of the battle came racing back. I hadn't thought about that song in years, and I'd never told her what happened on the raft that day. But she must have seen something in my expression because she looked up at me.

"From our anniversary," she said before going back to her knitting. "I never told you this, but while you were in the Navy, I had a dream one night," she added. "I was in this field of wildflowers, and even though I couldn't see you, I could hear you singing this song to me, and when I woke up, I wasn't afraid anymore. Because up until then, I was always afraid that you weren't coming back."

I stood there dumbstruck. "It wasn't a dream," I finally said.

She just smiled and I had the sense that she'd been expecting my answer. "I know. Like I said, I heard you."

After that, the idea that Clara and I had something powerful—spiritual, some might say—between us never left me. So some years later, I decided to start the garden and I brought her up here on our anniversary to show it to her. It wasn't much back then, nothing like it is now, but she swore it was the most beautiful place in the world. So I tilled more ground and added more seeds the next year, all the while humming our song. I did the same thing every year of our marriage, until she finally passed away. I had her ashes scattered here, in the place she loved.

But I was a broken man after she died. I was angry and boozing and losing myself little by little in the process. I stopped tilling and planting and singing because Clara was gone and I didn't see the reason to keep it going. I hated the world and I didn't want to go on. I thought about killing myself more than once, but then Dawson came along. It was good to have him around. Somehow he helped remind me that I still belonged in this world, that my work here wasn't done. But then he got taken away, too. After that, I came up here and saw the place for the first time in years. It was out of season, but some of the flowers were still blooming, and though I don't know why, when I sang our song tears came to my eyes. I cried for Dawson, I suppose, but I also cried for me. Mainly, though, I was crying for Clara.

That was when it started. Later that night, when I got home, I saw Clara through the kitchen window. Even though it was faint, I heard her humming our song. But she was hazy, not really there, and by the time I got inside she was gone. So I went back to the cottage and started to till again. Got things ready, so to speak, and I saw her again, this time on the porch. A few weeks later, after I scattered seeds, she started coming around regularly, maybe once a week, and I was able to get closer to her before she vanished. But then, when the flowers bloomed, I came out here and wandered among the flowers, and by the time I got home I could see and hear her plain as day. Just standing right there on the porch, waiting for me, as if wondering why it took me so long to figure things out. That's the way it's been ever since.

She's part of the flowers, you see? Her ashes helped to make the flowers grow, and the more they grew, the more alive she became. And as long as I kept the flowers going, Clara could find a way to come back to me.

So that's why you're here, and that's why I asked you to do this for me. This is our place, a tiny corner of the world where love can make anything possible. I think that the two of you, more than anyone else, will understand that.

But now it's time for me to join her. It's time for us to sing together. It's my time and I have no regrets. I'm back with Clara again, and that's the only place I've ever wanted to be. Scatter my ashes to the wind and flowers, and don't cry for me. Instead, I want you to smile for the both of us; smile with joy for me and my gal.

Tuck

Dawson leaned forward, resting his forearms on his thighs, trying to imagine Tuck as he wrote the letter. It sounded nothing like the laconic, rough-hewn man who'd taken him in. This was a Tuck that Dawson had never met, a person Dawson had never known.

Amanda's expression was tender as she refolded the letter, taking extra precaution not to tear it.

"I know the song he talks about," she said after she had stowed the letter safely in her purse. "I heard him singing it once while he sat in the rocker. When I asked him about it, he didn't really answer. Instead, he played it for me on the record player."

"At the house?"

She nodded. "I remember thinking it was catchy, but Tuck had closed his eyes and he just seemed . . . lost in it. When it was over, he got up and put the record away, and at the time I didn't know what to make of it. But now I understand." She turned toward him. "He was calling to Clara."

Dawson slowly rotated his wine glass. "Do you believe him? About seeing Clara?"

"I didn't. Not really, anyway. But now I'm not so sure."

Thunder rumbled in the distance, reminding them again of what they had come here to do. "I think it's probably time," Dawson said.

Amanda stood, brushing off her pants, and together they descended to the garden. The breeze was steady now, but the mist had grown even thicker. The crystalline morning was gone, replaced by afternoon weather that reflected the murky weight of the past.

After Dawson retrieved the box, they found the path that led to the center of the garden. Amanda's hair rippled in the breeze, and he watched as she ran her fingers through it, trying to keep it under control. They reached the center of the garden and stopped.

Dawson was conscious of the weight of the box in his hands. "We should say something," he murmured. At her nod, he went first, offering a tribute to the man who'd given him shelter and friendship. Amanda, in turn, thanked Tuck for being her confidant and told him that she'd come to care about him like a father. When they were finished, the wind picked up almost on cue, and Dawson lifted the lid.

The ashes took flight, swirling together over the flowers, and as she watched, Amanda couldn't help thinking that Tuck was looking for Clara, calling out to her one last time.

*

They retreated to the house afterward, alternately reminiscing about Tuck and sitting in companionable silence. Outside, the rain had begun to fall. It was steady but not hard, a delicate summer rain that felt like a blessing.

When they grew hungry, they ventured out into the rain, taking the Stingray down the twisty drive onto the highway again. Though they could have returned to Oriental, they drove instead to New Bern. Near the historic downtown district, they found a restaurant called the Chelsea. It was nearly empty when they arrived, but by the time they left, every table was occupied.

There was a short break in the rain, and they spent it strolling the quiet sidewalks, visiting the shops that were still open. While Dawson browsed in a secondhand bookstore, Amanda took the opportunity to step out and call home. She spoke to both Jared and Lynn before touching base with Frank. She called her mom, too, leaving a message on the answering machine telling her that she might be late and asking her to leave the door unlocked. She hung up just as Dawson approached, feeling a stab of grief at the thought that the night was almost over. As if reading her mind, Dawson offered his arm, and she clung to it as they slowly made their way back to the car.

Back on the highway, the rain started again. The mist grew thicker almost as soon as they crossed the Neuse River, tendrils stretching from the forest like ghostly fingers. The headlights did little to illuminate the road, and trees seemed to absorb what little light there was. Dawson slowed the car in the wet, murky darkness.

The rainfall was steady on the soft-top, like the passing of a distant train, and Amanda found herself thinking about the day. Over their meal, she'd caught Dawson staring at her more than once, but rather than feeling self-conscious, she didn't want him to stop.

She knew it was wrong. Her life didn't allow for that kind of desire; society didn't condone it, either. She could try to dismiss her feelings as temporary, a by-product of other factors in her life. But she knew that wasn't true. Dawson wasn't some stranger that she happened to rendezvous with; he was her first and only true love, the most enduring of all.

Frank would be crushed if he knew what she was thinking. And despite their troubles, she knew she loved Frank. Yet even if nothing happened—even if she went home today—she knew that Dawson would continue to haunt her. Although her marriage had been troubled for years, it wasn't simply that she was seeking solace elsewhere. It was Dawson—and the *us* they created whenever they were together—that had made all of this both natural and inevitable. She couldn't help thinking that the story between them was somehow unfinished; that both of them were waiting to write the ending.

After they passed through Bayboro, Dawson slowed the car. Coming up was the turn onto another highway, one that led south, to Oriental. Straight ahead lay Vandemere. Dawson would make the turn, but as they approached the intersection, she wanted to tell him to keep going. She didn't want to wake tomorrow wondering if she'd ever see him again. The thought was terrifying, and yet somehow the words wouldn't come.

There was no one else on the road. Water flowed from the macadam into shallow gullies on either side of the highway. When they reached the intersection, Dawson gently applied the brakes. Surprising her, he brought the car to a stop.

The wipers moved the water from side to side. Raindrops glittered in the reflection of the headlights. As the engine idled, Dawson turned toward her, his face in shadow.

"Your mom is probably expecting you."

She could feel her heart beating, speeding up. "Yes." She nodded, saying nothing more.

For a long moment, he simply stared at her, reading her, seeing all the hope and fear and desire in the eyes that held his own. Then, with a flicker of a smile, he faced the windshield, and ever so slowly the car began to roll forward, toward Vandemere, and neither one of them was willing or able to stop it.

There was no awkwardness at the door when they returned to the cottage. Amanda made for the kitchen as Dawson turned on the lamp. She refilled their glasses of wine, feeling both unsettled and secretly thrilled at exactly the same time.

In the living room, Dawson turned the radio dial until he found some old-time jazz, keeping the volume low. From the shelf above, he pulled down one of the old books and was thumbing through the yellowed pages when Amanda approached him with the wine. Returning the book to its spot on the shelf, he took the glass and followed her to the couch. He watched as she slipped off her shoes.

"It's so quiet," she said. Setting her glass on the end table, she pulled her legs up and wrapped her arms around her knees. "I understand why Tuck and Clara wanted to remain here."

The dim light of the living room lent her features a mysterious cast, and Dawson cleared his throat. "Do you think you'll ever come back here again?" he asked. "After this weekend, I mean?"

"I don't know. If I knew it would stay like this, then yes. But I know it won't, because nothing lasts forever. And part of me wants to remember it just like it was today, with the flowers in full bloom."

"Not to mention a clean house."

"That, too," she agreed. She reached for her wine, swirling it in the glass. "Earlier, when the ashes were floating away, do you know what I was thinking about? I was thinking about the night we were on the dock watching the meteor shower. I don't know why, but all of a sudden it was like I was there again. I could see us lying on the blanket, whispering to each other and listening to the crickets, that perfect, musical echo. And above us, the sky was just so...alive."

"Why are you telling me this?" Dawson's voice was gentle.

Her expression was melancholy. "Because that was the night I knew I loved you. That I'd really and truly fallen in love. And I think my mom knew exactly what had happened."

"Why do you say that?"

"Because the next morning, she asked me about you, and when I told her how I felt, we ended up in a screaming match—a big one, one of the worst we ever had. She even slapped me. I was so shocked, I didn't know how to respond. And all the while she kept telling me how ridiculous my behavior was, and that I didn't know what I was doing. She made it sound like she was angry because it was you, but when I think back on it now, I know she would have been upset no matter who it was. Because it wasn't about you, or us, or even your last name. It was about her. She knew I was growing up, and she was afraid of losing control. She didn't know how to handle that—not then, and not now." She took a sip and lowered the glass, spinning the stem with her fingers. "She told me I was self-centered this morning."

"She's wrong."

"I thought so, too," she said. "At first anyway. But now I'm not so sure."

"Why would you say that?"

"I'm not exactly acting like a married woman, am I?"

Watching her, he held his silence, giving her time to consider what she was saying. "Do you want me to bring you back?" he finally asked.

She hesitated before shaking her head. "No," she said. "That's the thing. I want to be here, with you. Even though I know it's wrong." Her eyes were downcast, lashes dark against her cheek-bones. "Does that make any sense?"

He traced a finger along the back of her hand. "Do you really want me to answer?"

"No," she answered. "Not really. But it's...complicated. Marriage, I mean." She could feel him weave delicate patterns across her skin.

"Do you like being married?" Dawson asked, his voice tentative.

Instead of answering right away, Amanda took a sip of her wine, collecting herself. "Frank is a good man. Most of the time, anyway. But marriage isn't what people think it is. People want to believe that every marriage is this perfect balance, but it isn't. One person always loves more deeply than the other. I know Frank loves me, and I love him, too...just not as much. And I never have."

"Why not?"

"Don't you know?" She looked at him. "It's because of you. Even when we were standing in the church and I was getting ready to take my vows, I can remember wishing that you were standing there, instead of him. Because I not only still loved you, but loved you beyond measure, and I suspected even then that I would never feel the same way about Frank."

Dawson's mouth felt dry. "Then why did you marry him?"

"Because I thought it was good enough. And I hoped I could change. That over time, maybe I would come to feel the same way about him as I did about you. But I didn't, and as the years went on, I think he came to see that, too. And it hurt him, and I knew it hurt him, but the harder he tried to show me how important I was to him, the more suffocated I felt. And I resented that. I resented him." She winced at her own words. "I know that makes me sound like an awful person."

"You're not awful," Dawson said. "You're being honest."

"Let me finish, okay?" she said. "I need you to understand this.

You need to know that I do love him, and I cherish the family we've created. Frank adores our children. They're the center of his life, and I think that's why losing Bea was so hard on us. You have no idea how terrible it is to watch your child get sicker and sicker and know that there's nothing you can do to help her. You end up riding this roller-coaster of emotions, feeling everything from anger at God to betrayal to a sense of utter failure and devastation. In the end, though, I was able to survive the pain. Frank never really recovered. Because underlying all those other things is this bottomless despair and it just... hollows you out. There's a gaping hole where all this joy used to be. Because that's what Bea was. She was joy in living form. We used to joke that she came out of the womb smiling. Even as a baby, she hardly ever cried. And that never changed. She laughed all the time; to her, everything new was a thrilling discovery. Jared and Lynn used to compete for her attention. Can you imagine that?"

She paused, her voice becoming more ragged. "And then, of course, the headaches started and she began bumping into things as she toddled around. So we visited a host of specialists, and each of them told us there was nothing he could do for her." She swallowed hard. "After that...it just started getting worse. But she was who she was, you know? Just happy. Even toward the end, when she was barely able to sit up on her own, she still laughed. Every time I heard that laugh, I'd feel my heart break just a little bit more." Amanda was quiet then, absently staring toward the darkened window. Dawson waited.

"At the end, I used to lie in bed with her for hours, just holding her as she slept, and when she'd wake up we'd lie there facing each other. I couldn't turn away, because I wanted to memorize everything about the way she looked: her nose, her chin, her little curls. And when she'd finally fall asleep again, I'd hold her close and just weep at the unfairness of it all."

When Amanda finished she blinked, seemingly unaware

of the tears spilling down her cheeks. She made no move to wipe them away, and neither did Dawson. Instead, he sat perfectly still, attuned to every word.

"After she died, part of me died, too. And for a long time, Frank and I could barely look at each other. Not because we were angry, but because it hurt. I could see Bea in Frank, and Frank could see her in me, and it was...unbearable. We barely held ourselves together, even though Jared and Lynn needed us more than ever. I started to drink two or three glasses of wine every night, trying to numb myself, but Frank would drink even more. Finally, though, I recognized that it wasn't helping. So I stopped. But for Frank, it wasn't so easy." She stopped to pinch the bridge of her nose, the memory awakening the familiar traces of a headache. "He couldn't stop. I thought that having another child might heal him, but it didn't, really. He's an alcoholic, and for the last ten years he's lived half a life. And I've reached the point where I don't know how to give him back that other half."

Dawson swallowed. "I don't know what to say."

"I don't, either. I like to tell myself that if Bea hadn't died, this wouldn't have happened to Frank. But then I wonder whether his decline was partly my fault, too. Because I'd been hurting him for years, even before Bea. Because he knew that I didn't love him in the same way he loved me."

"It's not your fault," he said. Even to him, the words sounded inadequate.

She shook her head. "That's kind of you to say, and on the surface I know you're right. But if he's drinking to escape these days, it's probably to escape from me. Because he knows I'm angry and disappointed and he knows there's no way he can erase ten years of regret, no matter what he does. And who wouldn't want to escape from that? Especially when it comes from someone you love? When all you really want is for that person to love you as much as you love them?"

"Don't do that," he said, capturing her gaze with his own. "You can't take the blame for his problems and make them yours."

"Spoken like someone who's never been married." She gave him a crooked smile. "Let me just say that the longer I've been married, the more I've come to realize that few things are ever black and white. And I'm not saying that the problems in our marriage are entirely my fault. I'm just saying that there might be a few shades of gray somewhere in there. Neither one of us is perfect."

"That sounds like something a therapist would say."

"It probably is. A few months after Bea died, I started seeing a therapist twice a week. I don't know how I would have survived without her. Jared and Lynn saw her, too, but not as long. Kids are more resilient, I guess."

"I'll take your word on that."

She rested her chin on her knees, her expression reflecting her turmoil. "I never really told Frank about us."

"No?"

"He knew I'd had a boyfriend in high school, but I didn't tell him how serious it was. I don't think I've ever even told him your name. And my mom and dad, obviously, tried their best to pretend it had never happened at all. They treated it like this deep, dark family secret. Naturally, my mother breathed a sigh of relief when I told her I was engaged. She wasn't thrilled, mind you. My mom doesn't get thrilled about anything. She probably considers it beneath her. But if it makes you feel better, I had to remind her of Frank's name. Twice. Your name, on the other hand..."

Dawson laughed before suddenly growing quiet. She took a sip of wine, feeling the heat as it slid down her throat, barely aware of the soft music still playing in the background. "So much has happened, hasn't it? Since we last saw each other?" Her voice was small.

"Life happened."

"It was more than just life."

"What are you talking about?"

"All this. Being here, seeing you. It makes me think back to a time when I still believed that all my dreams could come true. It's been a long time since I've felt like that." She turned toward him, their faces inches apart. "Do you think we could have made it? If we'd moved away and started our lives together?"

"It's hard to say."

"But if you had to guess?"

"Yes. I think we would have made it."

She nodded, feeling something crumble inside at his answer. "I think so, too."

Outside, a squall began to force waves of rain against the windows like handfuls of tossed pebbles. The radio played softly, music from another time, blending with the steady rhythm of the rain. The warmth of the room was cocoonlike, and Amanda could almost believe that nothing else existed.

"You used to be shy," she murmured. "When we were first paired together in class, you barely spoke to me. I kept dropping hints, waiting for you to ask me out and wondering whether you ever would."

"You were beautiful." Dawson shrugged. "I was no one. It made me nervous."

"Do I still make you nervous?"

"No," he said, then reconsidered. A slight smile eased onto his face. "Maybe a little."

She raised an eyebrow. "Is there anything I can do?"

He took her hand and turned it this way and that, noting how perfectly their hands seemed to fit together, reminding him again of what he had given up. A week ago, he'd been content. Maybe not perfectly happy, maybe a bit isolated, but content. He'd understood who he was and his place in the world. He was alone, but that had been a conscious choice, and even now he didn't regret it. Especially now. Because no one would have been able to take Amanda's place, and no one ever would.

"Will you dance with me?" he finally asked.

She answered with the ghost of a smile. "Yes."

He rose from the couch and gently helped her up. She stood, her legs feeling shaky as they moved toward the center of the small room. The music seemed to fill the room with longing, and for a moment neither of them knew what to do. Amanda waited, watching as Dawson turned to her, his face unreadable. Finally, placing a hand on her hip, he drew her closer. Their bodies came together then and she leaned into him, feeling the solidness of his chest as his arm circled her waist. Ever so slowly, they began to turn and sway.

He felt so good to her. She breathed in the smell of him, clean and real and everything she remembered. She could feel the taut plane of his stomach and his legs against hers. Closing her eyes, she laid her head on his shoulder, flooded with desire, thinking of the first night they'd ever made love. She'd been trembling that night and she was trembling now.

The song ended but they continued to hold each other as another song started. His breath was hot on her neck and she heard him exhale, a kind of release. His face inched even closer, and she leaned her head back in abandon, wanting the dance to last forever. Wanting them to last forever.

His lips grazed her neck first, then gently brushed her cheek, and though she heard a faraway warning echo, she strained toward the butterfly touch.

They kissed then, first hesitantly, then more passionately, making up for a lifetime apart. She could feel his hands on her, all of her, and when they finally separated, Amanda was conscious only of how long it had been since she'd ached for this. Ached for him. She stared at Dawson through half-closed eyes, wanting him more than anyone she'd ever known, wanting all of him, here and now. She could feel his desire as well, and with a movement that seemed almost preordained, she kissed him once more before leading him to the bedroom.

13

—— ✣ ——

The day was crap. Started like crap, the afternoon and eve-ning were crap, even the weather was crap. Abee felt like he was dying. It had been raining for hours, the water soaking through his shirt, and he couldn't stop the alternating bouts of shivering and sweating no matter how hard he tried.

He could tell Ted wasn't doing much better. When he'd checked himself out of the hospital, he'd barely made it to the car with-out falling. But that didn't stop him from making directly for the back room of his shack, where he kept all his weapons. They'd loaded up the truck before setting out for Tuck's.

Only problem was, no one was here. There were two cars parked out front but no sign of either of their owners. Abee knew that Dawson and the girl were coming back. They had to, since their cars were here, so he and Ted had split up before settling in to wait.

And wait. And *wait*.

They'd been there at least two hours before the rain started to fall. Another hour in the rain, and the chills started up. Every time he shivered, his eyes flashed white because of the pain in his gut. Swear to God, he felt like he was dying. He tried think-ing about Candy to pass the time, but all that did was make him wonder whether *that guy* would be there again tonight. The thought enraged him, which made him shiver even more, and the whole thing would start over. He wondered where the hell Dawson was and what he was doing out here in the first place. He wasn't even sure whether he believed Ted about Dawson—in fact, he was pretty sure he didn't—but catching the look on Ted's face, he decided to keep his mouth shut. Ted wasn't going to give up on this. And for the first time in his life, Abee was a little afraid of what Ted would do if he walked over and announced that they were going home.

Meanwhile, Candy and *that guy* were probably at the bar right now. Both of them laughing it up, sharing those special smiles. Just picturing it made his pulse race with fury. The pain flashed then, and for a second he was sure he was going to pass out. He was going to kill that guy. Swear to God. Next time he saw him, he was going to kill him and then make sure Candy understood the rules. He just had to get this piece of family business out of the way first, so Ted would be around to help him. God knows he was in no condition to handle it himself.

Another hour passed and the sun sank lower in the sky. Ted felt like he was going to puke. Every time he moved, his head felt like it was going to explode, and his arm was already itching so bad beneath the cast that he wanted to tear the damn thing off. He couldn't breathe through his swollen nose and all he wanted was for Dawson to show up so he could end this thing here and now.

He didn't even care whether little miss cheerleader was with him. Yesterday, he'd worried about witnesses, but not anymore. He'd just hide her body, too. Maybe folks would think the two of them had run off together.

Even so, where the hell was Dawson? Where could he have gone for the whole damn day? And in the rain? He sure as hell hadn't planned on this. Across the way, Abee looked like he was dying. Guy was practically green, but Ted couldn't do this alone.

Not one-handed, while his brain was swooshing from side to side inside his skull. It hurt to breathe, for God's sake, and whenever he moved he got so dizzy he had to hold on to something to keep from toppling over.

As darkness fell and the mist rolled in, Ted kept telling himself that they'd be back any minute, but it was getting harder to convince himself of that. He hadn't eaten since the day before, and his dizziness was getting worse.

By ten o'clock, there was still no sign of them. Then eleven. Then midnight, with the stars between the clouds a blanket of flickering lights above them.

He was cramped and cold, and the dry heaves started. Ted began to shake uncontrollably, unable to stay warm.

One o'clock and still nothing. At two, Abee finally came staggering up, barely able to stay upright. By then, even Ted knew they weren't coming back that night, and the two of them staggered to the truck. He barely remembered the trip back to the property or the way he and Abee clung to each other as they stumbled up the drive. All he could really recall was the feeling of rage as he collapsed in bed, and after that everything went black.

14

When she woke on Sunday morning, it took Amanda a few seconds to recognize her surroundings before the evening came rushing back. Outside, she could hear birds singing while sunlight streamed through the small opening between the drapes. Cautiously, she rolled over and found the space beside her empty. She felt a stab of disappointment followed almost immediately by confusion.

Sitting up, she held the sheet against her as she peered toward the bathroom, wondering where Dawson was. Seeing that his clothes were gone, she swung her feet down, wrapped the sheet around her, and went to the bedroom door. Peeking around the corner, she caught sight of him sitting on the steps of the front porch. Turning around, she dressed hurriedly and stepped into the bathroom. She ran a quick brush through her hair and padded to the front door, knowing she needed to talk to him. Knowing he needed to talk to her.

Dawson turned when he heard the squeak of the door opening behind him. He smiled at her, the darkening stubble on his face adding a bit of roguishness to his appearance. "Hey, there," he said and reached beside him. He held out a Styrofoam cup; another was cradled in his lap. "I figured you might need some coffee."

"Where did you get this?" she asked.

"The convenience store. Just down the road. As far as I can tell, it's the only place in Vandemere that sells coffee. It's probably not as good as what you had Friday morning, though."

He watched her as she took the cup and sat beside him. "Did you sleep okay?"

"Yes," she said. "And you?"

"Not really." He shrugged slightly before turning away, focusing on the flowers again. "The rain finally stopped," he commented.

"I noticed."

"I should probably wash the car when I get it back to Tuck's," he said. "I can call Morgan Tanner if you want me to."

"I'll call him," she said. "I'm sure we'll be talking, anyway." Amanda knew the meaningless chatter was simply a way to avoid talking about the obvious. "You're not okay, are you?"

His shoulders drooped, but he said nothing.

"You're upset," she whispered, feeling sick at heart.

"No," he answered, surprising her. He slipped his arm around her. "Not at all. Why would I be upset?" He leaned over then, kissing her tenderly before slowly drawing back.

"Look," she started, "about last night—"

"Do you know what I found?" he interrupted. "While I was sitting out here?"

She shook her head, mystified.

"I found a four-leaf clover," he said. "By the steps here, just before you came out. Poking out of the ground in plain sight." He presented her with the delicate green wisp, sandwiched in the folds of a piece of scrap paper. "It's supposed to be lucky, and I've been thinking a lot about that this morning."

Amanda heard something troubled in his voice, and she felt a flash of foreboding. "What are you talking about, Dawson?" she asked quietly.

"Luck," he said. "Ghosts. Fate."

His words did nothing to ease her confusion and she watched

as he took another sip of coffee. He lowered the cup and stared into the distance. "I almost died," he said finally. "I don't know. I probably should have died. The fall alone should have killed me. Or the explosion. Hell, I probably should have died two days ago..."

He trailed off, lost in thought.

"You're scaring me," she finally said.

Dawson straightened, coming back to her. "There was a fire on the rig in the spring," he began. He told her everything: the fire turning into an inferno on the deck; how he'd hit the water and seen the dark-haired man; how the stranger had led him to the life preserver; how he'd reappeared with a blue windbreaker, then suddenly vanished in the supply ship afterward. He told her all that had happened over the next few weeks—the feeling that he was being watched, and how he'd seen the man again at the marina. Finally, he described his encounter with Ted on Friday, including the dark-haired man's inexplicable appearance and disappearance in the woods.

By the time he finished, Amanda could feel her heart racing as she tried to comprehend it. "Are you saying that Ted tried to kill you? That he went to Tuck's place with a gun to hunt you down, and you didn't feel the need to even mention this yesterday?"

Dawson shook his head in apparent indifference. "It was over. I took care of it."

She could hear her voice rising. "You dump his body back at the old homestead and call Abee? You take his gun and dump it? That's taking care of it?"

He sounded too tired to argue. "It's my family," he said. "That's how we handle things."

"You're not like them."

"I've always been one of them," he said. "I'm a Cole, remember? They come, we fight, they come again. It's what we do."

"So what are you saying? That it's not over?"

"Not to them."

"Then what are you going to do?"

"Same thing I've been doing. Try my best to stay out of sight, keep out of their way as much as possible. It shouldn't be too hard. Other than cleaning up the car and maybe swinging by the cemetery again, I've got no reason to stick around."

A sudden thought, liquid and blurry at first, began to crystallize in her mind, one that led to the first stirrings of panic. "Is that why we didn't go back last night?" she demanded. "Because you thought they might be at Tuck's?"

"I'm sure they were," he said. "But no, that's not the reason we're here. I didn't think about them at all yesterday. I had a perfect day with you instead."

"You're not angry with them?"

"Not particularly."

"How can you do that? Just turn it off like that? Even when you know they're out there hunting you down?" Amanda could feel adrenaline flooding her body. "Is this some crazy idea about your destiny as a Cole?"

"No." He shook his head, the movement almost imperceptible. "I wasn't thinking about them because I was thinking about you. And since you first came into my life, that's the way it's always been. I don't think about them because I love you, and there isn't room for both."

Her gaze fell. "Dawson..."

"You don't have to say it," he hushed her.

"Yes, I do," she pressed, and she leaned in, her lips meeting his. When they separated, the words flowed as naturally as her breath. "I love you, Dawson Cole."

"I know," he said, gently sliding his arm around her waist. "I love you, too."

※

The storm had wrung the humidity from the air, leaving blue skies and a sweet floral aroma behind. The occasional drop of water still fell from the roof, landing on ferns and ivy, making them shimmer in the clear golden light. Dawson had kept his arm around Amanda, and she leaned into him, savoring the pressure of her body against his.

After Amanda rewrapped the clover and tucked it into her pocket, they got up and walked the property, their arms around each other. Skirting the wildflowers—the path they'd used the day before was muddy—they made their way around the back. The house was set into a small bluff; beyond that, the Bay River stretched out, almost as wide as the Neuse. At the water's edge, they spotted a blue heron high-stepping through the shallows; a little farther down, a clutch of turtles was sunning on a log.

They stayed for a while, taking it all in before slowly circling back to the house. On the porch, Dawson pulled her close, kissing her again, and she kissed him back, flooded by the knowledge of her love for him. When they finally drew back, she heard the faint sound of a cell phone as it began to ring. Her phone, reminding her of the life she still had elsewhere. At the sound, Amanda bowed her head reluctantly, as did Dawson. Their foreheads came together as the ringing continued, and she closed her eyes. It seemed to go on forever, but once it was finally quiet, Amanda opened her eyes and looked at him, hoping he'd understand.

He nodded and reached for the door, opening it for her. She stepped inside, turning when she grasped that he wasn't going to follow. Instead, after watching as he took a seat on the step, she forced herself in the direction of the bedroom. Reaching for her bag, she fished out her cell phone, turned it on, and looked at the list of missed calls.

Suddenly, she was sick to her stomach and her mind began to race. She went to the bathroom, shedding clothes as she walked. Instinctively, she made a mental list of what she had to do, what she was going to say. She turned on the shower and searched the cabinets for shampoo and soap, fortunately finding both. Then she stepped in, trying to wash off the feeling of panic. Afterward, she toweled off and slipped back into her clothes, drying her hair as best she could. Carefully she applied the little makeup she always carried with her.

She moved quickly through the bedroom, tidying up. She made the bed and put the pillows back in place; from there, she retrieved the nearly empty bottle of wine and poured what remained down the sink. Sliding the bottle into the garbage pail beneath the sink, she thought twice about bringing it with her, then decided to leave it in place. From the end tables, she collected the two half-empty glasses. After rinsing them with water, she dried them and replaced them in the cupboard. Hiding the evidence.

But the phone calls. The missed calls. The *messages.*

She was going to have to lie. The thought of telling Frank where she'd been struck her as utterly impossible. She couldn't bear the thought of what her children might think. Or her mother. She needed to fix this. Somehow, she needed to fix everything, yet underneath that thought lurked a persistent voice, whispering the question: *Do you know what you've done?*

Yes. But I love him, another voice answered.

Standing in the kitchen, overcome by emotion, she felt like she was going to cry. And maybe she would have, but a moment later, anticipating her turmoil, Dawson walked into the small kitchen. He took her in his arms and whispered again that he loved her, and for just an instant, as impossible as it seemed, she felt that everything was going to be all right.

❦

They were both quiet as they made the drive back to Oriental. Dawson could sense Amanda's anxiety and knew enough to stay quiet, but his grip was tight on the wheel.

Amanda's throat felt raw—nerves, she knew. Having Dawson beside her was the only thing that kept her from breaking down.

Her mind shifted from memories to plans to feelings to worries, one right after the other, a kaleidoscope that changed with every turn. Lost in her thoughts, she barely noticed the miles going by.

They reached Oriental a little before noon and drove past the marina; a few minutes later, they were turning up the drive. She vaguely noticed that Dawson had grown tense, his eyes scanning the trees lining the drive as he leaned over the wheel. Cautious, even. His cousins, she thought suddenly, and as the car began to slow, Dawson's expression suddenly took on a look of disbelief.

Following his gaze, Amanda turned toward the house. The house and garage appeared exactly the same; their cars were still parked in the same spot. But when Amanda saw what Dawson had noticed already, she found that she felt almost nothing. She'd known all along that it would come down to this.

Dawson slowed the car to a stop and she turned toward him, flashing a brief smile, trying to reassure him that she could handle it.

"She left three messages." Amanda gave a helpless shrug. Dawson nodded, recognizing that she needed to confront this alone. With a deep breath, Amanda opened the door and stepped out, not at all surprised that her mom looked as though she'd taken time to dress for the occasion.

15

━━━ 🍂 ━━━

Dawson watched as Amanda made straight for the house, allowing her mother to follow if she wished. Evelyn didn't seem to know what to do. She obviously hadn't been to Tuck's place before; it wasn't an ideal destination for anyone in a cream pantsuit and pearls, especially after a rainstorm. Hesitating, she looked toward Dawson. She stared at him, her face impassive, as if reacting to his presence were somehow beneath her.

She finally turned and followed her daughter to the porch. By then Amanda was already seated in one of the rocking chairs. Dawson put the car back into gear and slowly drove it toward the garage.

He climbed out and leaned against the workbench. From where he was standing, he could no longer see Amanda, nor could he imagine what she would say to her mother. As he looked around Tuck's garage, something pricked Dawson's memory, something that Morgan Tanner had said while he and Amanda had been in his office. He'd said that both Dawson and Amanda would know when to read the letter he'd written each of them, and all at once he knew that Tuck had meant for him to read it now. Tuck probably foresaw how things would play out.

Reaching into his back pocket, he pulled out the envelope. Unfolding it, he ran his finger over his name. It was the same shaky scrawl he'd noticed in the letter he and Amanda had read together. Turning the envelope over, he pried it open. Unlike the previous letter, this one was only a single page, front and back. In the quiet of the garage that Dawson once called home, he focused on the words and began to read.

Dawson,

I'm not exactly sure how to start this letter, other than to tell you that over the years, I've come to know Amanda pretty well. I'd like to think she hasn't changed since I first laid eyes on her, but I can't honestly say for sure. Back then, you two kept pretty much to yourselves, and like a lot of young folk you both went still whenever I came around. Had no problem with that, by the way. Did the same thing with Clara. Don't know if her daddy heard me talk until after we were married, but that's another story.

My point is, I don't really know who she was, but I know who she is now, and let's just say I know why you never got over her. She's got a lot of goodness inside her, that one. Lots of love, lots of patience, smart as a whip, and she's just about the prettiest thing that ever walked the streets of this town, that's for sure. But it's her kindness I think I like best because I've been around long enough to know how rare something like that really is.

I'm probably not telling you anything you don't already know, but over the last few years, I've come think of her as something like a daughter. That means I have to talk to you like maybe her daddy would have, because daddies ain't worth much if they don't worry just a little. Especially about her. Because more than anything else, you should understand that Amanda's hurting, and I think she's been hurting for a while now. I saw it when she first came to see me, and I guess I hoped it was a phase, but the more she came to visit, the worse she seemed to be feeling. Every now and then, I'd wake up and see her poking

around the garage, and I began to understand that you were
part of the reason she was feeling the way she was. She was
haunted by the past, haunted by you. But trust me when I say
that memories are funny things. Sometimes they're real, but
other times they change into what we want them to be, and in
her own way, I think Amanda was trying to figure out what the
past really meant to her. That's the reason I set up the weekend
like I did. I had a hunch that seeing you again was the only way
she was going to find her way out of the darkness, whatever that
might mean.

But like I said, she's hurting, and if there's one thing I've
learned, it's that people in pain don't always see things as clearly
as they should. She's at the point in her life where she has to
make some decisions, and that's where you come in. Both of you
need to figure out what happens next, but keep in mind that she
might need more time than you do. She might even change her
mind once or twice. But once it's finally decided, both of you
need to accept the decision. And if it somehow doesn't work
out between you, then you've got to understand that you can't
look back anymore. It'll destroy you in the end, and destroy her
as well. Neither one of you can keep living with regret, because
it drains the life right out of you, and the very idea is enough to
break my heart. After all, if I've come to think of Amanda as
my daughter, I've come to think of you as my son. And if I had
a single dying wish, it would be to know that both of you, my
two children, are somehow going to be all right.

Tuck

Amanda watched her mom test the decaying floorboards of the
porch, as though fearing she might fall through. She hesitated
again at the rocker, trying to decide whether it was actually necessary to sit down.

Amanda felt a familiar weariness as her mother lowered herself carefully into the chair. She perched in such a way as to touch as little of it as possible.

Once settled, her mother turned to regard her, seemingly content to wait for Amanda to speak first, but Amanda stayed quiet. She knew there was nothing she could say that would make this conversation easier, and she deliberately faced away, watching the play of sunlight as it filtered through the canopy.

Finally, her mother rolled her eyes. "Really, Amanda. Stop acting like a child. I'm not your enemy. I'm your mother."

"I know what you're going to say." Amanda's voice was flat.

"That may very well be the case, but even so, one of the responsibilities of being a parent is to make sure your children know when they're making mistakes."

"Is that what you think this is?" Amanda's narrowed gaze snapped back to her mother.

"What would you call it? You're a married woman."

"You don't think I know that?"

"You're certainly not acting like it," she said. "You're not the first woman in the world who's been unhappy in her marriage. Nor are you the first to act on that unhappiness. The difference with you is that you continue to think that it's someone else's fault."

"What are you talking about?" Amanda could feel her hands tightening around the arms of her rocker.

"You blame people, Amanda." Her mother sniffed. "You blame me, you blame Frank, and after Bea, you even blamed God. You look anywhere besides the mirror for the cause of the problems in your life. Instead, you walk around feeling like a martyr. 'Poor little Amanda struggling against all odds in a hard and cruel world.' The truth is, the world isn't easy for any of us. It never has been, and it never will be. But if you were honest with yourself, you'd understand that you're not entirely innocent in all this, either."

Amanda clenched her teeth. "And here I was, hoping that you

were capable of even the tiniest flicker of empathy or understanding. I guess I was wrong."

"Is that what you really think?" Evelyn asked, picking at an imaginary piece of lint on her clothing. "Tell me then—what should I be saying to you? Should I hold your hand and ask how you're feeling? Should I lie to you and tell you that everything is going to be just fine? That there aren't going to be any consequences, even if you somehow manage to keep Dawson a secret?" She paused. "There are always consequences, Amanda. You're old enough to know that. Do you really need me to remind you?"

Amanda willed herself to keep her voice steady. "You're missing my point."

"And you're missing mine. You don't know me as well as you think you do."

"I know you, Mom."

"Oh, yes, that's right. In your words I'm incapable of even a flicker of sympathy or understanding." She touched the small diamond stud in her earlobe. "Of course, that begs the question as to why I covered for you last night."

"What?"

"When Frank called. The first time, I acted like I suspected nothing at all while he rambled on about some golf thing he planned to do tomorrow with a friend named Roger. And then later, when he called back a second time, I told him that you were already asleep, even when I knew exactly what you were up to. I knew you were with Dawson, and by dinner, I knew that you weren't coming back."

"How could you know that?" Amanda demanded, trying to mask her shock.

"Have you never noticed how small Oriental is? There are only so many places to stay in town. On my first call, I spoke to Alice Russell at the bed-and-breakfast. We had a pleasant conversation, by the way. She told me that Dawson had checked out, but simply knowing that he was in town was enough for me to figure out what was going on. I suppose that's why I'm here, instead of waiting for you at the house. I thought we could just skip the lying and denying altogether. I thought it would make our conversation a bit easier for you."

Amanda felt almost dizzy. "Thank you," she mumbled. "For not telling Frank."

"It's not my place to tell Frank anything, or to say anything that would add more trouble to your marriage. What you tell Frank is your own business. As far as I'm concerned, nothing happened at all."

Amanda swallowed the bitter taste in her mouth. "Then why are you here?"

Her mother sighed. "Because you're my daughter. You may not want to talk to me, but I do expect you to listen." Amanda caught the whiff of disappointment in her mom's tone. "I have no desire to hear the tawdry details of what went on last night, or hear how awful I was for not accepting Dawson in the first place. Nor do I want to discuss your problems with Frank. What I'd like to do instead is to give you some advice. As your mother. Despite what you might think sometimes, you are my daughter and I care about you. The question is, are you willing to listen?"

"Yes." Amanda's voice was barely audible. "What should I do?"

Her mother's face lost all its stiff artifice and her voice was surprisingly soft. "It's really very simple," she said. "Don't take my advice."

Amanda waited for more but her mother remained quiet, adding nothing to her comment. She wasn't sure what to make of it. "Are you telling me to leave Frank?" she finally whispered.

"No."

"Then I should try to work things out with him?"

"I didn't say that, either."

"I don't understand."

"Don't read so much into it." Her mother rose, straightening her jacket. She moved toward the steps.

Amanda blinked, trying to grasp what was happening. "Wait . . . you're leaving? You didn't say anything."

Her mom turned. "On the contrary. I said everything that matters."

"Don't take your advice?"

"Exactly," her mom said. "Don't take my advice. Or anyone's advice. Trust yourself. For good or for bad, happy or unhappy, it's your life, and what you do with it has always been entirely up to you." She placed one polished leather pump on the creaky first step, her face becoming masklike again. "Now, I suppose I'll see you later? When you come home to get your things?"

"Yes."

"Then I'll put out some finger sandwiches and fruit." With that, she continued down the steps. At her car, she noticed Dawson standing in the garage and she studied him briefly before turning away. Once behind the wheel, she started the engine, and then, all at once, she was gone.

❧

Putting the letter aside, Dawson left the garage and focused his gaze on Amanda. She was staring out at the forest, more composed than he'd imagined she would be, but he was unable to read anything more from her expression.

As he walked toward Amanda on the porch, she offered a weak smile before turning away. Somewhere in the pit of his stomach, he felt the stirrings of fear.

He took a seat in the rocker and leaned forward, clasping his hands together and sitting in silence.

"Aren't you going to ask me how it went?" she finally asked.

"I figured you'd get around to telling me sooner or later," he said. "If you wanted to talk about it, I mean."

"Am I that predictable?"

"No," he said.

"Yes, I am. My mother, on the other hand . . ." She tugged at her earlobe, buying time. "If I ever tell you that I think I have my mom figured out, remind me of what happened today, okay?"

He nodded. "Will do."

Amanda drew a long, slow breath, and when she finally spoke, her voice sounded strangely distant. "When she was walking up to the porch, I knew exactly how our conversation was going to unfold," she said. "She was going to demand to know what I was doing and tell me what a terrible mistake I was making. Next to come would be the lecture about expectations and responsibility, and then I'd cut her off, telling her that she didn't understand a thing about me. I was going to tell her that I've loved you all my life and that Frank didn't make me happy anymore. That I wanted to be with you." She turned toward him, pleading for him to understand. "I could hear myself saying the words, but then..." Dawson watched her expression close in on itself. "She has this way of making me question everything."

"You mean about us," he said, the knot of fear growing tighter.

"I mean about me," she said, her voice barely a whisper. "But yes, I'm also talking about us. Because I did want to say those things to her. I wanted to say them more than anything, because they're true." She shook her head, as if trying to clear her mind of the remnants of a dream. "But as my mom started talking, my real life came flooding back, and all of a sudden I could hear myself saying something different. It was like there were two radios tuned to different stations, each one playing an alternate version. In the other version I heard myself saying that I didn't want Frank to know about any of this. And that I have children waiting for me back home. And that no matter what I said or how I tried to explain it to them, there would still be something inherently selfish about all of this."

When she paused, Dawson watched as she absently twirled her wedding band.

"Annette is still a little girl," she went on. "I can't imagine leaving her, and at the same time I can't imagine taking her away from her father, either. How could I explain something like this to her? So that she would understand? And what about Jared and Lynn? They're almost adults, but would it be any easier on them? To know that I broke up the family so I could be with you? Like I was trying to relive my youth?" Her voice was anguished. "I love my kids, and it would break my heart to see their disappointment whenever they looked at me."

"They love you," Dawson said, swallowing the lump in his throat.

"I know. But I don't want to put them in that position," she said, picking at some flaking paint on the rocker. "I don't want them to hate me or be disappointed in me. And Frank..." She drew an unsteady breath. "Yes, he has problems, and yes, I struggle with my feelings toward him all the time. But he's not a bad man and I know that part of me will always care for him. Sometimes, I feel like I'm the reason he's able to function as well as he still does. But he's not the kind of man who would be able to wrap his mind around the idea that I'd left him for someone else. Believe me when I tell you that he wouldn't be able to recover from something like that. It would just...destroy him, and what then? Would he drink even more than he already does? Or sink into some deep depression that he couldn't escape? I don't know if I can do that to him." Her shoulders drooped. "And then, of course, there's you."

Dawson sensed what was coming next.

"This weekend was wonderful, but it isn't real life. It was more like a honeymoon, and after a while the excitement will wear off. We can tell ourselves it won't happen, we can make all the promises we want, but it's inevitable, and after that you'll never look at me the way you do now. I won't be the woman you dream about, or the girl you used to love. And you won't be my long-lost love, my one true thing anymore, either. You'll be someone my kids despise because you ruined the family, and you'll see me for who I really am. In a few years, I'll simply be a woman pushing fifty with three kids who might or might not hate her, and who might end up hating herself because of all this. And in the end, you'll end up hating her, too."

"That's not true." Dawson's voice was unwavering.

Amanda did her best to act brave. "But it is," she said. "Honeymoons always come to an end."

He reached for her then, his hand coming to rest on her thigh. "Being together isn't about a honeymoon. It's about the real you and me. I want to wake up with you beside me in the mornings, I want to spend my evenings looking at you across the dinner table. I want to share every mundane detail of my day with you and hear every detail of yours. I want to laugh with you and fall asleep with you in my arms. Because you aren't just someone I loved back then. You were my best friend, my best self, and I can't imagine giving that up again." He hesitated, searching for the right words. "You might not understand, but I gave you the best of me, and after you left, nothing was ever the same." Dawson could feel the dampness in his palms. "I know you're afraid, and I'm afraid, too. But if we let this go, if we pretend none of this ever happened, then I'm not sure we'll ever get another chance." He reached up, brushing a strand of hair from her eyes. "We're still young. We still have time to make this right."

"We're not that young anymore—"

"But we are," Dawson insisted. "We still have the rest of our lives."

"I know," she whispered. "That's why I need you to do something for me."

"Anything."

She pinched the bridge of her nose, trying to keep the tears at bay. "Please . . . don't ask me to go with you, because if you do, I'll go. Please don't ask me to tell Frank about us, because I'll do that, too. Please don't ask me to give up my responsibilities or break up my family." She inhaled, gulping air like someone drowning. "I love you, and if you love me, too, then you just can't ask me to do these things. Because I don't trust myself enough to say no."

When she finished, Dawson said nothing. Though he didn't want to admit it, he knew there was truth in what she had said. Breaking up her family would change everything; it would change her, and though it scared him, he recalled Tuck's letter. She might need more time, Tuck had said. Or perhaps it really was over and he was supposed to move on.

But that wasn't possible. He thought about all the years he'd dreamed of seeing her again; he thought about the future they might never spend together. He didn't want to give her time, he wanted her to choose him now. And yet he knew that she needed this from him, maybe more than anything she'd ever needed, and he exhaled, hoping that it might somehow make the words come easier.

"All right," he finally whispered.

Amanda began to cry then. Wrestling with the emotions raging through him, Dawson stood. She did, too, and he pulled her close, feeling her collapse against him. As he breathed her in, images began to cycle through his mind—the sunlight striking her hair as she stepped from the garage when he first arrived at Tuck's; her natural grace as she moved through the wildflowers at Vandemere; the still, hungry moment when their lips had first touched in the warmth of a cottage he'd never known existed. Now it was coming to an end, and it was like he was watching the last flicker of light wink out in the darkness of an endless tunnel.

They held each other on the porch for a long time. Amanda listened to the beating of his heart, sure that nothing would ever feel so right. She longed, impossibly, to start all over. She would do it right this time; she would stay with him, never abandoning him again. They were meant for each other, and they belonged together. *There was still time for both of them.* When she felt his hands in her hair, she almost said the words. But she couldn't. Instead, all she could do was murmur, "I'm glad I got to see you again, Dawson Cole."

Dawson could feel the smooth, almost luxurious, silkiness of her hair. "Maybe we could do it again sometime?"

"Maybe," she said. She swiped at a tear on her cheek. "Who knows? Maybe I'll come to my senses and just show up in Louisiana one day. Me and the kids, I mean."

He forced a smile, a desperate, futile hope leaping in his chest. "I'll make dinner," he said. "For everyone."

But it was time for her to go. As they left the porch, Dawson reached for her hand and she took it, squeezing so tight it was almost painful. They retrieved her things from the Stingray before slowly walking to her car. Dawson's senses felt acutely heightened—the morning sun pricked the back of his neck, the breeze was feathery light, and the leaves were rustling, but none of it seemed real. All he knew was that everything was coming to an end.

Amanda clung to his hand. When they reached her car, he opened the door and turned toward her. He kissed her softly before trailing his lips down her cheek, chasing the pathway of her tears. He traced the line of her jaw, thinking about the words that Tuck had written. He would never move on, he understood with sudden clarity, despite what Tuck had asked of him. She was the only woman he'd ever love, the only woman he ever wanted to love.

In time, Amanda forced herself to take a step away from him. Then, slipping behind the wheel, she started the engine and closed the door before lowering the window. His eyes were bright with tears, mirroring her own. Reluctantly, she put the car in reverse. Dawson backed away, saying nothing, the ache he felt etched in her own anguished expression.

She turned the car around, pointing it in the direction of the road. The world had gone blurry through her tears. As she rounded the curve in the drive, she glanced into the rearview mirror and choked out a sob as Dawson grew smaller behind her. He hadn't moved at all.

She cried harder as the car picked up speed. The trees pressed in all around her. She wanted to turn the car around and go back to him, to tell him that she had the courage to be the person she wanted to be. She whispered his name, and though there was no way he could have heard her, Dawson raised his arm, offering a final farewell.

❧

Her mother was seated on the front porch when Amanda arrived. She was sipping a glass of iced tea while music played softly on the radio. Amanda passed her without a word, climbing the stairs to her room. Turning on the shower, she removed her clothes. She stood naked in front of the mirror, as drained and spent as an empty vessel.

The stinging spray of the shower felt like punishment, and when she at last stepped out, she pulled on a pair of jeans and a simple cotton blouse before packing the rest of her things in her suitcase. The clover went into a zippered compartment of her purse. As she usually did, she stripped the sheets from the bed and brought them to the laundry room. She put them into the washer, moving on autopilot.

Back in her room, the list of things to do continued. She reminded herself that the ice maker in the refrigerator back home needed to be fixed; she'd forgotten to arrange that before she'd left. She also needed to start planning the fund-raiser. She'd been putting that off for a while, but September would be here before she knew it. She needed a caterer, and it would probably be a good idea to start soliciting donations for the gift baskets. Lynn had to sign up for SAT prep classes, and she couldn't remember whether they'd put the deposit down on Jared's dorm room. Annette would be coming home later this week, and she'd probably want something special for dinner.

Making plans. Moving past the weekend, reentering her real life. Like the water in the shower washing Dawson's scent from her skin, it felt like a kind of punishment.

But even when her mind finally began to slow, she understood that she still wasn't ready to go downstairs. Instead, she sat on the bed as sunlight streamed gently through the room, and all at once she remembered the way Dawson had looked when he'd been standing in the drive. The image was clear, as vivid as if it were happening all over again, and despite herself—despite everything—she suddenly knew that she was making the wrong decision. She could still go to Dawson and they could find a way to make it work, no matter what the challenges might be. In time, her children would forgive her; in time, she would even forgive herself.

But even then she was paralyzed, unable to bring herself to move.

"I love you," she whispered into the silent room, feeling her future being swept away like so many grains of sand, a future that already felt almost like a dream.

16

---- 🌿 ----

Marilyn Bonner stood in the kitchen of the farmhouse, idly watching the workers make adjustments to the irrigation system in the orchard below. Despite yesterday's downpour, the trees still needed to be watered, and she knew the men would be out there most of the day, even though it was the weekend. The orchard, she'd come to believe, was like a spoiled child, always needing just a bit more care, a bit more attention, never quite satisfied.

But the real heart of the business lay beyond the orchard, in the small plant where they bottled the jellies and preserves. During the week, it housed a dozen people, but on weekends the place was deserted. When she'd first built it, she could remember townspeople whispering that there was no way her business could support the cost of such a facility. And maybe it *had* been a stretch at the time, but little by little the whispers had been silenced. She'd never get rich making jelly and jam, but she knew the business was good enough to pass down to her kids and allow them both a comfortable living. In the end, that was all she'd really wanted.

She still had on the same outfit she'd worn to church and her visit to the cemetery. Usually, she changed immediately after returning home, but today she couldn't seem to summon the energy. Nor was she hungry, and that was unusual, too. Someone else might think she was coming down with something, but Marilyn knew well enough what was bothering her.

Turning from the window, she inspected the kitchen. She'd had it renovated a few years ago, along with the bathrooms and most of the downstairs, and she found herself thinking that the old farmhouse had finally begun to feel like home—or rather, the kind of home she'd always wanted. Until the renovation, it had felt more like her parents' house, a feeling that didn't sit well with her as she'd gotten older. A lot of things didn't sit well with her as she struggled through adulthood, but as hard as some of the years had been, she'd learned from the experiences. Despite it all, she had fewer regrets than people might imagine.

Still, she was bothered by what she'd seen earlier that day, and she debated what to do. Or even whether she should do anything at all. She could always pretend that she didn't know what it meant and let time do its magic.

But she'd learned the hard way that ignoring a situation didn't always work out for the best. Reaching for her purse, she suddenly knew what she had to do.

After cramming the last of the boxes into the passenger seat of the car, Candy went back inside her house and removed the gold Buddha statue from the living room windowsill. As ugly as it was, she'd always kind of liked it, imagining that it had brought her luck. It was also her insurance policy; and lucky or not, she planned to pawn it as soon as she could, knowing she'd need the money to start over.

She wrapped the Buddha in some newspaper and put it in the glove compartment before stepping back to survey her packing. She was amazed that she'd been able to get everything into the Mustang. The trunk could barely close, the passenger seat was piled so high it would be impossible to see out the side window, and items had been stuffed in every nook and cranny. She really needed to stop the Internet shopping. In the future, she'd need a bigger car, or quick getaways would be that much more difficult. She could have left some items behind, of course. The cappuccino maker from Williams-Sonoma for instance, but in Oriental she'd needed it, if only to feel like she wasn't living completely in the sticks. A little touch of the city, so to speak.

In any case, this part was done. She'd finish up her shift at the Tidewater later tonight, then hit the highway, turning south as soon as she reached I-95. She'd decided to relocate to Florida. She'd heard a lot of promising things about South Beach, and it sounded like the kind of place she might end up staying in for a while. Even settle down. She knew she'd said that before and it had yet to work out that way, but a girl had to dream, right?

Tip-wise, Saturday night had been a bonanza, but Friday had been disappointing, which was why she'd resolved to stick it out one last night. Friday night had started out well—she'd dressed in a halter and short shorts, and guys were practically emptying their wallets trying to get her attention, but then Abee had showed up and ruined everything. He'd taken a seat at a table, looking sick as a dog and sweating like he'd just walked out of a sauna, and he'd spent the next half hour staring at her with that crazed expression of his.

She'd seen it before—a kind of paranoid possessiveness—but Abee brought it to a whole new level on Friday night. For her, the weekend couldn't end soon enough. She had the sense that Abee was on the verge of doing something stupid, maybe even dangerous. She'd been sure he was going to start something that night and maybe he would have, but fortunately, he'd gotten a call on his cell phone and had left the bar in a rush. She'd halfway expected to find him outside her front door on Saturday morning, or waiting for her at the bar on Saturday night, but strangely, he hadn't shown up. To her relief, he hadn't shown up today, either. A good thing, considering the loaded car made her plans pretty obvious, and it was clear that he wouldn't be too happy about the idea. Although she didn't want to admit it, Abee scared her. Scared half the bar on Friday night, too. The place had begun to clear out as soon as he entered, which was why her tips had dried up. Even after he left, the crowds had been slow to come back.

But it was almost over. One more shift and she'd be out of here. And Oriental, like all the other places she'd lived, would soon be nothing but a memory.

For Alan Bonner, Sundays were always a little depressing, because he knew the weekend was almost at an end. Work, he'd decided, wasn't all it was cracked up to be.

Not that he had much of a choice. His mom was big on him *making his own way in the world* or however she phrased it, and that was kind of a bummer. It would have been nice had she hired him as the manager at the plant, where he'd be able to sit in an air-conditioned office issuing orders and overseeing things as opposed to delivering snacks to convenience stores. But what could he do? Mom was the boss, and she was saving that position for his sister, Emily. Unlike him, Emily had actually graduated from college.

It wasn't all bad, though. He had his own place, courtesy of Mom, and the utilities were paid by the orchard, which meant any money he earned was pretty much his own. Even better, he could come and go as he pleased, a definite step up compared to the years he'd lived in the house. And besides, working for Mom, even in an air-conditioned office, wouldn't have been easy. First, if he worked for her, they'd be around each other all the time, which neither of them would have enjoyed. Taken together with the fact that Mom was kind of a stickler for paperwork—never one of his strengths—he knew things were better the way they were. For the most part, he could do what he wanted, when he wanted, with evenings and weekends entirely his own.

Friday night had been especially fun, because the Tidewater wasn't nearly as crowded as usual. Not after Abee showed up, anyway. People couldn't get out of there fast enough. He'd stayed at the bar, though, and for a while, it was downright... *pleasant*. He could talk to Candy and she actually seemed interested in what he was saying. Of course, she was flirty with all the guys, but he'd kind of gotten the sense that she liked him. He'd been hoping for more of the same on Saturday, but the place had been a zoo. The bar was packed three deep and every table was filled. He could barely hear himself think, much less talk to Candy.

But every time he'd called out an order, she'd smiled at him over the other guys' heads, and that gave him hope for tonight. Sunday nights were never crowded, and he'd been working up the courage all morning to ask her out. He wasn't sure she'd say yes, but what did he have to lose? It wasn't like she was married, right?

🌿

Three hours to the west, Frank stood on the putting green at the thirteenth hole, drinking his beer as Roger lined up for a putt. Roger had been playing well, much better than Frank. Today, Frank couldn't hit a shot to save his life. His drives were slicing, his chips were falling short, and he didn't even want to think about his putting.

He tried to remind himself that he wasn't out here to worry about his score. It was a chance to escape the office and spend time with his best friend; it was a chance to get some fresh air and relax. Unfortunately, the reminders weren't working. Everyone knew that the true joy of golf lay in hitting that wonderful shot, that long arcing drive straight down the fairway, or the chip that ended up two feet from the hole. So far, he hadn't hit a single shot that was worth remembering, and on the eighth hole he'd five-putted. *Five!* He might as well have been trying to putt the ball through the windmill and into the clown's mouth at the local putt-putt place, considering how well he'd been playing today. Even the fact that Amanda was coming home couldn't lighten his mood. The way things were going, he wasn't even sure he wanted to watch the game afterward. It wasn't like he was going to enjoy it.

He took another pull from the beer can, finishing it, thinking it was a good thing he'd packed the cooler. It was going to be a long day.

Jared loved the fact that his mom was out of town, since he could stay out as late as he wanted. The whole curfew thing was ridiculous. He was in college and people in college didn't have curfews, but apparently no one had ever informed his mom about that. When she got back from Oriental, he'd have to get her to see the light.

Not that it had been a factor this weekend. When his dad fell asleep, he was dead to the world, meaning that Jared was free to come in as late as he wanted. Friday night he'd been out until two, and last night he hadn't come in until after three. His dad had been none the wiser. Or maybe he was, but Jared had no way of knowing. By the time he'd gotten up this morning, his dad was already at the golf course with his friend Roger.

The late nights had taken their toll, though. After foraging in the fridge for something to eat, he figured he'd lie down in his room and take a nap. Sometimes there was nothing better than crashing in the middle of the afternoon. His little sister was off at camp, Lynn was up at Lake Norman, and both his parents were gone. In other words, it was quiet in the house, or at least as quiet as it ever was around here during the summer.

Stretching out on his bed, he debated whether to turn off his cell phone. On the one hand, he didn't want to be disturbed, but on the other hand, Melody might call. They'd gone out on Friday night, then gone to a party together last night, and though they hadn't been dating long, he liked her. Actually, he liked her a lot.

He left the phone on and crawled into bed. Within minutes, Jared was asleep.

❦

As soon as Ted woke, he felt a flash of pain in his head, and though the images were fragmented they slowly began to come together. Dawson, his broken nose, the hospital. His arm in a cast. Last night, waiting out in the rain while Dawson had kept his distance, playing him...

Dawson. Playing. Him.

He sat up gingerly, his head pounding as his stomach did a flip-flop. He winced, but even that hurt, and when he touched his face the pain was excruciating. His nose was the size of a potato, and nausea washed over him in waves. He wondered if he could make it to the bathroom to take a leak.

Ted thought again about the tire iron smashing into his face, he thought again about the miserable night he'd spent in the rain, and he felt his anger begin to rise. From the kitchen, he heard the baby wail, the high-pitched whine rising above the blare of the television. He squinted, trying and failing to block out the sounds, then finally staggered from the bed.

His vision went black at the corners; he reached toward the wall to keep from falling over. He drew a deep breath, gritting his teeth as the baby continued to cry, wondering why the hell Ella didn't shut the damn kid up. And why the TV was so damn loud.

He stumbled on the way to the bathroom, but when he raised the cast too quickly to catch himself on the way out, it felt like his arm had been attached to an electric wire. At his scream, the bedroom door burst open behind him. The baby's cries were like a knife blade between his ears, and when he turned, he saw two Ellas and two babies.

"Do something about the kid, or I will," he snarled. "And shut off the damn TV!"

Ella backed out of the room. Turning around, Ted closed one eye, trying to find his Glock. His double vision slowly subsided, and he spotted the gun on the bed stand, next to his truck keys. It took two attempts to grab it. Dawson had gotten the better of him all weekend, but it was time for it to end.

Ella was staring at him as he stepped out of the bedroom, her eyes as big as saucers. She'd gotten the baby to stop crying but had forgotten about the TV. The sound pounded into his skull. Lurching into the small living room, he kicked the TV over, sending it crashing to the floor. The three-year-old began to scream and Ella and the baby started wailing. By the time he stepped outside, his stomach had begun to roil and nausea came in waves.

He bent over and vomited off the edge of the porch. He wiped his mouth before shoving his gun in his pocket. Gripping the railing, he carefully descended the steps. The truck was blurry now, but he made his way toward its outline.

Dawson wasn't going to get away. Not this time.

🌿

Abee was standing at the window of his house while Ted staggered toward the truck. He knew exactly where Ted was going, even if he was taking the long way to reach the truck. Veering left and right, Ted seemed unable to walk a straight line.

As miserable as he'd felt last night, Abee had woken up feeling better than he had in days. The veterinary drugs must have worked, because his fever was gone, and though the gash in his gut was still tender to the touch, it wasn't quite as red as it had been yesterday.

Not that he was feeling a hundred percent. Far from it. But he was doing a whole lot better than Ted, that's for sure, and the last thing he wanted was for the rest of the family to see the shape Ted was in. He'd already heard some talk around the property about how Dawson had gotten the better of Ted *again*, and that wasn't good. Because it might mean they were wondering whether they could get the better of him, too, and that was the last thing he needed right now.

Someone needed to nip that problem in the bud. Opening the door, Abee started toward his brother.

17

After rinsing the rain-washed grime from the Stingray, Dawson set down the hose and walked to the creek behind Tuck's house. The afternoon had grown warm, too warm for the mullets to jump, and the creek had taken on the lifeless quality of glass. There was no movement at all, and Dawson found himself remembering those final moments with Amanda.

As she'd pulled away, it had been all he could do not to chase after her and try one more time to convince her to change her mind. He wanted to tell her again how much he loved her. Instead, he'd watched her go, knowing in his heart that this was the last time he'd see her, and wondering how on earth he'd let her slip away again.

He shouldn't have come back home. He didn't belong here, he'd never belonged here. There was nothing here for him, and it was time to leave. As it was, he knew he'd been pressing his luck with his cousins by staying as long as he had. Turning around, he walked along the side of the house, toward his car. He had one last stop to make in town, but after that, he'd leave Oriental behind forever.

Amanda wasn't sure how long she stayed in the room upstairs. An hour or two, maybe more. Whenever she peered out the window, she could see her mother sitting on the porch below, a book open in her lap. Her mother had placed covers over the food to keep the flies away. Never once had her mother risen to check on Amanda since she'd gotten back home, nor had Amanda expected her to. They knew each other well enough to know that Amanda would come down when she was ready.

Frank had called earlier from the golf course. He kept the conversation short, but she could already hear the booze in his voice. Ten years had taught her to recognize the signs instantly. Although she hadn't been inclined to talk, he hadn't noticed. Not because he was drunk, which he obviously was, but because despite a horrible start to his game, he'd finished with four straight pars. Perhaps for the first time ever, she was actually glad he was drinking. She knew he'd be so tired by the time she got home that he'd probably fall asleep long before she went to bed. The last thing she wanted was for him to be thinking about sex. She just couldn't handle something like that tonight.

Still, she wasn't ready to go downstairs. Rising from the bed, she went instead to the bathroom and rummaged through the medicine cabinet, finding a bottle of Visine. She blinked a few drops into her red, swollen eyes, then ran a brush through her hair. It didn't help much and she didn't really care, and she knew Frank wouldn't notice.

But Dawson would have noticed. And with Dawson, she would have cared how she looked.

She thought of him again, as she'd been doing since she'd returned to the house, trying to keep her emotions in check. Glancing toward the bags she'd packed earlier, she spotted the corner of an envelope sticking out from her purse. She pulled it out, catching sight of her name scrawled in Tuck's shaky script. Taking a seat on the bed again, she broke the seal and lifted the letter out thinking, strangely, that Tuck had the answers she needed.

Dear Amanda,

By the time you read this, you'll probably be facing some of the hardest choices of your life, and no doubt it will feel like your world is falling apart.

If you're wondering how I know, let's just say that I've come to know you pretty well over the last few years. I've always worried about you, Amanda. But that's not what this letter is about. I can't tell you what to do, and I doubt if there's anything I can say that'll make you feel any better. Instead, I want to tell you a story. It's about me and Clara, and it's one that you don't know, because I could never find the right way to tell you. I was ashamed, and I think I was afraid that you'd stop coming back to see me, because you might think I'd been lying to you all along.

Clara wasn't a ghost. Oh, I saw her all right, and I heard her, too. I'm not saying those things didn't happen, because they did. Everything in the letter I wrote to you and Dawson was true. I saw her that day when I came back from the cottage, and the more I tended the flowers, the more plainly I could see her. Love can conjure up many things, but deep down, I knew that she wasn't really there. I saw her because I wanted to, I heard her because I missed her. I guess what I'm really trying to say is that she was my creation, nothing more, even if I wanted to fool myself into thinking otherwise.

You might wonder why I'm telling you this now, so I might as well get to it. I married Clara at seventeen, and we spent forty-two years together, fusing our lives, ourselves, into what I thought was a whole that couldn't ever be broken. When she died, the next twenty-eight years pained me so much that most folks—including me—thought I'd plumb lost my mind.

Amanda, you're still young. You may not feel it, but to me, you're just a child with a long life yet to come. Listen to me when I say this: I lived with the real Clara, and I lived with Clara's

*ghost, and of the two, one filled me with joy while the other was
only a dim reflection. If you turn away from Dawson now,
you'll live forever with the ghost of what might have been yours.
I know that in this life, innocent people inevitably get hurt by
the decisions we make. Call me a selfish old man, but I never
wanted you to be one of them.*

Tuck

Amanda put the letter back into her purse, knowing Tuck was
right. She could feel the truth as deeply as she'd ever felt anything, and she could barely breathe.

With a feeling of desperate urgency she didn't quite comprehend, she gathered her bags and carried them down the stairs.
Normally, she would have placed them near the door until
she was ready to leave. Instead, she found herself reaching for the
knob and making her way directly to her car.

She tossed her bags into the trunk before moving around the
car. Only then did she notice her mother standing on the front
porch, watching her.

Amanda said nothing, nor did her mother. They simply stared
at each other. Amanda had the uncanny feeling that her mother
knew exactly where she was going, but with Tuck's words still
ringing in her ears, Amanda was beyond caring. All she knew
was that she needed to find Dawson.

Dawson might still be at Tuck's, but she doubted it. It wouldn't
have taken him long to wash the car, and with his cousins on the
loose she knew that he wouldn't stay in town.

But there was someplace else he said he might go . . .

The words came into her mind suddenly, without conscious
thought, and she slipped behind the wheel, knowing exactly
where he might be.

🌿

At the cemetery, Dawson stepped out of the car and made the short walk toward David Bonner's headstone.

In the past, whenever he visited the cemetery, he came at odd hours and did his best to remain unnoticed and anonymous.

Today, that wouldn't be possible. Weekends tended to be busy, and there were clusters of people walking among the headstones. No one appeared to pay any attention to him as he walked, but he kept his head bowed nonetheless.

Finally reaching the site, he noticed that the flowers he'd left on Friday morning were still there, but they'd been moved to the side. Probably by the caretaker when he'd mowed. Squatting, Dawson plucked at a few of the longer blades of grass near the headstone that had been missed.

His thoughts drifted back to Amanda, and he was gripped by a sense of intense loneliness. His life, he knew, had been cursed from the beginning, and closing his eyes, he said a final prayer for David Bonner, unaware that his shadow had just been joined by another. Unaware that someone was standing right behind him.

Reaching the main street that ran through Oriental, Amanda stopped at the intersection. A left turn would bring her past the marina and eventually to Tuck's. A right turn would lead her out of town, eventually becoming the rural highway she'd follow on her way back home. Straight ahead, beyond a wrought-iron fence, was the cemetery. It was the largest in Oriental, the place where Dr. David Bonner had been laid to rest. Dawson, she remembered, had said he might drop by on his way out of town.

The gates to the cemetery were open. She scanned the half-dozen cars and trucks in the parking lot, searching for his rental car, and her breath caught when she spotted it. Three days ago, he'd parked it beside hers when he'd arrived at Tuck's. Earlier that morning, she'd stood beside it as he'd kissed her one last time.

Dawson was here.

We're still young, he'd told her. *We still have time to make this right.*

Her foot was on the brake. On the main road, a minivan rumbled past, momentarily obscuring her view, heading toward downtown. The road was otherwise deserted.

If she crossed the road and parked, she knew she'd be able to find him. She thought of Tuck's letter, the years of grief he had endured without Clara, and Amanda knew she'd made the wrong decision. She couldn't imagine a life without Dawson.

In her mind's eye, she could see the scene unfold. She would surprise Dawson at Dr. Bonner's grave and could hear herself saying that she'd been wrong to leave. She could feel her happiness as he took her in his arms once more, knowing they were meant to be together.

If she went to him again, she knew she'd follow him anywhere. Or he'd follow her. But even then, her responsibilities continued to press down on her, and ever so slowly, she removed her foot from the brake. Instead of going straight, she found herself suddenly turning the wheel, a sob catching in her chest as she headed onto the main road, the car pointing toward home.

She began to speed up, trying again to convince herself that her decision was the correct one, the only one she could realistically make. Behind her, the cemetery receded into the distance.

"Dawson, forgive me," she whispered, wishing he could somehow hear her, wishing she'd never had to say those words at all.

🌿

A rustling behind him interrupted Dawson's reverie, and he scrambled to his feet. Startled, he recognized her instantly but found himself speechless.

"You're here," Marilyn Bonner stated. "At my husband's grave."

"I'm sorry," he said, dropping his gaze. "I shouldn't have come."

"But you did," Marilyn said. "And you came here recently, too." When Dawson didn't respond, she nodded at the flowers. "I make it a point to come by after church. They weren't here last weekend, and they're too fresh to have been placed here earlier in the week. I'm guessing...Friday?"

Dawson swallowed before answering. "In the morning."

Her gaze was unflinching. "You used to do that a long time ago, too. After you got out of prison? That was you, right?"

Dawson said nothing.

"I thought so," she said. She sighed as she took a step closer to the marker. Dawson moved aside, making room as Marilyn focused on the inscription. "A lot of people put flowers out for David after he died. And that went on for a year or two, but after that, people stopped coming by, I guess. Except for me. For a while, I was the only one bringing them, and then, about four years after he died, I started seeing other flowers again. Not all the time, but enough to make me curious. I had no idea who was responsible. I asked my parents, I asked my friends, but none of them would admit to it. For a short time, I even wondered if David had been seeing someone else. Can you believe that?" She shook her head and drew a long breath. "It wasn't until the flowers stopped arriving that I realized it was you. I knew you'd gotten out of jail and that you were on probation here. I also learned that you left town about a year later. It made me so...*angry* to think you'd been doing that all along." She crossed her arms, as if trying to close herself off from the memory. "And then, this morning, I saw the flowers again. I knew it meant that you'd come back. I wasn't sure you'd come here today...but sure enough, you did."

Dawson shoved his hands in his pockets, suddenly wanting to be anywhere but here. "I won't visit or bring flowers again," he muttered. "You have my word."

She looked at him. "And you think that makes it okay that you've come here at all? Considering what you did in the first place? Considering that my husband is here, instead of with me? That he missed the chance to watch his children grow up?"

"No," he said.

"Of course you don't," she said. "Because you still feel guilty about what you did. That's why you've been sending us money all these years, am I right?"

He wanted to lie to her but couldn't.

"How long have you known?" he asked.

"Since the first check," she said. "You'd stopped by my house just a couple of weeks earlier, remember? It wasn't too hard to put two and two together." She hesitated. "You wanted to apologize, didn't you? In person. When you came to the porch that day?"

"Yes."

"I didn't let you. I said...a lot of things that day. Things that maybe I shouldn't have said."

"You had every right to say what you did."

A flicker of a smile formed on her lips. "You were twenty-two years old. I saw a grown man on the porch, but the older I've gotten, the more I've come to believe that people don't really grow up until they're at least thirty. My son is older than you were then, and I still think of him as a child."

"You did what anyone would do."

"Maybe," she said, offering the slightest of shrugs. She stepped closer to him. "The money you sent helped," she said. "It helped a lot over the years, but I don't need your money anymore. So please stop sending it."

"I just wanted—"

"I know what you wanted," she interrupted. "But all the money in the world can't bring David back, or undo the loss I felt after he died. And it can't give my children the father they never knew."

"I know."

"And money can't buy forgiveness."

Dawson felt his shoulders sag. "I should go," he said, turning to leave.

"Yes," she said. "Yes, you probably should. But before you leave, there's something else you should know."

When he turned, she willed him to meet her eyes. "I know that what happened was an accident. I've always known that. And I know you'd do anything to change the past. Everything you've done since then makes that clear. And yes, I'll admit that I was angry and frightened and lonely when you came to my house, but I never, ever believed there was anything malicious about your actions that night. It was just one of those awful, terrible things that happen sometimes, and when you came by, I took it out on you." She let the words sink in, and when she went on, her voice was almost kind. "I'm fine now, and my kids are fine, too. We've survived. We're okay."

When Dawson turned away, she waited until he finally faced her again.

"I came here to tell you that you don't need my forgiveness anymore," she said, drawing out the words. "But I also know that's not what any of this has ever been about. It's never been about me, or my family. It's about you. It's always been about you. You've been clinging to a terrible mistake for too long, and if you were my son, I'd tell you that it was time you finally let this go. So let it go, Dawson," she said. "Do that for me."

She stared at him, making sure he understood her, then turned and walked away. Dawson remained frozen as her figure receded, winding through the sentinel gravestones until she eventually vanished from sight.

18

---- 🌿 ----

Amanda drove on autopilot, oblivious to the crawling weekend traffic. Families in minivans and SUVs, some towing boats, thronged the highway after spending the weekend at the beach.

As she drove, she couldn't imagine going home and having to pretend that the past few days hadn't happened. She understood that she could tell no one about them, yet, strangely, she felt no guilt about the weekend, either. If anything, she felt regret, and she found herself wishing that she had done things differently. Had she known from the beginning how their weekend would end, she would have stayed longer with Dawson on their first night together, and she wouldn't have turned away when she'd suspected that he was going to kiss her. She would have seen him Friday night as well, no matter how many lies she had to tell her mother, and she would give anything to have spent all of Saturday wrapped in his arms. After all, had she given in to her feelings sooner, Saturday night might have had a different ending. Perhaps the barriers, the ones that came with her marriage vows, would have been overridden. And they almost were. As they'd danced in the living room, letting him make love to her was all she could think about; as they'd kissed, she'd known exactly what would happen. She wanted him, in the way they'd once been together.

She'd believed she could go through with it; she'd believed that once they reached the bedroom, she would be able to pretend that her life in Durham no longer existed, if only for a night. Even as he undressed her and carried her to the bed, she thought she could set aside the reality of her marriage. But as much as she wanted to be someone else that night, someone free of responsibilities and untenable promises, as much as she wanted Dawson, she knew she was about to cross a line from which there would be no return. Despite the urgency of his touch and the feel of his body against hers, she couldn't give herself over to her feelings.

Dawson hadn't become angry; instead, he held her against him, his fingers moving through her hair. He kissed her cheek and whispered assurances; that this wasn't important, that nothing would ever change the way he felt about her.

They stayed that way until the sky began to lighten and exhaustion settled in; in the early predawn hours, she finally fell asleep, cradled in his arms. When she woke the following morning, her first thought was to reach for Dawson. But by then, Dawson was already gone.

At the bar in the country club, long after they'd finished their round of golf, Frank signaled to the bartender for another beer, unaware of the inquiring glance the bartender shot at Roger. Roger just shrugged, having switched to Diet Coke himself. The bartender reluctantly put another bottle in front of Frank as Roger leaned closer, trying to make himself heard above the noise in the crowded bar. Over the past hour, it had become packed. The game was tied at the top of the ninth inning.

"You do remember that I'm meeting Susan for dinner, so I'm not going to be able to drive you home. And you can't drive, either."

"Yeah, I know."

"Do you want me to call you a cab?"

"Let's just enjoy the game. We'll figure it out later, okay?" Frank raised the bottle and took another drink, his glassy eyes never leaving the screen.

Abee sat in the chair beside his brother's bed, wondering again why Ted lived in a crap hole like this. The place reeked, some disgusting combination of soiled diapers and mold and God knows what else had died around here. Combined with the baby that never stopped crying and Ella skittering around the house like a frightened ghost, it was a wonder that Ted wasn't even crazier than he already was.

He wasn't even sure why he was still here. Ted had been unconscious for most of the afternoon, ever since he'd collapsed on the way to his truck. Ella was already screaming about taking him back to the hospital by the time Abee scooped him up and brought him inside.

If Ted took a turn for the worse, he might just do that, but there wasn't much the doctors could do. Ted just needed his rest, same as he could get in the hospital. He had a concussion and should have taken it easy last night, but he hadn't and now he was paying the price.

Thing was, Abee didn't want to spend another night sitting with his brother in the hospital, not when he was feeling better himself. Hell, he didn't even want to be here with Ted, but he had a business to run, a business that depended on the threat of violence, and Ted was a big part of that. It was lucky that the rest of the family hadn't seen what happened, and that he'd been able to get him back inside before anyone noticed.

Christ, it stank in here—like a damn sewer—and the late afternoon heat only intensified the smell. Pulling out his cell phone, he cycled through his contacts, finding Candy, and hit send. He'd called her earlier but she hadn't answered, nor had she returned his call. He wasn't happy about being ignored like that. Not happy at all.

But for the second time that day, Candy's phone just rang and rang.

❦

"What the hell's going on?" Ted suddenly croaked out. His voice was gravelly and his head felt like it had been subjected to a jack-hammer.

"You're in bed," Abee said.

"What the hell happened?"

"You didn't make it to the truck and ended up eating a pile of dirt. I dragged you in here."

Ted slowly raised himself into a sitting position. He waited for the spinning and it came, but not as violently as it had that morning. He wiped his nose. "You find Dawson?"

"I didn't go huntin' for him. I've been watching over your sorry ass all afternoon."

Ted spat onto the floor, near a pile of dirty clothes. "He might still be around."

"He might. But I doubt it. He probably knows you're after him. If he's smart, he's long gone by now."

"Yeah, well, maybe he ain't so smart." Leaning heavily on the bedpost, Ted finally stood, tucking the Glock into his waistband. "You're driving."

Abee had known Ted wouldn't let things drop. But maybe it would be good for his kin to know that Ted was up and around and ready to take care of business. "And if he ain't there?"

"Then he ain't there. But I gotta know."

Abee stared at him, preoccupied with the unanswered phone calls and Candy's whereabouts. Thinking about the guy he'd seen flirting with her at the Tidewater. "All right," he said. "But after that, I might just need you to do something for me, too."

Candy held the phone as she sat in the parking lot of the Tide-water. Two calls from Abee. Two unanswered and so far unre-turned calls. The sight of them made her nervous, and she knew she should call him back. Just do a little purring and say all the right things, but then he might get it into his head to come and visit her while she was at work, and that was the last thing she wanted. He'd probably notice her packed car in the parking lot, figure out that she was planning on clearing out, and who knew what that psycho would do.

She should have packed up later, after work, and left from home. But she hadn't been thinking, and her shift was about to start. And while she could cover maybe a week in a motel and the food, she really needed tonight's tips for gas.

There was no way she could park out front—not where Abee could see the car. Slipping into reverse, she pulled out of the lot and rounded the highway curve, back toward downtown Orien-tal. Behind one of the antiques stores at the edge of town was a small lot, and there she turned in and parked out of sight. Better. Even if that did mean she had to walk a bit.

But what if Abee showed up and *didn't* see her car? That might be a problem, too. She didn't want him asking too many ques-tions. She thought about it, deciding that if he called again she'd answer and maybe mention in an offhand way that she'd had car trouble and had been dealing with that all day. It was trouble-some, but she tried to console herself with the fact that she had only five hours to go. By tonight, she'd be able to put this whole thing behind her.

Jared was still sleeping at quarter past five, when his cell phone began to ring. Rolling over, he reached for it, wondering why his dad was calling.

Except it wasn't his dad. It was his dad's golf buddy, Roger, asking him to come and pick up his dad at the country club. Because his dad had been drinking and shouldn't be driving.

Gee, really? he thought. *My dad? Drinking?*

Jared didn't say that, even if he'd wanted to. Instead, he promised to be there in about twenty minutes. Getting out of bed, he threw on the shorts and T-shirt he'd been wearing earlier, then slid into his flip-flops. He collected his keys and wallet from the bureau. Yawning, he descended the steps, already thinking about calling Melody.

Abee didn't bother to hide the truck on the road outside Tuck's and hike through the woods like he'd done the night before. Instead, he sped up the uneven drive and came to a gravel-spraying halt directly in front of the house, driving like a SWAT team leader on a mission. He was out of the truck with his gun drawn before Ted, but his brother clambered out of the truck with surprising agility, especially considering the way he looked. The bruises beneath his eyes had already turned blackish purple. The guy was a human raccoon.

No one was around, just like Abee had expected. The house was deserted, and there was no sign of Dawson in the garage, either. His cousin certainly was a slippery bastard. It was a shame he hadn't stuck around all these years. Abee could have found good use for him, even if Ted would have had a fit.

Ted wasn't all that surprised that Dawson was gone, either, but that didn't mean he was any less angry about it. Abee could see Ted's jaw muscles clenching in sporadic rhythm, his finger stroking the Glock trigger. After a minute of seething in the driveway, he marched toward Tuck's house and kicked in the door.

Abee leaned against the truck, deciding to let him be. He could hear Ted cursing and shouting and tossing crap around inside the house. While Ted was throwing his tantrum, an old chair came crashing through the window, the glass exploding into a thousand shards. Ted finally appeared in the doorway but barely broke stride, walking furiously toward the old garage.

A classic Stingray was housed inside. It hadn't been there last night, another indication that Dawson had come and gone. Abee wasn't sure whether Ted had figured that out yet, but he supposed it didn't matter. Let Ted get this fit out of his system. The sooner it passed, the sooner things would return to normal around here. He needed Ted to start focusing less on what he wanted and more on what Abee told him to do.

He watched as Ted grabbed a tire iron from the workbench. Heaving it high above his head, he brought the tire iron down on the front windshield of the car with a scream. Then he began hammering the hood, denting it immediately. He smashed the tire iron into the headlights and knocked off the mirrors, but he was just getting started.

For the next fifteen minutes, Ted tore the car apart, using every tool at his disposal. The engine, the tires, the upholstery, and the dashboard were crushed and slashed to pieces, Ted venting his fury at Dawson with manic intensity.

A shame, Abee reflected. The car was a beauty, a serious classic. But the car wasn't his, and it made Ted feel better, so Abee supposed it was for the best.

When Ted was finally finished, he started back toward Abee. He was less wobbly on his feet than Abee expected and was breathing hard, his eyes still a little wild. It occurred to him that Ted might just point the gun and shoot him out of sheer rage.

But Abee hadn't become head of the family by backing down, even when his brother was at his worst. He continued to lean against the truck with studied nonchalance as Ted approached. Abee picked at his teeth. He examined his finger when he was done, knowing Ted was right there.

"You done?"

Dawson was on the dock behind the hotel in New Bern, boats in the slips on either side of him. He'd driven here straight from the cemetery, sitting at the water's edge as the sun began its descent.

It was the fourth place he'd stayed in the last four days and the weekend had left him both physically exhausted and emotionally spent. Try as he might, he couldn't envision his future. Tomorrow, and the day after that, and the endless stretch of weeks and years seemed to hold no purpose at all. He'd lived a specific life for specific reasons, and now those reasons were gone. Amanda, and now Marilyn Bonner, had released him forever; Tuck was dead. What should he do next? Move? Stay where he was? Keep his job? Try something new? What was his purpose now that the compass points of his life were gone?

He knew he wouldn't find the answers here. Rising from his spot, he trudged back to the lobby. He had an early flight on Monday and knew he'd be up long before the sun so he could drop off the rental car and check in. According to his itinerary, he'd be back in New Orleans before noon, and home not long after that.

When he reached his room, he lay down on his bed fully clothed, as adrift as he'd ever been in his life and reliving the feel of Amanda's lips against his. *She might need time*, Tuck had written, and before slipping into a fitful sleep he clung to the hope that Tuck was somehow right.

Stopped at a red light, Jared regarded his dad in the rearview mirror. He must have been trying to pickle himself, Jared decided. When he'd pulled up to the country club a few minutes earlier, his dad had been leaning against one of the columns, his eyes bleary and unfocused, and his breath alone could have fueled the gas grill in the backyard. Which was probably the reason he wasn't talking. No doubt he wanted to hide how drunk he actually was.

Jared had gotten used to these kinds of situations. He wasn't as angry about his dad's problem as he was sad. His mom would end up in one of her moods, though—trying to act completely normal while her husband lurched around the house dead drunk. It wasn't worth the energy to get angry, but he knew that beneath the surface, she'd be boiling. She'd do her best to keep her tone civil, but no matter where his dad ended up sitting, she'd settle herself in a different room, like that was a perfectly ordinary thing for couples to do.

Things weren't going to be pretty tonight, but he'd let Lynn deal with that, assuming she got home before his dad passed out. As for him, he'd already called Melody and they were going over to a friend's to go swimming.

The stoplight finally turned green, and Jared, preoccupied by the image of Melody in a bikini, pressed down on the accelerator, unaware that another car was still speeding through the intersection.

The car slammed into his with an ear-shattering crash, spraying glass and metal shards everywhere. Part of the door frame, mangled and bent, exploded inward toward his chest in the same instant that the air bag inflated. Jared jerked against the restraints of the seat belt, his head whipping around as the car began to spin through the intersection. *I'm going to die*, he thought, but he couldn't draw enough breath to make a sound.

When the car finally stopped moving, it took a moment for Jared to understand he was still breathing. His chest hurt, he could barely move his neck, and he thought he was going to choke on the overwhelming odor of gunpowder from the air bag's deployment.

He tried to move but was hit with searing pain in his chest. The door frame and steering wheel were wedged against him and he struggled to free himself. Squirming to the right, he was suddenly released from the weight pressing down on him.

Outside, he caught sight of other cars that had stopped in the intersection. People were getting out, some of them already calling 911 on their cell phones. Through the jagged web of glass, he noticed that the hood of his car was pitched like a small tent.

As if from a great distance, he heard people shouting at him not to move. He turned his head anyway, thinking suddenly of his dad, and saw the mask of blood covering his father's face. Only then did he begin to scream.

❧

Amanda was an hour from home when her cell phone rang. Reaching over to the passenger seat, she had to dig through her purse to find it, finally answering on the third ring.

As she listened to Jared's shaky account, an icy paralysis gripped her. In a disjointed fashion, he told her about the ambulance at the scene, about all the blood on Frank. He himself was fine, he reassured her, but they were making him get into the ambulance along with Frank. He told her that both of them were being taken to Duke University Hospital.

Amanda clenched the phone. For the first time since Bea's illness, she felt a gut-wrenching fear take root. Real fear, the kind that left no room to think or feel anything else.

"I'm coming," she said. "I'll be there as quick as I can—"

But then, for some reason, the call was cut off. She redialed immediately, but there was no answer.

Veering into the opposite lane, she floored the gas pedal and passed the car in front of her, flashing her lights. She had to get to the hospital *right away*. But the beach traffic had yet to thin.

❧

After their little excursion to Tuck's, Abee realized he was starving. Since the infection, he hadn't had much of an appetite, but now it was back with a vengeance, another sign of how well the antibiotics were working. At Irvin's he ended up ordering a cheeseburger, along with a side of onion rings and chili-cheese fries. Though he wasn't finished yet, he knew he'd end up cleaning every plate. He figured he'd even have room for a piece of pie and a scoop of ice cream later.

Ted, on the other hand, wasn't doing so well. He, too, had ordered the cheeseburger, but he was taking small bites and chewing slowly. Smashing up the car had apparently used up the last bit of strength he had.

While they'd been waiting for their food, Abee had called Candy. This time, she'd answered on the first ring and they'd talked for a little while. She told him she was already at work and apologized for not returning his calls, mentioning that she'd had car trouble. On the phone, she sounded like she was glad to hear from him, flirting just the way she always had. When he hung up, he felt a lot better about the situation and even wondered if he'd been reading too much into what he'd seen the other night.

Maybe it was the food or his general recovery, but as he continued to work through his burger, he found himself thinking back on the conversation again, trying to figure out what was bothering him about it. Because something *was* bothering him about the call. Part of it was that Candy had said she was having *car* trouble, not *phone* trouble, and busy or not, she probably could have called him back if she'd wanted to. But he wasn't sure that was it.

Ted got up halfway through the meal and spent some time in the bathroom before coming back. As Ted walked toward the table, Abee thought his brother could have been in the cast of some cheap horror flick, but others in the restaurant were doing their best not to notice, staring at their plates instead. He smiled. It was good to be a Cole.

Still, he couldn't stop thinking about his conversation with Candy, and he sucked on his fingers between bites, pondering it.

Frank and Jared had been in an accident.

The words scrolled through her mind like some terrible ticker tape, making Amanda more frantic with every passing minute. Her grip on the wheel was white-knuckled as she flashed her lights again, then again, willing the car in front of her to allow her to pass.

They'd been taken away in an ambulance. Jared and Frank were being rushed to the hospital. Her husband and her son . . .

Finally, the car ahead of her changed lanes and Amanda roared past it, quickly closing the gap to the cars that were farther ahead.

She reminded herself that Jared had sounded shaken, nothing more.

But the blood . . .

Jared had mentioned in a panicky voice that Frank was covered in blood. Clutching the phone, she tried to call her son again. He hadn't answered a few minutes ago, and she told herself that it was because he was in the ambulance or in the emergency room, where phones were forbidden. She reminded herself that paramedics or doctors or nurses were caring for Frank and Jared now, and that when Jared finally answered, she'd no doubt regret her needless panic. In the future, it would be a story to be told around the dinner table, about how Mom drove like a bat out of hell, for no reason at all.

But Jared didn't answer again, and neither did Frank. When both calls went to voice mail, she felt the pit in her stomach become a wide and bottomless chasm. She was suddenly certain that the car accident was serious, far worse than Jared had let on. She wasn't sure how she knew, but the idea wouldn't leave her.

She dropped her phone on the passenger seat and slammed her foot down on the accelerator, racing up to within inches of the car in front of her. Whoever was driving finally made room, and she blew past without a sidelong nod.

19

In the dream, Dawson was back on the rig, just as the series of explosions began to rock the platform, but this time everything was silent and the events unfolded in slow motion. He watched the sudden rupture of the storage tank, followed by flames that leapt outward and skyward; he traced the blackened smoke as it formed into sluggish, mushroomlike shapes. He saw the shimmery ripple of shock waves move across the deck, unhurriedly felling everything in its path, tearing posts and machinery from their housings. Men were hurled overboard as other explosions followed, every twitch of their arms plainly visible. The fire began to consume the deck in a ponderous, dreamlike way. All around him, everything was slowly being destroyed.

But he remained rooted in place, immune to the shock waves and the flying debris that magically veered around him. Straight ahead, near the crane, he saw a man emerge from an oily cloud of smoke, but like Dawson, he was immune to the ongoing devastation. For an instant, the smoke seemed to cling to him before being pulled away like a curtain. Dawson gasped as he glimpsed the dark-haired man in the blue windbreaker.

The stranger stopped moving, his features indistinct through the shimmering distance. Dawson wanted to call out to him, but no sound came to his lips; he wanted to get closer, but his feet seemed glued in place. Instead, they simply stared at each other across the rig, and despite the distance Dawson thought he felt the beginnings of recognition.

Dawson woke up then, blinking at his surroundings as adrenaline surged through his system. He was in the hotel in New Bern, right on the river, and though he knew it had been only a dream, he felt a chill run through him. Sitting up, he swung his feet toward the floor.

The clock showed that he'd slept for over an hour. Outside, the sun was almost down and the colors in his hotel room were muted.

Dreamlike . . .

Dawson stood and glanced around, spotting his wallet and keys near the TV. Seeing them jogged his memory about something else, and striding across the room he riffled through the pockets of the suit he'd been wearing. He checked them again to make sure he wasn't mistaken, then quickly rummaged through his bag. Finally, he grabbed his wallet and keys and hurried downstairs to the parking lot.

He searched every inch of the rental car, working methodically through the glove compartment, the trunk, between the seats, the floor. But he was already beginning to recall what had happened earlier that day.

He'd set Tuck's letter on the workbench after reading it. Amanda's mother had walked by and he'd turned his attention to Amanda on the porch, *and he'd forgotten to retrieve the letter.*

It must still be on the workbench. He could leave it, of course . . . except that he couldn't imagine doing that. It was the last letter that Tuck had written to him, his final gift, and Dawson wanted to take it home.

He knew that Ted and Abee would be scouring the town to find him, but nonetheless he found himself driving across the bridge, on his way back to Oriental. He'd be there in forty minutes.

After taking a deep breath to steel himself, Alan Bonner entered the Tidewater, noting an even smaller crowd than he'd expected. There were a couple of guys at the bar and a few toward the rear playing pool; only one of the tables was occupied, by a couple that was counting out cash and appeared to be leaving any minute. Nothing like Saturday night, or even Friday night for that matter. With the jukebox playing in the back and the television near the cash register on, the place seemed almost cozy.

Candy was wiping down the bar, and she smiled at him before waving with the towel. She was dressed in jeans and a T-shirt, with her hair in a ponytail, and though she wasn't quite as dolled up as usual, she was still prettier than anyone else in town. The butterflies in his stomach began to flutter as he wondered whether she'd agree to have dinner with him.

He stood straighter, thinking, *No excuses.* He'd take a seat at the bar, just be his normal self, and gradually work the conversation to the point where he could ask her out. He reminded himself that she'd definitely been flirting with him, and while she might be a flirt by nature, he was sure there'd been more to it than that. He could tell. He *knew* it, and with a deep breath, he started toward the bar.

Amanda burst through the door of Duke University Hospital's emergency room, staring wildly at the crowd of patients and families. She'd continued to call Jared and Frank over and over, but neither of them had answered. Finally, she'd phoned Lynn in frantic desperation. Her daughter was still at Lake Norman, a few hours away. Lynn had broken down at the news and promised to be there as quickly as she could.

Standing inside the doorway, Amanda scanned the room, hoping to find Jared. She prayed that her worries had been for nothing. Then, to her bewilderment, she spotted Frank at the far end of the room. He stood and began walking toward her, appearing less injured than she'd assumed he would be. She peered over his shoulder, trying to locate her son. But Jared was nowhere to be seen.

"Where's Jared?" she demanded when Frank reached her side. "Are you okay? What happened? What's going on?"

She was still barking out questions when Frank took her arm and led her back outside.

"Jared's been admitted," he said. Despite the hours that had passed since he'd been at the club, his words were still slurred. She could tell he was trying to sound sober, but the sour smell of booze saturated his breath and his sweat. "I don't know what's going on. No one seems to know anything. But the nurse said something about a cardiologist."

His words only amplified the anxiety coursing through her. "Why? What's wrong?"

"I don't know."

"Is Jared going to be okay?"

"He seemed fine when we got here."

"Then why is he seeing a cardiologist?"

"I don't know."

"He said you were covered in blood."

Frank touched the swollen bridge of his nose, where a black-and-blue crescent surrounded a small cut. "I banged my nose pretty good, but they were able to stop the bleeding. It's no big deal. I'll be fine."

"Why didn't you answer your phone? I called a hundred times!"

"My phone is still in the car..."

But Amanda had stopped listening as the weight of everything Frank had said sank in. Jared had been admitted. Her son was the one who was hurt. Her son, not her husband. Jared. Her firstborn...

Feeling like she'd been punched in the stomach and suddenly sickened by the sight of Frank, she marched past him, heading

straight for the nurse behind the admitting desk. Doing her best
to control her rising hysteria, she demanded to know what was
going on with her son.

The nurse had few answers, repeating only what Frank had
already told her. *Drunk Frank*, she thought again, unable to stem
the tide of rage. She slapped both hands down on the desk, star-
tling everyone in the waiting room.

"I need to know what's going on with my son!" she cried. "I
want some answers *now*!"

Problems with her car, Abee thought. That's what had been bothering him about his earlier conversation with Candy. Because if
her car was having problems, then how had she gotten to work?
And why hadn't she asked him if he could drive her to work, or
back home?

Had someone else driven her? Like the guy in the Tidewater?

She wouldn't have been that stupid. Of course, he could call
her to find out, but there was a better way to get to the bottom
of this. Irvin's wasn't very far from the small house where she
lived, so he might as well swing by to check if her car was there.
Because if it was there, it meant that someone had driven her,
and then they'd definitely have something important to talk
about, wouldn't they?

He tossed a few bills onto the table and motioned for Ted to
follow. Ted hadn't talked much during the dinner, but Abee had
the sense he was doing a little better, despite his poor appetite.

"Where we going?" Ted asked.

"I want to check something out," Abee answered.

Candy's place was located just a few minutes away, toward the
end of a sparsely inhabited street. The house was a ramshackle
bungalow, fronted with aluminum siding and hemmed in by
overgrown bushes. It wasn't much, but Candy didn't seem to care,
and she hadn't done much to make it any homier.

As Abee pulled into the drive, he saw that her car was missing. Maybe she'd got it working, he reasoned, but while he sat in the truck and stared at the house, he noticed that something wasn't quite right. Something was missing, so to speak, and it took a few minutes before he figured out what it was.

The Buddha statue was missing, the one she kept in the front window, framed by a gap in the bushes. Her good luck charm, she'd called it, and there was no reason she should have moved it. Unless...

He opened the door of the truck and got out. When Ted glanced over at him, he shook his head. "I'll be back in a minute."

Abee pushed past the overgrown bushes and climbed onto the porch. Peering through the front window, he saw that the statue was definitely gone. The rest of the place looked the same. Of course, that didn't mean much, since he knew it had come furnished. But the missing Buddha bothered him.

Abee worked his way around the house, peering in the windows, though curtains blocked most of the views. He couldn't make out much.

Finally tiring of his efforts, he simply kicked in the back door, just like Ted had done at Tuck's house.

He stepped inside, wondering what the hell Candy might be up to.

*

Just as she had every fifteen minutes since she'd arrived, Amanda approached the nurses' station to ask if they had any further information. The nurse responded patiently that she had already given Amanda all the information she had: Jared had been admitted, he was being seen by a cardiologist, and the doctor knew they were waiting. As soon as she learned anything, Amanda would be the first to know. There was compassion in her voice as she said it, and Amanda nodded her thanks before turning away.

Even with the reality of her surroundings, she still couldn't make sense of what she was doing here or how any of this had happened. Though Frank and the nurse had tried to explain it to her, their words meant nothing in the here and now. She didn't want Frank or the nurse to tell her what was going on, she wanted to talk to *Jared*. She needed to see Jared, she needed to hear his voice to know that he was okay and when Frank had tried to put a comforting hand on her back, she'd jerked away as if scalded.

Because it was his fault that Jared was here in the first place. If he hadn't been drinking, Jared would have stayed at home, or been out with a girl, or at a friend's house. Jared would never have been anywhere near that intersection, would never have ended up in the hospital. He'd just been trying to help. He was being the responsible one.

But Frank . . .

She couldn't bear to look at him. It was all she could do not to scream at him.

The clock on the wall seemed to be keeping time in slow motion.

Finally, after an eternity, she heard the door that led to the patients' rooms swing open, and she turned to see a doctor emerge wearing surgical scrubs. She watched as he approached the duty nurse, who nodded and pointed in her direction. Amanda was paralyzed with trepidation as the doctor came toward her. She searched his face for a sign of what he might say. His expression gave nothing away.

She stood, Frank following her lead. "I'm Doctor Mills," he said, and he signaled them to follow him through a set of double doors that led to another corridor. When the doors closed behind them, Dr. Mills turned to face them. Despite the gray in his hair, she could see that he was probably younger than her.

It would take more than one conversation for her to fully absorb what he told them, but this much she grasped: Jared, while appearing fine, had been injured by the blunt impact of the smashed car door. The attending physician had detected a trauma-induced heart murmur, and they'd taken him in for evaluation. While there, Jared's condition had deteriorated markedly and rapidly. The doctor went on to mention words like *cyanosis* and told them that a transvenous pacemaker had been inserted, but that Jared's heart capacity kept diminishing. The doctor suspected that the tricuspid valve had ruptured, that her son needed valve replacement surgery. Jared was already on bypass, he explained, but they now needed permission to perform heart surgery. Without surgery, he told them bluntly, their son was going to die.

Jared was going to die.

She reached for the wall to keep from falling down as the doctor glanced from her to Frank and back again.

"I need you to sign the consent form," Dr. Mills said. In that instant, Amanda knew that he'd also smelled the booze on Frank's breath. She began to hate her husband then, truly *hate* him. Moving as though in a dream, she deliberately and carefully signed her name on the form with a hand that barely seemed her own.

Dr. Mills led them to another part of the hospital and left them in an empty waiting room. Her mind was numb with shock.

Jared needed surgery, or he would die.

He couldn't die. Jared was only nineteen years old. He had his whole life in front of him.

Closing her eyes, she sank into a chair, trying and failing to make sense of the world crumbling around her.

🌿

Candy didn't need this. Not tonight.

The young guy at the end of the bar, Alan or Alvin or whatever his name was, was practically panting to ask her out. Even worse, business was so slow tonight, she probably wouldn't make enough to fill her car with gas. Great. Just great.

"Hey, Candy?" It was the young guy again, leaning over the bar like a needy puppy. "Can I have another beer, please?"

She forced a smile as she popped the top off a bottle and walked it down to him. As she neared the end of the bar, he called out a question, but headlights suddenly flashed on the door, either from a passing car or someone pulling into the lot, and she found herself glancing toward the entrance. Waiting.

When no one came in, she heaved a sigh of relief.

"Candy?"

His voice brought him back to her. He pushed his shiny black hair off his forehead.

"I'm sorry. What?"

"I asked how your day's been going so far."

"Peachy," she answered with a sigh. "Just peachy."

❧

Frank sat in a chair across from her, still slightly swaying, his gaze unfocused. Amanda did her best to pretend he wasn't there.

Other than that, she couldn't concentrate on anything except her fear and thoughts of Jared. In the silence of the room, entire years of her son's life were magically compressed. She remembered how small he'd felt when she'd held him in her arms in his first weeks of life. She remembered combing his hair and packing a sandwich in a Jurassic Park lunch box on his first day of kindergarten. She recalled his nervousness before his first middle school dance; the way he drank milk from the carton, no matter how many times she'd asked him not to. Every now and then, she'd be startled from her memories by the sounds of the hospital and remember where she was and what was happening. And then the dread would take hold of her once again.

Before he'd left, the doctor had told them the surgery might take hours, might even last until midnight, but she wondered whether someone would give them an update before then. She wanted to know what was happening. She wanted someone to explain it to her in a way she'd understand, but what she really wanted was for someone to hold her and promise that her little boy—even if he was now almost a man—was going to be okay.

Abee stood in Candy's bedroom, his lips forming a tight line as he took it all in.

Her closet was empty. Her drawers were empty. The damn bathroom vanity was empty.

No wonder she hadn't answered the phone earlier. Candy had been busy packing her things. And when she had finally answered the phone? Why, she must have forgotten to mention anything about her little plans to leave town.

But no one left Abee Cole. No one.

And what if it was because of that new boyfriend of hers? What if they planned to run off *together*?

The idea was enough to make him bolt out the shattered back door. Rounding the house, he hurried to the truck, knowing he had to get to the Tidewater *now*.

Candy and her little boy were going to learn a lesson tonight. Both of them. The kind of lesson neither was likely to forget.

20

The night was as dark as any Dawson could remember. No moon, only endless black above, punctuated by the faint flicker of stars.

He was getting close to Oriental now and couldn't escape the feeling that he was somehow making a mistake by returning. He'd have to pass through the town to reach Tuck's, and he knew his cousins could be waiting for him anywhere.

Up ahead, beyond the curve where his life had changed forever, Dawson noticed the glow of Oriental's lights, rising beyond the tree line. If he was going to change his mind, he needed to do it now.

Unconsciously, he eased his foot off the pedal, and it was then, as the car slowed down, that Dawson felt suddenly that he was being watched.

Abee squeezed the wheel tight as the truck roared through town, tires squealing. He took a hard left into the parking lot of the Tidewater, sending the truck skidding as he slammed on the brakes in a handicapped spot. For the first time since smashing up the Stingray, even Ted was showing signs of life, the anticipation of violence heavy in the truck.

The truck had barely come to a halt before Abee leapt out, Ted close behind. Abee couldn't get his mind around the fact that Candy had been lying to him. She'd obviously been planning her little escape for some time and believed that he wouldn't find out. It was time to teach her just who made the rules around here. *Because you see, Candy, it sure as hell ain't you.*

As he stormed toward the entrance, Abee noticed that Candy's Mustang convertible wasn't in the lot, which meant she'd probably parked it somewhere else. At some guy's house, both of them probably laughing behind Abee's back. He could just hear Candy laughing at what a fool Abee was, and the thought made him want to blast through the door, aim the gun in the direction of the bar, and just start pulling the trigger.

But he wasn't going to do that. Oh, no. Because first, she had to *understand* exactly what was going on. She had to *understand* that he made the rules.

Beside him Ted was remarkably steady on his feet, almost excited. Faint strains of music from the jukebox came from inside, the neon rope that spelled out the name of the bar painting their faces with a reddish glow.

Abee nodded at Ted before raising his leg to kick open the door.

❧

Dawson slowed the car to a crawl, every nerve ending on high alert. In the distance, he could just make out the lights of Oriental. He was overcome by a sudden sense of déjà vu, as if he already knew what was coming but was powerless to stop it, even if he wanted to.

Dawson leaned over the wheel. If he squinted, he could make out the convenience store, the one he'd passed on his morning jog. The spire of the First Baptist Church, illuminated by floodlights, seemed to hover above the business district. The halogen streetlights cast an eerie glow on the macadam, highlighting the route that led to Tuck's, taunting him with the possibility that he might never make it there. The stars he'd seen before had vanished, the sky above the town was almost unnaturally black. Up ahead on the right squatted the low-slung building that had replaced the original copse of trees, almost exactly central to the curve in the highway at the edge of town.

Dawson scanned the landscape closely, waiting for...something. Almost immediately, he was rewarded by a flash of movement beyond the driver's side window.

He was there, standing just outside the edges of the headlights' beams, in the meadow that bordered the highway. The dark-haired man.

The *ghost*.

It happened so fast, Alan couldn't even comprehend it.

There he was, chatting up Candy—or trying to, anyway—as she was getting ready to drop off another beer, when all of a sudden the front door of the bar was shoved open with such force that the upper half was torn from its hinge.

Before Alan had time to flinch, Candy had already begun to react. Recognition flashed across her face, the beer bottle halting in mid-delivery. Candy mouthed the words *Oh, shit* before she suddenly let go of the bottle.

By the time the bottle burst into splinters on the concrete floor, Candy had already turned and was sprinting away from him, a scream rising in her throat.

Behind him, a roar echoed off the wall.

"WHO IN THE HELL DO YOU THINK YOU ARE?!"

Alan shrank into himself as Candy raced for the far end of the bar, toward the manager's office. Alan had been coming to the Tidewater long enough to know that the manager's office had a reinforced steel door with dead bolts, because that was where the safe was kept.

Cringing, Alan watched Abee zero in on her as he rushed past him, chasing Candy's blond ponytail to the end of the bar. Abee, too, knew where she was going.

"OH, NO, YOU DON'T, YOU BITCH!"

Candy threw a terrified look over her shoulder before grabbing the doorjamb of the office. With a cry, she catapulted herself through the opening.

She swung the door closed just as Abee planted a hand and lunged over the bar. Empty bottles and glasses went flying. The register crashed to the floor, but he got his legs out in front of him.

Almost.

He hit the floor, stumbling, knocking liquor bottles off the shelf below the mirror as though they were bowling pins.

They barely slowed him down. In a flash, he was solidly on his feet and at the manager's door. Alan saw everything, each scene unfolding individually with surreal, violent precision. But when his thoughts caught up with what was actually happening, panic flooded every inch of his body.

This isn't a movie.

Abee began to pound on the door, hurling himself against it, his voice a hurricane. *"OPEN THE DAMN DOOR!"*

This is real.

He could hear Candy screaming hysterically from the locked office.

Oh, my God . . .

In the rear of the bar, the guys who'd been playing pool suddenly bolted toward the emergency exit, dropping their pool cues as they ran. It was the slapping sound the cues made as they hit the concrete floor that caused Alan's heart to hiccup in his chest, kicking into gear a primitive instinct for survival.

He had to get out of here.

He had to get out of here *now!*

Alan shot off the stool like he'd been jabbed with an ice pick, sending it toppling backward and grabbing at the bar to keep from falling down. Turning toward the cockeyed front door, he could see the parking lot beyond. The main road out front beckoned, and he surged toward it.

He was only vaguely aware that Abee was pounding and shouting that he was going to kill Candy if she didn't open the door. He barely noted the overturned tables and chairs. The only thing that mattered was reaching that opening and getting the hell out of the Tidewater as fast as he possibly could.

He heard his sneakers hitting the concrete floor, but the cockeyed door seemed to be getting no closer. Like one of those doors at a carnival funhouse...

From far away, he heard Candy scream, "Leave me alone!"

He didn't see Ted at all, nor did he see the chair that Ted heaved in his direction until it smashed into his legs, sending him sprawling. Alan instinctively tried to break his fall, but he couldn't stop the momentum. His forehead hit the floor hard, the impact stunning him. He saw bursts of white light before everything went black.

Only slowly did the world come into focus again.

He could taste blood as he struggled to untangle his legs from the chair and turn over. He felt a boot step down hard on the side of his face, the heel cutting sharply into his jaw as his head was pressed to the floor.

Above him, Crazy Ted Cole stood pointing a gun right at him, looking faintly amused.

"Just where do you think you're going?"

🌾

Dawson pulled the car to the side of the road. He half-expected the figure to vanish in the shadows as he stepped out of the car, but the dark-haired man stood in place, surrounded by knee-high grass. He was perhaps fifty yards away, close enough for Dawson to notice the windbreaker rippling in the evening breeze. At a sprint, even fully clothed and running through high grass, Dawson could reach the man in less than ten seconds.

Dawson knew he wasn't imagining the stranger. He could *feel* him, could sense him as plainly as the beating of his heart. Without taking his eyes from the man, Dawson stretched his arm into the car and turned off the engine, killing the headlights. Even in the darkness, Dawson could see the splash of the man's white shirt, framed by the open windbreaker. His face, however, was too vague to make out, as always.

Dawson stepped from the road, onto the narrow gravel median beside it.

The stranger didn't move.

Dawson ventured farther into the meadow grass, and still the figure remained, unmoving.

Dawson kept his eyes trained on him as he slowly began to close the distance. Five steps. Ten. Fifteen. Had it been daylight, he knew he would have seen the man plainly. He would have been able to make out the distinct features of his face; but in the darkness, those details remained obscured.

Closer now. Dawson moved deliberately, feeling a wave of disbelief wash over him. He was as close as he'd ever been to the ghostlike figure, near enough to reach him in a single burst.

He continued to watch, debating when to break into his run. But the stranger seemed to read Dawson's mind. He took a step backward.

Dawson paused. The figure paused as well.

Dawson took another step; he watched as another step backward was taken. He took two quick steps, his movement mirrored precisely by the dark-haired man.

Throwing caution to the wind, Dawson broke into a run. The dark-haired man turned then and began to run as well. Dawson sped up, but the distance between them stayed eerily constant, the windbreaker flapping as if trying to taunt him.

Dawson accelerated and the stranger veered, changing direction. No longer running away from the road, he began to run parallel to it, and Dawson followed suit. They were heading toward Oriental, toward the blocky squat building at the head of the curve.

The curve . . .

Dawson wasn't gaining, but the dark-haired man wasn't pulling farther ahead, either. He'd stopped changing directions, and for the first time Dawson had the sense that the man had some distinct purpose in mind as he led him forward. There was something disconcerting about that, but lost in the chase, Dawson had no time to consider it.

*

Ted's boot pressed down hard on the side of Alan's face. Alan felt his ears being crushed from both directions and could feel the heel of the boot cutting painfully into his jaw. The gun pointed at his head appeared huge, crowding everything else from his vision, and his bowels suddenly went watery. *I'm going to die*, he suddenly thought.

"I know you seen this," Ted said wiggling the gun but still keeping it aimed. "If I let you up, you ain't gonna try to run, are you?"

Alan tried to swallow, but his throat wasn't working. "No," he croaked out.

Ted shifted even more weight onto the boot. The pain was intense and Alan screamed. Both his ears were on fire and felt like they'd been flattened into paper-thin disks. Squinting up at Ted as he babbled for mercy, he noted that Ted's other arm was in some sort of cast and that his face was black and purple. Dimly, Alan found himself wondering what had happened to him.

Ted stepped back. "Get up," he said.

Alan struggled to untangle his leg from the chair and slowly got up, almost buckling as a sharp bolt shot through his knee. The open doorway was only a few feet away.

"Don't even think it," Ted snarled. He motioned to the bar. "Git."

Alan limped back toward the bar. Abee was still at the office door, cursing and hurling himself at it. Finally, Abee turned toward them.

Abee cocked his head to one side, staring, looking deranged. Alan's bowels went watery again.

"I've got your boyfriend out here!" he shouted.

"He's not my boyfriend!" Candy screamed back, but the sound was muffled. "I'm calling the police!"

By then, Abee was already walking toward him, around the bar. Ted kept the gun trained on Alan.

"You think the two of you could just run off?" Abee demanded.

Alan opened his mouth to answer, but terror robbed him of his voice.

Abee bent over, grabbing one of the fallen pool cues. Alan watched as Abee adjusted his grip on the cue, like a batter getting ready to walk to home plate, crazy and out of control.

Oh, God, please, no . . .

"You think I wouldn't find out? That I didn't know what you were planning? I saw the two of you on Friday night!"

Just a few steps away, Alan stood riveted, unable to move while Abee cocked back the pool cue. Ted took a half step backward.

Oh, God . . .

Alan choked out a response: "I don't know what you're talking about."

"Did she leave her car at your place?" Abee demanded. "Is that where it is?"

"What—I—"

Abee stepped toward him, swinging the cue, before Alan had the chance to finish. The cue smashed into his skull, making the world erupt in blinding starbursts before going black again.

Alan hit the floor as Abee swung the pool cue again, then again. Alan tried weakly to cover himself, hearing the sickening sound of his arm breaking. When the cue snapped in half, Abee swung his steel-toed boot hard into his face. Ted started kicking him in the kidneys, yielding bursts of white-hot agony.

As Alan began to scream, the beating began in earnest.

❧

Running through the meadow grass, they were now closing in on the squat, ugly building. Dawson could see a few cars and trucks out front, and for the first time he noted a faint red glow above the entrance. Slowly, they'd begun to angle in that direction.

As the dark-haired stranger glided effortlessly ahead of him, Dawson felt a nagging sense of recognition. The relaxed position of the shoulders, the steady rhythm of his arms, the high-stepping cadence of the legs...Dawson had seen that particular gait before, and not just in the woods behind Tuck's house. He couldn't quite place it yet, but the knowledge hovered ever closer, like bubbles rising to the surface of the water. The man glanced over his shoulder, as if attuned to Dawson's every thought, and Dawson got his first clear glimpse of the stranger's features, knowing he'd seen the man before.

Before the explosion.

Dawson stumbled, but even as he righted himself, he felt a chill pass through him.

It wasn't possible.

It had been twenty-four years. Since then, he'd gone to prison and been released; he'd worked on oil rigs in the Gulf of Mexico. He'd loved and lost, then loved and lost again, and the man who'd once taken him in had died of old age. But the stranger—because he was, and always had been, a stranger—hadn't aged at all. He looked exactly the same as he had on the night he'd been out running after seeing patients in his office, a day on which it had rained. It was him, and he could see it now: the surprised face Dawson had seen as he'd swerved off the road. He'd been carrying the load of tires that Tuck had needed, returning to Oriental—

It was here, Dawson remembered again. It was here where Dr. David Bonner, husband and father, had been killed.

Dawson drew a sharp breath and stumbled again, but the man seemed to have read his thoughts. He nodded once without smiling just as he reached the gravel drive of the parking lot. Facing forward again, he sped up, parallel now to the front of the building. Dawson felt the sweat as he stumbled into the parking lot behind him. Up ahead, the stranger—Dr. Bonner—had stopped running and was standing near the building's entrance, bathed in the neon sign's eerie red light.

Dawson drew near, focusing on Dr. Bonner, just as the ghost turned and entered the building.

Dawson sped up, bursting through the doorway of a dimly lit bar seconds later, but by then, Dr. Bonner was gone.

It took only an instant for Dawson to register the scene: the toppled tables and chairs, the muffled sound of a woman screaming in the background while the TV continued to blare. His cousins Ted and Abee bent over someone on the ground, beating him savagely, almost ritualistically, until they suddenly stopped to look up at him. Dawson caught a glimpse of the bloodied figure on the ground, recognizing him instantly.

Alan . . .

Dawson had studied the young man's face in countless photos over the years, but now he also noticed the striking resemblance to his father. The man Dawson had been seeing all these months, the man who'd led him here.

As he took in the scene, all went still. Ted and Abee froze, neither of them apparently able to believe that someone—anyone— had suddenly arrived. Their breaths came in rasps as they stared at Dawson like wolves interrupted during a feeding frenzy.

Dr. Bonner had saved him for a reason.

The thought rushed into his head in the same instant that

Ted's eyes flashed with comprehension. Ted began to raise his gun, but by the time the trigger was pulled, Dawson was already diving out of the way, taking cover behind a table. He suddenly understood why he had been brought here—and perhaps even what his purpose had been all along.

※

With every gurgling breath, Alan felt as though he were being stabbed.

He couldn't move from the floor, but through his blurriness, he could just make out what was happening.

Ever since the stranger had burst into the bar, craning his head around wildly as if pursuing someone, Ted and Abee had quit beating him and for some reason turned their entire focus on the newcomer. Alan didn't understand it, but when he heard gunshots he curled himself into a ball and started to pray. The stranger had thrown himself behind some tables and Alan could no longer see him, but the next thing he knew, bottles of liquor were sailing over his head at Ted and Abee while gunshots ricocheted around the bar. He heard Abee cry out and the muted sound of cracking wood as pieces of a chair splintered around him. Ted had scrambled out of sight, but he could still hear his gun firing wildly.

As for himself, Alan was sure that he was dying.

Two of his teeth were on the floor and his mouth was filled with blood. He'd felt his ribs snapping as Abee had kicked him. The front of his pants was damp—either he'd wet himself or he'd started to bleed because of the blows to his kidney.

He distantly registered the sound of sirens, but convinced of his imminent demise, he couldn't summon the energy to care. He heard the banging of chairs and the clank of bottles. From somewhere far away, he heard Abee grunt as a bottle of liquor connected with something solid.

The stranger's feet raced past him toward the bar. Immediately thereafter, shouts were followed by a shot, shattering the mirror behind the bar. Alan felt the slivers of glass rain down, nicking his skin. Another shout and more scuffling. Abee began a high-pitched wail, the shriek ending abruptly with the sound of something being smashed against the floor.

Someone's head?

More scuffling. From his vantage point on the floor, Alan saw Ted stumble backward, narrowly missing stepping on Alan's foot. Ted was shouting something as he caught his balance, but Alan thought he heard a trace of alarm in his voice as another gunshot echoed through the small bar.

Alan squinched his eyes shut, then opened them again just as another chair came flinging through the air. Ted fired another wild shot toward the ceiling, and the stranger bull-charged him, driving Ted into the wall. A gun rattled across the floor as Ted was thrown to the side.

The man was on Ted as Ted tried to scramble away out of his sight line, but Alan couldn't move. Behind him, he heard the sound of fist against face, over and over...heard Ted shouting, the hammering against his chin making the sound rise and fall with the blows. Then Alan just heard the strikes, and Ted was silent. He heard another, then another and another, slowing.

Then there was nothing at all but the sound of a man's heavy breathing.

The howl of sirens was closer now, but Alan, on the floor, knew his rescue had come too late.

They killed me, he heard in his head as his vision turned black around the edges. Suddenly, he felt an arm grasp him around his waist and begin to lift.

The pain was excruciating. He screamed as he felt himself being dragged to his feet, an arm looping around him. Miraculously, he felt his legs move of their own accord as the man half-dragged, half-carried him toward the entrance. He could see the dark window of sky out front, could just make out the cock-eyed door they were moving toward.

And though he had no reason to say it, he found himself croaking out, "I'm Alan." He sagged against the man. "Alan Bonner."

"I know," the man responded. "I'm supposed to get you out of here."

I'm supposed to get you out of here.

Barely conscious, Ted couldn't fully register the words, but instinctively, he knew what was happening. *Dawson was getting away again.*

The rage he felt was volcanic, stronger than death itself.

He forced open one blood-slicked eye as Dawson staggered toward the doorway, Candy's boyfriend draped over him. With Dawson's back turned, Ted scanned the area around him for the Glock. *There.* Just a few feet away, beneath a broken table.

The sirens had become loud by then.

Summoning his last reserves of strength, Ted lunged toward the gun, feeling its satisfying weight as he tightened his grip. He swiveled the gun toward the door, toward Dawson. He had no idea whether any rounds were left, but he knew this was his last chance.

He zeroed in, taking aim. And then he pulled the trigger.

21

By midnight, Amanda felt numb. Mentally, emotionally, and physically drained, she'd been simultaneously exhausted and on edge for hours as she'd sat in the waiting room. She'd flipped through pages of magazines seeing nothing at all, she'd paced back and forth compulsively, trying to stem the dread she felt whenever she thought about her son. As the hours circled toward midnight, however, she found her acute anxiety draining away, leaving only a wrung-out shell.

Lynn had rushed in an hour earlier, her panic evident. Clinging to Amanda, she'd peppered her mom with endless questions that Amanda couldn't answer. Next she'd turned to Frank, pressing him relentlessly for details about the accident. Someone speeding through the intersection, he'd said, with a helpless shrug. By now he was sober, and though his concern for Jared was apparent, he failed to make any mention of why Jared had been driving through the intersection in the first place, or why Jared had even been driving his father at all.

Amanda had said nothing to Frank in the hours they'd been in the room. She knew that Lynn must have noticed the silence between them, but Lynn was quiet as well, lost in her worries about her brother. At one point, she did ask Amanda whether she should go pick up Annette from camp. Amanda told her to wait until they had a better sense of what was happening. Annette was too young to comprehend the full extent of this crisis, and in all honesty Amanda didn't feel capable of caring for Annette right now. It was all she could do to hold herself together.

At twenty past midnight on what had been the longest day of her life, Dr. Mills finally entered the room. He was obviously tired, but he'd changed into clean scrubs before coming to talk to them. Amanda rose from her seat, as did Lynn and Frank.

"The surgery went well," he said straight off. "We're pretty sure Jared is going to be fine."

Jared was in recovery for several hours, but Amanda wasn't allowed to see him until he was finally moved to the ICU. Though it was normally closed to visitors overnight, Dr. Mills made an exception for her.

By then Lynn had driven Frank home. He claimed to have developed an intense headache from the blow to his face, but he promised to be back the following morning. Lynn had volunteered to return to the hospital afterward to stay with her mom, but Amanda had vetoed the idea. She'd be with Jared all night.

Amanda sat at her son's bedside for the next few hours, listening to the digital beeps of the heart monitor and the unnatural hiss of the ventilator slowly pushing air in and out of his lungs. His skin was the color of old plastic and his cheeks seemed to have collapsed. He didn't look like the son she remembered, the son she'd raised; he was a stranger to her in this foreign setting, so removed from their everyday lives.

Only his hands seemed unaffected, and she held on to one of them, drawing strength from its warmth. When the nurse had changed his bandage, she'd caught a glimpse of the violent gash that split his torso, and she'd had to turn away.

The doctor had said that Jared would probably wake later that day, and as she hovered at his bedside she wondered how much he would remember about the accident and his arrival at the hospital. Had he been frightened when his condition suddenly worsened? Had he wished that she'd been there? The thought was like a physical blow, and she vowed that she would stay with him now for as long as he needed her.

She hadn't slept at all since she'd arrived at the hospital. As the hours passed with no sign of Jared waking, she grew sleepy, lulled by the steady, rhythmic sound of the equipment. She leaned forward, resting her head on the bedrail. A nurse woke her twenty minutes later and suggested that she go home for a little while.

Amanda shook her head, staring at her son again, willing her strength into his broken body. To comfort herself, she thought of Dr. Mills's assurances that once Jared recovered, he would lead a mostly normal life. It could have been worse, Dr. Mills had told her, and she repeated that sentiment like a charm to ward off greater disaster.

As daylight seeped into the sky outside the ICU's windows, the hospital began to come to life again. Nurses changed shifts, breakfast carts were loaded up, physicians began to make their rounds. The noise level rose to a steady buzz. A nurse pointedly informed Amanda that she needed to check the catheter, and Amanda reluctantly left the ICU and wandered to the cafeteria. Perhaps caffeine would give her the energy surge she needed; she had to be there when Jared finally awoke.

Despite the early hour, the line was already long with people who, like her, had been up all night. A young man in his late twenties took his place behind her.

"My wife is going to kill me," he confessed as they lined up their trays.

Amanda raised an eyebrow. "Why is that?"

"She had a baby last night and she sent me here for coffee. She told me to hurry, because she was getting a caffeine headache, but I just had to make a detour to the nursery for another peek."

Despite everything, Amanda smiled.

"Little boy or little girl?"

"Boy," he said. "Gabriel. Gabe. He's our first."

Amanda thought of Jared. She thought about Lynn and Annette, and she thought about Bea. The hospital had been the site of both the happiest and saddest days of her life. "Congratulations," she said.

The line crawled along, customers taking their time with their selections and ordering complicated breakfast combinations. Amanda checked her watch after finally paying for her cup of coffee. She'd been gone for fifteen minutes. She was pretty sure she wouldn't be able to bring the cup into the ICU, so she took a table by the window while the parking lot out front slowly began to fill.

When she had drained her coffee cup, she visited the bathroom. The face reflected in the mirror was haggard and sleep deprived, barely recognizable. She splashed cold water on her cheeks and neck and spent the next couple of minutes doing the best she could to make herself presentable. She took the elevator back up, then retraced her steps to the ICU. When she neared the door, a nurse stood and intercepted her.

"I'm sorry, but you can't go in right now," she said.

"Why not?" Amanda asked, coming to a standstill. The nurse wouldn't answer, and her expression was unyielding. Amanda felt the coils of panic tighten inside her once more.

She waited outside the door of the ICU for almost an hour, until Dr. Mills finally emerged to talk to her.

"I'm sorry," he said, "but there's been a serious development."

"I was j-j-just with him," she stammered, unable to think of anything else to say.

"An infarction occurred," he went on. "Ischemia in the right ventricle." He shook his head.

Amanda frowned. "I don't know what you're trying to tell me! Just say it so I can understand!"

His expression was compassionate, his voice soft. "Your son," he finally said, "Jared...he had a massive heart attack."

Amanda blinked, feeling the corridor close in. "No," she said. "That's not possible. He was sleeping...he was recovering when I left."

Dr. Mills said nothing and Amanda felt light-headed, almost disembodied as she babbled on. "You said he was going to be fine. You said the surgery went well. You said he'd wake up later today."

"I'm sorry—"

"How could he have had a heart attack?" she demanded, incredulous. "He's only nineteen!"

"I'm not sure. It was probably a clot of some sort. It might have been related to either the original trauma or the trauma from surgery, but there's no way to know for certain," Dr. Mills explained. "It's unusual, but anything can happen after the heart sustains such a serious injury." He touched her arm. "All I can really tell you is that if it had happened anywhere other than the ICU, he might not have made it at all."

Amanda's voice began to quiver. "But he did make it, right? He's going to be okay, isn't he?"

"I don't know." The doctor's face was shuttered again.

"What do you mean, you don't know?"

"We're having difficulty keeping a sinus rhythm."

"Stop talking like a doctor!" she cried. "Just tell me what I need to know! Is my son going to be all right?"

For the first time, Dr. Mills turned away. "Your son's heart is failing," he said. "Without...intervention, I'm not sure how long he's going to last."

Amanda felt herself stagger, as if the words were actual blows. She steadied herself against the wall, trying to absorb the doctor's meaning.

"You're not saying that he's going to die, are you?" she whispered. "He can't die. He's young and healthy and strong. You have to do something."

"We're doing everything we can," Dr. Mills said, sounding tired.

Not again, was all she could think. *Not like Bea. Not Jared, too.*

"Then do more!" she urged, half-pleading, half-shouting. "Take him to surgery, do what you have to do!"

"Surgery isn't an option right now."

"Just do what you have to do to save him!" Her voice rose and cracked.

"It's not that simple—"

"Why not?" Her face reflected her incomprehension.

"I have to call an emergency meeting with the transplant committee."

Amanda felt her last threads of composure give way as he said those words. "Transplant?"

"Yes," he said. He glanced toward the ICU door, then back to her. He sighed. "Your son needs a new heart."

❧

Afterward, Amanda was escorted back to the same waiting room she'd occupied during Jared's first surgery.

This time, she wasn't alone. There were three others in the room, all wearing the same tense, helpless expression as Amanda. She collapsed into a chair, trying and failing to suppress a horrible feeling of déjà vu.

I'm not sure how long he's going to last.

Oh, God...

Suddenly, she couldn't stand the confines of the waiting room anymore. The antiseptic smells, the hideous fluorescent lighting, the drawn, anxious faces...it was a repeat of the weeks and months they'd spent in rooms identical to this one, during Bea's illness. The hopelessness, the anxiety—she had to get out.

Standing, she threw her purse over her shoulder and fled down the generic tiled hallways until she reached an exit. Stepping into a small terraced area outside, she took a seat on a stone bench and drew a deep breath of the early morning air. Then she pulled out her cell phone. She caught Lynn at home, just as she and Frank were about to leave for the hospital. Amanda related what had happened as Frank picked up the other extension and listened in. Lynn was again full of unanswerable questions, but Amanda interrupted to ask her to call the sleepaway camp where Annette was staying and arrange to pick up her sister. It would take three hours round trip and Lynn protested that she wanted to see Jared, but Amanda said firmly that she needed Lynn to do this for her. Frank said nothing at all.

After hanging up, Amanda called her mother. Explaining what had happened in the last twenty-four hours somehow made the nightmare even more real, and Amanda broke down before she was able to finish.

"I'm coming," her mother said simply. "I'll be there as fast as I can."

🌿

When Frank arrived, they met with Dr. Mills in his office on the third floor to discuss the possibility of Jared receiving a heart transplant.

Though Amanda heard and understood everything that Dr. Mills said about the process, there were only two details that she later truly remembered.

The first was that Jared might not be approved by the transplant committee—that despite his grave condition, there was no precedent for adding a patient to the waiting list who'd been in an automobile accident. There was no guarantee that he would be eligible.

The second was that even if Jared was approved, it was a matter of pure luck—and long odds—whether a suitable heart would become available.

In other words, the odds were slim on both counts.

I'm not sure how long he's going to last.

On their way back to the waiting room, Frank looked as dazed as she felt. Amanda's anger and Frank's guilt formed an impenetrable wall between them. An hour later, a nurse stopped by with an update, saying that Jared's condition had stabilized for the time being, and that they would both be allowed to visit the ICU if they wanted to.

Stabilized. For the time being.

Amanda and Frank stood beside Jared's bed. Amanda could see the child he'd been and the young man he had become, but she could barely reconcile those images with the prone, unconscious figure in the bed. Frank whispered his apologies, urging Jared to "hang in there," his words triggering a flood of rage and disbelief in Amanda that she struggled to control.

Frank seemed to have aged ten years since the night before; disheveled and downcast, he was the picture of misery, but she could summon no feeling of sympathy for the guilt she knew that he was feeling.

Instead, she ran her fingers through Jared's hair, marking time with the digital beeps of the monitors. Nurses hovered over other patients in the ICU, checking IVs and adjusting knobs, acting as though the day were completely ordinary. An ordinary day in the life of a busy hospital, but there was nothing ordinary about any of this. It was the end of life as she knew it for her and her family.

The transplant committee was meeting soon. There was no precedent for a patient like Jared to be added to the waiting list. If they said no, then her son was going to die.

❧

Lynn showed up at the hospital with Annette, who was clutching her favorite stuffed animal, a monkey. Making a rare exception, the nurses allowed the siblings into the ICU together to see their brother. Lynn went white in the face and kissed Jared on the cheek. Annette placed the stuffed animal next to him on the hospital bed.

In a conference room several floors above the ICU, the transplant committee met for an emergency vote. Dr. Mills presented Jared's profile and case history as well as the urgency of the situation.

"It says here that he's suffering from congestive heart failure," one of the committee members said, frowning at the report before him.

Dr. Mills nodded. "As I detailed in the report, the infarction severely damaged the patient's right ventricle."

"An infarction that most likely stemmed from injury sustained in an automobile accident," the member countered. "As a general policy, hearts aren't given to accident victims."

"Only because they don't generally live long enough to benefit," Dr. Mills pointed out. "This patient, however, survived. He's a young, healthy male with otherwise excellent prospects. The actual cause of the infarction is still unknown, and as we know, congestive heart failure does meet the criteria for transplantation." He set the file aside and leaned forward, facing each of his colleagues in turn. "Without a transplant, I doubt this patient will last another twenty-four hours. We need to add him to the list." A note of pleading crept into his voice. "He's still young. We have to give him the chance to live."

A few of the committee members exchanged skeptical glances. He knew what they were thinking: Not only did this case lack precedent, but the time frame was too short. The odds were almost nonexistent that a donor could be found in time, which meant the patient was likely to die no matter what decision they made. What they didn't mention was a colder calculation, though no one on the committee gave voice to it. It had to do with money. If Jared was added to the list, the patient would be counted as either a success or failure for the overall transplant program, and a higher success rate meant a better reputation for the hospital. It meant additional funds for research and operations. It meant more money for transplants in the future. In the big picture, it meant more lives could be saved in the long run, even if one life had to be sacrificed now.

But Dr. Mills knew his colleagues well, and in his heart he knew they also understood that each patient and set of circumstances was unique. They understood that numbers didn't always tell the whole story. They were the kind of professionals who sometimes took risks in order to help a patient now. For most of them, Dr. Mills guessed, it was the reason they'd gone into medicine in the first place, just as he had. They wanted to save people, and they decided to try again that day.

In the end, the recommendation from the transplant committee was unanimous. Within the hour, the patient was given 1A status, which awarded him the highest priority—if a donor could miraculously be found.

❧

When Dr. Mills broke the news to them, Amanda jumped up and hugged him, clinging to him with desperate force.

"Thank you," she breathed. "Thank you." Over and over, she repeated the words. She was too afraid to say anything more, to hope aloud for the miracle of a donor.

❧

When Evelyn entered the waiting room, one glimpse at the shell-shocked family was enough for her to know that someone had to assume control of their care. Someone who could support them, not someone who needed supporting.

She hugged each of them in turn, holding Amanda longest of all. Stepping back to inspect the group, she asked, "Now, who needs something to eat?"

❧

Evelyn promptly herded Lynn and Annette off to the cafeteria, leaving Frank and Amanda alone. Amanda couldn't fathom the thought of eating. As for Frank, she didn't really care. All she could do was think about Jared.

And wait.

And pray.

When one of the ICU nurses passed by the waiting room, Amanda raced after her, catching her in the hallway. Voice trembling, she asked the obvious question.

"No," the nurse answered, "I'm sorry. So far, there's no word on a possible donor."

Still standing in the hallway, Amanda brought her hands to her face.

Unbeknownst to her, Frank had emerged from the waiting room, reaching her side as the nurse hurried away.

"They'll find a donor," Frank said.

At his tentative touch, she wheeled around.

"They'll find one," he said again.

Her eyes flashed. "You of all people can't *promise* me that."

"No, of course not..."

"Then don't say anything," she said. "Don't say things that are meaningless."

Frank touched the swollen bridge of his nose. "I'm just trying to—"

"What?" she demanded. "Make me feel better? My son is dying!" Her voice rang out in the tiled hallway, turning heads.

"He's my son, too," Frank said, his voice quiet.

Amanda's anger, so long suppressed, suddenly exploded to the surface. "Then why did you make him come and get you?" she cried. "Why were you too drunk to drive yourself?"

"Amanda..."

"You did this!" she screamed at him. Up and down the

corridor, patients craned to peer out their open doors, and nurses froze midstride. "He shouldn't have been in the car! There was no reason for him to be there! But you got so damn drunk that you couldn't take care of yourself! Again! Just like you always do!"

"It was an accident," Frank tried to interject.

"But it wasn't! Don't you understand that? You bought the beer, you drank it—*you* set all this in motion. You put Jared in the path of that car!"

Amanda was breathing hard, oblivious to anyone in the hallway. "I've asked you to stop drinking," she hissed. "I've begged you to stop. But you never stopped. You never cared about what I wanted, or what was best for the kids. The only thing you ever thought about was yourself and how much you hurt after Bea died." She drew a harsh breath. "Well, you know what? I was crushed, too. I'm the one who gave birth to her. I'm the one who held her and fed her and changed her diapers while you were at work. I was the one who never left her side when she was sick. That was me, not you. *Me.*" She stabbed her own chest with her finger. "But somehow you became the one who couldn't cope. And you know what happened? I ended up losing the husband I married, along with my baby. Yet even then I was somehow able to soldier on and make the best of things." Amanda turned away from Frank, her face twisted with bitterness.

"My son is on life support and his time is running out because I never had the courage to leave you. But that's what I should have done a long time ago."

Halfway through her outburst, Frank had dropped his gaze, focusing instead on the floor. Spent, Amanda began to walk down the hall, away from him.

She stopped for a moment, turned, and added, "I know that it was an accident. I know you're sorry. But being sorry isn't enough. If it wasn't for you, we wouldn't be here, and both of us know that."

Her last words were a challenge that echoed through the hos-

pital ward, and she half-expected him to respond. But he said
nothing, and Amanda finally walked away.

🌿

When family members were allowed to visit the ICU again,
Amanda and the girls took turns sitting with Jared. She stayed
with him for almost an hour. As soon as Frank arrived, she left.
Evelyn went in to see Jared next, staying only a few minutes.

After the rest of the family was shepherded off by Evelyn,
Amanda returned to Jared's bedside alone, remaining there until
after the nurses changed shifts.

There was still no word on a donor.

🌿

The dinner hour arrived and more time passed. Evelyn finally
showed up and frog-marched Amanda out of the ICU, leading
her down to the cafeteria. Although the thought of food made
her feel almost nauseated, her mother personally supervised
Amanda's eating of a sandwich in silence. Swallowing each taste-
less mouthful with mechanical effort, Amanda finally choked
down the last bite and crumpled the cellophane wrapper.

With that, she stood and went back to the ICU.

🌿

By eight o'clock, when visiting hours were officially over, Evelyn determined that it would be best for the kids to go home
for a while. Frank agreed to accompany them, but again Dr.
Mills made an exception for Amanda, allowing her to stay in the
ICU.

The frenetic activity of the hospital slowed as evening settled
in. Amanda continued to sit unmoving by Jared's bedside. Feeling dazed, she noticed the rotation of nurses, unable to remember
their names as soon as they left the room. Amanda begged God

over and over to save her son's life, in the same way she'd once begged God to save Bea.

This time, she could only hope God would listen.

❧

Sometime after midnight, Dr. Mills stepped into the room.

"You should go home and get some rest," he said. "I'll call you if I hear anything at all. I promise."

Amanda refused to release Jared's hand, raising her chin in stubborn defiance.

"I won't leave him."

❧

It was nearly three in the morning when Dr. Mills returned to the ICU. By then, Amanda was too exhausted to rise.

"There's news," he said.

She turned toward him, suddenly sure that he was going to tell her their last best hope had been exhausted. *This is it*, she thought, feeling numb. *This is the end.*

Instead, she saw something akin to hope in his expression.

"We found a match," he said. "A one-in-a-million shot that somehow came through."

Amanda felt adrenaline surge through her limbs, every nerve awakening as she tried to grasp his full meaning. "A match?"

"A donor heart. It's being transported to the hospital right now, and the surgery has already been scheduled. The team is being assembled as we speak."

"Does that mean Jared is going to live?" Amanda asked, her voice hoarse.

"That's the plan," he said, and for the first time since she'd been in the hospital, Amanda began to cry.

22

---- ❧ ----

At Dr. Mills's urging, Amanda finally went home. She'd been told that Jared would be taken into pre-op, where he would be readied for the procedure, and she wouldn't be able to spend time with him. After that, the actual surgery would take anywhere from four to six hours, depending on whether there were complications.

"No," Dr. Mills said, even before she had a chance to ask. "There's no reason to expect any complications."

Despite her lingering anger, she'd called Frank after getting the news and before she left the hospital. Like her, he hadn't been sleeping, and while she'd expected to hear the slurring she'd grown used to, he was sober when she reached him. His relief about Jared was obvious, and he thanked her for calling him.

She didn't see Frank once she arrived home, and she suspected that since her mother was in the guest room, Frank was sleeping on the couch in the den. Though exhausted, what she really needed was a shower, and she spent a long time standing beneath the luxurious flow of water before finally crawling into bed.

Sunrise was still an hour or two away, and as Amanda closed her eyes she told herself she wasn't going to sleep long, just a quick catnap before heading back to the hospital.

Her dreamless sleep lasted for six hours.

Her mother was holding a cup of coffee when Amanda came rushing down the hall, frantic to get to the hospital and struggling to remember where she'd left her keys.

"I called just a few minutes ago," Evelyn said. "Lynn said they hadn't heard anything at all, aside from the fact that Jared was in surgery."

"I still have to go," Amanda mumbled.

"Of course you do. But not until you have a cup of coffee." Evelyn held out the cup. "I made this for you."

Amanda pawed through the piles of junk mail and odds and ends on the counters, still searching for her keys. "I don't have time..."

"It'll take five or ten minutes to drink," her mother said, in a voice that brooked no protest. She put the steaming cup in Amanda's hand. "It won't change anything. Once you get to the hospital, we both know that all you're going to do is wait. The only thing that will matter to Jared is whether you're there when he wakes up, and that's not going to happen for several hours. So take a few minutes before you rush out of here." Her mother sat down in one of the kitchen chairs and pointed to the seat next to her. "Have a cup of coffee and something to eat."

"I can't have breakfast while my son is in surgery!" she argued.

"I know you're worried," Evelyn said, her voice surprisingly gentle. "I'm worried, too. But as your mother, I also worry about you, because I know how much the rest of the family depends on you. We both know that you function much better after you've eaten and had a cup of coffee."

Amanda hesitated then raised the cup to her lips. It *did* taste good.

"You really think it's okay?" She gave an uncertain frown as she took a seat next to her mother at the kitchen table.

"Of course. You have a long day ahead of you. Jared is going to need you to be strong when he sees you."

Amanda clutched the cup. "I'm scared," she admitted.

To Amanda's astonishment, her mother reached out and covered her hands with her own. "I know. I am, too."

Amanda stared at her hands, still laced around the coffee cup, surrounded and supported by her mother's tiny manicured ones. "Thanks for coming."

Evelyn allowed herself a small smile. "It's not like I had a choice," she said. "You're my daughter, and you needed me."

Together, Amanda and her mother drove to the hospital, meeting up with the rest of the family in the waiting room. Annette and Lynn ran to give her a hug, burying their faces in her neck. Frank merely nodded and mumbled a greeting. Her mother, instantly sensing the tension between them, whisked the girls off to an early lunch.

When Amanda and Frank were alone, he turned to her.

"I'm sorry," he said. "For everything."

Amanda looked at him. "I know you are."

"I know it should be me in there, instead of Jared."

Amanda said nothing.

"I can leave you alone if you want," he said into the silence. "I can find someplace else to sit."

Amanda sighed before shaking her head. "It's fine. He's your son. You belong here."

Frank swallowed. "I've stopped drinking, if that means anything. Really, this time. For good."

Amanda waved to cut him off. "Just...don't, okay? I don't want to get into this now. This isn't the time or place, and all it's going to do is make me angrier than I already am. I've heard it all before, and I can't deal with this on top of everything else right now."

Frank nodded. Turning around, he went back to his seat. Amanda sat in a chair along the opposite wall. Neither of them said another word until Evelyn returned with the kids.

A little after noon, Dr. Mills entered the waiting room. Everyone stood. Amanda searched his face, expecting the worst, but her fears were allayed almost immediately by his air of exhausted satisfaction. "The surgery went well," he began, before walking them through the steps of the procedure.

When he'd finished, Annette tugged at his sleeve. "Jared is going to be okay?"

"Yes," the doctor answered with a smile. He reached down to touch her head. "Your brother is going to be fine."

"When can we see him?" Amanda asked.

"He's in recovery right now, but maybe in a few hours."

"Will he be awake then?"

"Yes," Dr. Mills answered. "He'll be awake."

When the family was informed they could go in and visit Jared, Frank shook his head.

"Go ahead," he said to Amanda. "We'll wait. We'll see him after you come out."

Amanda followed the nurse to the recovery room. Up ahead, Dr. Mills was waiting for her.

"He's awake." He nodded, falling into step with her. "But I want to warn you that he had a lot of questions and didn't take the news too well. All I ask is that you do your best not to upset him."

"What should I say?"

"Just talk to him," he answered. "You'll know what to say. You're his mother."

Outside the recovery room, Amanda took a deep breath, and

Dr. Mills pushed open the door. She entered the brightly lit room, immediately spotting her son in a bed with the curtains drawn back.

Jared was ghostly pale, and his cheeks were still hollowed out. He rolled his head to the side, a brief smile crossing his face.

"Hi, Mom," he whispered, his words fuzzy with the remnants of anesthesia.

Amanda touched his arm, careful not to disturb the countless tubes and swaths of medical tape and instruments attached to his body. "Hey, sweetheart. How are you?"

"Tired," he mumbled. "Sore."

"I know," she said. She brushed the hair from his forehead before taking a seat in the hard plastic chair beside him. "And you'll probably be sore for a while. But you won't have to be here long. Just a week or so."

He blinked, his eyelids moving slowly. Like he used to do as a little boy, right before she turned out the lights at bedtime.

"I have a new heart," he said. "The doctor said I had no choice."

"Yes," she answered.

"What does that mean?" Jared's arm jerked in agitation. "Am I going to have a normal life?"

"Of course you will," she said soothingly.

"They took out my *heart*, Mom." He gripped the sheet on the bed. "They told me that I'm going to be taking drugs forever."

Confusion and apprehension played across his youthful features. He understood that his future had been irrevocably altered, and while she wished she could shield him from this new reality, she knew she couldn't.

"Yes," she said, her gaze never wavering. "You had a heart transplant. And yes, you'll be on drugs forever. But those things also mean you're alive."

"For how long? Even the doctors can't tell me that."

"Does that really matter right now?"

"Of course it matters," Jared snapped. "They told me that the average transplant lasts fifteen to twenty years. And then I'll probably need another heart."

"Then you'll get another one. And in between, you're going to live, and after that, you'll live some more. Just like everyone else."

"You don't understand what I'm trying to say." Jared turned his face away, toward the wall on the far side of the bed.

Amanda saw his reaction and searched for the right words to reach him, to help him accept this new world he'd woken up to. "When I was waiting in the hospital for the last couple of days, do you know what I was thinking?" she began. "I was thinking that there were so many things that you still haven't done, things you still haven't experienced. Like the satisfaction of graduating from college, or the thrill of buying a house, or the excitement of landing that perfect job, or meeting the girl of your dreams and falling in love."

Jared didn't show any signs of having heard her, but she could tell by his alert stillness that he was listening. "You'll still be able to do all those things," she went on. "You'll make mistakes and struggle like everyone, but when you're with the right person, you'll feel almost perfect joy, like you're luckiest person who ever lived." She reached over to pat his arm. "And in the end, a heart transplant has nothing to do with any of those things. Because you're still alive. And that means you'll love and be loved...and in the end, nothing else really matters."

Jared lay without moving, long enough to make Amanda wonder if he'd fallen asleep in his postoperative haze. Then he gradually turned his head.

"You really believe everything you just said?" His voice was tentative.

For the first time since she'd heard about the accident, Amanda thought of Dawson Cole. She leaned in closer.

"Every word."

23

Morgan Tanner stood in Tuck's garage, his hands clasped before him as he examined the wreckage that had once been the Stingray. He grimaced, thinking that the owner wasn't going to be happy about this.

The damage was obviously recent. There was a tire iron protruding from a quarter panel that had been partially peeled back from the frame, and he was certain that neither Dawson nor Amanda would have let it remain so, had they seen it. Nor could they be responsible for the chair that had been tossed through the window onto the porch. All of this was likely the work of Ted and Abee Cole.

Though he wasn't native to Oriental, he had become attuned to the rhythms of the town. He'd learned over time that if he listened carefully at Irvin's, it was possible to learn a great deal about the history of this part of the world, and the people who lived here. Of course, in a place like Irvin's, any information had to be taken with a grain of salt. Rumors, gossip, and innuendo were as common as actual truth. Still, he knew more about the Cole family than most people would have expected. Including quite a bit about Dawson.

After Tuck had spoken to him about his plans for Dawson and Amanda, Tanner had been concerned enough for his own safety to learn what he could about the Coles. Though Tuck vouched for Dawson's character, Tanner had taken the time to talk to the sheriff who'd arrested him, as well as the prosecutor and public defender. The legal community in Pamlico County was small, and it was easy enough to get his colleagues talking about one of Oriental's most storied crimes.

Both the prosecutor and public defender had believed there'd been another car on the road that night, and that Dawson had swerved out of the way to avoid it. But given that the judge and sheriff back then were friends of Marilyn Bonner's family, there was little they could do. It was enough to make Tanner frown at the realities of small-town justice. After that, he spoke to the retired warden of the prison in Halifax, who informed him that Dawson had been a model inmate. He also called some of Dawson's prior employers in Louisiana, to verify that his character was sound and trustworthy. Only then did he agree to Tuck's request for assistance.

Now, aside from finalizing details of Tuck's estate—and handling the situation with the Stingray—his role in all of this was over. Considering all that had happened, including the arrests of both Ted and Abee Cole, he felt fortunate that his name had not been dragged into any of the conversations he'd overheard at Irvin's. And like the good lawyer he was, he had volunteered nothing.

Still, the entire situation troubled him more deeply than he let on. He'd even gone so far as to make some unorthodox calls during the past couple of days, putting him squarely outside his comfort zone.

Turning away from the car, he scanned the workbench, hunting for the work order, hoping it included the phone number of the Stingray's owner. He found it on the clipboard, and a quick perusal gave him all the information he needed. He was setting the clipboard back onto the bench when he spotted something familiar.

He picked it up, knowing he'd seen it before, and examined

it for a moment. He considered the ramifications before reaching into his pocket for his cell phone. He scrolled through his contact list, found the name, and hit CALL.

On the other end, the phone began to ring.

❧

Amanda had spent most of the past two days at the hospital with Jared, and she was actually looking forward to sleeping in her own bed later that night. Not only was the chair next to his bed incredibly uncomfortable, but Jared himself had urged her to leave.

"I need some time alone," he'd told her.

While she sat in the small terraced garden enjoying a bit of fresh air, Jared was upstairs meeting with the psychologist for the first time, much to her relief. Physically, she knew he was making excellent progress. Emotionally, however, was another matter. Though she wanted to think their conversation had opened the door at least a crack to a new way of thinking about his condition, Jared was suffering from the sense that years had been stolen from his life. He wanted what he'd had before, a perfectly healthy body and a relatively uncomplicated future, but that was no longer possible. He was on immunosuppressants so his body wouldn't reject the new heart, and since those made him prone to infection, he was taking high doses of antibiotics as well, and a diuretic had been prescribed to prevent fluid retention. And though he'd be released the following week, he would have to attend regular appointments at the outpatient clinic to monitor his progress for at least a year. He would also be required to undergo supervised physiotherapy and was told that he'd be placed on a restrictive diet. All that in addition to talking with the psychologist on a weekly basis.

The road ahead would be challenging for the entire family, but where there had once been nothing but despair, Amanda now felt hope. Jared was stronger than he thought he was. It would take time, but he'd find a way to get through all this. In the past two days, she'd noticed flashes of his strength, even if he hadn't been aware of it himself. And the psychologist, she knew, would help him as well.

Frank and her mom had been shuttling Annette to and from the hospital; Lynn had been driving here on her own. Amanda knew she hadn't been spending as much time with her girls as she should. They were struggling, too, but what choice did she have?

Tonight, she decided, she'd pick up a pizza on the way home. Afterward, maybe they'd watch a movie together. It wasn't much, but right now it was all she could really do. Once Jared got out of the hospital, things would start getting back to normal again. She should call her mother to tell her of her plans...

Digging into her purse, she pulled out her phone and noticed a number on the screen she didn't recognize. Her voice-mail icon was blinking as well.

Curious, she called up voice mail and put the phone to her ear, listening as Morgan Tanner's slow drawl came through, asking her to call when she had the chance.

She dialed the number. Tanner picked up immediately.

"Thank you for returning my call," he said, with the same cordial formality he had shown when Amanda and Dawson had met with him. "Before I get started, please know that I'm sorry to call at such a difficult time for you."

She blinked in confusion, wondering how he'd known. "Thank you ... but Jared is doing much better. We're very relieved."

Tanner was silent, as if trying to interpret what she'd just said. "Well, then ... I was calling because I went to Tuck's house earlier this morning and while I was examining the car—"

"Oh, that's right," Amanda interrupted. "I meant to tell you about that. Dawson finished repairing it before he left. It should be ready to go."

Again, Tanner took a few seconds before going on. "My point

is, I found the letter that Tuck had written to Dawson," he continued. "He must have left it here, and I wasn't sure whether you wanted me to forward it to you."

Amanda moved the phone to her other ear, wondering why he was calling her. "It was Dawson's," she said. "You should probably send it to him, shouldn't you?"

She heard him exhale on the other end. "I take it you haven't heard what happened," he said slowly. "On Sunday night? At the Tidewater?"

"What happened?" Amanda frowned, now utterly confused.

"I hate to have to tell you this over the phone. Would it be possible for you to come by my office this evening? Or tomorrow morning?"

"No," she said. "I'm back in Durham. What's going on? What happened?"

"I really think this should be done in person."

"That's not going to be possible," she said with a trace of impatience. "Just tell me what's going on. What happened at the Tidewater? And why can't you just send the letter to Dawson?"

Tanner hesitated before he finally cleared his throat. "There was an...altercation at the bar. The place was pretty much torn apart, and numerous shots were fired. Ted and Abee Cole were arrested, and a young man named Alan Bonner was seriously injured. Bonner is still in the hospital, but from what I could learn, he's going to be okay."

Hearing the names, one after the other, made the blood pound in her temples. She knew, of course, the name that linked them all. Her voice was almost a whisper.

"Was Dawson there?"

"Yes," Morgan Tanner answered.

"What happened?"

"From what I was able to gather, Ted and Abee Cole were assaulting Alan Bonner when Dawson suddenly entered the bar.

At which point, Ted and Abee Cole went after him instead."
Tanner paused. "You have to understand that the official police
report has yet to be released—"

"Is Dawson okay?" she demanded. "That's all I want to know."

She could hear Tanner breathing on the other end. "Dawson
was helping Alan Bonner out of the bar when Ted managed to
fire off a last round. Dawson was shot."

Amanda felt every muscle in her body tense, bracing for what
she already knew was coming. These words, like so many in the
past few days, seemed impossible to comprehend.

"It...he was shot in the head. He had no chance, Amanda.
He was brain-dead by the time he reached the hospital."

Even as Tanner spoke, Amanda could feel her grip loosening
on the phone. It clattered to the ground. She stared at it, lying in
the gravel, before finally reaching down to punch the OFF button.

Dawson. Not Dawson. He couldn't be dead.

But she heard again what Tanner had told her. He'd gone to
the Tidewater. Ted and Abee were there. He'd saved Alan Bonner and now he was gone.

A life for a life, she thought. God's cruel trick.

She suddenly flashed on the image of the two of them holding hands and wandering in a field of wildflowers. And when the
tears finally came, she wept for Dawson, and for all of the days
they would never know together. Until perhaps, like Tuck and
Clara, their ashes somehow found each other in a sunny field, far
away from the beaten path of ordinary lives.

Epilogue

⚬

Two years later

Amanda slipped two pans of lasagna into the refrigerator, before peering into the oven to check on the cake. Though Jared wouldn't turn twenty-one for another couple of months, she'd come to think of June 23 as a kind of second birthday for him. On this day two years ago, he'd received a new heart; on that day he'd been given a second chance at life. If that wasn't worth celebrating, she wasn't sure that anything was.

She was alone in the house. Frank was at work, Annette hadn't yet returned from a slumber party at her friend's house, and Lynn was working her summer job at the Gap. Meanwhile, Jared planned to enjoy one of his last free days before his internship at a capital management firm began, by playing softball with a group of friends. Amanda had warned him that it was going to be hot out there and made him promise to drink lots of water.

"I'll be careful," he'd assured her before leaving for the softball field. These days, Jared—maybe because he was maturing, or maybe because of all that had happened to him—seemed to understand that worry went hand in hand with motherhood.

He hadn't always been so tolerant. In the aftermath of the accident, everything seemed to rub him the wrong way. If she looked at him with concern, he claimed she was suffocating him; if she tried to start a conversation, he often snapped at her. She understood the reasons behind his ill temper; his recovery was painful, and the drugs he took often made him nauseated. Muscles that had once been strong began to atrophy despite physiotherapy, underscoring his sense of helplessness. His emotional recovery was complicated by the fact that unlike many transplant patients, who'd been waiting and hoping for a chance to add years to their lives, Jared couldn't help feeling that years of his life had been taken away. He sometimes lashed out at friends when they came to see him, and Melody, the girl he'd been so interested in that fateful weekend, informed him a few weeks after the accident that she was dating someone else. Visibly depressed, Jared decided to take the year off from school.

It was a long and sometimes discouraging road, but with the help of his therapist, Jared gradually began to rebound. The therapist also suggested that Frank and Amanda meet with her regularly to talk about Jared's challenges, and how they could best respond to and support him. Given their own marital history, it was sometimes hard for them to set aside their own conflicts in order to provide Jared with the security and encouragement he needed; but in the end, their love for their son came before everything else. They did what they could to support Jared as he moved steadily through periods of grief, loss, and rage to get to a point where he finally began to accept his new circumstances.

Early last summer, he'd signed up for an economics class at the local community college, and to Amanda and Frank's enormous pride and relief he announced soon thereafter that he'd decided to re-enroll full-time at Davidson in the fall. Later that same week he'd mentioned over dinner, in an almost offhand way, that he'd read about a man who'd lived thirty-one years after his heart transplant. Since medicine was improving every year, he figured he'd be able to live even longer.

Once he was back in school, his spirits continued to lift. After consulting with his doctors, he took up running, working up to the point where he now ran six miles a day. He started going to the gym three or four times a week, gradually regaining the physique he'd once had. Fascinated by the course he had taken in the summer, he decided to focus on economics when he returned to Davidson. Within weeks of returning to school, he met another prospective economics major, a girl named Lauren. The two of them had fallen head over heels in love, and they'd even begun to talk about getting married after they graduated. For the past two weeks, they'd been on a mission trip to Haiti, sponsored by her church.

Aside from diligently taking his medications and abstaining from alcohol, Jared, for the most part, now lived the life of an ordinary twenty-one-year-old. Even so, he didn't begrudge his mother's desire to bake him a cake to celebrate the transplant. After two years, he'd finally reached the point where, despite everything, he considered himself lucky.

There was, however, a recent twist in Jared's thinking that Amanda wasn't sure how to handle. A few evenings ago, while she'd been loading dishes into the dishwasher, Jared had joined her in the kitchen, stopping to lean against the counter.

"Hey, Mom? Are you going to do that charity thing for Duke this fall?"

In the past, he'd always referred to her fund-raising luncheons as *things*. For obvious reasons, since the accident, she hadn't hosted the event, nor had she been volunteering at the hospital. Amanda nodded. "Yes. They asked me to take over as the chairperson again."

"Because they botched it the last couple of years without you, right? That's what Lauren's mom said."

"They didn't botch the events. They just didn't go as well as planned."

"I'm glad you're doing it again. For Bea, I mean."

She smiled. "Me, too."

"The hospital likes it, too, right? Because you're raising money?"

She reached for a towel and dried her hands, studying him. "Why are you suddenly so interested?"

Jared absently scratched at his scar through his T-shirt. "I was hoping that you could use your contacts at the hospital to find something out for me," he said. "It's something I've been wondering about."

※

With the cake cooling on the counter, Amanda stepped out onto the back porch and inspected the lawn. Despite the automatic sprinklers that Frank had installed last year, the grass was dying in spots as the roots withered away. Before he'd gone to work this morning, she'd seen him standing over one of the dull brown patches, his face grim. In the past couple of years, Frank had become fanatical about the lawn. Unlike most of the neighbors, Frank insisted on doing his own mowing, telling anyone who asked that it helped him relax after a day spent filling cavities and shaping crowns at the office. Though she supposed there was some truth in that, there was also something compulsive about his habits. Rain or shine, he mowed every other day, making checkerboard patterns in the lawn.

Despite her initial skepticism, Frank hadn't had a single beer or even a sip of wine since the day of the accident. At the hospital, he'd sworn he was stopping for good, and to his credit, he'd kept his vow. After two years, she no longer expected him to slip back into his old ways at any moment, and that was a big part of the reason things between them had improved. It wasn't a perfect relationship by any means, but it wasn't as terrible as it once had been, either. In the days and weeks following the accident, arguments between them had been an almost nightly occurrence. Pain and guilt and anger had sharpened their words into blades, and they often lashed out at each other. Frank slept in the guest room for months, and in the mornings, eye contact between them was rare.

As difficult as those months had been, Amanda could never bring herself to take the final step of filing for divorce. Given

Jared's fragile emotional state, she couldn't imagine traumatizing him any further. What she didn't realize was that her resolve to keep the family intact wasn't having the intended effect. A few months after Jared came home from the hospital, Frank was talking to Jared in the living room when Amanda walked in. As had become the pattern by then, Frank got up and left the room. Jared watched him go before turning to his mom.

"It wasn't his fault," Jared said to her. "I was the one driving."

"I know."

"Then stop blaming him," he said.

Ironically, it was Jared's psychologist who ultimately convinced her and Frank to seek counseling for their troubled relationship. The tension at home was affecting Jared's recovery, she pointed out, and if they truly cared about helping their son, they should consider seeking couples counseling themselves. Without a stable home environment, Jared would have difficulty accepting and coping with his new circumstances.

Amanda and Frank drove in separate cars to their first appointment with the counselor, who Jared's psychologist had referred them to. Their first session degenerated into the kind of argument they'd been having for months. By the second session they were actually able to talk without raising their voices. And at the counselor's gentle but firm urging, Frank began attending AA meetings as well, much to Amanda's relief. In the beginning, he went five nights a week, but lately it was down to one, and three months ago Frank had become a sponsor. He met regularly for breakfast with a thirty-four-year-old recently divorced banker who, unlike Frank, had been unable to achieve sobriety. Until then Amanda had not allowed herself to believe that Frank was actually going to be successful in the long term.

There was no question that Jared and the girls had benefited from the improved atmosphere at home. There had even been moments recently when Amanda considered it a new beginning for her and Frank. When they talked these days, the past was

seldom front and center; now they were able to laugh occasionally in each other's company. Every Friday, they went on a date—
another recommendation of the couples counselor—and while
it still felt stilted at times, both of them knew it was important.
They were, in many ways, getting to know each other again, for
the first time in years.

There was something satisfying in that, but Amanda knew
that theirs would never be a passionate marriage. Frank wasn't,
nor ever had been, wired that way, and it didn't bother her. After
all, she had known the kind of love that was worth risking everything for, the kind of love that was as rare as a glimpse of heaven.

&

Two years. Two years had elapsed since her weekend with Dawson Cole; two long years since the day Morgan Tanner had called
to tell her that he'd passed away.

She kept the letters, along with Tuck and Clara's photograph
and the four-leaf clover, stashed in the bottom of her pajama
drawer, a place where Frank would never look. Every now and
then, when the ache she felt at his loss was especially strong,
she'd pull those items out. She'd reread the letters and twirl the
four-leaf clover between her fingers, wondering who they'd truly
been to each other that weekend. They were in love, but they
hadn't been lovers; they were friends and yet also strangers after
so many years. But their passion had been real, as undeniable as
the ground she stood on.

Last year, a couple of days after the anniversary of Dawson's
death, she'd made a trip to Oriental. Turning in at the town cemetery, she'd hiked out to the very edge of the property, where a small
rise overlooked a copse of leafy trees. It was here that Dawson's
remains were buried, far from the Coles, and even farther from the
plots of the Bennetts and the Colliers. As she stood over the simple headstone, gazing at the freshly cut lilies that someone had laid
there, she imagined that if by some twist of fate she was buried in

the Collier plot of this very same cemetery, their souls would eventually find each other—just as they had in life, not once but twice.

On the way out, she made a detour to pay respects on Dawson's behalf at the grave of Dr. Bonner. And there, before his
headstone, she saw an identical bouquet of lilies. Marilyn Bonner's handiwork on both counts, she guessed, because of what
Dawson had done for Alan, and the realization left her wiping
her eyes as she made her way back toward her car.

Time had done nothing to diminish her memories of Dawson; if anything, her feelings for him had deepened. In a strange
way, his love had given her the resolve she'd needed to make it
through the hardships of the last two years.

Now, sitting on her porch as the late afternoon sun slanted
through the trees, she closed her eyes and sent a silent message to
him. She remembered his smile and the way his hand had felt in
hers, she remembered the weekend they'd spent, and tomorrow,
she'd remember it all once more. To forget him or anything about
the weekend they'd shared would be a betrayal, and if there was
anything Dawson deserved, it was loyalty—the same kind of loyalty he'd showed her in the long years they had spent apart. She'd
loved him once and had loved him again, and nothing would
ever change the way she felt. After all, Dawson had renewed her
life in a way she'd never imagined possible.

Amanda put the lasagna into the oven to bake and was tossing a
salad just as Annette returned home. Frank walked in a few minutes later. After giving Amanda a quick kiss, he caught up briefly
with her before heading down the hall to change. Annette, chat-
tering nonstop about the slumber party, added frosting to the
cake.

Jared was next to arrive, with three friends in tow. After down-
ing a glass of water, he went off to shower while his friends settled
on the couch in the den to play video games.

Lynn pulled in half an hour later. To her surprise, Lynn was accompanied by two friends of her own. All of the young people instinctively migrated to the kitchen, Jared's friends flirting with Lynn's, asking what the girls were going to do later and hinting that they might be interested in coming along. Annette hugged Frank, who'd returned to the kitchen, begging him to take her to see some tween girls' movie; Frank chugged his Diet Snapple, teasing her with promises of seeing something with guns and explosions instead, eliciting squeals of protest from Annette.

Amanda watched all of it as a casual observer might, a bemused smile lighting up her face. Getting the whole family together for dinner wasn't exactly rare these days, but it wasn't all that common, either. The fact that there were others here didn't bother her in the slightest; it would make dinner a lively affair for all.

Pouring herself a glass of wine, she stole out onto the back porch, watching a pair of cardinals as they flitted from branch to branch.

"You coming?" Frank called out from the doorway behind her. "The natives are getting restless."

"Go ahead and have them serve up," she said. "I'll be there in a minute."

"Do you want me to get you a plate?"

"That would be great," she said, nodding. "Thank you. But make sure everyone gets theirs first."

Frank turned from the doorway, and through the window she watched as he moved among the crowd into the dining room.

Behind her, the door opened again.

"Hey, Mom? Are you okay?"

The sound of Jared's voice brought her back into the moment, and she turned.

"I'm fine," she said.

After a beat, he stepped out onto the porch, closing the door gently behind him. "You sure?" he asked. "You look like something's bothering you."

"I'm just tired." She managed a reassuring smile. "Where's Lauren?"

"She'll be here in a little while. She wanted to go home and shower."

"Did she have fun?"

"I think so. She hit the ball, at least. She was pretty excited about that."

Amanda looked up at him, tracing the line of his shoulders, his neck, the plane of his cheek, still able to see the way he'd looked as a little boy.

He hesitated. "Anyway...I wanted to ask you if you thought you could help me. You never really answered me the other night." He kicked at a tiny scuff mark on the porch. "I want to send a letter to the family. Just to thank them, you know? If it wasn't for the donor, I wouldn't be here."

Amanda lowered her eyes, remembering Jared's question of the other night.

"It's natural to want to find out who the donor of your heart was," she finally said, choosing her words with care. "But there are good reasons why the process is supposed to remain anonymous."

There was truth in what she said, even if it wasn't the whole truth.

"Oh." His shoulders slumped. "I thought that might be the case," he said. "All they told me was that he was forty-two when he died. I just wanted...to find out more about what kind of person he was."

I could tell you more, Amanda thought to herself. *A lot more.* She'd suspected the truth since Morgan Tanner had called, and she'd made some calls to confirm her suspicions. Dawson, she'd learned, had been taken off life support at CarolinaEast Regional Medical Center late Monday night. He'd been kept alive long after doctors knew he would never recover, because he was an organ donor.

Dawson, she knew, had saved Alan's life—but in the end, he'd saved Jared's as well. And for her that meant...everything. *I gave you the best of me,* he'd told her once, and with every beat of her son's heart, she knew he'd done exactly that.

"How about a quick hug," she said, "before we go inside?"

Jared rolled his eyes, but he opened his arms anyway. "I love you, Mom," he mumbled, pulling her close.

Amanda closed her eyes, feeling the steady rhythm in his chest. "I love you, too."

Reading Group Guide

Discussion Questions

1. Though he was raised in Oriental, North Carolina, Dawson never felt he belonged there. Why not? Have you ever felt like an outsider or a misfit?

2. Tuck is more of a parent to Dawson than his own father. What needs do Dawson and Tuck fulfill for one another?

3. Growing up, Dawson tried to blend in with his family, going so far as to fail classes on purpose. Have you ever sabotaged yourself for the sake of others? Why does Dawson provoke such a strong reaction from his family?

4. When Amanda's parents threaten not to pay for college, Dawson decides it would be best if they broke up, saying, "If you love someone, you're supposed to let them go" (pg. 19). Do you agree with him? What would you have done in Dawson's position?

5. As Amanda learns more about Tuck and Clara's quiet life together, she concludes that they lived "in the middle ground, where contentment and love were found in the smallest details of people's lives" (pg. 31). In your opinion, is

this kind of life enough, or do people need excitement and passion to be happy? Where do you find contentment in life?

6. Why does Dawson plead guilty in the trial regarding Dr. Bonner's accident? Do you think his decision makes sense?

7. Why is Amanda angry when she learns that Dawson hasn't dated anyone in the past 24 years? How would you feel if an ex wasn't able to move on after your breakup?

8. Though they've been apart for more than twenty years, Dawson and Amanda's feelings for each other are as strong as ever. Why has their love endured over the years? In your experience, is love eternal, or does it grow weaker with time and distance?

9. Why does Dawson have the Bonners followed? Do you think he goes too far?

10. Amanda admits to Dawson that she went to Tuck's place to be alone after her father died. Why does Tuck's home hold so much significance for Amanda? Are there any places you feel a strong emotional attachment to?

11. Compare Abee and Ted's motivations throughout the novel. Why is it so important to Ted that he teach Dawson a lesson?

12. Why did Tuck plot to get Dawson and Amanda back together? Why did he wait until he died to do so?

13. In his letter to Dawson, Tuck says that memories are funny things because, "sometimes they're real, but other times they change into what we want them to be" (pg. 192). Have

you ever realized you were remembering the past differently than it actually happened? Do you think Amanda's marital problems affected her memories of Dawson?

14. Throughout the novel, Dawson repeatedly makes sacrifices for others. Do you think that he sacrifices too much? In what situations is it fair to put yourself before others?

15. What do you think Amanda learns from her reunion with Dawson? How do you understand her choice at the end of the novel? What would you have done if you were in her shoes?

Early February 2011

Ira

I sometimes think to myself that I'm the last of my kind.

My name is Ira Levinson. I'm a southerner and a Jew, and equally proud to have been called both at one time or another. I'm also an old man. I was born in 1920, the year that alcohol was outlawed and women were given the right to vote, and I often wondered if that was the reason my life turned out the way it did. I've never been a drinker, after all, and the woman I married stood in line to cast a ballot for Roosevelt as soon as she reached the appropriate age, so it would be easy to imagine that the year of my birth somehow ordained it all.

My father would have scoffed at the notion. He was a man who believed in rules. "Ira," he would say to me when I was young and working with him in the haberdashery, "let me tell you something you should never do," and then he would tell me. His *Rules for Life*, he called them, and I grew up hearing my father's rules on just about everything. Some of what he told me was moral in nature, rooted in the teachings of the Talmud; and they were probably the same things most parents said to their children. I was told that I should never lie or cheat or steal, for instance, but my father—a sometimes Jew, he called himself back then—was far more likely to focus on the practical. Never go out in the rain without a hat, he would tell me. Never touch a stove burner, on the off chance it still might be hot. I was warned that I should never count the money in my wallet in public, or buy jewelry from a man on the street, no matter how good the deal might seem. On and on they went, these *nevers*, but despite their random nature, I found myself following almost every one, perhaps because I wanted never to disappoint my father. His voice, even now, follows me everywhere on this longest of rides, this thing called life.

Similarly, I was often told what I *should* do. He expected honesty and integrity in all aspects of life, but I was also told to hold doors for women and children, to shake hands with a firm grip, to remember people's names, and to always give the customer a little more than expected. His rules, I came to realize, not only were the basis of a philosophy that had served him well, but said everything about who he was. Because he believed in honesty and integrity, my father believed that others did as well. He believed in human decency and assumed others were just like him. He believed that most people, when given the choice, would do what was right, even when it was hard, and he believed that good almost always triumphed over evil. He wasn't naive, though. "Trust people," he would tell me, "until they give you a reason not to. And then never turn your back."

More than anyone, my father shaped me into the man I am today.

But the war changed him. Or rather, the Holocaust changed him. Not his intelligence—my father could finish the *New York Times* crossword puzzle in less than ten minutes—but his beliefs about people. The world he thought he knew no longer made sense to him, and he began to change. By then he was in his late fifties, and after making me a partner in the business, he spent little time in the shop. Instead, he became a full-time Jew. He began to attend synagogue regularly with my mother—I'll get to her later—and offered financial support to numerous Jewish causes. He refused to work on the Sabbath. He followed with interest the news regarding the founding of Israel—and the Arab-Israeli War in its aftermath—and he began to visit Jerusalem at least once a year, as if looking for something he'd never known he'd been missing. As he grew older, I began to worry more about those overseas trips, but he assured me that he could take care of himself, and for many years he did. Despite his advancing age, his mind remained as sharp as ever, but unfortunately his body wasn't quite so accommodating. He had a heart attack when he was ninety, and though he recovered, a stroke seven months later greatly weakened the right side of his body. Even then, he insisted on taking care of himself. He refused to move to a nursing home, even though he had to use a walker to get around, and he continued to drive despite my pleas that he forfeit his license. It's dangerous, I would tell him, to which he would shrug.

What can I do? he would answer. How else would I get to the store?

My father finally died a month before he turned 101, his license still in his wallet and a completed crossword puzzle on the bed-stand beside him. It had been a long life, an interesting life, and I've found myself thinking about him often of late. It makes sense, I suppose, because I've been following in his footsteps all along. I carried with me his *Rules for Life* every morning as I opened the shop and in the way I've dealt with people. I remembered names and gave more than was expected, and to this day I take my hat with me when I think there's a chance of rain. Like my father, I had a heart attack and now use a walker, and though I never liked crossword puzzles, my mind seems as sharp as ever. And, like my father, I was too stubborn to give up my license. In retrospect, this was probably a mistake. If I had, I wouldn't be in this predicament: my car off the highway and halfway down the steep embankment, the hood crumpled from impact with a tree. And I wouldn't be fantasizing about someone coming by with a thermos full of coffee and a blanket and one of those movable thrones that carried the pharaoh from one spot to the next.

Because as far as I can tell, that's just about the only way I'm ever going to make it out of here alive.

I'm in trouble. Beyond the cracked windshield, the snow continues to fall, blurry and disorienting. My head is bleeding, and dizziness comes in waves; I'm almost certain my right arm is broken. Collarbone, too. My shoulder throbs, and the slightest twitch is agonizing. Despite my jacket, I'm already so cold that I'm shivering.

I'd be lying if I told you I wasn't afraid. I don't want to die, and thanks to my parents—my mother lived to ninety-six—I long assumed that I was genetically capable of growing even older than I already am. Until a few months ago, I fully believed I had half a dozen good years left. Well, maybe not *good* years. That's not the way it works at my age. I've been disintegrating for a while now—heart, joints, kidneys, bits and pieces of my body beginning to give up the ghost—but recently something else has been added to the mix. Growths in my lungs, the doctor said. Tumors. *Cancer.* My time is measured in months now, not years . . . but even so, I'm not ready to die just yet. Not today. There is something I have to do, something I have done every year since 1956. A grand tradition is coming to an end, and more than anything, I wanted one last chance to say good-bye.

Still, it's funny what a man thinks about when he believes death to be imminent. One thing I know for sure is that if my time is up, I'd rather not go out this way—body trembling, dentures rattling, until finally, inevitably, my heart just gives out completely. I know what happens when people die—at my age, I've been to too many funerals to count. If I had the choice, I'd rather go in my sleep, back home in a comfortable bed. People who die like that look good at the viewing, which is why, if I feel the Grim Reaper tapping my shoulder, I've already decided to try to make my way to the backseat. The last thing I want is for someone to find me out here, frozen solid in a sitting position like some bizarre ice sculpture. How would they ever get my body out?

The way I'm wedged behind the wheel, it would be like trying to get a piano out of the bathroom. I can imagine some fireman chipping away at the ice and wobbling my body back and forth, saying things like "Swing the head this way, Steve," or "Wiggle the old guy's arms that way, Joe," while they try to manhandle my frozen body out of the car. Bumping and clunking, pushing and pulling, until, with one last big heave, my body thumps to the ground. Not for me, thanks. I still have my pride. So like I said, if it comes to that, I'll try my best to make my way to the backseat and just close my eyes. That way they can slide me out like a fish stick.

But maybe it won't come to that. Maybe someone will spot the tire tracks on the road, the ones heading straight over the embankment. Maybe someone will stop and call down, maybe shine a flashlight and realize there's a car down here. It isn't inconceivable; it could happen. It's snowing and people are already driving slowly. Surely someone's going to find me. They have to find me.

Right?

❧

Maybe not.

The snow continues to fall. My breath comes out in little puffs, like a dragon, and my body has begun to ache with the cold. But it could be worse. Because it was cold—though not snowing—when I started out, I dressed for winter. I'm wearing two shirts, a sweater, gloves, and a hat. Right now the car is at an angle, nose pointed down. I'm still strapped into the seat belt, which supports my weight, but my head rests on the steering wheel. The air bag deployed, spreading white dust and the acrid scent of gunpowder throughout the car. It's not comfortable, yet I'm managing.

But my body throbs. I don't think the air bag worked properly, because my head slammed into the steering wheel and I was knocked unconscious. For how long, I do not know. The gash on my head continues to bleed, and the bones in my right arm seem to be trying to pop through my skin. Both my collarbone and my shoulder throb, and I'm afraid to move. I tell myself it could be worse. Though it is snowing, it is not bitterly cold outside. Temperatures are supposed to dip into the mid-twenties tonight but will climb into the high thirties tomorrow. It's also going to be windy, with gusts reaching twenty miles an hour. Tomorrow, Sunday, the winds will be even worse, but by Monday night, the weather will gradually begin to improve. By then, the cold front will have largely passed and the winds will be almost nonexistent. On Tuesday, temperatures are expected to reach the forties.

I know this because I watch the Weather Channel. It's less depressing than the news, and I find it interesting. It's not only about the expected weather; there are shows about the catastrophic effects of weather in the past. I've seen shows about people who were in the bathroom as a tornado ripped the house from its foundation, and I've seen people talk about being rescued after being swept away by flash flooding. On the Weather Channel, people always survive catastrophe, because these are the people who are interviewed for the program. I like knowing in advance that the people survived. Last year, I watched a story about rush-hour commuters who were surprised by a blizzard in Chicago. Snow came down so fast, the roads were forced to close while people were still on them. For eight hours, thousands of people sat on highways, unable to move while temperatures plummeted. The story I saw focused on two of the people who'd been in the blizzard, but what struck me while watching was the fact that neither of them seemed prepared for the weather. Both of them became almost hypothermic as the storm rolled through. This, I must admit, made no sense to me. People who live in Chicago are fully aware that it snows regularly; they experience the blizzards that sometimes roll in from Canada, they must realize it gets cold. How could they not know these things? If I lived in such a place, I would have had thermal blankets, hats, an additional winter jacket, earmuffs, gloves, a shovel, a flashlight, hand warmers, and bottled water in the trunk of my car by Halloween. If I lived in Chicago, I could be stranded by a blizzard for two weeks before I began to worry.

My problem, however, is that I live in North Carolina. And normally when I drive—except for an annual trip to the mountains, usually in the summer—I stay within a few miles of my home. Thus, my trunk is empty, but I'm somewhat comforted by the fact that even if I had a portable hotel in my trunk, it would do me no good. The embankment is icy and steep, and there's no way I could reach it, even if it held the riches of Tutankhamun. Still, I'm not altogether unprepared for what's happened to me. Before I left, I packed a thermos full of coffee, two sandwiches, prunes, and a bottle of water. I put the food in the passenger seat, next to the letter I'd written, and though all of it was tossed about in the accident, I'm comforted by the knowledge that it's still in the car. If I get hungry enough, I'll try to find it, but even now I understand that there's a cost to eating or drinking. What goes in must go out, and I haven't yet figured out how it will go out. My walker is in the backseat, and the slope would propel me to my grave; taken with my injuries, a call of nature is out of the question.

About the accident. I could probably concoct an exciting story about icy conditions or describe an angry, frustrated driver who forced me off the road, but that's not the way it happened. What happened was this: It was dark and it began to snow, then snow even harder, and all at once, the road simply vanished. I assume I entered a curve—I say *assume*, because I obviously didn't see a curve—and the next thing I knew, I crashed through the guardrail and began to careen down the steep embankment. I sit here, alone in the dark, wondering if the Weather Channel will eventually do a show about me.

I can no longer see through the windshield. Though it sends up flares of agony, I try the windshield wipers, expecting nothing, but a moment later they push at the snow, leaving a thin layer of ice in their wake. It strikes me as amazing, this momentary burst of normalcy, but I reluctantly turn the wipers off, along with the headlights, though I'd forgotten they were even on. I tell myself that I should conserve whatever is left of the battery, in case I have to use the horn.

I shift, feeling a lightning bolt shoot from my arm up to my collarbone. The world goes black. Agony. I breathe in and out, waiting for the white-hot agony to pass. Dear God, please. It is all I can do not to scream, but then, miraculously, it begins to fade. I breathe evenly, trying to keep the tears at bay, and when it finally recedes, I feel exhausted. I could sleep forever and never wake up. I close my eyes. I'm tired, so tired.

Strangely, I find myself thinking of Daniel McCallum and the afternoon of the visit. I picture the gift he left behind, and as I slip away, I wonder idly how long it will be until someone finds me.

🌿

"Ira."

I hear it first in my dream, slurry and unformed, an underwater sound. It takes a moment before I realize someone is saying my name. But that is not possible.

"You must wake up, Ira."

My eyes flutter open. In the seat beside me, I see Ruth, my wife.

"I'm awake," I say, my head still against the steering wheel. Without my glasses, which were lost in the crash, her image lacks definition, like a ghost.

"You drove off the highway."

I blink. "A maniac forced me off the road. I hit a patch of ice. Without my catlike reflexes, it would have been worse."

"You drove off the road because you are blind as a bat and too old to be driving. How many times have I told you that you are a menace behind the wheel?"

"You've never said that to me."

"I should have. You didn't even notice the curve." She pauses. "You are bleeding."

Lifting my head, I wipe my forehead with my good hand and it comes back red. There is blood on the steering wheel and the dash, smears of red everywhere. I wonder how much blood I've lost. "I know."

"Your arm is broken. And your collarbone, too. And there is something wrong with your shoulder."

"I know," I say again. As I blink, Ruth fades in and out.

"You need to get to the hospital."

"No argument there," I say.

"I am worried about you."

I breathe in and out before I respond. Long breaths. "I'm worried about me, too," I finally say.

My wife, Ruth, is not really in the car. I realize this. She died nine years ago, the day I felt my life come to a full stop. I had called to her from the living room, and when she didn't answer, I rose from my chair. I could move without a walker back then, though it was still slow going, and after reaching the bedroom, I saw her on the floor, near the bed, lying on her right side. I called for an ambulance and knelt beside her. I rolled her onto her back and felt her neck, detecting nothing at all. I put my mouth to hers, breathing in and out, the way I had seen on television. Her chest went up and down and I breathed until the world went black at the edges, but there was no response. I kissed her lips and her cheeks, and I held her close against me until the ambulance arrived. Ruth, my wife of more than fifty-five years, had died, and in the blink of an eye, all that I'd loved was gone as well.

"Why are you here?" I ask her.

"What kind of question is that? I am here because of you."

Of course. "How long was I asleep?"

"I do not know," she answers. "It is dark, though. I think you are cold."

"I'm always cold."

"Not like this."

"No," I agree, "not like this."

"Why were you driving on this road? Where were you going?"

I think about trying to move, but the memory of the lightning bolt stops me. "You know."

"Yes," she says. "You were driving to Black Mountain. Where we spent our honeymoon."

"I wanted to go one last time. It's our anniversary tomorrow."

She takes a moment to respond. "I think you are going soft in your head. We were married in August, not February."

"Not that anniversary," I say. I don't tell her that according to the doctor, I will not last until August. "Our other anniversary," I say instead.

"What are you talking about? There is no other anniversary. There is only one."

"The day my life changed forever," I say. "The day I first saw you."

For a moment, Ruth says nothing. She knows I mean it, but unlike me, she has a hard time saying such things. She loved me with a passion, but I felt it in her expressions, in her touch, in the tender brush of her lips. And, when I needed it most, she loved me with the written word as well.

"It was February sixth, 1939," I say. "You were shopping downtown with your mother, Elisabeth, when the two of you came into the shop. Your mother wanted to buy a hat for your father."

She leans back in the seat, her eyes still on me. "You came out of the back room," she says. "And a moment later, your mother followed you."

Yes, I suddenly recall, my mother did follow. Ruth has always had an extraordinary memory.

Like my mother's family, Ruth's family was from Vienna, but they'd immigrated to North Carolina only two months earlier. They'd fled Vienna after the *Anschluss* of Austria, when Hitler and the Nazis absorbed Austria into the Reich. Ruth's father, Jakob Pfeffer, a professor of art history, knew what the rise of Hitler meant for the Jews, and he sold everything they owned to come up with the necessary bribes to secure his family's freedom. After crossing the border into Switzerland, they traveled to London and then on to New York, before finally reaching Greensboro. One of Jakob's uncles manufactured furniture a few blocks from my father's shop, and for months Ruth and her family lived in two cramped rooms above the plant floor. Later, I would learn that the endless fumes from the lacquer made Ruth so sick at night, she could barely sleep.

"We came to the store because we knew your mother spoke German. We had been told that she could help us." She shakes her head. "We were so homesick, so hungry to meet someone from home."

I nod. At least I think I do. "My mother explained everything after you left. She had to. I couldn't understand a word that any of you were saying."

"You should have learned German from your mother."

"What did it matter? Before you'd even left the store, I knew that we would one day be married. We had all the time in the world to talk."

"You always say this, but it is not true. You barely looked at me."

"I couldn't. You were the most beautiful girl I'd ever seen. It was like trying to stare into the sun."

"*Ach, Quatsch . . . ,*" she snorts. "I was not beautiful. I was a child. I was only sixteen."

"And I had just turned nineteen. And I ended up being right." She sighs. "Yes," she says, "you were right."

I'd seen Ruth and her parents before, of course. They attended our synagogue and sat near the front, foreigners in a strange land. My mother had pointed them out to me after services, eyeing them discreetly as they hurried home.

I always loved our Saturday morning walks home from the synagogue, when I had my mother all to myself. Our conversation drifted easily from one subject to the next, and I reveled in her undivided attention. I could tell her about any problems I was having or ask any question that crossed my mind, even those that my father would have found pointless. While my father offered advice, my mother offered comfort and love. My father never joined us; he preferred to open the shop early on Saturdays, hoping for weekend business. My mother understood. By then, even I knew that it was a struggle to keep the shop open at all. The Depression hit Greensboro hard, as it did everywhere, and the shop sometimes went days without a single customer. Many people were unemployed, and even more were hungry. People stood in lines for soup or bread. Many of the local banks had failed, taking people's savings with them. My father was the type to set money aside in good times, but by 1939 times were difficult even for him.

My mother had always worked with my father, though seldom out front with the customers. Back then, men—and our clientele was almost exclusively men—expected another man to help them, in both the selection and the fitting of suits. My mother, however, kept the storeroom door propped open, which allowed her a perfect view of the customer. My mother, I must say, was a genius at her craft. My father would tug and pull and mark the fabric in the appropriate places, but my mother in a single glance would know immediately whether or not to adjust the marks my father had made. In her mind's eye, she could see the customer in the completed suit, knowing the exact line of every crease and seam. My father understood this—it was the reason he positioned the mirror where she could see it. Though some men might have felt threatened, it made my father proud. One of my father's *Rules for Life* was to marry a woman who was smarter than you. "I did this," he would say to me, "and you should do it, too. I say, why do all the thinking?"

My mother, I must admit, really was smarter than my father. Though she never mastered the art of cooking—my mother should have been banned from the kitchen—she spoke four languages and could quote Dostoyevsky in Russian; she was an accomplished classical pianist and had attended the University of Vienna at a time when female students were rare. My father, on the other hand, had never gone to college. Like me, he'd worked in his father's haberdashery since he was a boy, and he was good with numbers and customers. And like me, he'd first seen his wife-to-be at the synagogue, soon after she'd arrived in Greensboro.

There, however, is where the similarity ends, because I often wondered whether my parents were happy as a couple. It would be easy to point out that times were different back then, that people married less for love than for practical reasons. And I'm not saying they weren't right for each other in many ways. They made good partners, my parents, and I never once heard them argue. Yet I often wondered whether they were ever in love. In all the years I lived with them, I never saw them kiss, nor were they the kind of couple who felt comfortable holding hands. In the evenings, my father would do his bookkeeping at the kitchen table while my mother sat in the sitting room, a book open in her lap. Later, after my parents retired and I took over the business, I hoped they might grow closer. I thought they might travel together, taking cruises or going sightseeing, but after the first visit to Jerusalem, my father always traveled alone. They settled into separate lives, continuing to drift apart, becoming strangers again. By the time they were in their eighties, it seemed as though they'd run out of anything at all to say to each other. They could spend hours in the same room without uttering a single word. When Ruth and I visited, we tended to spend time first with one and then the other, and in the car afterward, Ruth would squeeze my hand, as if promising herself that we would never end up the same way.

Ruth was always more bothered by their relationship than either of them seemed to be. My parents seemed to have little desire to bridge the gap between them. They were comfortable in their own worlds. As they aged, while my father grew closer to his heritage, my mother developed a passion for gardening, and she spent hours pruning flowers in the backyard. My father loved to watch old westerns and the evening news, while my mother had her books. And, of course, they were always interested in the artwork Ruth and I collected, the art that eventually made us rich.

❦

"You didn't come back to the shop for a long time," I said to Ruth.

Outside the car, the snow has blanketed the windshield and continues to fall. According to the Weather Channel, it should have stopped by now, but despite the wonders of modern technology and forecasting, weather predictions are still fallible. It is another reason I find the channel interesting.

"My mother bought the hat. We had no money for anything more."

"But you thought I was handsome."

"No. Your ears were too big. I like delicate ears."

She's right about my ears. My ears are big, and they stick out in the same way my father's did, but unlike my father, I was ashamed of them. When I was young, maybe eight or nine, I took some extra cloth from the shop and cut it into a long strip, and I spent the rest of the summer sleeping with the strip wrapped around my head, hoping they would grow closer to my scalp. While my mother ignored it when she'd check on me at night, I sometimes heard my father whispering to her in an almost affronted tone. *He has my ears*, he'd say to her. *What is so bad about my ears?*

I told Ruth this story shortly after we were married and she laughed. Since then, she would sometimes tease me about my ears like she is doing now, but in all our years together, she never once teased me in a way that felt mean.

"I thought you liked my ears. You told me that whenever you kissed them."

"I liked your face. You had a kind face. Your ears just happened to come with it. I did not want to hurt your feelings."

"A kind face?"

"Yes. There was a softness in your eyes, like you saw only the good in people. I noticed it even though you barely looked at me."

"I was trying to work up the courage to ask if I could walk you home."

"No," she says, shaking her head. Though her image is blurred, her voice is youthful, the sixteen-year-old I'd met so long ago. "I saw you many times at the synagogue after that, and you never once asked me. I even waited for you sometimes, but you went past me without a word."

"You didn't speak English."

"By then, I had begun to understand some of the language, and I could talk a little. If you had asked, I would have said, 'Okay, Ira. I will walk with you.'"

She says these last words with an accent. Viennese German, soft and musical. Lilting. In later years her accent faded, but it never quite disappeared.

"Your parents wouldn't have allowed it."

"My mother would have. She liked you. Your mother told her that you would own the business one day."

"I knew it! I always suspected you married me for my money."

"What money? You had no money. If I wanted to marry a rich man, I would have married David Epstein. His father owned the textile mill and they lived in a mansion."

This, too, was one of the running jokes in our marriage. While my mother had been speaking the truth, even she knew it was not the sort of business that would make anyone wealthy. It started, and remained, a small business until the day I finally sold the shop and retired.

"I remember seeing the two of you at the soda parlor across the street. David met you there almost every day during the summer."

"I liked chocolate sodas. I had never had them before."

"I was jealous."

"You were right to be," she says. "He was rich and handsome and his ears were perfect."

I smile, wishing I could see her better. But the darkness makes that impossible. "For a while I thought the two of you were going to get married."

"He asked me more than once, and I would tell him that I was too young, that he would have to wait until after I finished college. But I was lying to him. The truth was that I already had my eye on you. That is why I always insisted on going to the soda parlor near your father's shop."

I knew this, of course. But I like hearing her say it.

"I would stand by the window and watch you as you sat with him."

"I saw you sometimes." She smiles. "I even waved once, and still, you never asked to walk with me."

"David was my friend."

This is true, and it remained true for most of our lives. We were social with both David and his wife, Rachel, and Ruth tutored one of their children.

"It had nothing to do with friendship. You were afraid of me. You have always been shy."

"You must be mistaking me for someone else. I was debonair, a ladies' man, a young Frank Sinatra. I sometimes had to hide from the many women who were chasing me."

"You stared at your feet when you walked and turned red when I waved. And then, in August, you moved away. To attend university."

I went to school at William & Mary in Williamsburg, Virginia, and I didn't return home until December. I saw Ruth twice at the synagogue that month, both times from a distance, before I went back to school. In May, I came home for the summer to work at the shop, and by then World War II was raging in Europe. Hitler had conquered Poland and Norway, vanquished Belgium, Luxembourg, and the Netherlands, and was making mincemeat of the French. In every newspaper, in every conversation, the talk was only of war. No one knew whether America would enter the conflict, and the mood was grim. Weeks later, the French would be out of the war for good.

"You were still seeing David when I returned."

"But I had also become friends with your mother in the year you were gone. While my father was working, my mother and I would go to the shop. We would speak of Vienna and our old lives. My mother and I were homesick, of course, but I was angry, too. I did not like North Carolina. I did not like this country. I felt that I did not belong here. Despite the war, part of me wanted to go home. I wanted to help my family. We were very worried for them."

I see her turn toward the window, and in the silence, I know that Ruth is thinking about her grandparents, her aunts and uncles, her cousins. On the night before Ruth and her parents left for Switzerland, dozens of her extended family members had gathered for a farewell dinner. There were anxious good-byes and promises to stay in touch, and although some were excited for them, nearly everyone thought Ruth's father was not only over-reacting, but foolish to have given up everything for an uncertain future. However, a few of them had slipped Ruth's father some gold coins, and in the six weeks it took to journey to North Carolina, it was those coins that provided shelter and kept food in their stomachs. Aside from Ruth and her parents, her entire family had stayed in Vienna. By the summer of 1940, they were wearing the Star of David on their arms and largely prohibited from working. By then, it was too late for them to escape.

My mother told me about these visits with Ruth and their worries. My mother, like Ruth, still had family back in Vienna, but like so many, we had no idea what was coming or just how terrible it would eventually be. Ruth didn't know, either, but her father had known. He had known while there was still time to flee. He was, I later came to believe, the most intelligent man I ever met.

"Your father was building furniture then?"

"Yes," Ruth said. "None of the universities would hire him, so he did what he had to do to feed us. But it was hard for him. He was not meant to build furniture. When he first started, he would come home exhausted, with sawdust in his hair and bandages on his hands, and he would fall asleep in the chair almost as soon as he walked in the door. But he never complained. He knew we were the lucky ones. After he woke, he would shower and then put on his suit for dinner, his own way of reminding himself of the man he once had been. And we would have lively conversations at dinner. He would ask what I had learned at school that day, and listen closely as I answered. Then he would lead me to think of things in new ways. 'Why do you suppose that is?' he would ask, or, 'Have you ever considered this?' I knew what he was doing, of course. Once a teacher, always a teacher, and he was good at it, which is why he was able to become a professor once again after the war. He taught me how to think for myself and to trust my own instincts, as he did for all his students."

I study her, reflecting on how significant it was that Ruth, too, had become a teacher, and my mind flashes once more to Daniel McCallum. "And your father helped you learn all about art in the process."

"Yes," she says, a mischievous lilt in her voice. "He helped me do that, too."